THE
VERY
BAD
THING

THE VERY BAD THING

NED WHITE

VIKING

To my Father and Mother

VIKING
Published by the Penguin Group
Viking Penguin, a division of Penguin Books USA Inc.,
40 West 23rd Street, New York, New York 10010, U.S.A.
Penguin Books Ltd, 27 Wrights Lane,
London W8 5TZ, England
Penguin Books Australia Ltd, Ringwood,
Victoria, Australia
Penguin Books Canada Ltd, 2801 John Street,
Markham, Ontario, Canada L3R 1B4
Penguin Books (N.Z.) Ltd, 182–190 Wairau Road,
Auckland 10, New Zealand

Penguin Books Ltd, Registered Offices:
Harmondsworth, Middlesex, England

First published in 1990 by Viking Penguin,
a division of Penguin Books USA Inc.

10 9 8 7 6 5 4 3 2 1

LIBRARY OF CONGRESS CATALOGING IN PUBLICATION DATA
White, Ned.
The very bad thing / White, Ned.
p.   cm.
ISBN 0-670-82375-9
I. Title.
PS3573.H4745V47   1990
813'.54—dc20   89–40312

Printed in the United States of America
Set in Times Roman

Acknowledgments

This novel would not have been possible without the expert advice of a number of people. Special among them: Steve Barry, local rock and roll aficionado, manager, and promoter; Ted McDonough, who helped me understand the real world of the private detective; and Steve Rowley, whose ongoing tutorial in matters of computers and artificial intelligence was persistently thorough, forbearing, and congenial.

The author is especially grateful to the "home team"—Marnie, Sam, Amy, and Molly—for their continuing patience and support.

1

For Dred Balcazar, this second Monday in March was an unlikely day to fall either in lust or in love. An androgynous sexless nothing kind of day, sky the color of stone, the air cold and heavy with the smell of low tide and the threat of drizzle. A day for ice in the heart. True and proper Bostonians, Dred thought, got their stiff upper lips from this kind of weather, took a deviant pride in merely surviving it, weather that attacked the bones, late winter days that could stretch out for weeks and weeks, like empty promises, deep into May. On hateful Mondays like this one, when there was little else to do, he often found refuge a few blocks from his Beacon Hill apartment, on the fifth floor of the Boston Athenaeum.

As a regular "reader" he had come to know the Athenaeum well: its dusty corners, sibilant radiators fighting off the chill, its grim-visaged staff, ashen-faced patrons, and sense of Brahmin propriety—a notion to which he was just becoming acquainted—and in the fifth-floor balcony "his" chair, with its thick, soft green leather where today he would sit and advance himself with the last three issues of *American Science*, except that it was not his today. It was hers. With Goethe, as heavy as a watermelon, in her lap. Across a hunched shoulder she smiled politely, and then returned to the book, leaving him no choice but to sit down in one of the hard-backed chairs at the reading table on the opposite side.

He pushed the chair back a few inches so that a soapstone bust in the middle of the table (a very fine likeness of George Bernard Shaw) now obscured his eyes from her view.

Dozens of times on Monday afternoons he had ascended to this remote perch, the loftiest habitable part of the building and one of the world's best places to enjoy a catnap without fear of interruption. There was a single, unmarked entrance: From the floor narrow stairs led up into the stacks, taking a surprising turn toward a short hallway before opening up into this dimly lit oak-paneled alcove, set back far enough from the Main Reading Room below to be safely, cozily out of sight.

If you hadn't been told it was here, you'd never find it on your own.

Stars in space emblazoned the cover of the February issue of *American Science*. He thumbed quickly to the article boldly titled "Grand Unification Theory: The Final Grail," a topic he hoped that someday he would begin to understand, but now he noticed his enthusiasm waning. He sighed audibly and edged his chair an inch to the right to look at her again.

Recently he had trained himself to become more patient in observing very small things, and so it was only later that he would come to see past the details to determine that she was, her whole self, very beautiful. He noticed first that her eyes, long-lashed and a soft smoky gray, were moving far too quickly across the printed page for her to absorb anything by Goethe. He strongly doubted that she was rereading something already familiar to her. She was too young to be that confident, that educated. Late twenties probably, a decade younger than he, a different generation.

Over the top lip of *American Science* and past G. B. Shaw's left ear he watched her toy with her hair, freshly washed bright blond. Very pretty thick hair that didn't like dry heat. Tufts of cowlicks. Her jeans were new, stone-washed, a designer label somewhere. Old home-knit light gray sweater, fluffy sleeves bunched at the elbows. She was strong, athletic-looking, strength in her forearms when she shifted Goethe in her lap. Big strong legs, a horsewoman?

For an instant she lifted her eyes at him; he looked back, then down at the blur of words and dappling of stars on the pages before him. Leaning into the table, he angled to the left, Shaw once again slipping between them.

Now it was her turn, shifting herself into view, leaning toward the lamp next to her on the end table, pulling the chain and turning the light on and not looking up. Stroking the hair away from her face.

Now catching his eye for a second and turning away.

Yes, very pretty. Breasts unknown, not enormous. No jewelry except what looked like a turquoise ring on her left pinkie. And her mouth rubbery, always in motion, biting her lip, chewing a pencil that she otherwise didn't seem to use, her tongue pushing inside her cheek.

He was not reading about cosmology any more than she seemed to be reading Goethe. Regressing, more and more like a young kid, risking these eye games with her. Ducking her glances, she ducking his. Finally the game ended with a brief locked gaze, and she smiled at him, closed the book, and stood up.

"Is everything all right?" she asked, with evident concern.

"Yes, fine," he said.

"Would you mind saving my seat? I'd appreciate it." She left Goethe there as she almost touched him, brushing past him into the hall and out of sight, her footsteps clicking down the stairs.

Two things: the very light scent of her perfume as she moved past him, and the sound of her voice. A gentle voice like a soft hand on his shoulder or how her sweater might feel, a voice all in her throat, with no power to it. A voice with the easy friendly drawl of the West.

Cowgirl, he imagined, just as he had frequently and vividly dreamed she would be, coming to him as a gift of his own wishful thinking, in the dream leaning over him, her face, smooth bronze skin, bending to his lips, her hair tumbling in a blond thicket, the trace odors of sweat and trail dust, her body all over him. Waking up laughing, tingling, and wondering that such a woman might ever materialize, precipitously freed from his imagination, flesh pulled together from this dream cartoon, and then what? How does one say to her: I've dreamed of someone a whole lot like you?

Ten minutes later he was still saving her seat, his chair for her. If he reclaimed it as his own until her return, she might ask if perhaps he'd like to sit there instead of her. If he occupied it strictly as a custodial service and vacated before she saw him there, she would feel his warmth in the leather and make the same point, or at least marvel at his penchant for servility. Both scenarios were unattractive and clumsy and so he stayed in the wooden chair.

Wanting to catch up on these back issues of *American Science*, he couldn't. It annoyed him because there was a part of him that very much wanted to make good logical sense of monstrously difficult ideas like the origins of the universe and a single unifying force binding everything we'll ever touch or think about into a stable, fixed fabric. He knew literature and history and music and some French and Latin—enough to feel comfortable with them, unlike math, which he grasped only as chunks of broad ideas—and fragments of biology and chemistry, but he was eager to push himself deeper into more science like astronomy and physics, just to stay even with it, stuff that often made headlines in the papers because of the sheer vastness of the subject matter, the genius required to understand it better: black holes, supernovas, string theories, mysterious rings of light. Fitfully here at the Athenaeum, he struggled not to have it all pass him by. But not now; the more pressing mystery was how a dream-woman bronze-faced cowgirl slips through a cosmological membrane into the fifth floor of the nation's oldest private library.

Save her seat. Arising from his own, he gathered the magazines and deposited them neatly atop Goethe in the chair, suggesting possibly (to any wandering interloper) a lone scholar pursuing a kind of dangerous, maniacal synthesis of great thinking from different centuries. Someone whose chair definitely is not to be taken while he is off in search of a very sexy woman.

There was in the fifth-floor reading room of the Athenaeum a distinct Monday afternoon group, and many of the faces were familiar. But hers didn't fit—too pretty and fresh and unbookish. He took the elevator to the first-floor mezzanine and its narrow balcony overlooking the grand lobby, saw no one below who might be her.

At this level the Athenaeum seemed its most architecturally complex, with mazes of thin corridors, unnamed offices, snugly turning stairways, and other novelties—like the corner Children's Reading Room where now behind a glass door a knot of toddlers enjoyed afternoon Storytime, ministered by a young black woman with an eager voice. Dred sidled past unnoticed, between long, heavy glass display cases now exhibiting obscure pamphlets and austere old ledgers, over to the stairs leading down to the main floor. In the center of the room was the circulation desk, the library's principal command post, where John, radiating irritation, was doing something overtly tiresome with file cards. John was a graduate student at Harvard writing a paper on some arcane sliver of sixteenth-century English literature. Bristling with smarts, and easily aroused to combat.

"John."

"Mr. Balcazar." Not delighted to be diverted from his file cards.

"A young woman left some things on a table, fifth-floor reading room. I wonder if maybe she left. Just a few minutes ago."

"A young woman."

"Late twenties, blondish hair, pretty. Gray sweater, jeans."

"Oh, that one. Yes. I saw her come in but I haven't seen her leave."

"Is she a reader here?"

John seemed astonished by the question. People were either readers or tourists in a group. "I should hope so." This was a *private* library.

John delighted in illuminating the obvious for this man who claimed to be an educated man as well as a private investigator.

"Meaning, do you know her?"

"I know far fewer people here by name than you might imagine."

He went back to his shuffling and stacking of cards. Without looking up, he said, "If she left personal items on the table just bring them down and I'll keep them here until she asks for them."

"Thanks, John."

"If you're bored to tears a week from Wednesday night you might want to catch the lecture." Still without looking at him.

"What is it?"

"Walt Whitman, and a discourse on his—how do we say?—universal sexuality. Otherwise put, his rampaging, nondiscriminatory hormones."

Dred smiled. "Sorry, I can't make it."

He turned and had a glimpse of gray sweater behind closing elevator doors at the far end of the hall. Same color gray? Close enough. Going up.

"Think I just saw her."

"Well. You have fun," said John. A self-delighted twinkle in his eye, John was hormonally volatile in his own right. Dred believed him a latent heterosexual who for unknown reasons enjoyed posturing as effeminate.

He pressed the call button and waited for the floor indicator to reach 5. When it stopped at 4 and started down again, he moved off to the stairwell and climbed to the fourth floor. Here on the landing there was only the sound of his heavy breathing and the faint awareness of her perfume, or perhaps it was just a bath soap, but she must have gotten off here. The floor was carved up into odd-shaped rooms warehousing books that were very old and largely unread, municipal records and family histories and obscure subjects with thunderous Latin titles embossed on flaking leather bindings. Most of these rooms stored books on movable Spacemaster shelves that glided on tracks, sandwiching together or pulling apart with a few turns of a crank handle. Stepping into a corridor that led to Room 2 and Room 3, he stopped and listened for her.

Yes, someone was in Room 3, ratcheting the Spacemaster stacks apart. This was the horror movie section, dusty, thickly bound tracts on what the Athenaeum genteelly termed "controversial religious subjects." Exorcisms, black masses, Rosicrucians, mystics and metaphysicists, alchemists and astrologers and witches. He stepped in and slid along the first open aisle of books, two or three aisles apart from the sound of this other person still unseen, heels snapping on the hard floor, hesitating between stacks, finding a book whose heft was signaled by the slap of pages being turned in blocks. The swelling of these sounds through the room suggested maleness, and now an audible sigh confirmed it: if she was here too, she remained perfectly still.

The man flashed by, out the door at the limit of Dred's peripheral vision, leaving not even a sense of color, but in his wake a radiator clanged and hissed from the far wall. Then nothing. Down in the center of this aisle were books about dreams and visions and hidden powers of the mind, and at the end things more grim: studies of pagan rituals and sacrifices, Druids and Aztecs donating willing victims to their gods.

Her scent was here. But she was not.

He retreated to the door, back into the lobby, up to the fifth floor, up the stairs into the stacks to the hallway to the alcove to find her back in her place as if she'd never left. Smiling openly and sweetly.

"Hey, I thought you'd gone," she said in that loping lazy accent of hers, really not much of a drawl but certainly not New England or Midwest. Her stony gray eyes were now warm and kind. Eloquent, perhaps, with an entirely revised opinion of him.

"Glad you got your seat again. Although you can see crowding is not a problem." Cotton in the mouth, tough talking at this altitude, high atop Beacon Hill. She was lustrously, dreamily pretty.

"Thanks."

Now he realized for the first time that her sweater was off, looped around her waist with the sleeves loosely knotted in front, and she was wearing a gray denim shirt, Western-style stitching over the pockets, sleeves rolled up. Top two buttons unbuttoned at her throat. Sure, it's warm in here, that's all. Showing something of her collarbone, her skin a buttery gloss, and shadow of cleavage and a white lacy edge of bra, hardly visible.

And she'd very nicely set his three back issues of *American Science* on the table in front of his chair and moved G. B. Shaw a foot or so toward the end of the table, leaving a dustless square where the base had been. He sat down and debated whether to make a show of starting to read again.

"Is everything okay? You look worried."

Correct. He was worried that if he was already feeling this way about her he would soon be flying blind. "If you don't mind, I think you're quite—" and he decided not to say "interesting to watch." Better to be blind than stupid. "You're very pretty."

"Thanks. No, I don't mind."

He'd been honest before with women he was attracted to. Some of those women were still his friends.

"You're nice-looking yourself," she continued. "You have a friendly face. It's not just men who notice women."

"Can I ask your name?"

She wrinkled her nose. "Does it matter? I don't really like my name so much."

"Try me."

She snorted. "Lauren."

"Why are you here?" he asked. "I haven't seen you before."

"Just came to read, like you. Visit with old Socrates here."

Well, dimly, remotely, Shaw could pass for Socrates. "I'm pretty sure this is George Bernard Shaw." Immediately he wished he'd not said that.

"Yeah? Really?"

"Pretty sure."

Lauren got up and grabbed the bust and moved it back to the center of the table between them, examining his face critically.

"I'll be. Guess it is."

Then sitting down, damned if she didn't start to hum "Wouldn't It Be Loverly" from *My Fair Lady* from Shaw's *Pygmalion*, and then slouch down in the chair hiding again behind the bust, and he could only see her arm as she fiddled with Goethe in her lap.

Wouldn't it. Be loverly. Loverly.

She finished the song and her arm, all he could see, was still. For a minute or more he imagined what he might say, but he felt embarrassed just being here. She started, "I'm looking for a job, actually. I've been visiting all these big office buildings around here. I need a break."

He stretched to peer over Shaw's head and made eye contact. "What kind of job?"

"Hey, I'll do anything. Right now I'd almost settle for secretary. Not really, but almost."

"Look. I might have something." Two weeks ago this would have been a lie, but not now. A job coming up: there was a computer company with an as yet undefined problem, and he might need support in his office.

"Really?"

He slid two feet to the right.

"If you'd like, we could talk it over during dinner. My treat."

She seemed to think this over, but not for long. "Okay." Her smile was *very* affectionate. "Before the universe ends?" A nod to the cover of the February issue with its spatter of stars.

"And before you finish *Faust*," he reciprocated.

"Outlive us both," is what he heard. "Actually it's *The Sorrows of Young Werther* I'm looking at."

"Haven't read it yet," he said, making a mental note that someday he should, knowing he wouldn't.

"And this Grand Unification thing. Do you really understand that?"

"No, not yet."

"So you're not a genius, then."

"Guess not." Her wide eyes, the little twist to her mouth gave him goose bumps.

"Here," she said, and then she did something else very strange. Opening Goethe to its front flyleaf, she ripped off a triangular swatch of the page, took her pencil, and jotted down a number.

"Yikes. The management would disapprove," he said. "Unless of course Goethe is not so popular this month." She smiled again, tossed her head, leaned forward and handed him the scrap of paper.

"This is my service, you can call and I'll call back. Right now I've got another interview, I gotta go."

She was up out of her chair, and she dumped Goethe ignominiously from her lap in a fluttering, crunching heap on the floor.

"Damn," she said, leaving it there and moving by him.

"Don't take the job. I want to talk to you."

She turned for a second and reached her hand out to his shoulder, grabbing it, a quick squeeze. "Okay, I won't." Then she disappeared out of the alcove, down the stairs into the reading room.

He found himself staring at her empty chair, and felt the tightness in his chest, the heat in his cheeks.

This is not right.

He called for the elevator but changed his mind and took the stairs two at a time, got outside onto Beacon Street, but there was no sign of her, feeling that he'd missed her by seconds. She'd probably headed onto the Common or deeper, downhill, into the labyrinth of the city.

In his apartment, some six blocks away at the corner of Willow Street and Acorn Lane, he poured a glass of jug white wine and sat in his Hitchcock rocker allowing himself a moment to contemplate this gentle pressure in his midsection. Perhaps the first time had been in high school with Amanda Drexler. Then sophomore year at Yale with Debbie Everton. And only once since then, a little crush that becomes puppy lust, young love, head-over-heels loss of appetite before the perfectly settled confidence of knowing we're on a higher plane of knowledge and life with the finest woman ever insinuated into the human race, Annie Shea, who, on the eve of Ronald Reagan's first inauguration, skippered her thirty-foot yawl from Fort Lauderdale generally vaguely south to the Caribbean and Central America without him, not to be seen since. She wanted him to come along with his proven job skills—bartending and yacht chartering. Yet he had feared the adventure would expand and continue around the world in a ceaseless string of aimless spontaneities that in time would sour what they already had. And he said no.

Her name was poisonous when he felt low, alone. He blotted it out, reminded himself there must be no conceivable link between Annie Shea (tumbling long blond hair, bronze skin, sneak attacks in the night) and the cowgirl cartoon woman of his dreams, who may have just become corporeal in the Athenaeum.

And love, love with these symptoms, didn't happen with Elaine Prescott, who since Florida was the one most likely to be his wife. No, not with her or anyone else.

The wine helped ease the tightness and soon the feeling was no longer a threat. He poured another, drank it in the kitchen. Better if she hadn't flattered him that women notice men too. In the fall one of his best friends from college, visiting from California, had taken him aside and talked of women, of marriage and love, thinking this might help him understand his problems with Elaine, who was then living with him. His friend fully believed that his own wife was ordained to be so from birth. Two folks out of four billion, give-or-take, prearranged by God to marry. Fair enough: could this be the prelude to a perfect pairing, cowgirl and investigator? Across yawning abysses and continental divides, two can be arranged to be together, blind-date synchronicity by the Great Unseen. Perhaps to be covered in a future issue of *American Science*.

He stepped from the living room through double doors into his office and called her answering service, asked the operator to take the message word for word. "Scientist wants to talk to Goethe about possible job. Shaw not invited. Thursday. Oyster House?" And then his listed office phone number.

Remembering and assessing the impression he'd made. He'd been horrible. She'd seen him at his worst, his least prepared, his most unsophisticated. Running around after her and she'd probably been in the bathroom the whole time. Damn, he'd said "Yikes," an epithet he reserved for the shower, or occasionally the middle of the night alone, half in a dream, no other time. Next time around she'd have much to learn from him and about him, that he knew a great deal, that he could handle the world and could do so with more aplomb than she'd yet seen. Musical: he owned an antique Martin small-body guitar, what they called an 017. Composed music on it. And his piano, an old Jurgens upright in prime condition. That he was an investigator doing uptown work under the license of a down-and-dirty downtown agency in the heart of the real city. Did push-ups and sit-ups to stem the negative effects of age and his use of alcohol. An expert driver, even in a battered old mustard-yellow rust-scarred Subaru. An exceptional friend, deeply loyal. Average height and weight with a strong body and enormous capacity for love. Of women. Dark eyes, some had said, teasing, bedroom eyes, good legs, good health, solid glutei maximi. All this and more: you also get a good singing voice. Romantic. Pliant, uncertain view of the world. The important things. Vague distrust of men with unknown motives. And of the human race a clear-eyed pessimism that needed an infusion of contradiction and hope.

She could get to know these things. Not all at once. But dinner was a start, if she wanted to risk it with him, as he was confident she did.

She called back on Tuesday, a message on his tape. "Goethe accepts. Seven-thirty? Glad Shaw can't make it. Let me know if there's a change. And thanks."

Thursday evening he walked from under the Central Artery toward Union Street, feeling less and less easy as he approached the Oyster House. After one taunting day of sun, the creeping gloom of mid-March had returned. Undifferentiated dreariness that belied what the local weathermen had loosely, even recklessly, defined as "light rain." Neither word was correct. The precipitation was more an enveloping contagion, smelling of diesel. Something even a proper Bostonian could hate.

He was purposely five minutes late, and now very edgy about seeing her again. He'd forgotten much of her face, the tonal shadings of her voice, that indifferent drawl, if she was kind. Tearing the flyleaf from Goethe and dropping the book *pages down* on the floor—perhaps a signature to some larger compulsive psychopathology that might explode full force during dinner. At the front door he hesitated, peered through the glass to find her, then discovered her arm slipping through his and giving it a squeeze.

"Damn, you scared me."

She smiled as she had before, and she started to come back to him. "Didn't mean to. Good to see you." She was half a head shorter; if she leaned on him her head would fit very neatly on his shoulder.

Inside, they stood waiting to be seated. She took his arm again and he felt better about her. "You've given me plenty to do the last couple of days, Mr. Balcazar."

Right. Incredibly, he'd never said his name; somehow he assumed she must have already known it.

"I had your number, and I had Beacon Hill, and that's how I started. T. D. Balcazar. I just found it yesterday."

"Lauren, I'm sorry to put you to all that work." She looked sparkling in white cotton pants, bright blue silk blouse, a heavy strand of cloisonné beads, green veined with gold, around her neck.

"So what's the T. D.? Is that what they call you?"

"Thomas Dreddiker. Dred, normally."

"Dred. Wow. That's wild. Like Dred Scott."

"Kind of the same."

"If I called you T. D. instead, would you mind?"

"No, if you'd like." Some did, some of the time. "And Lauren. Lauren what."

"McHalick," it sounded like. "Like Kevin McHale, with a lick at the end. What's Balcazar? Is that Greek or something?"

"Curbside setter, really."

"Excuse me?" She leaned forward, cocked her head.

The waitress, Sherri, took orders for his martini with black olive, her white wine with a cube of ice, his "bowl of chowder immediately" and her "I'll have one, too" all with crisp efficiency, so that Lauren had not lost her thought.

"Curbside what?"

"Meaning, part Dutch, some Spanish—I figure a hundred and twenty-eighth, enough Anglo so I'm allowed my Beacon Hill apartment, but then there's a rogue chromosome from Morocco. Probably a saber-wielding Moor." Yes, right, she was very pretty. Very, very pretty.

"Wow. That's quite a mix. And I thought I was a hybrid."

"Are you?" Yes, of course. She was authentically blond, but her skin was possibly Mediterranean like his, her throat, the crescents of her breasts a creamy teak color.

"Polish Catholic, on my father's side. And Jewish—from my

mother's father. But my mother's mother is bedrock Episcopalian. English.''

When the drinks arrived she downed her wine in two enthusiastic gulps, clunked the ice cube around in her mouth, and started craning her neck for the waitress even as he sipped into the lower half of his martini. He felt ever more at ease with her, knowing she drank, as he felt instinctively friendlier toward men who drank. Drinkers like him, two or three cocktails a day, chronic, rarely excessive, were becoming an endangered species. Perhaps he was alcoholic. His last doctor didn't think so, declaring his liver to be normal size and suggesting alcohol is fine if you eat right, just take it easy. Perhaps he wasn't alcoholic. In fact he had taken take it easy, just about every single day for the last six or seven years. Happily, he rolled the olive around in his mouth. At last Lauren caught Sherri's eye and ordered another round for both of them.

"Lauren."

She smiled with wide eyes and mimicked him. "T. D." And then added, "Hot in here, isn't it?"

"It's fine." He smiled back. "I'm glad you're here."

The ice cube, lessened by a third, appeared on the tip of her tongue; she took it lightly in her hand, touched it to her collarbone.

"Yeah, me too, you're more relaxed now than Monday. That's good."

It was one of those cubes with a hole through the middle, for easy handling. At its touch to her skin she cringed slightly, then found the sensation agreeable, tracking it across the very top of her left breast and leaving a trail of dew.

"Hot in here," she reiterated. "It's nice." Now across the other side, finding the barely perceptible line where her breast lifted two finger-widths below the collarbone.

"You may have noticed," he said, entranced. "I was attracted to you. This can happen."

"I noticed. I think likewise." She brought the ice into the ridge above, at the base of her throat. Cooled, her skin flashed pink and goose-fleshed, distending the tiniest hairs along the column of her neck, these downy filaments visible only with the light *just so*. And now on the other side.

"Almost all gone," he said rather lamely. *What*, he wondered, *is she telling me*?

"The job," she said. "You have a job."

She plopped the remnants of the ice into her mouth, rolling it about with her tongue.

"Okay. Be that as it may, there actually is a job."

"Salty," she volunteered—how the ice tasted.

"Yes, the job. Maybe it has nothing to do with how pretty you are." She chewed on it, swallowed. Moisture where she'd traced the ice was evaporating. Her skin would be warming, drying, feeling good there.

He remembered that there could be, in fact, a real job. Existing as such only for the right person at the right time, it had been open on and off for six months, depending on business. Only one other candidate so far. Radcliffe, last fall. Gretchen Somethingburger, with an acquired case of Cambridge lockjaw, inclined to note abstruse and useless ironies that spilled forth from her in sputtering, self-conscious giggles of ill-timed glee. Ill-timed and ill-expressed with her ravenous consumption of an especially wet (too much Thousand Island dressing, as he recalled) taco salad, some of which ended up as soggy projectiles on his favorite and only wool blazer.

"Well, I'm interested, I hope you know. It is, in fact, a job with you?"

"Yes."

Sherri came back with the drinks and at last the servings of chowder, which lolled hazardously in shallow platters. Dred was no longer hungry, decided not to eat.

"I haven't really had a job in over six months."

"I was going to ask. Why not?"

"Wrong makeup, who knows?"

"I doubt it. What were you doing before then?"

"Before last summer I was in Ohio, Pennsylvania. Since then—well, it's a lot to go into. Maybe not now."

"Okay, not now."

"But it's stupid. I do need to make some money. When can we have an official interview?"

"We're having it," he said, with a quick smile. "The job itself is kind of secretarial, but there may be some more substantial stuff—"

The crash could have been a speeding car exploding through a plate glass window, it was that loud, right behind him. A fleeting second of not knowing if life was in the balance, fight-or-flight voltage singing through the nerves. Then a chill of cathartic silence and relief. Sherri in shock standing over an irretrievable mess of dinner on the floor, glasses and plates, with the man at the table beyond red-faced with rage.

"Christ, lady, you almost gave me a heart attack. What the hell."

"Henry," said the woman next to him, taking his arm.

Lauren was standing, glaring at the man. "She didn't mean it. Obviously."

"Sorry," said Sherri.

"Next time just say something, like 'Look out below.' Anything. I really do have a heart condition."

"What an ungodly mess," Henry's companion was saying, a fat older man with mean-spirited eyes. Now Lauren was bending over with Sherri, picking up gloppy chunks of crockery and glass. She scowled at the second man. "You'll get your dinner, in time."

Sherri didn't want her help. "You shouldn't be doing this."

"Hey, I used to waitress myself, I've been through it."

"Please don't, really, it's the rules."

"What am I going to do, sue you?"

"Right."

"Fuck that," said Lauren a little too loudly. Dred was fascinated, deciding to raise himself up and lend a hand. Lauren had seafood slop all over her hands, streaks on her white pants. Now one of the busboys was here, an older man who must have heard her last remark. He considered her sternly.

"Please, miss, go wash up. Or go to your seat."

Instantly she narrowed her eyes back at him. "Just trying to help." She glanced quickly at Dred, "Be right back," then turned and headed for the ladies' room.

Henry's evil-eyed companion was looking at him. "Spunky, isn't she?"

Dred thwarted him with an icy stare, then sat down again, not facing him, and finished his martini. In a minute, before he could wonder if she was all right, Lauren was coming back, with her sleeves rolled up and her thumb holding a small wad of tissue pressed against the underside of her wrist.

"Oops," he said.

"Don't worry, just a small cut."

He got up, grabbed both their glasses. "Let's go to another table. A noncretinous environment."

"A what?"

He said nothing but led her to another room, a far corner table away from people, sat with her, wanted to see the cut. She presented her arm to the center of the table, near the candle, her thumb still pressed against the tissue. "Take your thumb away." Instantly she did. He took her arm in his hand, just below her wrist, lifted the tissue from the wound. A small cut, yes, a thin slice under a flap of translucent skin, very little blood in an area thick with arteries and veins. "Might be glass in there." She shook her head. He gradually relaxed his hold on her arm, widened the circle till his hand barely touched the skin. She watched him, him looking at her. A slow sweep of his curled palm along her arm to her elbow, the tickle of these hairs, this filigree, silvery even in winter. His fingers moved to her cheek, shimmery down below her ear. Visible. Intangible.

"I'm a little fuzzy," she said, a loopy grin.

"Lauren. You're very beautiful."

"Thank you."

Her left hand came into his, and now her fingertips, little bumps of hardened skin.

"Guitar."

"Yes."

"Good calluses. You play a lot."

"Couple of nights a week."

Her eyes wouldn't leave him.

"You're not from around here."

"No. Born in Ohio. Then to Montana, then around and about and back East."

"Montana, neat. Great state. Big sky, horses."

"Yeah. I left there when I was sixteen."

"Are you seeing somebody? And happily?"

She laughed, but now a little hitch to her shoulder, a coolness in her widening eyes. "T. D., I like you but I'm not going to seduce you. I'm just here."

"Okay. Maybe I can seduce you."

"You're not doing badly. Do you think that's what you should do?"

He leaned back and allowed the new waitress to interrupt. An explanation for the move, a request for drinks, please pass apologies on to Sherri for any suggestion that they were hiding from her, and sorry we left the chowder and no thanks, we're not hungry right now.

"Steel strings. Tell me it's rock and roll and maybe I'll be in love."

"Hey, look, I like you, okay? It wasn't going to take long to tell you. But this job—I mean, there really is a job, right?"

"Okay, here we go." He drew a breath, leaned back, and prepared himself for business. "I have a new word processor I uncrated just last week that I'll never understand. It has a program on it called Wordmate that I can't even get onto the screen. I have two new answering machines, one for each phone, that I'm always screwing up, so we're lucky to be here at all. I have a cranky thermostat. I have a coffee maker—"

"Listen, I'm actually a very capable person, and I can probably do all these things. But I'm lost. I mean, what is it that you *do*?"

"Mostly I have to manage my enormous portfolio, untold millions that need constant attention."

"You're joking, of course."

"Of course."

"Still, you sound very Old Boston. As much as I know it."

"You'll know it soon enough, but not from me."

"Okay." She smiled. "What else?"

"Well, I enjoy music, piano and guitar, like you—this sounds like a first date, doesn't it? Okay, I dabble in investigative work, cook gourmet breakfasts, do crosswords, help counsel my older brother in keeping his marriage young and alive. And oh, so much more. End of commercial." He immediately regretted throwing in Kurt and Erica and their failing marriage.

"Investigative work. So you're a detective?" A wry grin that betrayed a trace of fascination.

"Strictly speaking, no. I don't have a license. I work off someone else's license, guy's name is Frank Cirione, he's the real thing, a real private detective, his father and my father were old school buddies in New York, and one thing led to another and technically I'm an employee of his. An operative. It sounds funny, but it's legal."

"So you're not really official?"

"I am as an operative, I'm just not licensed. Pure technicality."

"Okay. And you need help?"

"When I'm on a case, it's important to have someone in the office. I miss calls, some people don't talk to the machine. There's a new client, we've been playing phone tag. I hate to lose them, this is a chance to do some very good work with a very big client. There's some legwork, too."

"This could be wild. What's the case about?"

"Some sort of high-tech thing, maybe corporate fraud or sabotage, I'm not sure yet. Computer company. We keep missing each other, I don't have the details."

"Do you use a lot of other stuff, like hidden video cameras and things?"

"No, not yet. Someday maybe."

"Really? You really don't?" Her surprise was punctuated with a nervous toss of her head just as, behind her, the bartender was approaching to interrupt. "You're Mr. Balcazar?"

"Yes."

"Sir, there's a call for you at the bar. From a woman named Elaine."

With an apologetic glance to Lauren, he lifted himself from his chair. "Former colleague, that's all." For the first time Lauren looked lost in her own thoughts and became distant, smiling vacantly.

At the corner of the bar Dred found in the wall mirror one third of his guest reflected. Distracted by something out the window.

"What. I've got company."

"Dred, be nice. I'm in your apartment."

"Do me a favor and get out of it."

Lauren was waving at someone through a far window, now rising from the table.

"Dred, please, I'm trying to help. I mean, thank God you had the restaurant down in your appointment book, otherwise—"

"Elaine, *what* is going on?"

"You've got to come back—someone's broken in."

He turned and she had just shot a hasty look his way, was edging through the crowded tables to the door, signaling to the someone past the window—he couldn't see who.

"I mean, nothing's disturbed that I can tell, but the kitchen window's broken—the one to the roof. And I think your computer's been stolen."

She was gone.

"Are you all right?" Elaine asked. "Have you been drinking?"

"Sit down in one place and don't move."

He slapped a twenty and a ten on the table, grabbed his coat, and rushed outside onto Union Street. In this neighborhood a dozen street corners offered sanctuary, a part of the city whose peculiar geometry (the Old Boston and the New Boston rubbing elbows in awkward disharmony) was virtually unsurpassed for abrupt disappearance.

Elaine Prescott was old Old Boston, tracing her ancestors back to the kind of fringe Puritans who, Dred believed, were much more savage and far less noble than commonly portrayed, probably ate gravel with their food to help digest it, made friends with the

Indians in order to cheat them, prayed incessantly for long growing seasons, more real estate, regular bowel movements, and healthy genes to spawn as many offspring with as little effort as possible. The gene pool was drying up with Elaine. For all her connections, club memberships, and generally decorous behavior, he doubted Elaine could survive one week in this town—or any other—completely on her own. She simply could not handle the logistics of city living. She was a bad driver and the worst parallel parker he'd ever seen. She could never order in a restaurant without confusing even the most seasoned waitress. She didn't understand how the MBTA worked and vowed she never would. He couldn't simply dismiss these incompetencies as quaint; they were basic adult skills, and he decided he was not patient enough to wait for her to acquire them.

But her most offensive habit, now, was that she continued to love him in the face of his tireless campaign to give her every reason not to. Almost as irritating was her desultory use of his apartment for surprise visits, either to see him or some of the things she had left behind and refused to claim, using her old key, misinterpreting that Dred retained just enough affection for her not to change the lock.

He had tried once, but the locksmith never showed up.

Tonight everything in his two-floor apartment seemed to be just as he had left it, but for three differences, readily apparent: the double-hung window in the breakfast nook on the second floor, facing out on his neighbor's roof, had been opened; his new computer was missing from the table in his office; and Elaine was here to distract him from finding out why.

"Even if you don't have an alarm you should stick on those little stickers that say that you do. Especially on your windows to the roof—any burglar with a shred of imagination comes in the back way. You insist, of course, that the window was locked—"

"Elaine, if it wasn't, why would he break the glass?" Just below the latch of this nine-pane sash hung a sheet of gray shirt cardboard, lightly taped to the muntins around the pane. Inspecting behind it, Dred saw that the glass had been shattered by a blow from the outside, several small triangular shards still glazed in place, bent inward.

"You'll notice I cleaned it up for you. And covered over the hole."

It intrigued him that Elaine so readily took credit for any act of cleaning, when she was secretly a terrible slob. Far easier for her to pick up after someone else than to keep her own life in order. She traipsed along behind him as he moved through the living room toward his office. He hesitated, stooped to the carpet, and recognized black crumblings of asphalt, brought in from the flat roof, someday to be a patio, outside the kitchen window. Sneakers or running shoes with treads were most likely responsible.

The double doors to his office were open and his desk light on.

"Did you do anything in here?" he asked.

"No, nothing. Just looked."

"Meaning: did you open the doors and turn on the light?"

"Well, of course. How else—"

He turned to her. "Elaine. The office doors were closed when I left, and all the lights were out."

"Exactly. That's just how I found it."

"So if the burglar is going to steal my computer, he has to open the office door, a smooth brass doorknob, and turn on the light, probably the wall switch—"

"And if he had any brains he'd wear gloves and use a flashlight."

"I'd never make that assumption. And I hope you know me well enough to have learned that."

With all those generations of Brahmin inbreeding, Elaine Prescott somehow had lucked out with a very pretty face, soft freckled skin that went vulnerable when she believed she was being scolded, especially by him, for any kind of significant mistake (like contaminating the scene of the crime with her fingerprints), and now as she bit her tongue and looked chastened he fought off a twinge of sympathy. "But you didn't touch anything else."

"Absolutely nothing. Really."

His desktop was fine, the same mess he'd left it in. He unlocked the lower right drawer and determined that his files were okay, their heavy bulk undisturbed. Some should be boxed and taken to a clos-

et, like bank statements from his Florida days, and resolutely forgotten. Later.

"Front door was locked, you used your key and came in, the
lights were off, you felt a draft from the open window upstairs."

"Right."

"Then you turned the lights on, came upstairs to the kitchen, saw
what had happened. And you looked around."

"Right. And swept up the glass. And put cardboard in the hole."

He'd had the computer, a respectable Korean-made portable with
a hard disk, just long enough for its outline to be discerned where
dust could not gather. The cables were still there, the printer, the
manuals, the floppy disks—all the stuff he vowed one day to try to
understand. It wouldn't have been stolen if it weren't here in the
first place, came here only as the result of Elaine's nagging that he
"invest" in this kind of machinery, certain to pay dividends if he
wrote just five letters a week. She had a California contact who
could get this stuff to him at 10 percent over wholesale. She loved
the model she had at home, doing public relations work for her
women's club. She knew Wordmate. And she was going to enjoy
the rare opportunity of being his tutor.

Despite, or maybe because of, her intervention in the purchase of
the machine, it cost him 10 percent under list and only twice had
been deflowered by 120 volts flowing through its tiny, quirky veins.

"Funny they didn't take the printer, too," she said. "Twelve
hundred dollars."

"Why?" He was thinking, maybe there are prints on the pin hous-
ing of the cable, where computer spits its binary babble to printer.

"Why what?"

"Think why he, or they, didn't steal the printer, too."

"Too heavy?" she blurted. "Too heavy for one, anyway, carrying the computer, too."

"Possible." He turned to her. "You want a drink, don't you?"

She sighed, nodded. "I can project myself sitting down, having a
drink with you, yes."

The martini glow from the Oyster House had dissipated. He
guided her toward the kitchen, grabbed a Bass Ale for himself,

pulled out a jug of white wine for her, and poured it into a jelly glass with a threaded rim—the only clean small glass on the drainboard. Sitting at the drop-leaf pine table by the window where the burglar had entered, Elaine was still working on her problem.

"Maybe they thought there was something on the computer."

"That's my guess, too."

"But if they had time to boot it up and get into Wordmate, they'd see there was nothing there."

He stood with his back against the sink, drank half his glass of ale.

"Maybe there wasn't time."

"Maybe," she said.

"Elaine. Tell me just how it works. If I knew about computers, and I broke into a detective's office looking for confidential information somewhere in the guts of the machine, what would I do? What would I look for?"

She cleared her throat. "Well, with this machine, first I'd have to put in a boot disk and then turn the computer on. But I checked your box of floppies and it looked as though nothing had been touched."

"Go on."

"Well, maybe that doesn't matter because you can tell just looking at the computer it's got a hard disk, and if I were looking for something in there I would assume the detective was writing everything to the hard disk. So I'd boot up, get into Wordmate, and enter a 'wp' command. That's if I was looking for a text document, which I imagine I would be. Then I'd enter 'edit a document' to see what kinds of things you had in there."

Barely able to follow what she was saying, he finished his ale.

"See, when I talked to the guy in California, he said he would load everything you needed onto the hard disk, so you wouldn't be working on your *A* drive at all, and if I were a burglar who knew computers I'd make the same assumption. So, if I were short of time, I'd take my chances and steal the whole computer, but leave the floppies behind. Of course, this is the first time I've been here since you've had the computer, so I don't know what you've done with it. Maybe there's nothing on the hard disk at all. Maybe it hasn't even been formatted or initialized."

"Elaine. If you were tutoring me, would you talk to me like this?"

"It really isn't so terribly hard. You just have to know the language a little. I mean, you *asked* me—"

"If I just wanted to steal the thing, just to fence it somewhere, what would I do?"

"I guess I'd do just what happened. I'd pack it up and take it."

"Okay."

"Are you going to report this? Call the police?"

Dred reached into his refrigerator for another Bass Ale. "Not quite yet." Not until absolutely necessary. Partly through instinct, partly through Frank Cirione's repeated advice, Dred believed most encounters with the police to be questionably productive in matters of any subtlety. "Now, where's that glass."

"You left it on the counter, by the sink."

"I mean the broken glass, from the window. In the trash?"

Even as she said, "Is that all right?" he took out the grocery bag he used for trash, centered it on the floor under the overhead light, and stooped down to see what, if anything, these shards might tell him.

"Want some help?" she asked while he placed the larger pieces on the floor.

"No." The remains of breakfast were directly underneath; one large scepter-shaped piece had knifed into a bit of fried egg, another had snared a buttery crumb of English muffin. But laid out now in a puzzle replicating how the glass had been at the instant of impact, there was something here worth noting. "You found nothing inside— a rock, anything they might've used?"

"No." Elaine was up, moving around him to the jug of wine, pouring herself another. He stood up and glanced through the window to the rooftop as if this very familiar view needed one additional examination, confirmation that there was nothing there that could have been used to break window glass.

"You picked up these pieces with your bare hands, right?"

"For the smaller ones I used a paper towel. The long skinny ones are the baddies." True. The long skinny ones, treacherously sharp, revealed fluffy white filaments.

"And then I used your broom and dustpan."

He looked once again at the pattern of breakage in the center of the puzzle, where several seams rayed out to the edges. Even without use of a magnifying glass, a thread of dark-colored something was visible. Then a tiny triangular swatch of the same stuff.

"They couldn't have used their bare hands," she decided. "They'd cut themselves."

"Black leather. Probably a ski glove, something heavy."

"I'm sorry, Dred. I should've left everything alone. I was thinking, well, he's new at this kind of work, I can help—"

And now something else, a curl of bright green thread from a seam near the top of the puzzle. He rolled it between forefinger and thumb, ascertained its synthetic springiness.

"Poly something."

"You can tell?"

He could unequivocally. "You forget, my two years with Dad in the wool business, you get to know these things. The sweater you're wearing is probably Shropshire. This stuff is pure Texaco. Green parka or windbreaker of some kind. Broke the glass, reached in to undo the lock, snagged his sleeve."

She was biting her lip. "I'm sorry. Really."

"Elaine. Black gloves and green parka gets me nowhere. Don't sweat it."

"Still, I'm sorry—"

"You are chronically, compulsively sorry. Go sit down and relax."

The drizzle outside was strengthening into a steady, dull rain drumming on the rooftop, angling from the northeast away from the cardboarded hole. Through the rest of the window he peered out into the blackness and reconstructed what must have been the intruder's route from the street up here to this white, brightly lit bachelor's kitchen. He would need to get from the sidewalk through the neighbor's stockade fence door, normally unlocked, into the small yard. Easy enough. Then up onto the homebuilt trash enclosure, then onto the man's garage roof, heavily railed with wrought-iron fence and spikes, which, with one false step, would instantly have you singing tenor. Thence to the man's apartment roof, now a freshly built sundeck of pressure-treated parquet, and a five-foot hoist from the garage level—no mean feat for those not in tiptop physical shape. Across the sundeck to a four-, maybe four-and-a-half-foot-high wooden fence and into Balcazar property, the near half of the roof, unfinished. To risk entry this way, you'd probably want to think it through before actually doing it.

He seized the last bottle of ale from his refrigerator and against his better judgment slid into a chair opposite Elaine at the table. Her eyes wouldn't leave him alone. On his case. He wondered quickly about Lauren's disappearing act, why she could not be here tonight instead of Elaine. In his chest again, the slow squeeze of the vise.

"Drinking all that beer, how do you stay so thin?"

He pretended not to hear her. Elaine would do this to him from time to time, try to catch him off guard with this kind of backhanded compliment, well-meant but really very clumsy.

"Really," she said. "You look wonderful."

"Elaine. Please don't start." He was looking past her, recalling the details of Lauren's face and voice, what, if anything, had happened that suggested she was being less than honest with him. No. Nothing fit. Why did she leave?

"Why not? I mean it—you look wonderful."

As soon as he'd taken the phone call at the bar, at just that second when he'd turned his back, Lauren had left. "It doesn't go anywhere."

"I don't mind if it doesn't go anywhere. I love you anyway. You need someone to tell you these things." Her hand came to rest on his forearm, a gentle pressure. "You don't want to waste the best years of your life having only yourself to admire you."

"Elaine, give me a break, I've got to think this thing out a little bit."

"You mean there's hope?"

He pulled away and got up, remembering that Elaine too easily mistook mere physical proximity—face-to-face at this small table—for intimacy. At the sink he finished his ale, rinsed the glass, turned it upside down on the drainboard. Under the circumstances, it was "washed."

"Dred. I know you're bothered by this break-in. I'm sorry."

He was bothered less by the break-in than by Lauren's fast fade from dinner, that funny look on her face as he left the table to go to the phone. There was no way to guess at any possible connection between the two. It was safer to remember that strange things can happen simultaneously in different places without cause and effect arising to link them.

For a moment he worried about his security; that a flimsy sheet of cardboard was no deterrent to a repeat attack. The kitchen door, which Dred thought served no function at all but for banging into, was hinged near the outside wall, swung open into the kitchen so that it partially occluded the window overlooking the roof, kept colliding with his breakfast chair. Armed with a heavy antique brass hasp and latch, the door could be locked from inside the kitchen. Fortunately, the previous tenant had installed a dead bolt on the opposite side, in the hallway, so that an intruder, once gaining entry to the kitchen, might go no farther.

Elaine had stood up to put her glass in the sink. She took his hand.

"Hope you don't mind, but I want to go to bed with you."

"That's why you came over."

"Yes." He recalled that one night she had sealed herself in this kitchen, so angry with him she would not unlock the door. She chose to flee through the window to the roof and down to the street, not to show up until the next night.

"Not to get more of your things."

"No."

"I've got to sit down and think. Even if we were still together I couldn't go to bed with you right now." He could not have put it more gently. Anything else might reduce her to tears.

"I can change your mind," and she gave him her wild let's-do-it grin, moving in on him, her hand on the inside of his leg just as he edged around and moved past her, out of the kitchen, into the living room and his old faded wing chair. She did not immediately come after him; he heard her retrieving her wineglass, unscrewing the cap from the jug.

Lauren had waved at the restaurant window, at someone outside, and now Dred believed there was the slimmest of possibilities he'd seen that person too, at best a darkish hulk that may have been a person, leaning in toward the glass and seeing Lauren and waving to her to come outside. Or else, unless he believed this, there really was no one there, and she had slithered out into the night at the precise cue of Elaine's phone call. But it had not been the first opportunity for her to break away.

Elaine was here, kneeling at his side, stroking his arm, her chin poised weightless on his knee. Soon she would have her face in his lap and he would be arguing the merits of her body against the accumulated unpleasantness of their history together, the 90 Days' War last fall, punctuated by conciliatory bouts of frantic sex that left him feeling shamed and exhausted. Elaine, on the other hand, would become ever more invigorated, strengthened like Popeye inhaling spinach through his pipe.

"You're not concentrating," she said after grazing him with her cheek, a dot of her spittle spreading on his best gray wool slacks. "Think of this as a little fun—nothing else."

By thinking of Lauren and nothing else, his arousal surprised Elaine and empowered her with new energy. "That's better," she muttered, peering up at him with squinty eyes glazing with tears.

The day broke with the sun showering through tufts of gray clouds, chasing the tail of the miserable weather that had passed out to sea during the early morning hours. From the bedroom doorway near the foot of the stairs Dred watched Elaine clutch at his pillow and anxiously pull it to her before going limp in its embrace.

He'd been up an hour, since six, trying to remember. Polish father. Not "Mc" or "Mac," probably MIC or something. According to the phone directory, there was nothing under any of them, anywhere. All the *M*'s, and nothing.

Upstairs, on his second mug of coffee, he moved through the living room again, back into his office, where he felt more organized. He dialed her service.

"Lauren McHalick's line."

"Yes, message please. Could you have her call Dred Balcazar? As soon as possible?"

"Spell that please?"

He did. He gave his office number again. "I'm sending her something in the mail and I need a spelling for her last name."

"Just a minute."

She came back on. "I have 'M-I-C-H-A-E-L-E-C.' I don't know if that's right."

"Can you double-check? You must have a name for billing."

"Just a minute."

Another voice came on, an older-sounding woman. "Can I help you?"

Patiently Dred repeated his request.

"That's the spelling we have," she said. "It's her line, but billing is to someone else."

"So you don't have an address."

"No. We couldn't give that out anyway."

"Or her home number."

"Absolutely not."

"And the name for billing?"

"At the customer's request, no."

"Thanks. Appreciate the help."

He tried Boston area information, thinking she was listed but not published. She was evidently neither, not with that spelling.

He played back his most current office phone answering machine messages, the first from Elaine, the second from Harvey Monahan at American Data Corporation, the man he'd kept missing all week. Monahan was starting to lose his patience: "We've got to get moving on this thing before it starts to move on *us*, it's been what, two weeks since we first saw it, and as I've said, we're sure you're the man to do it. Sorry I'm hard to reach. Sorry *you're* hard to reach."

Elaine had sneaked up behind him, was working along his jaw-bone, under his chin, found his mouth, teased him with a light kiss and immediately pulled back.

"Let me get some coffee and then you can tell me about this Lauren creature." She was wearing his favorite blue terry-cloth bath-robe with the sleeves rolled back, much too big for her, as she turned and padded off to the kitchen. He got up and followed, tread-ing the patch of living room carpet and Navajo rug where last night they had made love, the last time (he swore), the very last time she would do this to him, saying it was all pure play and meant nothing. In the kitchen, barefoot, she seemed again very small, her chestnut hair unkempt and fluffy in the dusty morning light as she poured two fresh mugs of coffee.

"I never mentioned her name."

"Incorrect. She's in your appointment book for last night. And she was in your dreams. You forget you're a real blabber."

For the moment she seemed unconcerned, tossed her hair away from her eyes, challenged him with a grin. She wore an Indian neck-lace in three thin blades of hammered silver, small enough on her thin neck to be a choker, swelling a vein that columned up to the hollow below her ear. Making love, she would arch her neck, her face flushing with blood, the veins in her throat standing out hugely—as thick as crayons. When he was in love with her, these things were indiscriminantly attractive to him. She made love with the sin-ews and stamina of a panther, and this morning she would make him pay.

"Restless night. She's obviously on your mind."

"Elaine, you moved out in January. We can't go over all that again."

"Yes, I know. Let's not."

"Your father, I'm sure, is much happier for it."

"Yes, we've discussed that, and you're right. But my feelings for you. They're quite real."

Charles Baird ("call me Charlie") Prescott was so consummately

Old Boston that even Elaine could not describe who he was and what he did without acknowledging how ridiculous it sounded: senior partner in the fiduciary firm of Baird & Nichols, a colonial farmstead in Manchester-by-the-Sea, directorships of a dozen corporations, on the board of Massachussetts General Hospital (where Dred's brother, Kurt, practiced) and the Union Boat Club (where still, at the age of seventy, Charlie could be found any Tuesday or Thursday afternoon playing handball), patron of Symphony and Boston Ballet, ex-Commodore of the Eastern Yacht Club in Marblehead. A pragmatist of staggering ardor, Charlie's sole excursion into the impractical was his daily six o'clock gin-and-tonic with bitters, just *one*, regardless of season or weather, a ritual principally enforced (as Elaine told it) for the benefit of open communication with "the children" after work. Children meaning thirty-three-year-old Elaine and twenty-nine-year-old Henry (clerical gnome at Baird & Nichols, and too weak-brained for any significant advancement, regardless of connections).

At first Dred believed Charlie to have taken a shine to him, along with wife Elizabeth ("Beezey") when first they visited his Acorn Lane apartment in October. Then the moment when they arched their eyebrows at his garnishing of a martini with a black olive and he knew their respect for him could not last. Politically, of course, they were very conservative; he, if pressed, was diffidently left-of-center. They enjoyed making lots of money; Dred liked a fair wage. They wanted a son-in-law who would fill a Country Squire with enough little Prescott grandchildren to offset the procreational excesses of the Irish Catholics. Dred didn't care about Irish Catholics and didn't want kids of any kind. But mostly, he believed, the Prescotts were quintessentially blueblood and he was a mongrel of doubtful origin and genetic complexity.

Naturally they wanted to know what he "did." When he told them, they were visibly chagrined. Charlie's most damning observation, relayed to him by Elaine under some duress, was that "for all his travels and experience, I worry that you're involved with a man who seems so taken by the wonder of it all."

Like a hypodermic, the remark was both painful and sustaining.

"Elaine," he said, "I can't reconnect with a woman whose father says that I wonder too much."

She had to laugh. "I knew that would come back to haunt me. He just thought, what he meant was, you're kind of naive. Which we know is absolutely incorrect."

"I'm not so sure."

The infamous "wonder of it all" assessment came weeks before he sealed his doom with the entire Prescott clan just by *thinking* of taking on a case against Wilde, Tate & Tuttle, a competing but equally Brahmin fiduciary outfit that was probably in violation of every trusteeship statute in the Commonwealth. The plaintiff-in-waiting was a good friend whose modest portfolio had been brutalized by WT&T's blatant neglect. He hadn't taken it on, the case was now being settled out of court, but the mere possibility that he might become an adversary of one of Charlie Prescott's handball pals, Jack Tate, had fouled any chance he might have had with Elaine, their own considerable relationship problems notwithstanding.

"Jealousy aside, can you tell me about last night? At the Oyster House?"

"Not much to say. She took off right when you called."

"She got up and left?"

He nodded. "Want breakfast? I've got some eggs here, some sausage."

Elaine was pouring herself more coffee. "No appetite, really. Maybe some toast, if you've got it. I'll make it." She started flipping through cupboard doors in search of bread, which was never stored in the same place twice. "Why do you think she left?"

Right now he had no answer that made any sense. "Looked like she saw someone outside on the street, through the window. But I couldn't see."

"You think maybe it was just a coincidence, the burglary and dinner?"

"Hope so. If not, I don't understand it."

"Was she pretty?"

"Unfair question, but yes."

"I don't like her then. Where's the stupid bread?"

"In the fridge. Freezer." For a second, he felt something for her, sympathy more than tenderness. "Elaine. Let it never be said you're not pretty yourself."

Not looking at him, she was opening the bread and prying at two frozen slices with her fingernails. "I wish I liked myself a little more than I do, that's all."

"That has been a problem, yes. Now, unfortunately—"

"Maybe I should do Nautilus or something. Just to look better." She was cutting the slices free with a butter knife and jamming them into the toaster. He glanced at his clock, felt time slipping. She continued: "Muscle tone is what they say."

He took her hand, leaned over to kiss her on the forehead. "You're fishing for compliments, which is very unlike the Prescotts."

"Damn them all anyway."

"You are also quite pretty, which is also unlike the Prescotts."

She was leaning into him again, her body becoming just limp enough to fit his. "Dred." A faint smile. "I'm getting horny again."

A mistake to say that. "Don't, not now." He pulled away.

"Why not?"

"Elaine. Just. Because."

After toast with honey, just before nine, she was in his bedroom downstairs getting dressed for a morning of nothing to do before her afternoon shift at Shreve's gift department, and upstairs the office phone was ringing, Dred catching it just before its fourth ring, when the answering machine would kick in. Not Lauren, but Harvey Monahan of ADC.

"Mr. Balcazar."

Elaine was loudly griping, "Why don't men have full-length mirrors?"

"Mr. Monahan. I was just ten minutes from calling you."

"Please call me Harvey."

"Harvey."

"So when the hell can you start work? I don't even have time to see you and dicker, I want to retain you right now. I'm sick to death of your machine."

"Can't blame you. Just tell me what you need."

"I need *you*, and real soon. As I said like a week ago, Frank Cirione said you were the guy. People love Frank, and Frank loves you."

His manner, his voice, suggested a bear-sized man with a temperament to match, not one to waste anyone's time. A tough client, but fair.

"Okay. What's the problem?"

"Jesus, I had this long speech prepared, just to warm you up to it. You don't want the long speech, I can tell."

"No, I'll take the short version."

Harvey had to take another call, then came back. "We got a problem with a bug. Serious problem."

"A bug."

"Yeah, you're gonna have to bone up over the weekend, not here at ADC, somewhere else. Can you meet me Monday at, say, two? I'll give you directions."

The book was clear for Monday.

"Two o'clock, fine. What kind of a bug?"

"It's sabotage, of software. Really important, critical software, big-time stuff."

"Okay. Having to do with what?"

Harvey drew a breath. "Tell me what you know about artificial intelligence, and we'll take it from there."

2

After Harvey Monahan's call Elaine said she could spend Friday morning looking into it, making calls, asking around about artificial intelligence. Dred had his own lead, straight out of his alumni magazine, a guy he didn't like much but who might tell him where he could turn.

Some twenty years ago as a freshman across the hall, Todd Shaler was always the last guy to have fun, always ready with some excuse to hide in his room alone and then to appear later to offer a thorough and dispiriting critique of the kind of fun that he insisted they tell him they'd had. The safe assumption was, as Dred had learned, that college friends don't change. Not enough.

Ever the whiz in math and physics, he was now doing something unpronounceable in space research somehow linked, according to the alumni mag, with artificial intelligence. First stop in the ADC case, Friday afternoon, west of Boston in Bedford.

"How'd you find me?" Shaler asked over his Wild Turkey on the rocks. It was one of those mall restaurants that has too much brass and plants and croissant crumbs not wiped clean from the table.

"Phone book, called your wife, called Bedford Labs, fought my way through." Dred seasoned the moment with a shrug and a half smile, but Shaler would have none of it. Much heavier than he remembered, much sadder, with eyes that too easily got wet, Shaler had now become the fat man who would never be jolly.

"So you really are an investigator. I thought maybe you'd be a writer or philosophy type. Pretty scummy work, isn't it?"

Again Dred smiled, determined to keep Shaler from depressing himself. "Todd, it's a part-time pursuit for me. I take only certain kinds of things. It's not very lucrative."

Good, Shaler was brightening at his admission of misfortune. "How do you feed yourself? Got independent dough? Real estate?"

"I have some savings, a few stocks but not much. The investigative stuff pays most of the day-to-day bills, and I try to be a smart trader. That's it."

Dred sipped his martini, noted that Shaler was looking past him and not listening.

"Cute."

Dred turned and glanced at the object of Shaler's attention, a young waitress picking up drinks at the bar, pleasant-looking but otherwise unremarkable. Dred had long given up any systematic ogling of waitresses, but Shaler leaked a guttural noise of appreciation.

"You and I are both getting too old for that, Todd." Of doubtful sincerity, but one last effort to draw him into comradeship, old classmates together.

Shaler leaned in with a stage whisper. "I'm gonna wake up one of these years and look at my wife and know she's the last thing I'll ever fuck. You're not married, you wouldn't know about that."

"Maybe not."

"That's a conk on the head, and I'm not ready for it."

"You and Alexis doing okay?" Obviously not.

"Fine." Their own waitress brought Shaler's plate of tempura vegetables, set it in the middle of the table.

"You having dinner?" she asked.

"No," said Shaler. Then to Dred when she left: "Anthropologically, we're still hunters and gatherers." He popped something round, probably a mushroom, into his mouth. "Primal urges."

"We're also territorial." He hated how the conversation was going. "Creatures of habit, basically monogamous. Even," he added, "if it's serial monogamy."

"Give it up, Balcazar." The young waitress approached and brushed by them. "We're hunters. Gotta keep the cutlery sharp. Hey look, I got a wife who rolls over and plays dead in the sack, I don't think she's had an orgasm in ten years. Been married eleven. Maybe on our wedding night she faked it, who knows? Maybe you can't blame her. The thing is, whoever installed our ancestors on earth really screwed up, mucked up the formula for sex drives. A young guy in the right company, it's maybe twenty seconds from total inertia through arousal to ejaculation, the heart going bananas, the blood racing. A woman, you're talking two to three minutes at best, and that's a real prime filly. Figure two minutes, a hundred and twenty seconds, that's a six-to-one ratio. Women want to be loved, men want to attack."

Dred stared at him blankly, hating him. "Todd. Your math is lousy."

"Yeah, well, don't tell me it's not an attack, ninety percent of the time."

"Okay, I won't."

"Even with the women's movement, and all the sex books that tell you how to make it work for both of you, how to cut the ratio down, men are basically attackers and women basically expect it of them. Even Alexis—she says she just *wants* it, it doesn't matter how long it takes." He finished off his bourbon, rattling the ice. "Pain in the ass."

"Any chance I got you on a bad day?" A carefully contrived smile, trying to keep it light.

"Days are all the same." Now he pushed forward again with a wide-eyed intensity that was mildly alarming. "I got a hooker, once a week. Very pricey, two blocks off the Lexington Green, if you can believe it. She agrees with everything I said. Get to a certain age, almost any normal guy's got to have a hooker. If you're married."

The waitress came and took orders for a second round, the best chance to tolerate this guy for the twenty minutes they had left. On the Battle Green in the center of Lexington, maybe three miles away, there was the famous Minuteman statue with his musket cocked rakishly at his side. Modeled after Capt. John Parker, the man who organized the militiamen to stand up and fight for elemental political freedoms, among which was not the freedom for Todd Shaler to go fuck anybody he wanted.

"You never been married."

"No."

"Why not?"

"I was almost engaged once. Todd, let me confess, I'm not so good at other people's confessionals."

"Hey, nobody's confessing. Just saying what's on my mind. I happen to like women, so what? Don't you?"

He remembered: in college Shaler did not drink often, but when he did his dark temperament became marbled with real hostility. Happily, at that moment the second martini arrived, this time without a black olive, but it didn't matter anymore. Shaler took down half his bourbon in one vindictive gulp.

"Todd, I need your help with something, gotta get down to business."

"Sure. 'Course we don't see each other for fifteen years, seemed a good time to catch up. People have to say what's on their minds, otherwise they never have the chance."

"I know the feeling. Let's do this again sometime, now that I know you're here."

Shaler narrowed his eyes suspiciously. "Anytime."

"I told you on the phone I just started this case, and maybe there's something you can help me with."

"Maybe. So what is it? Or can't you talk about it."

"Right, I can't, not yet, I don't know much. I've got to get up to speed on artificial intelligence."

Shaler puffed his cheeks out, shifted his weight. "People spend their lives getting up to speed on that. Good luck, guy."

"Yeah, well, it's not a career. I just need a start."

"I should get paid for this."

It did not seem intended as a joke, but it needed to be played that way. "I can give you five bucks, not a penny more."

"I'm serious."

"Todd, just give me the nutshell. I'm buying the drinks, damn it."

Shaler chewed on his tongue. "You can say it different ways. AI is the conversion of human expertise into computer language. That's the one-liner on it."

"That's it? Any more?"

"That's it, unless you want to make a career of it."

"Any books I can read—with large type?"

"Hey, you want my advice, wait till next month, down in D.C. they're doing the annual AI symposium, you should go and just fight your way into it. To get any kind of sophistication with it, that's what you should do. It's the AI ego parade of the year, you'll love it."

"Can't. Too late. Tell me, does the computer actually think?"

"Christ, I hate it when people say that. The program, the computer, learns from the user. Asks questions. Gives advice. But it doesn't think, not yet, and when it does, tell me, I'm outa here."

"Okay, that's a help."

Shaler was finishing his drink, rattling his ice again, a guy who doesn't waste anything. "Might have another, if we got time."

"I can't, I'm gonna have to go."

"Yeah, too bad you missed the last conference, coupla weeks ago. Over at MIT."

"Tell me."

"The usual nerd herd. Fluid dynamics, wind tunnels. Stress types. Expert Systems types."

"Expert Systems?"

"That's a big part of AI. C'mon, Balcazar, where've you been? If you're gonna live in Boston you gotta know these things."

"I'll read up. Expert Systems." Dred made eye contact with their waitress, nodded when she mouthed "Check?," lifted his glass and regretted that there was no olive to tumble into his mouth.

"What the hell is Balcazar, anyway? Is that like Greek or something?"

"No, the name is Spanish."

Shaler crinkled his brow. "Well, you're Greek to me, Balcazar."

He decided he now understood about Shaler, that his view of the world was contorted equally by a lousy attitude and rank stupidity. It saddened him that after all this time Shaler was still a monumental asshole, would never surprise anyone, would never disappoint. An hour earlier, running ahead of schedule, Dred had driven by the Shaler house along a darkly wooded street of postwar-era split-level ranches with their false brick fronts and cheerless pastel colors, the Shaler place its original turquoise with incongruous barn-red trim, Alexis it must have been standing out in the driveway in her shiny green overcoat, arms akimbo, smoking a cigarette and staring balefully at their car, a large Chevy station wagon battered by long family trips to who-knows-where. Their son, it looked like, was shooting hoops with a deflated soccer ball, and as Dred parked on the opposite side of the road a few car lengths ahead and watched in the rearview mirror, the ball caromed off the hood of the car and splashed into a puddle, the kid uttering an epithet. What was most disturbing to Dred was that Alexis now was carrying on a heated conversation with *the car*, wagging her finger at its grille, sucking on her cigarette, unleashing a fresh tirade and not in the least bit breaking stride when the kid retrieved the soaking-wet soccer ball and tossed it at her back, quite hard.

Outside in the mall parking lot, Dred was saying good-bye to Todd, said he would call soon because there might be other things he might need to know. Alexis was two miles to the west, Shaler's whore two miles to the east, Bedford Labs two miles south, and here in the middle of this tidy triangle of shame and deceit, Shaler gave him a clammy, limp handshake, turned his body sideways to the cold wind, farted loudly, and walked off to his car.

Dred drove east on Route 2, through Lexington toward Boston, ADC, Harvey Monahan, AI, and Expert Systems slipping from his mind. Shaler's sour mug took over. Alexis talking to the car. Brother Kurt arguing with Erica. Elaine. Marriage might have worked for him, years ago, if someone had been there for him when he was less cautious, more open to risk—the way he'd been with Annie Shea, almost but not quite hopping aboard to sail away with her to places unknown. But not now. Marriage begins with love, has to turn practical, has to diminish into petty negotiations. I'll turn the lights off if you remember to turn the thermostat down. I won't leave my coat on the couch if you stop wearing that lousy perfume. I'll go to bed with you if you tell me you love me. All quotables from the 90 Days' War. I'll stop seeing my whore if you stop talking to the car.

He imagined himself with Lauren, invented a scheme to rescue her from her jobless nomadic life and whisk her to an island populated with intelligent and civilized people and make love till they were dizzy from exhaustion. Without words. Keep the feeling, don't talk, the way it had been with Annie, so many times.

Life plans always brought back Annie Shea. Life plans invariably included boats, warmer climes, less arduous work. It was astonishing to him that he really was an investigator, an operative for a tough city detective like Frank Cirione, even if he never imagined it to be a real career. It scared him in this business that the alarm would go off without warning, sooner rather than later, that it would be time to quit. Even simple jobs, like the first one Frank had offered him last fall—unauthorized depletion of inventory, stolen VCRs and toasters—could lead to dealings with ugly people, stupid people, jerks of all stripes, people who could hurt you. He'd never, even as a kid, had a punch thrown at him. He'd never had a gun pointed at him, never carried a gun, didn't intend to. He was the anonymous associate, the in-town brain. But the security of that kind of isolation couldn't last. As soon as somebody tried to hurt him, he'd be out of it in a minute. And Frank would be pissed as hell: I'm in the line of fire twice a month, what's the matter with *you*? One of these days you'll be in the heat and you won't be ready for it.

They had virtually nothing in common but their fathers, who were friends as kids, same P.S. 120 or something in Brooklyn back during the Depression. John Balcazar got into the wool business. Carmen Cirione became a cop. John got rich, moved into Manhattan. Carmen got shot in the stomach, took months to recover, quit the force and moved to Boston and became a private detective. Like his father, Frank became a cop, worked in homicide. Retired at thirty to join his dad. Carmen died from ailments related to his injury, Frank took over, moved the agency down to Fields Corner in Dorchester, light-years away from Beacon Hill into the heart and soul of the other Boston: working-class, short-tempered, combative, Irish Italian Black Hispanic in tense coexistence.

It was Frank who first sought him out, desperate for a contact with Boston's financial community, someone like John Balcazar's son who had a little free time and enough sense of adventure to do a little snooping. Somehow they hit it off. Frank was amazed that this well-bred, smart, nice-looking uptown sort of guy could handle street people and Brahmins with equal facility. Maybe you're not sure who you are, he ventured. Takes a while, Dred conceded, maybe a real long time. If you had a wife and kids you'd find yourself in no time, they won't put up with you if you don't.

No thanks, Dred would say. There were two big issues with Frank: having a wife and kids, and carrying a gun. He wanted Dred to do both. And the gun should be a very serious gun like a 9-millimeter Smith and Wesson, fifteen rounds to a clip, hollow point, aerate a guy with a hole you could toss a half dollar through.

No thanks, Frank.

Still, Frank was coming to think of him as his Secret Weapon. Few people who called the Cirione Agency needing surveillance or undercover work had any idea what resources Frank could marshal, technical and human. Anything corporate, anything reaching into the upper strata of Boston society at work or play would be Dred's domain, where you would need to put on the style. Odd, Dred believed, that whatever style was left to him was New York, Park Avenue, not Boston. There was a big difference. Frank agreed. You have to learn Boston, how Boston works. Boston doesn't know New York.

Where Route 2 swept over the crest of Belmont Hill there was a fine view of the city ahead, sparkling in the sun. Somewhere down there, Dred felt certain, Lauren was living, working, walking, talking. Now he recognized the ache again, that for whatever reason he was feeling too strongly about this girl too soon, all of forty minutes spent with her, hardly more than an introduction passing between them, her image again weakening, losing her face and her voice. Clear picture of her bending over helping pick up broken dishes and glass. A damn nice and unnecessary thing to do, something you stop doing later when you become colder, more thick-skinned, in your thirties, your forties. Her thigh stretching her white pants into egg-shaped flesh, something Renoir could do. Ice tracks on the skin of her chest. Clear picture of the cut on her wrist, the bump of her bone, the width of her arm, this softness in his hand. When he said he was an investigator she didn't run away. Only when he left to take the call from Elaine. Helping Sherri pick up broken plates was not an act. Having dinner with him was not an act. Leaving was not an act. Someone outside wanted to see her, pure, raw coincidence with Elaine's call. Maybe.

The ache went away, he looked at himself critically. It was not a good time to feel this way about a woman. Perhaps the three months with Elaine had weakened him more than he thought. Bad timing, just like a Christmas cold, to get the bug now, but the feeling had been missing for so long, missing since the final wave from the end of the dock in Fort Lauderdale. He'd never felt like this with Elaine. Insane even to begin feeling that way about this strange kid, to have so little to go on.

Kurt had told him before, warned him really, that he was romantic and led with his hormones, didn't check himself. Elaine, in the first few days with him, wondered about the music he liked, the stuff he rattled off on the piano when he was in the mood: Cole Porter, Rodgers and Hammerstein, the diminisheds and flatted ninths, the musical math of melancholy. Not from sympathy, but with a wrinkled-brow look of concern she'd say, "That stuff is so sad." True enough. Sad music was one of many things they could not share.

He pulled into the driveway of his rented garage off Willow Street, parked, then strolled up Acorn Lane toward 118. On the steps, with her arms wrapped around the cordovan valise in her lap, was Elaine, her small body curled up in a posture of pathos. She looked up at him.

"I thought you said five-thirty."

"I thought I said six-thirty," he told her, "and I was going to *call* you in Manchester. Not meet you here."

"I didn't want to go home," she said.

With this, he decided he couldn't risk moving a muscle. Too soon to tell if this was good news or bad.

"Well, you could've gone inside."

"I left my key on your night table. Stupid of me."

Possibly. "Want a drink?" he asked, stepping up to the door.

"Yes."

Once inside and upstairs in the kitchen, she seemed to recover from the gloom of her vigil. Without asking, he was making her a quick gin and tonic with bitters, and a martini for himself.

"You're acting different. It's something about the girl you had dinner with, isn't it?"

He pushed the drink into her hand. "Drink."

"What I mean is, I don't mean to suggest it's personal, just that something happened at dinner and you're more than just a little interested in knowing who she is. It would just help me to know, if I'm going to be much help to you. Even if I'm just stuck in the library."

Now she drank. Dred rescued a black olive from the open can in the refrigerator and tucked it into his martini.

"You have a lime?" she asked.

"No. Elaine, listen. The ADC thing is one thing, the break-in was another. Last night someone stole my computer. I think I might want it back, and I definitely want to know why it happened. I'm commissioning myself. You stick to the real job, I'll worry about the property crime." He took his drink into the office with Elaine following, sifted through the morning mail that he hadn't yet had a chance to identify.

"Okay. I'm doing artificial intelligence. We used to have limes."

There were two junk pieces for Elaine. Last fall she'd written all her catalogs with her new address. Mailing houses hear you live on Beacon Hill, 02108, they never leave you alone. He slapped the two pieces on the table next to her valise, where the computer used to be.

"So tell me, what do we know about AI?"

"Few things." She drank again. "Got some Xeroxes of stuff from the library, there in the valise. You owe me forty cents."

Damn it, now she was rattling her ice, finishing her drink already, one of those clunky twelve-ouncers with three ounces of booze. Four or five hits on the glass, it was gone.

"But I got, I think, a good lead," she said.

"You keep slugging them," he said gently, "you'll have problems."

"I'll be right back, then I'll tell you what I've got." She went off to the kitchen for a refill. Dred worried about her very little. After her blocked Fallopian tube she'd contemplated a hysterectomy. She had a charcoal-colored mole in the middle of her back that might have been melanoma, but wasn't. And then how she handled a car. For any of these ways that she might become hurt or sick or killed, he was simply philosophical. But he did worry about her drinking, with some of the same kind of anxiety that he worried about his own. Except that hers was worse than his.

"I'm back." She sat back in the leather client's chair, took a sip. "Okay. Through my friends in filmmaking I find there's a bunch of small television production companies that do a lot of training tapes for these high-tech types. Specifically, a place called Vidco, in Charlestown, that's worth a visit."

"How?"

"This was like ten phone calls later, but you can't beat it. Vidco did a show last summer, meaning a training program, for guess who?"

"I give up, tell me."

"The client, ADC. On Expert Systems." She looked very satisfied. "I assume that's close enough, for starters?"

"That's very nice work."

"Yeah, but get this. It's a program specially for knowledge engineers. That's what ADC calls them—the guys who make up the programs for AI."

"Knowledge engineers."

"I'm just reporting, Dred. I swear, that's what they call them."

Greater Boston—anything contained inside the arcing beltway

of I-495 forty miles outside of downtown—was swarming with household-name high-tech enterprises. Digital, Wang, ADC, Data General, Lotus, Cullinet, Polaroid, Commonwealth Data. Monsters doing unknowable things with electrons. All vigorously acculturating the entire population of Boston, directly or indirectly, as serfs to the industry. Sure, it made sense that television production companies would spring up just to feed them. There were probably new companies that did nothing but make toilet paper for their bathrooms.

"And you?" she pressed. "Did you see your friend?"

He told her quickly about his drinks with Shaler, but not Shaler's extraordinary gloom, his wife's bizarre penchant for talking to cars, or that Shaler had a whore two blocks from the Minuteman statue in Lexington.

"Good. You should see more of your old pals. You don't have enough men friends anymore."

"He's not a friend. So do I get to see this program?"

"I made a date Monday, ten o'clock." She finished the second drink and got ready to leave, disappearing downstairs to retrieve her front-door key from his night table, grabbing her coat off the back of the Parsons bench, puffing upstairs to leave her empty glass in the kitchen.

"My car's in the underground garage," she said. Under the Common, dangerous after dark. "Gotta go."

"Back to Manchester?"

She nodded. "Old friend, speaking of which. He's coming by after dinner." A wicked little grin calculated to prod his interest.

"Enjoy."

He helped her with her coat, feeding her small arms into the sleeves. She had a date, he didn't. Her night would be long and dull; he would catch some jazz down at Ryle's, or maybe Dave McKenna at the Plaza Bar, see someone he knew, go to bed when he liked.

"Not so old, actually. One of Henry's pals, seemed nice enough, though he's only thirty."

He took the bait. "Thirty is the Dark Ages of a person's life. Arrogance beyond measure, ignorance beyond belief."

"You remember it well then," she said slyly, coming close to him, presenting herself.

" 'Bye," he said. He leaned over and touched a kiss on her forehead. She scowled.

"Once again a shitty little kiss on the frontal lobe. Jesus, always it's the man who decides!" She wheeled, then spun back and went for him like a cat, grabbed his head with unusual strength, found his mouth, pulled him down to her level. He could only relax in her determined grip, then respond to her concerted effort with his own show of enthusiasm, his tongue moving into the hollow of her mouth, her body collapsing into curves that fit his. Even under the padding of her London Fog over her handmade cable-knit sweater over her heavy cotton white blouse, Elaine was small and pliant in his grip, and something of the pleasure he felt when he first hugged her almost a year ago was now coming back to him. Some of the old oom-pah-pah.

But not all of it, not enough. And she noticed it, turning to him before opening the door: "Something's happening with you. I hope it's okay, but it feels strange."

"I'm fine."

"Yeah. I wonder."

"Okay, you know how this works"—he was recording in the general direction of the answering machine's microphone—"and presumably so do I although very often the machine doesn't work, so if you have the least doubt that your message isn't being recorded, call back and do it again, and please never buy a TX-20 if your house is susceptible to voltage surges, which mine is. Thanks, talk to you soon, and good luck."

He went downstairs and put on blue jeans, a white cotton un-ironed shirt, his Harris tweed sport coat, boots, no tie, picked up the *Globe* off the floor where Elaine had left it in the morning, and looked to see who was playing at some of the smaller jazz clubs. Ryle's, SlimJim's, TT The Bear's. It would be good to settle back with a Manhattan on the rocks and hear Jeannie Jacobs again, one of those local jazz balladeers who popped in from time to time, usually at Ryle's, with a voice too sure, too sweet and full to stay local for long. Searching the ads, he saw the continuation of an article on John Williams's still-young career as conductor of the Boston Pops. There was also a short continuation of an article headed "COMPUTERS THAT THINK?"

He flipped back to the start of the story. "COMPUTERS THAT THINK? SOFTWARE DESIGNERS SAY YES, WITH 'EXPERT SYSTEMS.' "

First he scanned it to get a fix on the principals: interviews with people at Polaris Software in Tech Square, Digital Equipment Corp. in Maynard, and American Data Corp. headquartered in Westville. Expert Systems being one of the branches of artificial intelligence: such a system used software that replicated the knowledge and judgment ability of a given expert in a given field. Knowledge engineers. Defense applications, aircraft design, Star Wars stuff. It's here. It's real and it's Now. Knowledge engineers. "We're not overly comfortable with the term," said software designer Herb Tuckerman of Commonwealth Data, "but it's gaining currency in the industry. The knowledge engineer obviously doesn't engineer knowledge per se. He takes existing expertise and develops a way for a computer to accept it, to hold it, and to apply it."

Accept, Hold, Apply. Knowledge as something organic and malleable, yielding to the master, the hardware.

"Of course knowledge," Tuckerman went on, "isn't really something we know. It's what we seem to know. In this case it's not what it is, it's what it seems to be. That's all we can care about."

The bedside phone rang, his private unlisted number.

"What's with you, home on a Friday night?" It was Kurt.

"I was just headed out."

Any debate with Kurt about how to spend a Friday night was inevitably a losing proposition. He was extending a last-minute dinner invitation. It was eight o'clock, he'd just finished with an emergency heart patient, their guests, the Langleys, had canceled just at six when someone gave them Celtics tickets, and Erica was dolling up a tenderloin roast that had his name on it.

"Not that you're always our second choice," Kurt was saying. "But something told me my brother might be tired of potpies and doughnuts."

He ate neither. But he realized he hadn't eaten anything at all since the day before. "Be right over."

More important was simply seeing them together. Last summer Erica had moved to Santa Fe for at least a month. In October Kurt moved in with a friend on Pinckney Street for two months, then returned to their Harbor Towers condominium when their fourteen-year-old son, Tony, was home from his California prep school for Christmas vacation. In February, the last time Dred saw them, Erica was preparing to go to New York for a couple of weeks.

Of course there were no sides in their troubles. Impossible choice. They were both fine, very different people, whose worst lapse was the catastrophic stupidity they exhibited in marrying each other, notwithstanding her being pregnant with Tony. Anthony Strause Balcazar, a nice young kid with more than his share of experience in peacemaking at home, no doubt would enjoy a career in diplomacy, having never groused that his birthday and parents' wedding anniversary were eight months apart.

They lived on the ninth floor, had a fine vantage point of the city's rejuvenated waterfront and all the new construction downtown. Kurt met him at the door and immediately took him aside.

"Erica's in a real snit. She'll be out later."

"Okay. Sorry to hear it."

"She wants to see you, but right now she's too pissed off at me to come out."

The roast was about ready in the oven but there was time for a drink, and an obligatory moment by the full-length windows to appreciate what Kurt called the three-hundred-thousand-dollar view. They stood there silently, looking out over the city and the harbor. Kurt reveled in things money could buy—and the time to appreciate them, which for a heart surgeon at Massachusetts General was notably lacking. Three years older and an inch taller (six feet even, that magic number that he used to lord over him when they were in school in New York), Kurt had decided on a career in medicine largely out of a sense of duty, wide-reaching and deeply felt, to something having to do with the Balcazar name. Now, about to turn forty, he was smarter about it all: he was successful, respected by his peers, and ever richer. He'd also saved a lot of lives.

In the kitchen his awkwardness bespoke a telling unfamiliarity with basic cooking skills. He managed to pull the roast from the oven so that it could "repose," but he was at a loss to what else there might be for supper, flipping through cupboard doors with deepening irritation.

"Rice pilaf?" he asked.

"Takes about forty minutes, I think."

He gave Dred that hollow-eyed look, that this had been a bad fight with her. "Let me go back there and smoke her out." He disappeared around the corner and headed down the hall toward the bedroom. Dred finished his Manhattan, made another, and took it to the window to look at the view again. From behind the bedroom door he could now hear murmurs of conciliation from their two voices, the words incoherent except for "microwave," which rose up into a descant of frustration. Of course. If she'd planned to have the Langleys over, she'd have the side dishes standing by in the microwave. It seemed Kurt could have guessed this.

If Kurt hadn't married Erica, Dred possibly could have—if he had known her back then when marriage seemed more like a good idea than it did now. Several times Erica had been with him alone, both here in the condo and on Acorn Lane, and they had been very comfortable and easy in each other's company, sharing ideas and laughing at the same things. She was just his age, with a large-boned and yet graceful body, a knowing face that was still young, her warm, happy blue eyes. She'd told him they were contemplating a long separation. Yes, they'd had counseling, which had smoothed over their own rough spots but had not made them better as a couple. Kurt was hard-working, dedicated, competitive; she liked long moments of pure peace. He liked material comforts; she seemed indifferent to them. He was a convert to the Republican party, even if there might be stronger leaders than Ronald Reagan. Erica despised Reagan to the very depths of her soul.

That alone, Dred thought, could end a marriage.

Because she was his brother's wife, he hadn't risked imagining her as a lover, how her body would feel. It was all too family, too much, he thought, like being in an elevator stuck between floors, knowing people for how they smell, how their breathing sounds.

It would be different if he'd known her before she'd met Kurt.

She came out now with her eyes red but her head held high, a cheerful smile for him. Kurt followed with his ideas for the right wine to open. "Hi," she said, and kissed him.

"Sorry it's a bad time."

"Don't be. Glad you're here. It's been a while." Her voice was a friendly, throaty alto with the subtlest rasp.

"Dred, how about that Pommard you gave me last year?"

Erica was checking on a casserole dish in the microwave. "He's been ogling that bottle for weeks."

"Fine," he said. "Why not?"

Kurt did an aboutface, and with an air of servility to compensate for whatever he'd said or done to ruin the start of the evening headed down the hall to the utility room in back where they stored their wine.

Without catching his eye Erica said, "You're working on a new case."

It was not a question. Something else fundamentally askew in her relationship with Kurt: Erica had *some* real ESP, he was convinced. She truly did get phone calls from long lost friends she happened to be thinking about just moments before. She'd become nauseated in the middle of the night, deeply upset for no apparent reason, when John Balcazar, their father, had his fatal heart attack five years ago. And with Dred, she had an uncanny knack of knowing him very well with not much to go on, sporadic visits with polite conversation and long silences.

"Right. Sort of."

She was turning dials on the microwave, pulled out a vegetable dish from the freezer. "While I was alone with my thoughts, in there, I thought of you, and I felt something different. And it seemed to me you were—concerned about things."

Even with Kurt in the back room she kept her voice low. Kurt could accept some measure of the clichéd notion of woman's intuition, but he did not conceal his disdain for things paranormal. As a surgeon of great skill, he could not really be blamed; the body, however complex, was a machine whose individual parts were all readily quantifiable and comprehensible. The brain, of course, was somewhat less well known, but it was definitely not some sort of receiver picking up messages across space and time.

"Something like that." He smiled. "It's not the new case, it's something else."

"I bet she's very pretty. Is she?"

"Erica. This really isn't sporting, not having any secrets from you. C'mon, admit it."

"Dred, I'm looking at you and I see someone with a woman on his mind. It's also common sense. Seemed to me it was time— you're overdue in that department"

"I don't know anything about her."

"Well, she's got you, hasn't she?"

"It feels weird. It feels very childish."

"Nothing wrong with that. Does Elaine know? Or isn't that an issue for you?"

"Not since January." The day she moved out, he could still hear his front door slamming for the final time. "It's not going to work for us, never will. She's got a date tonight. Friend of her brother Henry's."

For a second he had a picture of Elaine with this unknown guy who looked like a Henry Prescott type, in a three-piece suit, with watch fob and sagging shoulders, a young banker, tragically constipated. Now Kurt came back with the bottle of Pommard, anxious to uncork it to give it time to breathe. "We can't forget about Tony's plane tomorrow. Logan at four-thirty."

"I haven't forgotten," said Erica.

Finding the corkscrew, Kurt said to Dred, "It's his spring break. Did I tell you we're going to the Bahamas? The three of us?"

"That's great. Next time invite me."

Erica gave him a knowing look—not a bad idea.

"And we're going to have the best damn time ever," Kurt proclaimed with more than his usual conviction as he worked the cork open. Then, to Erica: "If this roast reposes any longer it'll be comatose."

"The potatoes are almost ready, Kurt," she said.

For dinner they sat at one end of their enormous harvest table with their best china, crystal, and candles. They polished off the Pommard halfway through dinner and Kurt got up and brought back a serviceable Beaujolais for the next round. Erica asked about "the new case," and as had happened before, Kurt's initial skepticism that his younger brother should be involved in such matters gave way to wanting to know the details. But as yet there was almost nothing to report. Artificial intelligence, some kind of sabotage. And then the business of the burglary. No mention of his dinner with Lauren.

"Hope you're not going to waste a lot of time on a simple burglary."

"Wouldn't mind getting my computer back. If only to figure out how it works."

"Come on, Dred, it's insured, computers get replaced."

"I guess I have to know why. Why my place, why a computer."

"Money for drugs?" Kurt asked. "Seems logical."

"But nothing else was touched."

"Place was locked?"

"Of course. They came in through a window."

"And you were out."

"I was out. I do go out now and then."

"Don't get testy, okay? Wasn't implying anything."

Erica touched his arm. "Kurt."

Kurt leveled his eyes, gestured at him with a fork. "I think this guy goes out too much. I think he should settle in, just take it easy." Then directly to him: "You ever think maybe it's a problem? The women thing? I bet they've got support groups for guys like you."

"Jesus, Kurt, it's not like I'm a danger to anybody."

"Once you get your women straight, everything else will fall into place. Get your personal life in order first."

"So then I can go out and get a real job?" He said this with no enmity; they'd had many "career counseling" sessions before this, Kurt eventually advising him to do whatever he damn well pleased as long as he didn't start chewing up any of the principal in his trust fund, modest as it was.

"Admit to me you've had a slow start. That you've been too choosy."

"Yes, it's been slow."

"Even with this ADC thing, can you afford what you're doing now?"

"Don't worry about it, Kurt. You won't have to bail me out."

"Do us all a favor and marry Elaine, you'll be set for life."

"No thanks."

"Erica, talk sense to the boy."

She was rescued by the phone ringing, off in the corner of the living room. After she left, Kurt turned to him. "You hung out your shingle, what, last summer? You've turned away a lot of business—"

"I'm not going to spy on other people's wives. Or husbands."

"So how do you let people know you're not your average back-alley gumshoe? People hire detectives, nine times out of ten it's that kind of work. The ADC job, the way it sounds, could be a freak. That's not the usual thing, you're just lucky."

"You've got enough on your mind right now. Don't get into the big brother thing, okay?"

Ignoring it, Kurt lowered his voice at him. "One last question: how's the portfolio?"

Only with Erica out of earshot did Kurt work him over like this, but he didn't really mind. There were no big secrets between them and never had been.

"Hundred and twenty."

She came back and sat down, said simply, "They hung up."

"Heavy breather?" Kurt asked.

"No. Just someone who didn't talk. Then hung up."

Kurt finished his thought, bending forward to him in a whisper. "When Dad gave it to us fifteen years ago it was a hundred. You're losing ground."

"I'm aware of that," he said.

"You boys, please don't compare your money, not while I'm here."

"Sorry," Dred told her.

"Honey, we never get a chance to talk. I might have some stock tips for him."

"Here we go again," she said. "I'll do the wifely thing and cut up some fruit for dessert."

"That would be nice, sweetheart. Thanks." Kurt finished his wine, poured himself a new glass, passed the bottle to Dred. When Erica had turned the corner into the kitchen he said, "Speaking of artificial intelligence, don't pass it up as an investment. A little money you can afford to lose—it's a little dicey, but I think worth the risk."

"I'm not in a position to take chances, Kurt."

"Listen to me. Last week I saw an offering from an outfit that's really taking off. Polaris Software, in Cambridge."

"I've heard of them."

"Right. They're really heavily ventured out, but they've got this thing called the Financial Consultant. It's the first expert system for general business use, adaptable to any company. And would you believe the damn thing comes without a manual?"

"Tell me. I don't get it."

"The software's so damn smart any financial officer can sit down at the computer and turn it on and the program both teaches the guy at the keyboard and learns from him, too. Incredible. No manual. They say it's built around the top guy at Sloan Business School, Gerry Travers, all the stuff he knows."

Accept it, hold it, apply it. He was beginning to see. "It's everything Gerry Travers knows?"

"Right. Everything Gerry Travers knows—about corporate finance."

"His brain adapted to software."

"Dred, I'm telling you, this stuff is hot. You work for ADC, you ought to get the inside track, keep your ears open."

In the kitchen Erica let out a little yelp and cursed as something clattered to the tile floor. Kurt seemed barely to hear her, so Dred pushed his chair out and went into the kitchen. She was holding her hand under the faucet.

"As a scout mother for Tony I learned always point the blade away from you. Except when you're cutting pears, of course."

Dred picked up pear pieces and the large carving knife off the floor, caught a glimpse of her hand in the sink, the flowing tap water with a thin ribbon of pink from her blood.

"Nasty slice," he said. Testing the blade, he thought it extraordinarily sharp. She'd been sectioning the pear in her hand.

"It's long, not deep," she said. "That thing's like a razor. There's some gauze on the top shelf, over the microwave. Funny you're here, and not Kurt."

"Keep some pressure on it," he said. He found gauze pads, a roll of gauze, and adhesive tape.

"It's right in the palm." She turned the water off and wadded her hand with a paper towel, then took the gauze pad from him and pressed it against the wound. She let him wrap and tape an additional band of gauze around it. "It'll be okay," she said. "I do this at the strangest times."

"I'm sorry—what you're going through."

"Me too. But it's always good to see you. I'm glad you came." She leaned over against the counter and rested her right elbow on the chopping block to keep her hand elevated. "Dred. That last phone call, I have to tell you."

It had occurred to him but he hadn't had the chance to mention it. "Does it happen often?"

"No, that's the point. Never. Whoever he was, he was checking on you, just asked, 'Is Dred there?' "

"Nobody knows I'm here."

"I said no, he isn't. I said no because immediately I knew it was not a real call, not really for you, there was nothing in the voice, but there was something about him that made me think, 'This guy is bad news.' I got that clear and strong."

He hesitated. "Okay. I'll remember that."

"Is it possible it has something to do with Elaine? That's what I was thinking. Just bear with me."

"I'm certainly not ignoring you."

She smiled. "You might give her a call."

He left the kitchen, excused himself from Kurt, and went to the phone on Kurt's desk in the corner of the living room. Five rings.

"Hello?" Elaine answered. Very sleepy.

"Hi there, just called to see how it went."

"Dred. Lemme wake up."

"No, don't. Sorry to bother you."

"What a drip! The guy never showed. I'm thirty-three and I got stood up. What time is it, anyway?"

He checked his watch. "Just about ten. You pooped early."

"What a creep. Where are you, out having fun?"

"Kurt and Erica's. Go back to sleep, I'll give you a buzz this weekend."

"Yeah, thanks for calling. Love you. G'night."

"G'night."

Kurt was calling to him from the table. "Thanks for saving my wife! Couldn't have done better myself!"

He thought, just to be safe, to dial his own office number, just to check, heard his brand-new outgoing message and the beep, then punched in the double zero code to play back any messages. A long, faltering rewind of the tape, somebody with a lot to say.

"T. D. I gotta make up for the other night. Just want to see you, finish the job interview. Are you free Saturday? I can come at eight, about. I'll just knock. Can you call my service and just say yes? Say yes."

It took a long time for her to get it all out, staticky gaps between sentences. Now the end-of-message beeps.

He hung up and called back to hear it again, didn't know the remote code for skipping the outgoing message, listened to himself again, and then Lauren, now heard the distance in her voice, the effort just to speak, and now Erica was standing over him and biting her lip, and she reached over and rested her left hand gently on his shoulder.

3

His first impression of her arriving Saturday night was that she was smaller, as if she'd become magically capable of pulling her body more closely into itself. He suppressed the urge to hold her by these more compact shoulders, to offer even the most restrained welcoming kiss on the cheek or forehead. He simply gave her a quick smile and closed the door behind her. She slipped by him and took off her coat, beneath which she had the same gray sweater, collar of a pink shirt poking out. Cream-colored jeans, no jewelry except for the turquoise ring on her little finger. Battered running shoes with Velcro flaps.

"Job interview, part two," he said calmly, smiling and accepting her coat from her and laying it over the arm of the Parsons bench. Nodding with visible chagrin, she was peering through his bedroom door, opened a closet door next to the night table (on which he'd set a vase of freshly forced daffodils, one of the few flowers he could identify by name), then the guest bedroom, which was crammed with boxes of Elaine's stuff.

"So this is one of those up and down places."

"Downstairs is upstairs, right." Now he led her up the stairs, and while she started exploring, turning into the living room where he'd lit a very cheerful fire as the climax to an afternoon of frantic cleaning and dusting, he took from the fridge one of the two very fine long-necked bottles of *auslese* Riesling he'd just bought and uncorked it. He was not sure how he felt, missing the chance to grab her and startle her with a wild kiss.

She had come back into the hallway, watching him intently. "What really would be nice is some dope. I have some at home that I could've brought. But you're not the type, are you, who has it."

He occasionally did have it without actually buying it, guests sometimes brought it as a house present instead of wine. "I don't know what type I am." He handed her his only water goblet full of this excellent-tasting gleaming white wine, poured one for himself in the jelly jar from the drainboard. "I enjoy it, but I don't have any right now."

She was looking past him to the kitchen window facing the roof, the water-stained shirt cardboard still covering the broken windowpane. "So maybe you're the type who gets mad and throws things?"

His first chance Monday or Tuesday he would buy new glass and reglaze the window. In the interim he felt safe enough at night deadbolting the kitchen door from the hallway, effectively sealing off the rest of the apartment.

"Damnedest thing," he said, not entirely sure what she was thinking. "No, I almost never get mad, believe it or not, I was playing catch in here, with one of my many girlfriends, it was a regular hard baseball, and she's a sweetie but very clumsy and she didn't even get a glove on it, the ball ended up on Beacon Street two blocks away. Obviously I threw it too hard."

This piece of improvisational silliness had a peculiar effect on her: her laugh seemed to snag in her throat, her eyes widening, filling with sadness: he thought she might cry. Her neck stiffening, giving no indication if she had any knowledge of the truth behind the broken glass, but his feeling was that she didn't. She turned away, toward the fire that burned silently in the fieldstone fireplace, framed by his wall of books. He followed behind, and she pulled from her jeans hip pocket a squashed half-pack of cigarettes, took one out and stuck it in her lips.

He narrowed his eyes at her: she hadn't smoked before.

"I've been quitting for a few weeks, but now I'm not. This is not a good time. Fuck."

She patted her pockets looking for matches she didn't have; he stepped through the double doors into his office where he kept paper matches in the top desk drawer, noted the work table without the computer on it, wondered again what she knew, came back with the matches and stopped in his tracks; she had pulled the firescreen away and pushed back her right sleeve to poke the droopy weed into a thick veil of flame curling around the frontmost log. She held the cigarette there until her hand must have been in some considerable pain.

"Wait, I've got a light," he said, but already it was lit and she stuck it in her mouth with a very deep drag. Immediately clutching her hand and rubbing it, she dipped her fingers into the wine goblet, then rubbed the knuckles of her right hand. She looked up with a flash of a grin.

"Silly me."

"Silly you. What are you doing?"

She inhaled deeply again, let the smoke pour out her nostrils. "Just glad to be here." Then, staring deep into the flames: "Are you the type who can tell what a woman is thinking?"

"Not much. Help me out." At the least he believed she was apprehensive about something. Perhaps even frightened.

"You don't feel it, so I have to say it, right?"

"Lauren, Thursday night was a lot of fun. For about half an hour. After that—"

"I'm here to have you make me feel wonderful."

He was sitting next to her, taking in her secondary smoke and enjoying its sharpness in his nose. "Why the sudden disappearance? Looking for you, I find no phone number, no address, just an answering service that someone else is paying for. This is all strange stuff."

She closed her eyes, shook her head. "I can't talk about that."

"Why not?" he said. "Part of the interview."

"It's not so simple, can't we forget it?"

"Lauren, I don't want to lose track of you."

Her eyes still closed, she seemed to go limp with her head settling onto his shoulder with a tiny kiss on his cheek. "I can call you."

"No good," he said, his voice becoming low and soft. "What's the story?" The words vibrating with her jawbone nestling against his neck. Her thick cowlicky hair, tawny mane very soft. She said nothing, lifted her chin, took a long deep drag off the weed, then abandoned it prematurely to the fire. She touched the jelly glass he used for his wine.

"This is pathetic. The detective doesn't have another wineglass?"

"I use them so much they keep breaking." Not quite true, he had owned a pair of goblets years ago, but pairs of anything, like socks, were difficult to keep. "Lauren, tell me again why you left. Really."

She smiled, shook her head, nuzzled her face into his neck again, and now shocked him by grabbing his hair, yanking his head back to plant a large wet kiss hard on the middle of his throat. Suddenly he was falling back with her on the carpet, and she, her mouth in his hair, was mumbling something about Adam, to have some Adam. Did he hear it right? Adam, she said, is Ecstasy. "God, that would be great right now, to be with you and have that stuff, man, I'd tell you damn near *every*thing." He knew something of Ecstasy, the empathogen, the trust and love drug that he'd never had, and she was saying in his ear, "You're the kind of guy, where—" She didn't finish the sentence, patted his stomach, took a deep breath. "You're a real good guy. That's all."

She arose and went back into the kitchen with her wineglass and called out, "You really don't do video? Honest?"

"No, I don't. You asked that before."

"When are you going to fix this window?" she asked.

"Monday. Nobody works weekends."

"Can't you do it yourself? I could."

"Don't have the glass. It has to be cut."

"Someone could just bust right in here," she said, coming back, kneeling before him. "But that's a nice roof out there, you could make a deck. Lie out there in the sun. Have someone wait on you hand and foot."

"Someday I'll do that. On Beacon Hill you need all kinds of permits—"

"Stop." She touched her fingertip to the center of his lips, then to the corners of his mouth, to the end of his nose. She smiled, choked back a deep guttural laugh. "Maybe we don't talk and just go downstairs and screw."

But for her thumb and finger pinching his lips together he might have answered.

"Wanna?" she asked.

"What happened Thursday?" was his mumbled, closed-mouth response, and again she shook her head, dug her fingernail painfully into his upper lip. He wriggled free, then leaned in to her mouth to kiss her quickly but fully, retrieving the faint taste of wine when she pulled sharply back as police sirens flared up outside, very close, racing down Beacon Street.

"City living," she said, twisting away from him.

"Mr. Policeman is your friend," Dred reminded her as the sirens moved off. She curled onto her side with her face next to his knee.

"No, he's not. Mr. Zucchini is," and with absolutely no restraint or subtlety she thrust her head into his lap and attacked him with both her hands and her mouth, pulling him down onto the rug until he felt the heat in his groin rising too fast and decided, no, this should not happen.

He tumbled away from her to catch his breath, her fingers kneading at his cheeks. "Hold on," he said, struggling to his feet with his back turned to her.

"That was close," she said, pleased. "Quick."

"Yeah."

"Let me see it," she said. "Don't be shy."

"I'm getting some ice water." He turned and caught sight of her stunningly beautiful face burnished by firelight and rug-wrestling, her sweet mysterious smile by itself an aphrodisiac.

"You're shy because you're not big, you're not Mr. Zucchini. Turn around."

He was walking away, through the hall back into the kitchen. "Shit, Lauren, can you type?"

"I can see you're big, your jeans are pulled so tight over your buns they're about to split the seams."

"Do you know Wordmate? Can you do billing?"

He decided against ice water, chose instead to stick his face in the freezer, linger in its chill air, ponder some different form of flesh; behind a roasting chicken there was that slab of foil-wrapped, freezer-burned bluefish from last August hiding way in the back growing ice crystals and leaking its slow stink. Thawed, it would repel a starving buzzard. Good strategy. He could recall the image of this putrefying fish at any time it would be gentlemanly to do so, a good replacement for his old standby (with Elaine, who thrived on slowness) of his furry-limbed endodontist reaming out his root canals.

She'd finished her wine when he returned, was standing with her back to the fire, on her face a display of mock disappointment when she saw him. "Okay. So maybe show me your office. Where I'd be working."

He smiled, no. "I've been in there on the computer all day." Watching closely for any hint she knew this was impossible, he saw no hint that she did. "My workday is finished."

"So I won't see your office?"

"Lauren, the interview's over. Hope you don't mind."

"Can you play the piano for me?"

"Later, not now."

"Your guitar, then." She'd spotted it in its case, leaning in the shadows between the piano and the corner.

"No. Now that you're making more sense, I need to know, among other things, are you trying to decide, maybe, between two men?"

"Maybe." A wicked grin. "Tell me your life story, help me choose."

He pulled out the piano bench with the needlepoint cover on it, Montauk lighthouse, given to him by his mother when he got his first Manhattan apartment. He sat down, rolled the keyboard cover down, and leaned back on his elbows.

"Okay. Me first, then you."

"Good. Man goes first."

"It's not so exciting. Born in New York City. Father a wool importer. Mother a kind housewife. Older brother Kurt, a doctor. Summers on Long Island. Nice place in the East Eighties with a wafer-thin view of the park. Prep school and then Yale."

"Ivy League. Impressive." Without hesitating she sat down next to him at the piano, their legs touching.

"Ensign in the Navy and then Florida in the seventies to try an easy law school, it wasn't so easy, I came back to New York to work with Dad importing wool for two years, acquired enormous free wardrobe."

She was fiddling with his hair, behind his ear, curling it in her fingers.

"Back to Florida and did bartending and then charter boat work bumming around the islands, met a fine young woman who worked at a boatyard, fell in love, tell me when you're losing interest—" She was kissing him on the ear, shamelessly licking his hair, and now her tongue trailing down the back of his neck. "She had a boat. Wanted to sell all her life insurance. Take me around the world with her." Now chewing into his shirt under his shoulder blade, down his back. "Didn't go. Should have."

"Damn!" she said, pulling away. "Another guy on the rebound."

"That was six, seven years ago. I think I'm all right now."

"You should've gone. Don't ever pass those things up."

"So now I meet a very lovely and mysterious downy-skinned woman who's already driving me crazy."

She threw her head back, sighed deeply. "Oh, God."

"Who says nothing about herself, about Thursday night, when I didn't even get a good-bye. And I worried about her. And she seems the type to worry about. Your turn."

She said nothing, eyes downcast.

"Who's the other guy? I mean, it's understandable you have more than one who likes you."

"Yeah."

"It's happened before, no?"

"Yeah, nice guess." Twisting around, she was discovering on top of the piano a grouping of family pictures including the large one of Kurt and Erica and Tony and him with the senior Balcazars on their fortieth anniversary, a beachside clambake, all faces browned by sun and alcohol happiness.

"He is someone charming and loving and kind to you, no?"

"No. It was a mistake. Let's not talk."

"But it's your turn."

She slid across the piano bench to the corner, reached for his guitar case, he nodded yes. Taking it across the room, sitting and facing the fire like a counselor at camp, she cradled it expertly in her lap, pushed her sleeves up to her elbows, sighted along the neck.

"These steel strings." A subtle shift in her voice. "Be careful, it's pulling on the neck, right here, it'll go sharp way up here. But it's very nice all the same. I love these real old guitars."

He said, "Play me something. Something you wrote."

"Okay. 'Sidewalk Man.' "

> *"Sidewalk man, looking for his neon girl,*
> *Down the oily streets of rain. He sing,*
> *Neon Girl, Neon Girl, come let's find*
> *The very bad thing you mean to me."*

A true singing voice but at a whisper, her eyes fixed on the fire with a quick, very real smile once for him, her strong hands, fast fingers hammered on and off the steel strings. She was trained, maybe classical—but this music was soft and bluesy. His eyes fixed on her fingers, her hands, her arm flesh orange and blue in the firelight, shimmer of soft golden hairs, golden filigree, as her voice slid lazily through the song.

> *"Coming to the corner, Sidewalk Man*
> *Fevered of the night and pull the string*
> *Of Neon Girl, Neon Girl, come let's find*
> *The very bad thing you mean to me."*

Now just toying with her Velcro shoe flap, stupidly, a finger on her ankle, the bone a glossy bump.

"He say, 'There is a strong shadow where
There is very much light,
Dark at the top of your stairs.
And neon in your eyes.
Neon in your eyes.' "

And it ended with what sounded like the bridge, the middle part that wanted another refrain. Propped on his elbow, he just smiled and mouthed the word *nice*.

"That's the quiet fireside voice," she said. "With the band I really holler."

"The band?"

"Just a band. Like a thousand others in this town."

"Hope they appreciate you."

"No longer. We busted up."

He inched toward her, kissed her vacantly on her arm, tongue tickling her golden fuzziness till she giggled. "Damn you, stop that!" and she eased the Martin out of harm's way, grabbed him and kissed him hungrily on the face, tugged at his shirt button, reached in and stroked his chest, teeth on his jaw, muttering, "Pectoral analysis." She felt lightly through his chest hair, said, "Soft," was kissing him again and the other hand grabbing his thigh, rolled in this embrace one turn closer to the fire, bumping the fire screen, the heat instantly too intense. He found her resistant to retreat, tried to muscle her away, but her strength and leverage held him. "Say when," she said, biting his ear. "Into the inferno." Enough. He swung his legs over her, pulling both of them away just at the moment it was too hot to bear, and at the same time someone was downstairs, rapping the front door knocker four, five times. He was on top, his hands clasped around her upper arms to hold her still, she too was breathing hard and her face was flushed, as his must have been, from being too close to the fire. His back stung as if it had been repeatedly slapped.

Her nose wrinkled. "Your shirt smells like it got singed." She laughed crazily, as if there could be anything amusing about almost being set on fire.

Catching his breath, letting the pain lift from his skin. "Someone's at the door."

"T. D. Balcazar," she said, with another laugh and freeing her arm to pull his face down to hers, her mouth all over his face, growling, "Nobody needs to see you now, just me."

He pulled away and stood up as the knocker at last repeated its insistent rapping. "I better get that. Probably Willie Cuthbertson, across the street, that's her knock."

"She? Willie?"

"Wilhemina. She's your classic eccentric Beacon Hill widow, likes to drop by to interrupt things."

"I want to meet her," Lauren said, getting up, coming with him into the hall.

"Bad idea. She'll want to make friends with you, she'll invite herself in and stay all night."

"Then make her go away."

Dred got to the door in the middle of the third round of knocking, saw through his peephole that in fact it was Willie, but not looking in the mood for socializing. He opened the door.

"Willie. Something's the matter?"

"Can't you see for yourself, Dred Balcazar?" Her face screwed up in a scornful smirk. "There's a river running down the Lane!" True enough, the street's cobblestones were awash with water sluicing from Willow Street to this side of the Lane, spilling up onto the sidewalk just beyond her feet. "I do imagine its headwaters are the Fennelmans' hydrant, if you care to come exploring with me." She extended her hand. Dred immediately had to agree with her; the hydrant on Willow by the Fennelmans' apartment had let go sometime last year, with similar effect.

"I can't now, Willie, I've got company. But I'll telephone the fire department."

"Yes, I suppose you would. But it's curious, I think. The same man who performed this strange piece of theater should come knocking at your door just before me, and then dash over to Louisburg Square."

"Willie. The man who what?"

"I'm quite certain it was the same fellow, and not a well-dressed sort, no, not at all, not from *this* neighborhood."

"He knocked on my door? You're sure?"

"Dred, please. My eyes work quite well, thank you. I saw him standing by the Fennelmans' hydrant, and then he positively scampered down here to knock on your door."

"Willie, you say he opened the hydrant?"

"Why else would he have that huge wrench?"

"Okay, could you wait just a minute?" He turned, took the stairs three at a time to the upper hall, found Lauren in the kitchen with her back to the sink, her smile evaporating when she saw him.

"So tell me. You're not expecting any company, are you? 'Cause I'm not."

She scowled. "Company?"

"When I'm with you, strange things happen, and I'm not just talking hormones. I've got to look around outside, okay? Just a few minutes. You can do me a favor, call the fire department, or the police."

"Police are useless."

There was no time to argue. "Fire department then. Hydrant on Willow Street is open. I'll be back in no time."

"Dred!!" Willie's shriek from the front stoop pulled him out to the top of the stairs.

"Two seconds, Willie." He turned back to Lauren. "Gonna be okay?"

"I'm all right," she said.

"Dred!" cried Willie. "I think he just ran up to Louisburg Square!"

"I'll lock the door, you'll be fine. Just be a second." Now turning and leaping down the stairs three at a time again. He retrieved his keys from his bedside table, hurried out onto the stoop with Willie, who was pointing around the corner of Acorn and Willow. In those few seconds, even as he locked the door behind him, he decided the mischief maker, whoever he was and whatever he wanted, would not be so stupid as to hang around a neighborhood with Wilhemina Cuthbertson as Town Crier. He took her by the arm up to Willow where Godfrey Fennelman had come out just to display his disgust before retreating back into his home. Dred scanned both ends of Willow Street, down toward Beacon, up toward Louisburg Square with its towering elms and park benches.

"Well, I was *sure* he turned left up here."

"He's gone by now, Willie."

Difficult to hear yourself think with this high-pressure gush cascading down Acorn Lane. He walked Willie toward the lights of Louisburg Square until a normal level of conversation was possible.

"Did you get any kind of a look at his clothes? His features?"

"When he was knocking at your door he was standing right under your outdoor light."

"And?"

"Well, I made certain he didn't see *me*, for Heaven's sake. I crouched down behind the Cadwalladers' rhododendrons."

"Good. Did you see what he was wearing? What he looked like?"

"I could only see from behind. He wore one of those dark jackets, a heavy leather jacket. And dark gloves. And darkish trousers, I do believe."

"Color hair?"

"Oh, Lord, no, burglars always wear hats."

"Burglar?"

"I *assumed* he was a burglar, with that kind of hat. A watch cap sort of thing, that you roll down over your ears. Black, or perhaps navy."

"Tall? Short?"

"About your height. Very average, I'd say. Perhaps a tad taller."

"And you saw him uncap the hydrant with a big wrench."

"No, no, no, I simply saw him *with* the wrench near the hydrant."

Dred looked back toward 118-C, the warm glow of light from his bedroom, the upstairs office dark. To the right, the pantry windows were also dark.

He recalled how the kitchen looked when he'd left it. The pantry door was ajar, as it usually was, and there should have been some light coming through. But it was utterly dark.

"I need to get back to my guest," he said.

"I'm certain she'd enjoy that," said Willie, but Dred was already cutting hard around the back of the hydrant, across Willow to his front steps with keys in hand, quickly unlocking and throwing open the door.

"Lauren!"

The entire house reverberated with the sound of bodies colliding against walls and furniture. Upstairs, four steps at a time, finding the kitchen door shut and locked, Lauren behind it crying out "You fuck—," then her voice muffled. Dred heaved his shoulder against the door, immediately knew the heavy brass fittings wouldn't yield. Again, and again, with no effect.

"Lauren!"

"Fucker's got a *knife*—" and he heard someone strike the floor hard, his table or chairs overturning, Lauren yelping in pain, a metallic object clanging against metal, maybe the sink or the refrigerator. She raged against him, "You are *dead meat*, mister!" followed by a sickening thud and she groaned.

Thinking fast isn't always thinking best: he could risk the outdoor route down Willow to Marsden's stockaded yard, come in as the intruder must have, but if the guy had any brains at all he'd probably locked or somehow obstructed the gate from the inside. The other choice was to break through the old walled-up pass-through between the hall and the kitchen, reach around, and unlock the door.

He grabbed the poker from the fireplace set, ran headlong toward the section of wall, just at the top of the stairs, at kitchen counter height, rammed the iron through wallboard. Again with the poker, and now with his fists, and now tearing it apart with his hands, the wallboard crumbling into dust. The sounds inside were less violent, as though he'd subdued her, but now he heard her muffled whimpering, pleading with him, *oh no*. Stretching through the opening he'd made in the pass-through, his head and arm into the black of the kitchen, only a distant pinpoint of light was visible through the window, not enough to see. Dred reached far to the left near the doorjamb, found the face plate for the light switch, as far as he could reach, but couldn't get the switch itself. One more mighty stretch, the ragged edge of wall cutting into his armpit, no chance. The guy must have had her in a stranglehold, the way she was coughing and gagging. Dred chopped at the wallboard with his knuckles, breaking off another inch or two, reached in again and just did make contact with the switch, flipped it up to flood the kitchen with light.

He saw: the sonofabitch was already outside the window onto the roof, trying to drag her out with him, under the window, black leather sleeves, black gloves wrestling with her as her legs flailed at the overturned breakfast table and chairs. The window sash was a tangle of broken glass and splintered muntin latticework, the guy was doing his damnedest to haul her out underneath it, arm around her neck, but the sash never stayed up without some kind of prop, and he was having a very difficult time. And there on the linoleum was *the knife*, bloodless, Dred's serrated lemon/lime knife put away in the drawer earlier; this guy had been in the kitchen long enough to find it.

"Let her go, you bastard!" Another two inches and Dred would have his forefinger on the brass hasp, might be able to work it free, but the pass-through was designed for tea service, not full dinners, and there was no way to squeeze his body through any farther. Just far enough inside to watch and feel completely helpless, Lauren's body not eight feet away from him.

The guy had worked her arms through under the uncooperative sash, Lauren had her feet wrapped around the legs of the breakfast table, wouldn't go any farther, but now he wanted her head on the sill, grabbing her hair with one hand, the other to raise the sash and Lauren's arms wrestled free, interfered just in time as he tried to bring the sash down onto the side of her head.

"Fight him off," Dred cried. "Don't quit!"

"I'm *tryyyiiinng*," she cried out, and with a frenzied effort she raised the sash that tiny millimeter needed to free her head, wriggling away. But the bastard brought the window down onto her right hand, trapping her; she screamed, and then his other fist exploded through glass, an unbroken pane, to grab her face and jerk her head backwards, hard against the latticework.

Dred had one shoulder through the crumbled opening of the pass-through, tried every contortion possible to get the other one through, but couldn't. Exhausted, Lauren had all but ceased fighting, her nostrils flaring for air. Somehow with his other hand the intruder, now outside on the roof, had produced a length of electrical cable and snaked it through a broken pane next to her head, pulling it across her neck and outside again, no chance for Lauren to protect herself even now with both her hands free, reacting too late, blurting out, "You mother—"

The attacker's grip was swift and certain. Just a dark shadow on the roof, he worked furiously to twist the cable tightly around her neck, pulling her head sharply back against the remains of the sash. Lauren gasped with a sharp cry, instantly choked as the wire jerked hard up into her throat.

Dred pulled free of the pass-through, his stomach churning, knowing there was not enough time to risk the long way around outside, Marsden's gate sure to be locked. Not enough time.

The poker.

He was into the pass-through again, trying to hook either the tip or the barb of the poker under the hasp of the door, nicking it, but the far edge of the countertop, right next to the doorjamb, was higher than the hasp, made it impossible to see it. All his rational energy focused on using the poker as a lever against the far counter edge to hook that invisible hasp and lift it free, but his eyes were stuck on Lauren and this thick black wire wrapped very tight around her throat, her hands struggling but useless against it. Her face was deepening to crimson, with eyes squeezed closed and her frenzied resistance beginning to weaken. Instinctively he pleaded: "Shit, man, don't kill her. Whatever you want you can have, just don't kill her."

While Lauren fought fiercely for air, Dred was sure that the sonofabitch laughed. And his gloved hands, visible just behind the window, began to quiver with the increased strength required, the prodigious effort expended to keep the wire tight enough, long enough, to finish her off.

For an instant Lauren's eyes opened as narrow slits in her swollen face, must have seen him struggling with this ridiculous fireplace tool to get the door open. Three feet longer, the poker might hook around the cable and save her life, give her a few seconds of breath. Again he thought he'd made contact with the hasp; again the beveled tip of the poker slipped from its target. Her breathing had diminished to feeble, futile rasps, her hands now dropping away, falling limp against her sides as she started to lose consciousness.

"Don't quit, Lauren!"

Two, three more attempts with the poker failed. With the last bit of strength choked out of her, she was passing out, her head nodding forward on her chest. But her body still reacted, jerking and hiccuping for air.

Dred wriggled out of the hole, began stabbing the kitchen door with the poker, the middle panel near the latch where the wood was least thick, hundred-year-old pine that splintered under the attack of the weapon, again and again, and suddenly the panel cracked, revealing a hairline split, and Dred threw his shoulder into it. Still, it wouldn't give. High-density object needed. Rock, cinder block, lead ingot.

Computer printer.

Lugging it from his office with a long train of paper fanfolding out behind it to the door, all his adrenaline and strength focused on this target as he imagined that Lauren could be dead by now. He swung the printer back like a battering ram and crashed it into the door; again, and the panel ruptured apart, his hand was through it, onto the lock, releasing the door just as the assailant jerked Lauren's head back with such force that the remaining lattice in the window started to bend outward toward the roof. Dred leaped for the wire, got both hands on it but too close to her neck, the bastard had much more leverage and pulled with such strength that Dred's hands, his knuckles, were pulled into the reddened flesh of her throat. Freeing one hand from the cable, pulling back to give her the briefest respite—it was too much weight for the attacker. Dred's other hand found the serrated knife on the floor, but now the guy made his only mistake, yanking so hard on the wire the sash burst into splinters, exploding glass and wood onto the roof where he tumbled backwards. The cable slipped loose over her head, she slumped to the kitchen floor, and the man sprinted away across the roof, vaulting cleanly over Marsden's fence and out of sight.

Under any other circumstances, he would be a cinch to intercept, at Marsden's back gate.

"Okay, kiddo, back to life." Completely exhausted, trying to control his shaking, Dred knelt over her, felt a slow heartbeat tapping weakly in her throat. Hand under the nape of her neck, he arched her head back to open her windpipe, shoved his fingers between her teeth to spread them apart, pushed her tongue to one side. Deep inhale, then deep slow exhale into her. Now the shakes overwhelmed him, the panic of realizing how easily she could have died. And again breathing into her. "C'mon, wakeup call." Carefully massaging her throat, pinching her cheeks. "Damn you, your body's working, get with it." Again, forcing his air into her lungs. Getting the rhythm. Broken glass all over the floor. His right hand groping for the cordless phone kicked out of its cradle to the floor over by the bottom of the fridge, its antenna extended toward him. Pinching her cheeks again, and her wrist, and breathing into her; suddenly her body jerked underneath him, just as he was able to grasp the tip of the cordless antenna, pull it to him.

"Yay, Lauren." Her eyes flicked open, squinting in the harsh light.

She croaked her name, "Lauren," as he softly stroked her cheek, punched 911 on the cordless.

"You'll be okay," he said. And now to the police operator who had trouble understanding him as he fought to speak coherently: "Medical emergency—attempted strangulation—"

Her arms pulled him down to her, sandwiching the phone between them and muffling the police operator's protests into gibberish buzzing against his chest. She hugged him around the neck and held him tightly, long enough for the operator to lose interest and hang up. Dred's mouth was by her ear, he had to know from her if she was okay.

"Breathe all right?"

A little nod of her head.

"Are we in New York?"

A little shake, no.

"Is it summer? What's the date?"

"March. Sometime." Her voice thin and weak. "Don't let go."

"Okay," he said, and he didn't for many long seconds. Her breathing quickened, then gradually relaxed and deepened into the kind of cadence that presages sleep, but still she was holding him close.

"You have a dangerous house, Mr. Balcazar," she said finally.

"Don't talk. I need to call the cops."

"No. Hold me."

"At the least, you go to Mass General."

"No. I'm okay."

"Don't argue with me."

"I will." Long exhale. "I'm okay. Shit, it's cold in here."

With half the window gone, of course. He pulled far enough away from her to examine her face, her throat, the ligature mark clearly etched purple under her jaw. Some bruising on her face, her cheek-bone near her left eye, but apparently it was not serious. The only cut was a small slice of her ear lobe where the blood was already drying. Dots of blood on her pink collar.

"You are a beauty."

She smiled wanly. "Any marks?"

"Yes, but they won't last long. I've got a scarf you can wear."

"Thanks. So. You saved my life, right?"

He nodded. "Forever in my debt. Stay put, okay?" He struggled to his feet, out to the living-room couch to get cushions, and then a blanket from the top shelf of his office closet. Returning, he found her unsteadily erect, propped against the sink, leaning over it and vomiting.

He dumped the cushions and blanket on top of his battered computer printer in the hall, came in and held her carefully by the shoulders as she retched repeatedly until her stomach was empty.

When it was over, she could say with a short laugh, "Plumbing works."

She washed herself in the sink and rinsed her mouth as Dred started righting the table and chairs. From the floor beneath the broken window, he retrieved the weapon, some kind of black electrical cable, with a jack at one end. Maybe stereo cable of some sort. She turned and saw him holding it.

"Surprised I didn't shit in my pants," she said weakly.

"Lauren, I need to call the cops."

"Uh uh. Don't."

"Guy almost kills you, you don't want to call the cops."

"Right, I don't."

"Hold that thought. Let me get some ice for that bruise." Two cubes from the ice maker in a sandwich bag. He tucked them in, folded the flap over, secured it with a twist tie. "Now let's sit down and talk about this thing you have about the police."

"T. D., please." She was drying her face with a paper towel, accepted the little homemade ice pack from him, winced as she held it lightly to her cheek. "I gotta go to Ohio."

"*Ohio?* What for?"

"See my sister. I leave in the morning, I come back Wednesday."

"You lost some brain cells, kiddo. You almost get killed—"

"I'm *fine*, I keep telling you. The police are stupid. *I* don't know who the guy is, how the fuck will *they* know who he is? They gonna chase him all over the city? Gimme a break, I got through it. I do not want to fight with you, okay?"

All right. No police, and she could go to Ohio. It was her life.

"Just tell me what happened. How it happened."

"Simple. You went outside. I came down to the door to look outside and see what you were doing. Then I was back up in the living room. And I came in the kitchen because that's where the phone is, right? To call the fire department. Soon as I opened the door, the guy jumped me from behind."

"You didn't see him?"

"No. He killed the lights. Maybe he had a mask. A stocking or something. Hey, *you* saw him."

"Just a leather jacket, black gloves."

"Yeah. And a knife. I thought I had him, I knocked the knife out of his hand."

"So then he pulls you to the window and chokes you with this wire. Very unusual."

"T. D., I don't know the guy. Believe me."

He wasn't absolutely sure that he could, not with this display of defensiveness so soon after what she'd just been through. He took her by the hand from the kitchen, closing the partially shattered door behind them, found her shaky on her feet as they stepped over the blanket and cushions and the long path of fanfolded paper into the living room. He indicated the one cushion left, motioned her to sit. Dutifully, she did, a good girl, still applying the ice pack.

"Okay," he said. "Tell me what you know about this man."

"Strong."

"So I noticed. Anything else?"

"Little taller than you, maybe." Her voice was still hoarse. "I never saw him."

"Did he speak to you at all? In any way?"

She shook her head. "I thought he was going to rape me, kidnap me. That's why he wanted to haul me out onto the roof. Fucker."

"I believe this guy's only intention was to kill you. He knew you were here. How? He knew the layout of this place, knew how to lock the kitchen door from the inside, how to get in and out through the window, brought only that piece of wire as a weapon—"

She objected. "He started with a knife."

"Yeah, *my* knife, maybe just to persuade you somehow, keep you quiet. But he really wanted to strangle you. *You.* Not just any-one, but you. Stay put, I want to look around the roof, okay?"

She nodded, leaned back on the sofa, closed her eyes. Dred moved back into the kitchen, set one foot on the windowsill, grabbed the upper sash and pulled himself through onto the roof.

It was a perfectly clear, cool night, and you could make out individual window lights in the Prudential Tower a mile away. Saturday night, scored by bursts of police and ambulance sirens near and far. The hiss of water escaping under pressure, the Fennelmans' hydrant still uncapped and unattended, out of sight around the corner.

With just enough light from the kitchen he explored his section of the roof, stepping away from the broken glass and shattered wood toward Marsden's deck fencing, not quite shoulder-high. With your adrenaline pumping you might vault this height successfully, or you might not. Then you'd make it more easily over the iron railing at the far end, lower yourself another five feet to the shed roof of Marsden's garage, then down to the trash-can container and to ground level.

Marsden's stockade fence door creaked on its hinges, swinging freely.

And just beyond it on the sidewalk, centered in a circle of gaslight, was a shape recognizable even from this distance, an enormous spanner wrench. Just about the right size to open a fire hydrant and create an effective diversion.

Far too much had happened for him to believe Lauren Michaelec didn't have a central role in all this. The break-in and theft, the diversion and attack. She knew many things. She was saying nothing.

He turned back to the kitchen window, crawled through, opened the door into the hallway and the living room where she should have been resting, but wasn't.

"Down here," she called, her voice coming from the bottom of the stairs. When he was in the hallway again she held up her hand.

"What are you doing?" he asked. She was dressed to leave, her hand on the doorknob. Wound around her neck was his blue-and-white Yale scarf, which she must have taken off the hook of his bedroom door.

"I can't stay here."

"Where are you going?"

"The airport. I'll be back Wednesday. Hope you don't mind if I borrow your scarf. Obvious reason."

"Lauren—" When he took three quick steps down, she opened the door and stepped halfway outside.

"T. D., please. I have to get out of this town."

"You keep disappearing on me. Lauren, listen, who's flying to Ohio at this hour?" Two more steps down.

"No hugs good-bye, please. I'll be fine. 'Bye."

"The best thing to do is get you into a hotel for the night—"

She was through the door, pulling it closed behind her. Dred stood, then sat down on the stairs to think.

Sunday was long, empty, and dispiriting. Two cheerless handymen, recommended by a friend of Elaine's on Myrtle Street as being always available for a price, came over about noon to replaster and paint the wall around the pass-through and to frame up a temporary wall of two-by-fours and plywood in place of the kitchen window. They also attempted a temporary cosmetic reconstruction of the shattered panel in the kitchen door.

Dred called Lauren's answering service to have her call as soon as possible, in the event she was still in Boston. Fine, the Sunday operator obliged, we'll have her call when she checks in. She didn't call.

The handymen, Cliff and Sal, were less appalled by the damage they surveyed than titillated, expressed an acceptable level of sympathy for this messy, costly break-in. They wondered about the condition of the computer printer, with its tractor-feed apparatus contorted beyond repair, and the parts scattered about: the platen, a knob, a tiny spring, a cracked ribbon cartridge.

It was Sal's job to pick up the pieces of the window sash. "Most guys," he said, "would just break one pane and unlock the damn thing. This turkey must be new at this kinda work."

Elaine called in the afternoon, wondered about all the racket in the background. He told her, truthfully enough, that he was concerned about security and needed to wall up the window frame just for the time being. Later he would inquire into alarm systems or install some kind of iron grating to cover the window.

"Sorry," he added indifferently, "that you got stood up Friday night."

"What a creep! Henry's got the worst bunch of friends. This guy came with all kinds of credentials, only he didn't come."

"Yeah. Too bad."

"So the reason I called, remember Vidco, the production company that did the AI programs?"

"Yes, of course."

"Good, well, we're meeting there tomorrow, ten o'clock. Is that okay?"

"Fine," he said.

Monday morning he felt only marginally better. He had drunk too much Sunday night, slept badly, dreamed a sequence of loud and fiery anxious dreams about Lauren's safety, and had woken up remembering it was true she had almost been killed and that twice she had vanished without explanation. These were dreams of closeness thwarted by shapeless evil forces and things that in a dream have no real identity; dreams of needing to be together and having her swallowed up in a red cloud just as he reached for her outstretched arms. A final dream of guilt: that he successfully freed the kitchen door hasp with the fireplace poker but remained motionless in the pass-through to watch helplessly, his shoes nailed to the floor, as her face turned red, then purple, then blue-black as the wire slowly squeezed the last bit of life out of her. It was this last one that had him sitting bolt upright with a loud gasp and his eyes wide in the dark.

It was a morning of much water on the face and four cups of coffee.

Vidco, as he soon found out, was one of those split-personality production houses, half of it given over to high-art cinematic film work for expensive commercials and "image" pieces for corporations, the other half the down-and-dirty video end of things, training stuff for managers, three-day shoots on shoestring budgets with a lot of, as they called them, "talking heads." Dred was impressed that Boston had such an invisible industry churning out stuff that never got on TV, every year many hundreds of hours of training tapes and image pieces to be seen by mere handfuls of small specialized audiences.

Elaine met him in the huge marbled lobby of this old bank building recently gutted for new office space. The lobby may have been designed as an airy, sunny atrium, but something in the design had gone askew and it was plantless, just great empty space flanked by enormous Escher-like staircases. She got close enough to kiss him on the cheek. She toted her cordovan valise, bulging with papers on artificial intelligence. Dred had only a ballpoint pen inside his tweed jacket pocket.

Up the stairs to Vidco's third-floor offices, she was filling him in. "We're seeing this guy Herbert Fielding, he's the boss. I think I was lucky to connect with him and have him let us in."

"Why? What's the big deal?"

"Oh, you know, they have these nondisclosure agreements, showing this stuff to you. These programs, some of them are loaded with privileged information."

"But not highly confidential."

"I don't know, we'll see," Elaine said. "I'm still learning too." She took his arm when they got to the upper landing, both a little out of breath.

"Did you tell him what I do, why I want to see this stuff?"

"No. I told him you're a writer doing a story on AI."

"Terrific. This is my first shot at it, I know nothing?"

Herb Fielding was a soft, flaccid-faced man, maybe fifty, with wisps of unnaturally blond hair stretching over his baldness. A limp handshake, but clear blue eyes.

"I don't have too much time," he said to Elaine, "so I'll set you up in the screening room. We're in the middle of this horrendous slide show for the Tourist Bureau and we're just gasping."

Then, to him: "I hear you're a writer."

"Yes."

"Is this a commissioned job or on spec? No shame if it's on spec, of course."

"On spec," he said. "And I promise not to mention any names—I just need a feel for this stuff."

"Good, I was going to ask, in fact I was going to say, the client doesn't want people seeing this. I think you can understand."

"I appreciate it, Herb."

"So watch it, but just don't pay very close attention."

The screening room was set up for a small audience, three rows, thirty or thirty-five blue velvet theater seats. Impressed, Elaine showered Herb with compliments, but Herb was slithering off to the projection booth to start the program. Elaine moved in next to Dred in the middle row, sneaked her hand onto his arm as the houselights dimmed.

"I missed you this weekend. Really."

"Okay, everybody, show time," said Herb, returning during the 10-9-8 countdown, stepping in front of the screen to offer a very short and very odd speech, as if addressing a large crowd, his eyes fixed on somethiong above and past them. "This is video, but it is superbly cinematic video. Pure visual sorcery. Our entire crew deserves kudos on top of kudos. That's all I have to say. Enjoy."

He left. Elaine moved her hand on top of Dred's to pat it. And now the title: "Knowledge Engineering: Experience Makes It Real."

She said, "You're going to learn a whole new language."

"Not if I can help it."

"Have you read much of that stuff I gave you?"

"Very little," he lied. Zero.

In the fifteen-minute show there were principally four men who talked to the camera about their work, as Vidco tried diligently to keep the subject moving and interesting, but these men, these knowledge engineers, were at their best when lost in the vernacular of their work, which was all but incomprehensible. Still, these guys weren't nerds. They were in their thirties, fathers and husbands, attractive, sense of humor, wry irony, smart, squared away. Loved this argot they used, that they helped create. Music came up toward the end, the men had their last words about how "neat" life was at ADC in the AI Division, and then credits, with Elaine turning to say, "I like the guy with the pipe. The one who knew how silly all this sounded."

Producer, Maggie Wilder.

"Different breed," he said.

Associate Producer, Lauren Michalec.

"Test pilots, is what someone told me," she continued, not watching the screen. "So. Does this help?"

His eyes were closed tight, blocking out any distractions. *Lauren Michalec, Associate Producer.* When was it she planted herself in the Athenaeum to meet him? Monday. How long before had she been checking him out? Who decided to change the spelling to Michaelec, adding the "e"?

"Dred?"

"I don't need to see any more."

"Good, mission accomplished. Let's do some coffee and doughnuts someplace."

"I have to see Herb for a second, just a few words."

The receptionist guided him up one more flight to Vidco's slide room. She didn't think Herb would mind if he just poked his head in.

Herb was standing, chin in his hand, gazing at an enormous long light stand littered with hundreds of slides. One of his young associates, spiked hair, earring, was arguing with him enough so that Herb seemed relieved to be interrupted.

"Sam, excuse me a second. Yes?"

"Good show."

"Good, glad you liked it."

"Lauren Michalec, the Associate Producer. She still work here?"

"Lord, no." Herb ushered him out of the slide room into the hall. "Sorry, maybe you're a friend of hers."

"No, but the name rings a bell."

"I'm afraid I had to let her go. I certainly don't mind women of that persuasion but she was quite militant and could make life very unpleasant."

"Persuasion."

"Most lesbians are the nicest women I know. Not this one, not the way she acted, the way she carried herself."

"Blond?"

"Spare me, if only. Greasy brunette. Wicked Witch of the West. I'm absolutely *praying* you're not friends."

"Not at all. Somebody else, I guess. But thanks, Herb, it was a great show and I've got a lot to think about."

Herb was heading back to argue with Sam, turned for a second. "I trust you didn't pay too close attention to it."

He smiled, shook his head.

Elaine was waiting at the receptionist's desk, comparing notes with her on computer systems, Apples and IBMs, Elaine so proud of her literacy with computers. But lifting her head she saw the look on his face. "You all right?"

"I have to deal with some new stuff."

Was it possible someone had arranged for him to be here, to learn this apparently innocently on his own, that Lauren Michaelec and Lauren Michalec must be and at the same time could not be the same person?

There was just time before the two o'clock meeting at ADC's AI-3 building in Westville to race from Vidco in Charlestown down to Dorchester for a quick visit to the Cirione Detective Agency. The drive was on the Southeast Expressway, normally the most hair-raising vehicular adventure anywhere in the state but right now a hazy peripheral blur. Nothing mattered right now except the notion of two people with essentially the same very unusual name. One of whom had almost been murdered in his apartment.

Exiting in Dorchester, he readied himself to see Frank. The agency was in the neighborhood of Fields Corner, where kids grow up to become either cops or, without the right connections, robbers. Frank knew them both in large numbers, held them in equal disfavor.

Instead of Frank, he found his assistant, Kevin Ryan. Frank was in England, "on the Strohecker case," due back sometime tomorrow morning *maybe*. Depending on what he was doing and how enthusiastically, he was as likely as not to extend his stay, would think nothing of blowing off a cheap round-trip fare for an extra twenty-four hours of solid evidence. No matter: traditionally Frank was almost never in.

While Frank was the head gumshoe, Kevin was learning to be the business brains of the outfit, the one more inclined to observe the niceties of proper bookkeeping and how it was that Dred could work off Frank's "ticket" without a muddle of dubious paperwork. Some unlicensed operatives kept awful records and risked jeopardizing their "employer's" license renewal. Kevin must have been aware of that potential problem with Dred, but so far the paperwork had been lean, mean, and simple: the client paid Dred directly and Dred paid Cirione a 10 percent overhead fee. Nobody in state officialdom had yet found this objectionable, and barring Massachusetts' propensity for regulatory surprises, it didn't seem they would.

Dred had met Kevin only a couple of times but had liked him instantly. He was a former bouncer, sufficiently big and broadshouldered to discourage anyone who might take exception to his long sandy hair tied back in a ponytail or the weighty gold ring that he wore today, glinting from his left earlobe. He was also much smarter than he liked to be, or was likely to be, construed. A privately careful thinker with excellent recall. Still under thirty, single, and on the prowl. Knew his electronics and computers and video equipment. Right now in the office he was hunkering down over a calculator, apparently orchestrating checkbook stubs and receipts and invoices. It was March, corporate tax time, and the agency still didn't have an outside accountant.

Kevin was happy to be interrupted, but of ADC he knew no more than their original phone call to Frank sometime two or three weeks ago, when Frank had given them Dred's name as the operative who specialized in that sort of thing. He's our white-collar genius, Frank had said, our Beacon Hill Einstein.

"So what gives? Is this fraud or what?"

"Some kind of sabotage. He said 'a bug.' In artificial intelligence."

Kevin whistled through his teeth. "Like one of those viruses or something? That what we're dealing with?"

"I don't know yet."

"Shit, it had to happen. Too many smart people in Boston, you notice? One of them snaps, he can be very creative with the way he does his damage."

Dred heaved himself into the client's chair. "At the same time it's very weird that when this job's about to kick in, someone breaks in and steals my computer. And that the woman I'm having dinner with at the time isn't who she says she is. And on Saturday night she almost gets murdered. In my kitchen."

It still hurt just to say it. He now remembered Kevin's stone face, reserved for occasions of spectacular content, like murder or attempted murder, as a way of testing his ability to respond impassively. He amended the stone face this time with the slightest arching of his right eyebrow.

"How?"

"Guy tried to strangle her."

He nodded, as if this were the usual thing. "So who is she?"

"I have no idea."

"Cops?"

"Haven't been called."

Again the stone face, chased by a sardonic grin. "Attempted murder of a woman you don't know in your apartment, why call the cops, right?"

Dred backed up for him, assembled the relevant details from the Athenaeum, the Oyster House, 118-C Acorn Lane Saturday night, this woman's fear or distrust of cops, her Sunday-to-Wednesday trip to Ohio, her penchant for rapid disappearances, and the attack itself, which he abbreviated to a scope of much less danger, not as close a call as it really had been.

"No serious damage? Didn't pass out?"

He lied and shook his head. "She seemed okay, a little groggy maybe."

"No shit. But he could've killed her with the knife, right?"

"She disarmed him," he said. "But with the cable he was very

THE VERY BAD THING · 89

serious." Dred did not worry that Kevin probably considered him still pretty green about the dark corners of the criminal mind, the criminal world. That knowledge would come in time, they both knew.

Kevin was tapping his pencil like a drumstick. It might be a key point, he thought, that ADC and Harvey Monahan had called here two, maybe three weeks earlier looking for just the right person to help them, Frank not just recommending but sanctifying the name Dred Balcazar, and then there was nothing, no movement. Time enough for someone inside ADC, someone close to Monahan, to dig into his background, habits—everything.

Habits. Like his Monday afternoon study hall at the Athenaeum. Where he lived. The car he drove. His preference for women who were good-looking.

"She was pretty?"

"So-so."

"Frank'll never quite trust you till you're married, you know."

"Thanks a lot."

"And never quite feel secure about you till you're armed."

"No thanks."

"Any old piece, to win debates. Keep an open mind."

"Maybe someday." He instantly rejected the image of himself with a gun in his pocket. It was quarter of one, getting late, and Westville was impossible to get to from Fields Corner.

Kevin said, yes, when the time came everything was in place for some ID work, if needed. Which it probably would be. Sources were still on line at the phone company, state police, the Registry of Motor Vehicles, and the credit checkers, all you'd ever need to hit the ground running on knowing who a guy was and what his life was like. Kevin wanted to show him something new, speaking of the phone company and speaking of bugs, and led him down the hall into the small back room where he kept his electronics. He'd been repacking the innards of a surveillance briefcase, cutting Styrofoam to fit around a candy-bar-sized Pulnix video camera, recorder, transmitter, battery pack, and the like. Pulnix camera lens screwed into a pinhole fitting, virtually invisible from the outside but providing a wide-angle view of just about anything, perfect in very low light. On the floor of a dimly lit restaurant, for example, right by your chair. But what Kevin was most excited about was his purchase of a thing called "The Sweeper," which had just arrived today. A small metal box with just two features: an on/off switch and a small speaker. Simplicity itself. Get to a phone, call home, and stick the mouthpiece of the handset right over this little tiny speaker, it generates about a one-minute tone sweep from 300 to 2000 cycles per second and triggers any tone-activated bug on your home phone. When the sweep is done, if your home phone is still ringing, that means there's no bug on your line. If your phone has *stopped* ringing, that means The Sweeper has set off a bug, and you've got problems.

Dred had repeatedly told Frank it was unlikely he'd ever want to get too involved with this stuff. Frank tended to agree, but Kevin was nuts about these things and there were times they really needed this sort of gear. The problem, Kevin was telling him, was that tone-activated bugs, when attached to your home phone line, will pick up any conversation on that phone line *and* in the room where the phone is, even if the phone's not in use. They're clever little bugs, they activate the phone without making it ring.

Kevin came back to the office with The Sweeper and set it next to his phone, started dialing. Dred's office number.

"Ever think," he said, "that when you make a date with a pretty girl someone might want to listen in?"

"Occurred to me, but not seriously—"

"Maiden voyage, let's find out."

Handset mouthpiece next to the little speaker. On the first ring Kevin flicked the switch and The Sweeper started humming its whiny glissando from 300 cycles on up. At the fourth ring they both could hear from the handset's earphone that Dred's tape had interrupted with its outgoing message.

"Damn," said Kevin. "Your answering machine came on."

"It does that."

"This only works if your phone doesn't answer."

"Yeah."

"So when you get home, call me back, disconnect your machine, let's try it again."

"Okay."

"What about your other phone?"

Same problem, the bedroom phone downstairs, his unlisted personal line, had the same machine, another TX-20. Obviously The Sweeper needed simple virginal, uncomplicated telephones to whine at that would keep ringing dozens of times until it hit that special frequency to which the bug's transmitter was set.

Dred took the handset from him, thinking to check for messages, maybe something from "Lauren." He hit double zero.

Kevin noticed. "You should have a better code than that. You can set it to any number you like, but double zero, that's probably the factory setting, right?"

"Yeah. Well, one of these days." He had given his access code no thought at all.

The tape rewound to the start.

"The other thing is, of course, that a burglary could just be a cover, a diversion, for planting a bug, right in your home."

This was true, and yes, he'd have to get back home and disconnect the answering machines to let The Sweeper do its thing. But now he was hearing the only message on the tape.

From Harvey Monahan: he was very eager to move their afternoon meeting back from two to one because there was a lot more to talk about, the thing had arrived and was on the verge of sabotaging a million dollars' worth of work. Look forward to seeing you, more than I can say.

Terrific, it was already five of one.

ADC's AI-3 in Westville was a brand-new five-story gray brick building planted in a tidily landscaped wooded area, and around it on all sides were open fields belonging to an enormous dairy farm that seemed, judging by its apparent prosperity, still to be making milk. Beyond ADC and the dairy, there was nothing else suggestive of commercial activity. Just old farms and fields and woods.

Such was the burgeoning high-tech scene west of Route 128—
oases of unimaginable braininess popping up in brainless, raw-
boned agraria.

After checking in with the receptionist in the lobby and accepting
his stick-on visitor's badge (they had it waiting for him, his name
typed in), Dred did not wait more than thirty seconds before a wiry,
slightly built man rushed out into the lobby to greet him, and without introduction merely let the assumption rest that he was, in fact,
Harvey Monahan, but he was hardly the man Dred had anticipated.
In his late thirties, he seemed part spider, part bookkeeper, wet hair
with comb tracks swept tentatively across a balding crown. Son of
Wally Cox.

"Happens all the time. People expect some two-hundred-pound
black bear. Sorry about that. The voice is misleading." As it was
now—incongruous.

Harvey was in a hurry. Through the main entrance they strode
down a noiseless gray-padded corridor to the elevator banks. "I hope
you've done some homework. There's no time to lose."

"Just started." On the elevator, with a young woman joining
them, Harvey punched the third floor. "Very basic reading, nothing
fancy."

With his eyes at the level of Dred's chin Harvey spoke *sotto voce*,
his lips scarcely moving. "You're going to have to get up to some
kind of speed. After the warning this thing has finally arrived." The
young woman was looking at Dred's visitor's badge.

"Warning. The thing."

"My office is on the fifth floor, but I want to show you the
machines."

They got off on the third floor, alone, and as soon as the elevator
doors closed Harvey started to say more about it as they strolled
down a long corridor. "The warning is why I called you guys in the
first place. A few weeks ago our knowledge engineers came across
what looked like a little glitch in one of our compilers. Except then
they looked at it and said, hey, this thing is an exponential self-
copier *minus* the final little green-light command, the trigger, to set

it in motion. A virus with lots of horsepower but no ignition, if you get the idea."

"Virus."

"I assume you know the term?"

Dred nodded. "So that's what we're dealing with."

"Essentially. Close enough."

Dred let it pass for the moment. "I don't understand 'compiler.' "

"Okay. A compiler takes specifications written in English and produces a program that computers can execute. So. I write the word *go* in a program, and the compiler translates that word into digits—binary information. But look, don't worry, I'm not hiring you to be a hacker."

"So the compiler is like a translator. And the virus—"

"Understand, you probably know that most virus programs are self-copiers, they literally spread like wildfire, eating up memory and disk space, and sometimes destroy lots of data. The warning, again, was a bug without legs."

"And then you said, 'This thing has finally arrived.' "

"The thing is the real, complete virus itself. Ambulatory. It was triggered somehow, just this morning. So I'm glad you're here."

They opened an unmarked door and stepped into a wide, windowless, low-ceilinged room about as big as a basketball court. Perhaps a hundred ADC computers, many as big as vending machines, were arrayed in rows like soldiers. Trademark ADC gray everywhere. "So we call this the computer room. Obvious enough. Most of these machines are on right now. Most of them are talking to terminals throughout this building, and AI-5 in Cambridge and AI-2 in Framingham. And they're all talking to each other, fifty, a hundred conversations at once. There's nothing new or magical about any of this, but you have to remind yourself when you walk into a room like this that's what they're doing. So figure this is the nerve center of the entire AI program at American Data Corp. And someone's gotten into it."

At the far end of the room voices were rising over the hum of the cooling fans, a knot of a half dozen men in white shirts.

"Hardware guys," said Harvey. "They've been at it since breakfast."

They were hunched together like a team of surgeons picking through layers of flesh to locate some tiny but lethal tumor, as if this electronic predator were a physical creature, having organic mass, taking up fixed residence inside one of these machines. "What are their chances?"

Harvey snorted. "If I had any idea what they're doing, I'd tell you. We'll come back here later, let's go upstairs, I want to show you what it looks like when this thing hits."

The fourth floor, Harvey told him, was home to a lot of senior technical people and a handful of knowledge engineers, the "high priests" of artificial intelligence. Here they were clustering in the halls, unable to do any work. One of them, catching Harvey's eye, scooted over to be introduced.

"Ray Niles, this is our new special investigator, Dred Balcazar." His handshake was moist and fishy. Like many, if not most of the others, he was male and bearded, with a hairline in recession and a face trying to control a jumpy, nervous smile. But he was older, closing in on fifty, his black hair shaggy and speckled with gray. One of the masters. Studiously professorial, resplendent in lumpy tweed sport coat over a Red Sox T-shirt.

"Ray's a knowledge engineer, normally housed at AI-5 in Cambridge," said Harvey. "But he didn't want to miss the excitement, which is mostly right here."

"The floor's pretty much shut down," said Ray. "I'll show you what I can, but it's the nature of this thing to be elusive, if not invisible."

He led them to a bare office, a suite actually of countertops and terminals and an enormous confusion of papers and books and manuals and coffee cups and old food containers, the place smelling as much of yesterday's salad as the pervasive ADC ambience of heated plastic and static electricity.

Ray was soon doing things at one of the terminal keyboards when he suddenly turned to Dred and stood up. "I want to confess this right now, before you observe it on your own and decide that I might be classified as an eccentric."

"I'm sorry?" he said.

"Harvey will tell you the same thing: I'm going to laugh in the wrong places. Since you're a cop, I should tell you."

"Ray, I'm not a cop. I'm an investigator."

"Whatever. But I'm going to laugh at the wrong times. I think it can be funny, when machines misbehave, the way a child can be amusing when doing something—unsocial. It can be funny, in a primal autonomic reflex way. I just don't want to lose a lot of work. Okay? I'll shut up now. Let's find this nasty little bug and see if it makes me laugh."

"Do you find the bug?" Dred asked. "Or does it find you?"

"Better, more precise, yes, it finds us. But we're very hospitable, we open up our veins and invite it in for dinner. It loves us."

When Ray turned back to his keyboard and screen, Dred sought a signal from Harvey—that it might be agreed that Ray Niles was a bulb of too many watts—but now Harvey started to lean in over Ray's shoulder.

"Let's try Gondwana," Harvey urged.

"My sentiments exactly."

While Ray Niles's fingers started to dance all over the keyboard, Harvey began to describe what he was doing—in that anomalous (and yes) bearlike voice, now hushed so it cracked into a whisper.

"Gondwana is an early AI program we did here, it's all higher mathematics. We called it an expert system when we did it, five years ago. It's kind of old hat at this point."

"Gondwana." The name was thinly familiar.

Ray was happy to explain that it was the name for the original landmass of the earth, before continental drift, when everything was bonded together. Just then Dred spotted the source of the rancid salad smell, a half-eaten plastic tub from a fast-food place, maybe shrimp and pasta.

"I think the idea here was that this program would be the foundation for lots of others. Anyway, let's do this, simple polynomials, just to warm up." Keys clacked, and symbols jumped onto the screen, X plus Y and parentheses and squared and division lines and all those things he barely remembered from high school math, even the word *polynomial* an anxious, constricting recollection. He wished he'd had a better mind for fundamental math. The bigger, stormier concepts attracted him (infinity, imaginary numbers like the square root of a negative number or the impossibility of anything divided by zero, Mobius strips and Klein bottles that twist paradoxically into themselves, the topology of this spiral pasta poking into view from the tub, the shape of the universe mimicking either a doughnut or a saddle, depending on whom you ask) but the everyday arithmetic of tax forms, barrels of apples, and dynamics of bodies in space (Mrs. Jones driving her Buick forty miles an hour trying to meet Mr. Smith driving his Pontiac the other way at fifty, each gelatin-fleshed at the prospect of their turnpike Rest Area assignation) utterly baffled him.

"Where's it coming from?" he asked, believing there should be a specific source far beyond the terminal in front of them.

Ray turned to look at him. "Gondwana's down in the machines on the third floor, along with everything else. I want it to do something where it has to talk to a lot of other machines. This is a very fine program, and it can reach into a dozen other System 2000s. Let's make it do wing cross sections. Just the math, no graphics. It'll really start to hum."

Harvey told him, "You'll see a lot of Greek symbols here."

"Asymptotes, zillions of them," said Niles. An asymptote (Dred recalled uneasily from a freshman college course of "fun math" for English majors, his final foray into the field) was an expression for a line that continually approaches, but never quite meets, another. The train we chase in the dream and can't quite get to, the pasta salad we will never finish because there must always remain one atom or one half atom or one quarter atom of Creamy Italian dressing. "All right, here goes. We want a special kind of wing. I told it to give me a very fancy wing for a very fast but subsonic airplane, a highly compressed Joukowski airfoil."

After Ray entered a series of commands the screen began to

squeeze out long incomprehensible equations like enormous ten-story Erector sets—stacks of Greek letters in rhythmic repetitions of multiplication and division.

"Okay so far," Niles said. "It's not as fast as you might have expected. On a Cray, any one of those monster machines, this would be a lot quicker."

"That's a lot of computation," said Harvey, "but a wing cross section demands tons of math. Normally, most of what we do is symbolic, not numeric. So when a guy like Ray interviews an expert in, say, making soup recipes—"

"Shit, there it is!"

And Ray Niles laughed, just as he had warned, in a kind of startled whinny.

"Here they come." It was something anyone could see all too clearly.

"A new letter," said Harvey. The letter K, leaping into places on the screen where there had been a number or another letter.

"This is just one thing it does," Niles said. "It'll eat up the screen. So far it doesn't hurt Gondwana—all our files get backed up every day—it just wrecks the thing that you're doing right now." Little K's were devouring other letters and numbers, ever hungrier, faster. "It's not exponential, though it easily could be. It's just accelerating very comfortably." Niles turned to Harvey. "We saw it doing this on Doug's screen, couple of hours ago."

"Doug Kiskel," Harvey told him. "Another knowledge engineer."

"With an F. Zillions of them. When it runs out of numbers and characters on the screen, it starts chewing up empty space. Then it really fires up the afterburners."

"Like now," said Harvey, and Dred watched for a few seconds as black K's flicked into existence on the screen where the empty landscape had been pale silver.

"Can't turn it off. See?" Niles was slapping keys all over his keyboard. "*Nada*. Look, heavy breathing, now it's starting to come—"

The K's filled to big blotches spreading tendrils to other blotches and webbing together, and now silently, furiously, sucking up all empty space.

"Climax!" cried Niles with his gusty whinny of a laugh, throwing his head back and pulling at his hair.

Just before three, when most of the staff in AI-3 had been informed it was okay for them to go home early, word came up to Harvey Monahan in his office that in another experiment with Gondwana in a different office the letter that was chewing up phosphors on the terminal screen had become a *Y*. Most likely, Dred believed, given a few more exposures to this virus, other terminals would reveal other letters filling in the blanks, like high-tech Hangman, and the message would emerge as an anagram in all its witless and disaffected grunginess for a few privileged AI geniuses to see and ponder and keep in their hearts.

FucK You.

Some moments later it was with a sense of relief that he was at last alone with Harvey, at a big table in the cafeteria, with technical support from coffee and yellow legal pad, to focus for the moment only on obvious things. Harvey, insect body momentarily stilled, obliged him in his rumbling ursine voice. The problem was clear enough: nobody in the AI Division of ADC was going to get much work done with the machines acting this way. So far, there was no apparent damage to equipment or software, but viruses being what they were, that situation could change in an instant. Viruses could grow and replicate and infect other machines and in time destroy the host by wiping out its memory and all its programs. Tiny computer programs in their own right, viruses tended to occupy very little space, were hard to find and, once found, hard to disassemble. Simple, but elusive.

" 'Fuck You' isn't much of a signature," he was saying. "If it were just a little more advanced we might have a lead."

"What about access. Someone in this building?"

"Dred, understand: a virus program can be created on any computer and sent to damn near any other computer in the world, if you're smart enough. This could be an ADC person, or anyone in the world—a hacker in Des Moines or even Tehran. But we're starting to think, for a variety of technical reasons, that it's internal. Homegrown right here."

"Okay. And presumably you think the person can be found."

"Maybe, maybe not. In any case, forget access, think motive. And here's where you've got problems. We had layoffs three or four—five weeks ago, we lost a great many of our top software designers, cream of the senior technical staff, short of the knowledge engineers but still some of the best around. It was partly political, partly economic. The effect was a whole building full of hard feelings."

Dred was scribbling basics on the pad. AI-2, AI-3, AI-5. Fuck You. Ray Niles. Layoffs. Knldge Engs. "What about AI-1 and 4?"

"Don't exist," came the voice of a man from behind. Harvey invited him over to sit down, introducing him as Doug Kiskel, the knowledge engineer who got all the *F*'s. Dred stood and shook hands with him. He was tall, but otherwise forgettable; his coloring and clothing were various shades of pale.

"Shows you ADC doesn't do things in a linear fashion. Name a building AI-1, right away it's stigmatized, it's the earliest, the prototype." His voice a cool baritone of purely distilled confidence.

Spinning the table's third chair around backwards and mounting it cowboy style, Kiskel turned to Harvey, offered his latest ideas about what the virus was and where it might be from. Harvey would toss in an occasional apology or attempted explanation for Dred's benefit, but Kiskel had blinders on as he worked through his Byzantine logic in search of clues, just once or twice making eye contact with Dred. Fingers drumming frenetically on the chair's backrest, sound effects of cavalry coming to the rescue. The eyes very bright blue. Otherwise he was layers of beige, flawlessly smooth linen skin, a high forehead with thin sandy hair, cream cabled sweater with holes in the elbows. Probably mid-thirties, large-framed and athletic-looking, but the face was oddly delicate, as if expecting hurt. He never once smiled. He was finger-drumming and thinking and talking rings around Harvey Monahan, who, with his face rapturously upturned toward his colleague, several times betrayed astonishment that this wizard might be solving the virus problem *just by thinking it out*, but no, each track toward the solution branched with *buts* and *howevers* and a cascade of technical vernacular that kept the virus elusive, free.

Dred was scribbling other words onto his list. Knldge Base. Source code. Dirty binaries tacked onto the Compiler. Miriam. None of which meant anything to him. Only after Kiskel stood up, shook his hand, and left was there any chance to sift through it.

"Understand first about Doug Kiskel. He's the smartest man in the whole AI division, by half a head. Sometimes he's out here in Westville working with some of the newer staff, but most of the week he's in Cambridge at AI-5 developing extensions on a new language. When he mentioned Miriam, that's what Miriam is."

"Named for?"

Harvey shrugged. "No idea."

"Extensions. New language. What's the language do?"

"Okay." Harvey drew a deep breath, summoned his patience. Dred did not mind making him sweat a little to make the obscure clear and simple. "When we make an expert system, we have to know first what we want it to do. Let's say we want it to advise a soup company on new recipes, how to make them."

"Soup."

"Right, let's say the head chef at Campbell's is about to retire, and Campbell's wants an expert system that contains all his knowledge about how to make a good soup. So Campbell's hires ADC to send out a knowledge engineer, like Doug, to talk to the chef and accumulate everything he knows about how to make soup. The problem is, normally it takes months to get all that data collected. Months. Not recipes that already exist, but recipes he might create. Probably the guy knows more about soup than you'll ever need, so it's endless refining, shaping, sorting the guy's knowledge. That process is the bottleneck. The rest of it, believe me, is relatively easy. Or easi*er*."

"So now there's Miriam, is that the idea? That helps?"

"When he's finished, yes. Miriam as it is now translates what the guy knows about soup into computer code faster, easier. The *extensions* to Miriam are like new ways to make Miriam even faster, and therefore better. Miriam and its extensions are totally in Kiskel's domain. The guy's amazing, you can see the excitement there, what's going on in his head. Both those guys, Doug and Ray, are absolutely brilliant. In fact, they're both presenting demonstrations at the big AI Symposium in Washington next month. Kiskel's going to be the headliner, with Miriam."

Right, the same symposium Todd Shaler had talked about. The annual Biggie.

Moments later they were in his fifth-floor office with the door closed. There was a nice view over treetops toward the dairy farm and hills beyond. "I know you may be wondering about your role in all this."

He did. "What you're doing here is very impressive. And it's not likely I'll ever understand it."

"We don't need you to understand it." The great deep voice becoming almost inaudible. "We need you to understand people."

"Excuse me?"

"That's the part we're weak on. That's where you can help us. We'll do the technical stuff, you stick to flesh and blood. We're math, you're humanities. We'll teach each other."

"Harvey, what do you know about me?"

"Frank Cirione said you were new at this, but brilliant. He said something like Einstein-in-residence—is that his usual epithet for you?"

"One of Frank's few failings is his pathological admiration of me. Fortunately, I've gotten used to it."

Harvey laughed. "Let me say, my own view is you seem to be perceptive enough, and most important, you're normal."

"Compared to?"

"Most everyone I know at ADC."

"We started to talk about motive. What about something political—sabotaging software that ends up in the military?"

Harvey squinted at him. "Possible, but I doubt it. Most of what we do is pretty far afield of military applications. Very few government contracts here."

Dred remembered to ask what he thought to be an obvious question about the whole affair. "Back to the virus itself. Why not just shut down all your machines when it hits? Just unplug everything."

"Okay, bear with me. We can shut down some of the computers some of the time, like right now. But whether it's coming from the office next door or a hacker in Des Moines, it's most likely on the network. And we have a lot of users on the network, all over the country, who depend on us. Only in a real crisis would we pull up the drawbridge. So far our users don't seem to be affected. And inside the company itself, we seem to be okay, because of our backup procedures."

"Which are?"

"Every morning, seven to nine, guys in the computer room run backups of yesterday's work. These are called the incrementals. Every couple of weeks the incrementals—they're all on tape—get boxed up and shipped to an outside storage site. Then, twice a year, we do what we call a 'complete dump,' where everything gets copied and stored off site. Insurance reasons. So the virus *seems* to be trashing only the current day's work."

"Seems. You're not certain."

"Not yet. One reason we're letting the thing in so easily is to see if we can find it and take it apart. See what it really wants to do. Maybe it's just swearing at us. Or maybe it has something else in mind."

"And you do think it's someone within the company. Mad scientist in the basement, whatever the motive."

Harvey took another deep breath. "That's where we have to start. Of course with you we now have the flexibility of investigating the nonwork environment. Of anyone you wish to get to know better."

"Nonwork" meaning home, the community, friends and neighbors, background checks for possible scrapes with the law. "Above all, since we believe we're the only ones affected, this has to be treated strictly as an internal matter. The media finds out about this, we're sunk, so anything you do outside these walls must be very discreet. All that being said, I think I can assume you're interested?"

"You can." Very much so. A client of this size, with a problem of this intriguing nature, had been far too long in coming. The fee was as Frank had recently stipulated: four hundred a day, seventy-five an hour after eight hours, plus expenses. ADC wanted a "not to exceed" limit of five thousand dollars, continuance subject to negotiation. Very nice package.

From Harvey's office Dred could see his yellow Subaru among perhaps only a dozen other cars left in the lot. It was time to go, almost four o'clock; it would be at least an hour back into Boston at this time of day.

"Good." Harvey's narrow, bony hands opened a thickly packed manila envelope on the desk, took out an employee's badge, gave it to him. "Dred Balcazar, consultant. This is a class B-1 clearance, it'll get you into everything but Betty Ohlmeyer's panties."

"And she is?"

"My boss. VP for research operations, she's the one who's really sweating this thing right now."

Now he handed him a similar plastic thing.

"This is your card key. It's good for most of our buildings."

"So this is all aboveboard. I'm a private investigator, just as you've introduced me."

"Precisely, they'll figure that out anyway. Understand, with half a brain we'll get into the guts of this virus in a day or two, by ourselves. But we want a report from you, what you've seen about what we do, *your* expertise about something we're doing wrong to allow this sort of thing to happen. Not in a security sense—security is never perfect, never can be. We want to understand why, and if you're lucky, who. Maybe you can tell us."

"As long as it's no more technical than long division, fine."

"You're the people person. And to get you started . . ." He removed the last item in the envelope, a slab of a book. "These are all our AI employees, from top management down to touch labor and buildings and grounds. Their titles, home addresses, phone numbers. This was printed before the layoffs, so I've marked all those with an *X*, maybe about a hundred of them." Harvey passed it to him. A flick of his thumb through the pages and he guessed there were six or seven hundred names in here.

In the parking lot outside, the air had become warm, just as they had forecast, air that was soft and sweet-smelling of spring, the dairy farm, old leaves, thawing earth. Three hours inside AI-3 had given him an annoying case of the sticky sweats. He peeled off both his London Fog and tweed sport coat, swung them over his shoulder, faced the lowering sun and the breeze and let the air move through him, inside his shirt, over his skin. Airbath. Aftermath. Math hysteria. Choosing to be a real math person, sometime in high school it happens, is choosing to be visibly different from everyone else and electing to live with the social consequences. Or else one is visibly different to begin with, like a Ray Niles with his illogical high-register giggle, and math becomes the conventional sanctuary, the dark safe corner. Okay, so I'm strange, but after all I'm a math person, my mind is always busy busy busy with problems, problems that you'll never understand.

Driving along these winding country roads with the sun behind him, he strained to recall Lauren, how she looked before the occluding shock of the attack. At first she wasn't there, but in time she came back, crisply in profile, sitting cross-legged before the fire at a moment when she had just turned her head away. It was disturbing that this was the only view he remembered, when he had spent so much time building a picture of her at the Athenaeum, the Oyster House, his apartment. The attack had blotted everything else out, leaving only this image of Lauren in profile. And her name wasn't Lauren.

He recalled a minor unconscious act that had helped save her life. Leaving his apartment to join Willie Cuthbertson outside, he'd gone to his night table to take his keys with him, locking the door behind him as he stepped out onto the street. He could've left the keys inside and asked Lauren to let him back in when he rang, at exactly the time she was being assaulted in the kitchen. Had he not intuitively, thoughtlessly fetched his keys, she'd be dead.

He talked to her all the way home, rehearsing for his next meeting with her, if it should happen. "Whatever you're hiding," was how it took shape, "whomever you're protecting, whatever it is you're afraid of, I might've helped you."

She was in the Athenaeum, disappearing into the stacks. "Yes, I saw her," John would tell him at the Circulation Desk. "I believe she went into Room 3, you might look for her there." Off to Room 3 he would find her sidling between Spacemaster movable stacks far down the aisle, and he would take the crank handles of both stacks that flanked her and wind them in opposite directions, one in each hand, so that she was caught there, the stacks moving in on her. You couldn't actually hurt someone by squishing them between these stacks, the Spacemaster people made sure of that, the reduction gears didn't have enough oomph, but you could immobilize someone in there, simply capture them, as if for further study. He was holding the crank handles so that she was unable to push the stacks apart. "Why do you keep disappearing?"

"You're hurting me." Her head still in profile, that same flash-bulb memory.

"No, I'm not. Spacemaster stacks can't hurt you."

"I feel trapped."

And now let's crank them the other way and push them apart and let her turn this way, facing front. Light her face from front and back so her hair flames, her cheeks flush; her lips are full, her eyes squinting and smiling with love as now she is lying back on his bed naked with this great long lean thigh, this smoothly fluted quadricep.

He imagined dislocating her from Boston, sent her winging far south, far away from the grim hazards of the city. In pure Caribbean sunlight on an empty pink beach he was exploring her entire tanned upper thighs and flat abdomen and back and arms and shoulders, caramel skin ever so deliciously glazed with this fine blond down. Spun-sugar, waiting for enough time to be studied and loved and licked, tasting of salt and her soft sweet skin smell. Any twitch of movement, any repositioning of her body on this enormous white beach towel gave him new configurations to investigate, smooth striations of muscle and light and shadow. She would be reading a book plucked from the Goethe section of the Athenaeum and barely notice he was noticing.

Back home he would insist on the truth. Tell me why you're not Lauren. What do you know about the theft of my computer? Of the man who tried to kill you? They *are* the same man, are they not?

Tell me—or you can damn well forget about sunny beaches and instead cool your heels and almost perfectly proportioned breasts right where you are, trapped by Spacemaster stacks.

"I had to do it," she most likely would say.

"Why?"

At home he dumped his raincoat and tweed jacket on the Parsons bench and went upstairs with the mail and his ADC notes to his office and his machine. The message counter showed zero. He opened both windows to let in the warm air. Without needing to check the number, he dialed her answering service.

"I'm sorry," the woman said, "we no longer take calls for that person."

Unfortunate news. "You did yesterday."

"Well, sir, that's possible. Sunday is change day."

"Tell me how to reach her?"

"No, sir, I'm afraid I can't."

"You mean people come in, they use your service for a week, and then that's it? Isn't that a hassle for you?"

"I wouldn't know, really." She sounded sincere. "Normally a month is the minimum time, but sometimes there are exceptions."

"Well, she's in Ohio anyway, right?"

"I have no idea, sir."

"Thank you anyway. Sorry to trouble you."

4

If this girl played in a rock and roll band, Kevin Ryan had said, she must have made a stop or two at Jamais Vu, the kind of club you'd play either on your way up or on the way back down. Kevin knew that the current owner was a former friend of Frank's, a guy named Bunny McMahon, who did all his own booking for the club. If anyone had seen this girl perform in a band, Bunny had.

It was Dred's second trip to Jamais Vu. He'd come here with Elaine, learned the original owner was a local shrink who named it for the exotic psychological condition, the opposite of *déjà vu*, of feeling utterly estranged in familiar surroundings, which was precisely Elaine's reaction, trying to have fun with him and failing. No problem, he'd tried to assuage her: alienation is the proper state of mind at Jamais Vu, estrangement becomes a communal activity. But it was young people and their music that were the problem for Elaine; we are no longer young, she wanted it known. We don't understand the music or these people with short hair dyed in gumdrop colors.

The headliner for this Monday night was Just Three Chords, to follow Bazooka and Sarah Cries, and even on the slowest night of the week there were people gathering outside, Harvard Street in Brighton where you could leave your laundry off, play pool, and do a drug deal all within three doors of each other. If Dred and Kevin looked at all out of place here, no one seemed to mind.

Crowded but not too crazy tonight. There was a table and two stools near the back by the audio mixer, and you could actually talk and be heard. To a friendly girl whose hair fell softly across her forehead instead of sticking up in green spikes, Dred gave an order for two draft beers.

Sarah Cries, all girls with drums and two guitars, was finishing its set when the foamy glasses came.

"Bunny here tonight?" Kevin asked her.

"Always. He lives here. Think he's upstairs right now."

"Thanks." When she left, Kevin nodded to the stage where Sarah Cries were starting to pack up their instruments. "The all-girl bands. Mostly gay," he said. Even as Dred decided the remark didn't need a reply, a pretty young woman, strawberry blond, was standing behind Kevin kneading his shoulders.

"Kevvie."

With no hesitation, Kevin said, "Sheila."

"Two years later, not bad."

Without turning around Kevin glanced at Dred, stifling whatever chagrin he felt. "Sheila, this is my buddy Dred Balcazar. Sheila Corrigan."

She smiled at Dred as she continued her massage. "Hi, buddy. Kevvie and I were almost married."

"Not true," said Kevin. "That was your idea, not mine."

Out of the corner of his eye Dred caught sight of the TV planted up in the corner of the bar, offering a "Newsbreak" tease for the eleven o'clock news.

"Well, I'm married now," she said. "Gonna have a baby soon."

Here are the stories we're working on right now.

"Congratulations," Kevin offered indifferently, twisting away from her, concluding the massage. "So what brings you here?"

A fire in Chelsea leaves several people homeless.

"Music. Billy doesn't like to come, so I come alone."

Police discover the body of a young unidentified woman in a dumpster in the South End.

"Uh *huh*. You're not looking very pregnant."

"I'm not. Not yet. Trying real hard."

And: *Our Eyewitness News Team has learned that a computer virus has infected industry giant ADC.*

"Billy might be shooting blanks. Kid's gotta have a father."

Details coming up at eleven.

"Sheila, my buddy and I, we got work to do."

Dred got up from the stool, finished his beer. "You guys catch up. I'm going upstairs."

"Yeah, it's been two whole *years*." She threw an arm around Kevin, who did not fend her off. She might have been a little drunk.

Kevin turned and asked him, "Don't want any company?" He seemed to be thawing just enough not to want to leave her.

"No. Stay tuned."

"Billy must love you to pieces, the way you behave," Kevin told her, as Dred left and wormed his way through the mob of acid-washed blue jeans and black leather and vests and safari shirts, looking for the stairs in the back. This was a very young crowd, working-class kids, a few college types, pretty much the way they'd looked when Elaine had been here to spend most of her energy finding new ways to vent her general disapproval. Somewhere within her lived a seed of fun waiting to bloom, he believed, a precious plug of joy assiduously conserved beneath laminations of restraint. Someday the seed would root and flower, he hoped, with another man more patient than he to nurture it.

Bunny, he mouthed to himself as he moved past the stage and the remnants of Sarah Cries' equipment through a door to the stairs. You don't give yourself a nickname like that. Someone else gives it to you, and you survive it. Maybe by making yourself big and strong.

Bunny McMahon was, in fact, an enormous freckled man, early forties maybe, with a head of recently shaved red stubble, meaty tattooed arms declaring war on all comers, a soggy unfiltered cigarette dancing between his huge lips as he spoke.

"Balca-what?"

"Balcazar. Dred Balcazar. I work with Frank Cirione, I'm trying to locate a person, a rock and roll musician."

A derisive snort. Squatting on a big speaker, he hadn't moved. "Pal of Frank's no friend of mine."

Witlessly facetious, but with an edge of truth to it. Dred responded in kind: "You mean Frank gave me a bum steer? I got the wrong nightclub?"

With Bunny was a girl of twenty or so, swathed in leather, and he wanted her to leave. She nodded and ducked through the door, down the hall to the stairs. Now he removed the sopping butt from his mouth and smiled, flashing a solid gold bicuspid.

"Naahh. Kidding. Frank and me, we was bodyguards together, back a ways. You. You were never a cop? You don't look like a cop."

"No. And you?"

"Nah, I used to help Frank out, give him leads, shit like that. But he doesn't come back to me no more. So, hey. You need to talk? Business?"

"Looking for this woman. How many Boston rock bands have women guitar players?"

He found this question oddly amusing. "You mean, out of the one thousand six hundred and eighteen gigging bands in your greater metro demographic area how many have a girl in them who plays a guitar? Within two? Within a hundred?"

"You're saying quite a lot."

"Maybe a third." Bunny dug into his jeans pockets and pulled out another bent cigarette. "That's all you've got? No name?"

"I got a description."

"Tell me," Bunny said, lighting his cigarette. The smoke went down the wrong way and he coughed violently. The man was not so healthy.

"Pretty. Late twenties. Blond, medium height. And I think she's quite smart, a pretty good brain. So. This is like asking if you've got head sheets, glossies, I can look at."

"Hey, listen, I gotta tell you, there are a lot of women who might be her. They call up all the time, a lot of 'em come by ten o'clock in the morning, I hardly know my name and they're here with their tapes and they'd kill to get a gig here. Sure, Jammy Voo is the club, but I tell ya, they won't leave you alone, everyone's gotta be a star, know what I mean? Hey, I think I'm pretty fair, but you can't be Santa Claus to everybody, know what I mean?"

"She has a song she calls 'Sidewalk Man.' Slow reggae Caribbean kind of thing, something about neon in your eyes. Very pretty song. She's got a kind of breathy nodal voice."

Bunny sucked hard on his cigarette. If any of this registered with him he didn't show it. "Who else is in the band?"

"No idea. But if you've got photos, I'd recognize her."

"Okay. Show you my office. You're right, this is nothing to go on. Pretty blonde. They call up all the time." Bunny hoisted his great bulk up and Dred followed him into the hall and to another door, a rush of noise from below as the next band, Bazooka, was just starting its set. Bunny closed the door behind them, sealing out most of the din. From a bar refrigerator behind his desk he pulled out a Budweiser for himself, unsnapped the cap, winged it with thumb and forefinger across the room toward a wastebasket, missed, and then deposited himself in a great swivel chair. Photos all over the walls from bands and singers and politicians and God knows who else.

"There, on the table," he said, indicating a cardboard file box. "If she plays rock and roll in Boston, three to one she's in there."

Dred began leafing through glossy photos of bands, stapled to covering letters and promotional fliers. There was no special order to them. On most photos the band's name and musicians' names appeared in print on the border.

"What's the gig?" Bunny asked. "She singing off-key with the law?"

Waterworld. Clayface. Broken Molars. Happy Campers. "Client thinks she might be involved with the wrong elements, wants her to have a clean bill of health."

"Client may have a point, if she's been here." Bunny laughed.

The Black Moles. Extended Benefits. Circle Sky. Gorehounds.

"Turquoise ring," Dred thought aloud, realizing that the ring on her little finger might be the first thing to give her away, many of these female musicians so dolled up for the photograph, their hair electrically charged, smiles glued on, jutting plastic eyelashes, circles of paint around their eyes, she could hide in this photo even if you knew it was her.

Bunny had straightened up. "Yeah, turquoise ring. Some wear the Indian jewelry."

This was just one fraction off center, out of place. "I guess they do. Some don't," Dred replied.

"You mentioned turquoise, I was just answering."

Dred turned to him, surprised by the note of defensiveness. "Bunny. This is a large ring on her little finger, you'd remember it. It's a simple cross, in turquoise."

"Oh, my mistake. I don't know the kid. Usually I notice the jewelry, my woman taught me how to do that, see what other women wear, pay attention to it. Hey, knee-jerk reflex. Mighta been thinking of someone else." Another fraction off center.

Non Sequitur. White Heat. Llama and the Lips. "Someone else, other than who?"

"Hey, look, back off a notch, will ya? You got a thing for this girl? I'm talking about rock and roll women and their bands and the jewelry they wear."

Little Brother. Angel Hair and the Follicles.

"Sorry, Bunny. Damn, whole lotta bands here."

"Yeah, that's my business. So tell me about you and Frank Cirione. You old friends or something?"

Wetted Surface. Doctor Glassheart. And the turquoise ring.

"Our fathers."

Doctor Glassheart. Typeset under, her name was Stevie Bear.

"Huh?"

"Our fathers were buddies, back in New York. Same school. Carmen Cirione and my father. I got to know Frank when I moved here."

Forget the ring or anything else. She was exactly as she was, but with her hair swept to the side, and an amused, pouty smile that might be saying, "Can we meet somewhere and talk about all this?" Stevie Bear. The others in the band: Hank Proctor. Tom Carmody.

Bill Holland. He continued flipping through the glossies, book-marking her with his thumb.

"Yeah, well, he's an okay guy," Bunny was saying. "Don't see him much anymore, though. Funny, working for the same dick."

Thumbflips through the rest of the photos. "Well, I don't see her."

Bunny had eyes on him like the twin bores of a shotgun, skinny dark eyes that had a hard time looking anything but mean.

"Too bad."

"Lotta nice-looking women here. Wouldn't mind seeing them in person."

The girl with the punk hairdo and leather everything, the one who'd been with Bunny earlier, now stuck her face in.

"Not now, luscious," Bunny said, and she disappeared.

"Very pretty women," he said.

Bunny got up from his desk. "Yeah. Lot of them are faggots, but some of them—they'll come on to you, if they want to make a good impression. They do. Fact of life."

"Yeah, fact of life."

"No big deal," said Bunny.

"Yeah, no big deal. Unless music's so important to them they'll perform certain favors just to get an audition."

"I wish," Bunny said unconvincingly.

"Okay, I'm all done, I'll find some other leads."

"If she's not in there, she's real small time. 'Course you said turquoise ring, and I was thinking maybe it was one who came in, but no, she was brunette and a keyboard player." Stupidly trying too hard to backtrack.

"So, Bunny. I'll tell Frank we met. Take it easy. Thanks."

"Yeah, stay cool."

Downstairs, Bazooka was bouncing all over the stage. Dred ordered a martini, threw half of it back, snaked through the crowd to the back of the club where Sheila was still draped all over Kevin, her shoulders hitching to the heavy beat of the music. It was too loud to talk even back here, Kevin wriggled free of Sheila, they moved out into the front entry with the ticket taker.

"Thanks for the rescue. Good timing."

Dred took him aside out of earshot, next to the pay phone. "Got her name, the name of her band, and the other guys in it. And let it be noted that Bunny is a giant asshole."

"Frank warned me, yeah. He calls him Fartface."

Dred had a dime in the phone to call information. The book had been ripped out of its folder.

The ticket taker said, "Can't drink out here. Sorry."

The martini glass was on top of the phone. "I'm not drinking it."

"Can't *bring* your drink out here," he insisted.

"It's okay, pal, take it easy," Kevin said.

The operator told him there were no listings for Bear, Stevie, Stephanie, S, or S with middle initial. Not in Boston or Cambridge. He tried the same for Brookline, Newton, Somerville, Watertown. But Ticket Taker, a young guy who was clearly ill at ease being tough on them, would not yield to the impropriety of Dred's martini glass remaining in this entryway, perched on top of the phone. At last Kevin grabbed the offending drink and went back inside the club.

Dred continued with more dimes. Belmont, Waltham, Arlington. In the middle of the umpteenth "I show no listing for her," Ticket Taker surprised him. "She's a musician, right?"

"You know her?"

"What's the band?"

"Doctor Glassheart. I think they broke up." Dred hung up the phone.

"Yeah, they did. They were here couple months back, I think. January. She's pretty good, she fronts for them. Wild on the stage. I remember her."

"Know where she lives?"

The kid shook his head. "Mr. McMahon might. Y'ask him?"

"Not yet."

"He oughta know. Go ask him. He's prob'ly upstairs."

"Why would he oughta know?"

"Well, some of 'em he likes, and he gets to know them. I think she was one he liked."

Kevin returned to the entryway, took him aside. "So look, my old pal Sheila? She goes out two, three nights a week, don't ask *me* what her deal is with her husband. She knows this place, she knows Wings, The Chain, 18 Lansdale, she's a good source."

Dred took him inside. "I'm going to try upstairs once more."

Sheila told Kevin she didn't think she knew Doctor Glassheart or anyone in it. Dred downed a second martini strictly for its drug value and then another beer, he wanted the prop, the heft of the brown bottle in his hand to go upstairs. You couldn't hear yourself *think* in here—Bazooka a pretty apt description for their music. The dance floor was mobbed, kids dancing while holding bottles of beer. There couldn't have been anybody here over thirty, they all parted ways to let him through, thinking maybe he's a cop, a narc or something. Taking the steps two at a time, he wanted to barge in out of breath and looking desperate, like he just *knew* this fat fuck was lying to him.

Bunny's eyes wide as he threw the door open. Immediately Dred went to the table where the box of glossies was, and there was Doctor Glassheart pulled out on the table. Bunny knew her and had yanked her out.

"Well, there we are. Now we remember."

Backing away in his chair, pushing back. "Hey look, you're a friend of Frank's, you're okay, sit down."

"I'll stand."

"Now take it easy, pal, okay? You left, and then I thought, hey sure, I remember a girl like that. So I found her. So maybe you got something for this girl? No problem. Want the head sheet? Take it." Hands extended—help yourself. Dred obliged, also taking the promotional flier and the Doctor Glassheart cassette tape, tucking them into his pocket. "Yeah, that's it," Bunny continued. "Anything you want, you're a friend of Frank's. Just—unnerstand, I didn't remember her at first, that's all. Then I did. She was a weird one. Kind of a cocktease, you know the type."

"I know the type, Bunny. So you liked her so much, where's she live?"

"Boy, you're a real bad guy, you know that? Next time I see Frank, he should know how you operate."

"Where's she live?"

"Look. I ain't seen her since January." This was possibly true, matching what Ticket Taker had said.

"Okay." Dred just stared at him for several seconds, hating him. "I might want to call you back, Bunny. I might have some questions."

"Sure, no problem. You feeling better now?" Bunny tested. "You looked a little *annoyed* when you walked in here. Hope you're feeling better."

"I'm feeling better."

"Good."

"Hank Proctor, Tom Carmody, Bill Holland." Studying the head sheet, Kevin simply recited the names, for the third or fourth time, as if they were especially hard to remember. In fact, Kevin was quite a bit drunk.

"You want a ride home, or you want to take the T?" Dred asked him.

"No no no no, neither, I want to see the scene of the crime. Gee, she's a real looker. And she said, where was she going?"

"She said Ohio. Visit her sister."

"Ohio, geez. She comin' back?"

"Yeah, she said Wednesday. Now you sure you don't want to go home?"

"No, wanna see the scene. Listen, the audio mixer, I gotta tell you. He knows all the bands. Just before you came downstairs, I got him to twitch a little when I said the name Stevie Bear."

"Good," said Dred. "Sounds like everyone knows her but me."

"Nobody knows where she lives, though."

"No, that seems to be the pattern."

"No prints at the scene?" he asked.

"Guy wore gloves. Natch."

"So she's real cute, and someone wants to kill her. Why? Number one: jealousy. Insane jealous rage. Number two: money. Is that possible?"

"No. She's not the money type."

"Three: 'cause she knows too much about something. Why strangle her, though? Takes too long. Guy had a knife, he had all that broken glass around, he could've cut her throat, right? Smash her face in the glass. Geez, I had a lot of beer. I hate it when that happens."

"Gonna be okay?"

"Maybe not. Can you pull over?"

Dred wheeled the Subaru over next to the sidewalk at a corner. They were on Commonwealth Avenue, one of the city's great and beautiful thoroughfares, preparing to anoint it with Kevin Ryan's vomit. Kevin opened the door, leaned his head out over the curb. Nothing happened, just that rapid jerky breathing that usually foretells throwing up. At last Kevin pulled back into the car and they were off again.

"Thanks, all better now."

"Good."

"So the guy coulda killed her. With glass or a knife but he uses some, like, stereo cable, right? I'm thinking, what's that tell me? And now I'm thinking, I don't *know* what that tells me."

"Kev."

"Dred."

"I heard a newsbreak thing on the tube about a woman's body found in a dumpster in the South End. Today."

"Always the fuckin' dumpsters. Killers *love* the fuckin' dumpsters."

"I just hope like hell it isn't Stevie. Obviously."

"I'll call the precinct in the morning and find out for you." Kevin turned to him. "You okay to drive?"

Dred laughed. "You okay to ride?"

All the rest of the way to Acorn Lane, spaced between burps, Kevin laid out his theories of murder, liberally interrupted with apologies that it was just him talking, nothing official here. Women in dumpsters, he said, happen three, four times a year in the city. They are either stabbed or strangled, not so often shot. Men are stabbed or shot, are not strangled and do not end up in dumpsters. Why? Not *just* because they're too heavy. When men put women's bodies in dumpsters, they are making a statement about the victim. When men kill men, they don't traipse all over the city looking for dumpsters. Men usually stay where they die."

"Also," Dred told him, "somebody leaked the virus story. Saw it on the newsbreak thing."

"That's a problem?"

"My client said it would be, yes."

"I have a feeling I'm gonna be busy tomorrow."

They were silent the rest of the way to Beacon Hill. Kevin seemed to be dozing off. Dred began to feel he was slipping into that zone that shared something of both failure and triumph, that peculiar state of being where things begin to make less and less sense but it feels numb and not unpleasantly tingly, almost as if pharmaceutically induced. It felt good to have this cassette tape in his breast pocket, and the flier with the eight-by-ten photograph, a little package of success. Doctor Glassheart and Stevie Bear.

Parking on Willow Street, he nudged Kevin awake, helped him out, and they began the long, slow walk up Acorn Lane.

"Couldn't park farther away, couldja?" Halfway there, Kevin was already huffing.

"Not on Beacon Hill."

"Move somewhere that's got a driveway, will ya?"

On the front steps Kevin waited while Dred dug around for his keys. Here in the yew bushes by the steps, leaning against the wrought-iron fencing, was something wrapped in a trash bag, blocky and heavy with the plastic stretched tight around it and secured by a twist-tie.

"Kev. Check this."

"Another goddamn torso in a Hefty."

"No, it's something else."

Dred leaned over and grabbed the bag and tested its weight and hoisted it over the railing onto the top step, tearing at the plastic. Inside, the cream-colored case of a computer, his portable computer.

"So," Kevin said, "people break into your apartment to *borrow* things. Assholes."

With Kevin vaguely helping from below, he lugged the damn

thing upstairs through the living room into his office and set it on the table adjoining his desk. Kevin wanted to get it up and running to see if it had been damaged, but Dred didn't think that was very important right now. He had to think: why all the trouble to steal it simply to return it four days later?

In the living room he took the Doctor Glassheart cassette out of his pocket and looked at it closely for the first time. Handwritten on the label of the Glassheart cassette were the names of three songs.

"The Love I Dread." "Sidewalk Man." "Glassheart Theme." The first two written by S. Bear.

"Plugged in," called Kevin from the office. "And I'm struggling to stick in this little boot disk, be easier if I weren't so damn *drunk*."

For Christ's sake—"The Love I Dread."

"All right," Kevin declared. "It's in and booting. Does it always sound like a dog growling when it boots up?"

"Hell, Kev, I just bought it, who knows?" Okay, so maybe there was some sense to this after all: some very wise guy set her up to meet him at the Athenaeum, to catch his eye in his favorite fifth-floor balcony hangout, steal his seat, make a good impression.

"Got a *C* prompt.' Hard disk looks okay," said Kevin.

"Good." The good impression made, she'd arrange to be called at her answering service, hope for a dinner invitation, yes, Thursday, that's fine, she reports back to the guy that we're eating dinner Thursday at seven-thirty at the Oyster House, his apartment is *all yours*, and the crook tells her what to say and not say at dinner, how to act, certainly absolutely must have told her his name, this guy is Dred Balcazar, he's an investigator, an operative.

"Not a whole lot in your directory," Kevin noted.

And damn it, she said she'd spent all that time matching his phone number to his name, it took her forever. This was such bullshit, she already knew his name, she was a good actor. How would she be behaving if she truly felt the way she claimed to be feeling?

It was like their first fight. And she wasn't even here.

He turned the volume up on "The Love I Dread." It had to have been written months before she met him, didn't it occur to her this was kind of a *thing*, an amazing little coincidence of words foisted into her life?

It was pure heart-stopping shrieking rock and roll, the lead guitar squealing in constant pain over the heavy fuzzy rhythm guitar. A guy was singing "the love I dread," and she was echoing the line, until near the end when he thought he heard: "The love I dread is all I'll ever get."

Kevin called from the office, "So c'mon in, I got something to show you here."

"What?"

"A cute little ditty called BACKOFF.TXT. I bet it wasn't here before. I just *bet*."

On the tape, "The Love I Dread" ended and Stevie Bear started singing "Sidewalk Man," richer and more electric than what he remembered from Saturday night, but still a halting and plaintive kind of song. Singing it, she sounded hurt.

"Dred, you want to read this? You should."

He went in. Kevin was seated facing the little amber screen in which were centered two short sentences:

"Back off ADC and Lauren will be fine. If you don't, it will not be screwed up the way it was Sat. nite."

At first he tried to understand how it was these words had appeared here, what little animal in the computer had performed this weird and ugly bit of sorcery.

Kevin was trying to work it out in his head. "So. Maybe this asshole stole your computer just to send you a letter. No, Kevin, that's wrong. He stole the computer for some other reason, then something happened, and he decided to return it with this message on it. How 'bout that?"

"What happened was Saturday night. He tried to kill her and he failed."

"Okay, so he ups the ante with *this*, and he also says—" Kevin was up out of the chair, widening his eyes, getting excited. "He also says, 'Hey, gumshoe, guess what? It's all connected to ADC.' Jesus!"

"Right. Which we were just starting to see."

Kevin was still shaky on his feet. "Pure dumb luck you saw that video with the name on it, connected one Lauren Michalec with the other." He pronounced it *Micklick*. "He couldn't know about that."

"So maybe he's telling us what we're sure to find out anyway. Second guessing us."

"Chumming," said Kevin. "Stirring it up so we bite. Bite what, I dunno."

"Maybe."

"So lemme look at the scene of the crime." Kevin turned the computer off. They moved together to the kitchen and the smell of freshly painted wallboard sealing the window and pass-through. The weapon, the cable with the jack at the end, dangled snakelike over the back of one of the chairs.

"This wall is new," he noted with knit brows, facing the old window.

Neon girl, neon girl, come let's find the very bad thing you mean to me.

"And this is the weapon, right?" He had the cable in his hands, his thumb and fingers tracing its length.

"Yup."

Kevin was looking at the business end of it, this large stereophonic jack. "This is industrial-strength audio. Maybe you didn't see it, but at Jamais Vu this kinda shit was all over the place."

Dred slept on the couch in his clothes, fitfully dreaming of making phone calls, eager to get to work and call the band, maybe this guy Carmody, or maybe the guy who sang lead on "The Love I Dread," Bill Holland. Or the bassist Hank Proctor. He worried and dreamed about bodies in dumpsters. He awoke at three and then four and then five, and at six-thirty he got up and his back hurt from the couch.

Just starting his first cup of coffee, he went to his computer and with the help of some of Elaine's handwritten instructions learned how to make the machine tell him what was in it. Directories. Listing all these names of files, looking for the thing Kevin had unearthed the night before, *backoff* something, to recall it in the clear morning light and perhaps see it differently, understand it from a new angle.

There was no *backoff* anything in this directory.

Next to the computer Stevie Bear watched him from the photograph. Her face was fuller and younger-looking than he remembered, her head cocked and her lips parted as if in mid word. A petulant little-girl look, but with happy, smiling eyes.

"Stevie. The bastard wants me to back off. And now I can't find it."

As he dialed the Doctor Glassheart number printed on the flier, disregarding the basic courtesy that musicians be allowed to sleep late, Dred studied the faces of her former bandmates in the photo: first, Tom Carmody, sandy-haired with granny glasses, soft-featured and preppy, and then Bill Holland, a fiery-looking guy with curly black hair, here leering with upper lip curled and nostrils flared. And Hank Proctor, gangly and balding, cradling his bass and staring blankly.

After three rings, the phone company recording declared the number disconnected.

Information gave him the number for a Thomas P. Carmody in Brighton, which seemed like a safe bet. He dialed and got a tape: "This is Tom. I'm not here but please leave a message." He spoke just long enough for Dred to imagine this could have been the same voice he heard on "The Love I Dread."

"Yes, hi, Tom, I'm a friend of some very fine musicians who need a drummer, and you've been recommended. Could you call me back so we can talk more about this?" Without giving his name he left the office number.

More coffee, and he dialed a familiar number in Manchester, twenty miles to the north.

"Christ, who's this?"

"C'mon, kid, wake up, my computer's back."

Elaine snorted and harrumphed into the phone, her best early morning sounds of general world-weary disapproval.

"Seven-fifteen. I don't have to wake up till nine."

"You're awake now, aren't you?"

"Jesus, Dred, this isn't fair. Okay, I'm sitting up, listening."

"They returned my computer. Can you come over?"

"Christ. Why?"

"You don't have to do it right away, but I need some help with this thing. You know how it works. There's something in here I saw last night and I wanted to see it again and now I can't find it."

"You mean, like a file?"

"A file you can read. I really do need your help."

"Lord, why do I do these things? You can be such a waste of my time."

That hurt. Elaine was not generally inclined to sudden bursts of scorn. Possibly Charlie and Beezey were getting to her with their chronic acidity, the sour gas that emanates from Brahmin decay. She hadn't ever said anything to him like that before.

"I'm feeling a little punchy, normally I wouldn't call so early."

"Yeah, punchy, I've heard that before. Let me get up and call you back when I'm thinking straight, okay?"

She did, half an hour later.

"Okay, I'm coming into town anyway, I can swing by."

"Good."

"I've got a noon flight, I'm all packed, I'll come by right now."

"Flight. Where are you going?"

"Just one of those last-minute things, Bermuda. Tally Smith, she invited me, she has a house there."

He didn't know Tally Smith.

"Well, that's nice. Bermuda should be lovely. Taking company?"

"Possibly, we'll see."

"Okay. So you'll be here, what, maybe nine?"

More than anything before, the long-drawn-out battles during the 90 Days' War, the feisty encounters, the heated letters she wrote him, the post-breakup verbal brawls in his apartment, this insipid conversation seemed to him the utter end of it with her.

At nine he telephoned the Athenaeum, the circulation desk, and, upon discovering John was working a rare morning stint, prepared for battle.

"Mr. Balcazar. You certainly must know that the membership list is private."

"The last name is 'Bear,' like the animal. It's important."

"This has to do with . . . your investigative work?"

"Rules are to be bent, John, they are not to bend us."

"Spare me, I can't tolerate aphorisms, not at this hour. Bear, like the animal."

"Thanks, John."

A long pause. "Sorry, nothing female under Bear. Excuse any unintended *double entendre*." Pronounced very French: Doobla ontahnd.

"Stevie?"

"No, it's the Bears from Concord, and they certainly are not Stevie."

He asked him to try Michaelec, hoping that he had the spelling right.

"First name is Lauren."

"Yes, that is in fact correct. Now don't ask me to—"

"John, I need the address, before you go."

"Oh, of course. How stupid of me."

"And phone number."

"Sorry, no telephone. The address is a box number in Cambridge. Number 805."

"Shit."

"Shit it is then. So. Will we see you Wednesday night, for Walt Whitman?"

"Not likely," he said. "Appreciate the help."

Number 805. If all else failed, he could drop her a card. But Frank Cirione had said forget the post office, they hadn't yet divulged the name or address of any box holder.

Minutes later, opening the door with her duplicate key, Elaine shuffled in, toting a single suitcase, and, with hardly a hello as he greeted her, dropped the bag in the hall and trotted upstairs to the office.

"Bermuda," he said finally. "Should be nice."

"Iffy weather this time of year, but I don't care. Tally's a good friend." She sat at the computer keyboard like a concert pianist. "One day you'll be doing this on your own."

"Maybe. If they don't keep stealing it."

"Okay, directory . . ." She typed DIR next to the *C*, and file names started to rain down from the top of the screen. "What were you looking for?" And somehow, clacking keys, she froze the list so he could study it.

There was nothing there named *backoff*.

"Can you keep going?"

"What's it called?" she asked again.

"I'm not sure," he hedged. "But I don't see it."

The list unfroze and continued scrolling. In this directory, and in all the others Elaine called up, the *backoff* thing simply was no longer there. He watched as she unfroze the words for the last time, saw them sweep up to the top of the screen and vanish. She turned the machine off.

"What did it say that so intrigued you? You said it was a text file?"

"Yes. Just some messages from the software company, probably."

"Most text files have the extension TXT. I was looking for those, and I didn't see any."

"Maybe I was mistaken."

Elaine wasn't buying it. But she didn't seem to want to press him further. "At least you got it back," she said, as now she scrunched her nose to sniff. "You've been painting."

"Little repair work in the kitchen," he said. She got up to follow her nose, and when she'd stepped into its unnatural darkness she squealed her surprise. "Good *Gawwd*! Dred, what happened here?"

He came in behind her as she flipped on the overhead light.

"I mean, this is truly unattractive. You said a little repair—isn't this just a bit of an overreaction?"

"Security. I don't want this guy coming back."

A dubious twitch of her eyebrow while she assessed the graceless-ness of this new rectangular chunk of wall where once there had been a view to morning sun and the tops of buildings across the Common. A view they'd enjoyed together without quarrel, one of the few things they'd successfully shared. "You were so . . . cavalier the night of the break-in. So unthreatened."

"I changed my mind."

"*I'll* say. And you got mad and broke the door, too."

Cliff and Sal had done a pretty lousy job with the door.

"It's an old door. It just fell apart."

"Exploded is more like it." Turning back to him, she beamed with the certainty of her judgment that he was not telling the truth. "Something happened after Thursday night. Right? And you won't tell me."

He could go just so far with her. "The case has become more complicated, yes."

"I smell cigarettes."

"Sal, the carpenter, smoked," he lied.

"How more complicated? The break-in connects with ADC somehow?"

"I believe so, yes. Elaine, let's change the subject."

"Really? Must we?"

"Yes, I insist."

"Okay, new subject. I'd like a screwdriver, if you have the makings."

He showed faint disapproval. "If you must."

"Don't be a poop, Dred. You know how I hate flying, you know I always get a little tiny buzz before flying."

He made it for her in a tall glass and poured a final cup of coffee for himself. Elaine drank deeply, stepped through the hall into the living room, scoured the place with her eyes. Fireplace, couch, stereo, piano, guitar in its case with the lid ajar, unlatched; he could see her picking up clues.

Over the rim of the glass her dark eyes were daggers.

"You really like this girl, don't you?" she said.

"Just dinner, that's all."

Smiling, shaking her head. "Uh uh. She was here."

"We're through, Elaine," he shot back at her. "You're supposed to know that by now."

"She was here. On your first big date you have a fight, she flees in terror through the kitchen window, destroying it. Am I right?"

He let it pass. "Who you going to Bermuda with? With whom, rather."

"I'm not, I was just teasing you, I'm just going to see Tally." A big gulp. "So tell me why you like this girl so much. This girl who fled in terror through your window."

He didn't say anything because he didn't know, and it was rapidly becoming none of her goddamned business anyway.

"Okay, when you know, tell me. In the meantime can I beg a ride to Logan? Or should I call a cab?"

"Elaine, under the circumstances, maybe you should get all this stuff out of your system."

"This stuff?"

"This venom."

She wheeled by him to refill her glass, in the freezer dropping ice in like depth charges, fridge door slamming, and she came out and leaned against the window by the hallway door, drank, rolled up her sleeves, took two deep breaths before beginning.

"Dred Balcazar. I do not store venom."

"Okay," he said. "Mind if I make a few phone calls?"

"Snakes have venom."

"I'm sorry, Elaine. Let's just drop it."

"Fine. We'll drop it. No venom. I'll just fade pleasantly into the background, as always. While some ditsy bimbo takes my place." Pushing quickly past him, she was in his office retrieving the Doctor Glassheart photo from his desk, which had not been sufficiently concealed under a stack of stuff about artificial intelligence. "She is sort of pretty, in a vacant, airheady kind of way."

"She's involved in the case, Elaine. Back off." *Backoff*. Where the hell did it go?

"Okay, I will." She let the photo swoop to the floor, an autumn leaf. "But you do know, don't you? That I loved you?"

"Yes. Before we discovered—"

"I really did, Dred, but you go through these cycles, I think I know you and then you do something off-the-wall, something absolutely bewildering, and I don't know you. People have certain expectations of you and then you fool them."

"I've got to make some calls." But now a call came in, from Doug Kiskel at ADC in Cambridge, exhorting him to come over very soon to see the virus hunt in action, hear the latest news about how the thing was made and injected into the ADC system. There were reporters around; Harvey and Betty were apoplectic that somebody had spilled the beans. See you in a half hour, he replied to Kiskel.

Now Elaine started to dance around the apartment, winding up for the kill. "Who *are* you, anyway? People were always asking, who is this guy Balcazar you've chummied up with? And I'd say, oh, he's a Yalie from New York, and then I'd be saying he was a bartender in Florida for a while, he worked on charter boats, he was in the wool business, and pretty soon I realized, hey, *I* don't know who the hell he is, go ask him!"

"Elaine, just for now I need some peace. I'm calling Frank. Or Kevin."

He got Kevin as Elaine closed in, slopping part of her drink on the desk. "The Mad Moor is what I came to call you. The Mad Moor with the compulsive prick, trolling for bimbos."

Kevin had made it in at nine but was not yet fully functioning, nursing a Budweiser headache. Frank hadn't yet flown in from England.

"Not nice," Dred told her. Kevin was tuned in to all of it. "Kev."

"Ooo, boy, she's ripped," he said.

"So. If you want to fuck a punk rocker, maybe that's just what you deserve." Elaine was reducing herself to nothing more than a mean drunk.

"Kevin, I called Carmody's tape, left word. Can we get something on the other two guys? I don't see them in the book."

"As soon as I remember how to talk, yeah," he said.

"Dred, don't be such a *man*. You're into your man mode, it makes me ill."

"Elaine, please. So, Kev, I'm going to ADC pretty soon, can you talk to my tape?"

"I can meet you there later. I'll be outa here maybe eleven."

"Okay. About eleven then."

"Got woman trouble again," Kevin noted.

"Right, see you there." He hung up and dialed Yellow Cab and asked them to come to 118-C Acorn Lane right away.

Outside the AI-5 building in Tech Square, Cambridge, a van from Channel 5 had disgorged a crew now setting up a camera and lights. Inside the huge atrium-style lobby were a dozen or so reporters, variously harassing each other and the receptionist, a friendly-faced platinum blonde. Standing next to her was a man in a suit who seemed to be running interference with the reporters. He took a call at the desk and got their attention.

Dred decided to hear him out, see what the company was saying.

"Ms. Ohlmeyer will be coming down shortly to give you an update."

"Who's Ms. Ohlmeyer?" someone asked.

"She's a vice president for research operations. She's the company spokesman in this matter."

"Spokesperson," said a woman, correcting him.

"Go get 'em, Gail," said another.

Dred was wearing blue jeans and leather jacket and aviator sunglasses and the reporters ignored him. He clipped his B-1 badge to a belt loop on his left hip, fished out the card key Harvey had given him, and used it to open the main door. Inside, Doug Kiskel and a crisp-looking woman came toward him.

"Dred, this is Betty Ohlmeyer. Dred Balcazar."

She was older, very businesslike, with a strong handshake. "Harvey Monahan's been telling me about you for weeks," she said, with a trace of displeasure in her voice. "I'm glad you're finally with us. And I wish you luck."

"What do you tell them?" he asked, indicating the reporters now knotting near the door.

"We have a problem that we can solve. No permanent damage. Just a temporary breakdown. And that they should not believe any rumors or unauthorized leaks."

She smiled wanly as she pushed through into the lobby to face the reporters. Now Dred turned his attention to Kiskel, who was herding him toward the elevator. He sported a pale green sweater with moth holes. Stubble of blond beard, his hair uncombed, obviously it had been a long night, but still the guy seemed clear-eyed and totally alert.

"We think we know where it's coming from," he said.

There was no handshake; it was as if the two were old friends reconnecting after seeing each other in the hall moments earlier. In the elevator Kiskel hit the eighth-floor button and said nothing else, stared coolly ahead, until Dred decided to prompt him.

"So. Where do you think it's coming from?"

"I'll show you."

"Okay, fine, I'll wait."

A sudden, wide smile, and Kiskel seemed to shake something from his mind. "Hey, look, understand, I don't mean to be unfriendly, I spend all the time not talking, thinking. I have to keep thinking, this thing is a huge video game where you don't have the instruction book. I'm thinking, I'm not trying to ignore you."

He gave Dred a tap on the shoulder, and when the elevator doors opened added a hand at the small of his back, the cumulative effect not very pleasant. From one second to the next, Kiskel was either remote or jarringly familiar. They were walking shoulder to shoulder down a corridor past empty offices, until Dred slipped one step behind.

"Is everything still shut down?"

"Pretty much. We're receiving all six letters of the obscenity now at fairly regular intervals. With the *u* twice as often." He then squinted at Dred, as if seeing him closely for the first time. "You look like you haven't slept much. Everything okay?"

"Fine. It's a busy time, but I'm sleeping all right."

At the end of this hall was an open work area, a large table with chairs and men in shirtsleeves feverishly working with long accordion fanfolds of printout paper. One was Ray Niles, same ratty tweed coat and underneath this time a Bruins T-shirt.

"Ray's having a tough morning," Kiskel said with a sigh, as Ray looked up and came over to meet them.

"I suppose," Niles said to him (again no hello, no handshake), "that you read the paper this morning."

He hadn't, not past page 1, there had been too much Elaine. Wordlessly Niles led him away, around the corner to a room that served as an office kitchen/canteen, where the *Globe* lay on the counter, opened to the business section.

"This is one reason why we have the TV truck outside. Read this, and don't laugh."

AI SABOTAGE AT ADC?

CAMBRIDGE—Something, apparently, is bugging American Data Corporation.

The nation's fifth-largest computer firm, headquartered in Cambridge, is allegedly having problems with bugs—and not the kind with six legs and feelers.

They are instead a new strain of "virus," a program or series of programs that are created to sabotage other programs. They have in the past afflicted other computer firms, including the industry giant IBM. A particularly powerful virus can wreak havoc on an enormous scale while remaining essentially "invisible" and therefore highly elusive, perhaps uncatchable. Especially susceptible are programs that are networked from one computer system to another, like electronic mail networks.

Officially, ADC is saying nothing. But a well-placed source in its artificial intelligence division, who spoke under conditions of anonymity, told the *Globe* that a virus recently got into banks of computers used primarily for R&D in artificial intelligence. The bug, he said, "invited itself in, swore at us, then took its leave." The source adds that "there was no permanent damage," only "a memorable display of power and guttersnipe vitriol."

Other sources hinted that the virus temporarily disabled ADC's central AI computers, forcing early dismissal yesterday of most of its employees in that division.

A company spokesman said something slightly different: "Our main AI computers went down for a period today. There's no damage, no cause for concern."

But according to the source, the virus apparently "has attached itself to a part of our platform software that we can't locate—and it's right in the heart of our worldwide communications in AI."

With an ironic laugh, he implied that ADC's entire AI effort might be in jeopardy, if in fact it's as powerful and elusive as it has been portrayed.

At the same time, he said, ADC's best and brightest are hunting it down and hope to find it "within a day or two." Like a common cold, these things do come and go.

"Okay," Ray broke in, "they mention an ironic laugh and people think it's me. But it's not." Hissing whisper, the guy was clearly frightened. "I wanted to show this to you before you came to me. I don't even know what 'guttersnipe' means. That source wasn't me."

"Does it matter that much? Not that they think it's you, but that the word is out?"

"Stockholders, sure. Harvey Monahan. Burt Cooper. They're businessmen, of course." Cooper, the CEO, had left IBM when he was quite young and started ADC, back in the early 1960s. Like Digital Equipment's Ken Olsen, Data General's Edson deCastro, or Wang's An Wang, Burt Cooper was a high-tech celebrity, a household name around Boston, one of the entrepreneurial superheroes. "You've got to believe me, I didn't talk to the *Globe*."

"I do believe you, and it's not an issue."

Niles hadn't had a shower. The change of shirts notwithstanding, he smelled like feta cheese.

"Kiskel." The name like a snake spitting. "Kiskel's the guy. Has to be."

"Why?"

"He's not from my planet." Niles laughed. "He's not your typical computer jock. He ought to be in management. Okay, so he's got a 200 IQ, so what, why screw around with AI? He should be out making millions, he's that kind of guy. Instead he theorizes about Miriam and spends all his spare time just *thinking*!"

"Miriam. Remind me." Just to hear it from someone else.

"The new natural language system he's working on. How AI and humans can talk to each other." Closing in on him, eyes darting. "I have to tell you—from what I know, Miriam isn't going so well."

"How can you tell?"

"I haven't seen it, but I know he's losing it. He bit off more than he can chew. And he's got to make good in three weeks, at the big conference."

Dred pulled away. "Ray. You're his friend."

That nervous whinny of a laugh. "Not really."

"Still. You should be careful what information you volunteer."

Niles fidgeted, as if wrestling with a difficult choice, finally said, "I'm going to volunteer this, then you can see for yourself. Sandy Murchison. She lives in Arlington with her mother. She can help. She used to work here."

"Used to?"

Niles became very nervous. "Please. She was laid off, don't mention her name around here, and *please* don't say who told you about her. She's another resource, that's all." He tore off a corner of the *Globe* and was writing the name down: Sandy Murchison.

"Ray, this place is swarming with geniuses and I'm going to get help from someone who was laid off?"

A perplexing grin. "Exactly!" He gave the scrap of paper to Dred and scampered off like a frightened rabbit.

Out of the kitchen area, Dred found Kiskel with the other guys at the big table in the hall talking about things like source code and polluted binaries. And Kiskel started to try to explain, as he escorted him down the hall to a floor-length window and what looked like a small video camera, mounted above head height on the wall and pointed out the window.

"This is an infrared transceiver. It connects with that building over there. That's HRA."

Another acronym. "Meaning?"

"Heuristics Research Associates. It's part MIT, part ADC. Top floor, in the corner window, you'll see a small rectangular dark patch."

He saw it, a tiny piece of the window that seemed discolored. The building was several hundred yards away, diagonally across the street from them. This was Tech Square. Every building was aswarm with people working on the same kind of abstruse, incomprehensible stuff.

"The windows there have infrared filtering coating the glass. That little rectangle is where they scraped it off so that they could put an IR transceiver there."

"And you think that's how the virus came in?"

"We do. It seems that way to me. You should go over there and check it out."

"Can you help me to understand why?"

Without a word Kiskel shepherded him down past the kitchen, turned left into another corridor until they stopped in front of a poster-sized blueprint, a complex schematic with boxes and circles and lines. Here he continued to try to explain how it was that ADC computers were linked to different networks and different computers all over the world. How AI-5 in dryly intellectual Cambridge talked to AI-3 in down-home milk-fed Westville, where the huge computer room was, and also to AI-2 in suburban Framingham. And then to Pennsylvania and to Boulder, Colorado, to Albuquerque, and to California and Stanford Research Institute and points overseas. He tried to explain about protocol transactions and bridges and subnets, and that true viruses attached and replicated only when programs and "packets" were allowed in for execution, but this one was something different. This one was something exceptionally clever because it entered the constant flow of electrons in elaborate disguise, probably from HRA across the street over here to AI-5 and thence to the main computer room at AI-3 in Westville where yesterday Dred had watched men unscrewing the panels off the machines and working inside them as if the virus were a little biological blob of something tangible and extractable. The way the virus program was coded, Kiskel said, it seemed that it started at HRA across the street, which communicated here only via infrared.

"How do you know," Dred asked, "how the virus is coded?"

"We caught it and broke into it, that's what all the fuss is about. We see how it was written. It almost certainly started from a terminal at HRA. And it almost certainly was kicked into the system sometime Sunday afternoon, with a time delay on it, so it wouldn't show its hand till the next day, Monday."

Kiskel now led him to his office on the opposite side of the building, took him in, closed the door, slipped into his swivel chair behind his desk. Dred remained standing, not wanting to stay, feeling there was something very odd about this office.

"We can talk safely here," said Kiskel.

It was much less an office than a den. Home away from home. On one wall was a huge spatter painting, Jackson Pollock in kindergarten, with a display lamp underneath.

"We can't talk safely outside?" he asked, now scanning book titles on the shelf. *Structuring Heuristics. Strategies for Natural Language Processing. Downloading: Centering the Ethics of Immortality. Advanced Studies in Complexity Theory.*

"It's better here. No secret who you are, Dred. I can be seen helping you understand the problem, getting your feet wet. I probably can't be seen with you otherwise."

He now saw, for everything that was here, what wasn't.

"No computer."

Kiskel laughed. "Right, no terminal. I think I'm the only guy in

AI without one. I told them, I don't want it, when I need one I'll go to the office next door. Everything's on paper. Or in my head."

"Huh."

Also among the books, Kierkegaard, Hegel, Kant, Goethe.

"Computers are not important to me. As such."

"Then why are you here?"

"I'm a knowledge engineer. I'm very interested in how we know what we know, and how what we know can be understood by a machine. How a machine can differentiate between the way things are and the way things seem to be. Much more important that the machine understand the latter: to a machine, it's how it seems, not how it is. And of course, how the mind works. How it works well. How it works *not* well."

"You're starting to lose me." He wasn't listening closely, preferring to look around: hanging on a hook on the back of the door was a ski parka, dark blue.

"I'm as much interested in the minds of my colleagues as the minds of anyone else. These are very smart people. Mostly young, mostly nerdy types who remind you of being back in college, mostly social misfits of one kind or another. Ray Niles is a classic example— for twenty years he's been ADC's premier nerd in artificial intelligence. Ray can hardly tie his own shoes. His mind works extremely well most of the time, but he has no common sense, not much sense of balance, and no real ethical center that I can see."

He was listening again. "That's quite a statement." Perspiration on the back of his neck, white shirt just back from the cleaners, and it would have to go out again.

Now Kiskel rose from his chair, came around and sat on the corner of his desk. "Do you have your own ideas? Suspicions?"

Not looking at him. "Zillions of them. Pretty big field so far."

"Theoretically, yes. Like—everybody who's ever worked here?"

"Theoretically," Dred replied, discovering that Kiskel's home was 55 Hayes Terrace in Cambridge, according to a magazine mailing label upside down on his desk. Hayes Terrace, Dred knew, was in the Hills section of the city, an area of some pricey new condos.

"Doug, you just said something very intriguing. That Niles

doesn't have any ethical center. Why would you want to say something like that? Even if it's true?"

"Very simply because I think he might be involved." Kiskel became motionless. "Isn't the opinion alone more important than why I voiced it?"

Dred moved back to the bookcase to the right of the door. "But when you made that statement, Doug, I happened to be standing right here." Directly over his shoulder was the large book about downloading. "Okay. Downloading, I take it, means the transfer of information from one place to another, is that right?"

"Very roughly. What are you getting at?"

"Well, right here on the spine the words 'Centering' and 'Ethics' are very prominent, it was right over my shoulder in your line of sight when you made that statement about Ray Niles having no ethical center. Now I'm not sure what this title means, centering the ethics of immortality, but I do know that I have to think about motive all the time, and I have to consider the possibility that you just made that up. About Niles and his ethical center. For reasons I'm not sure of."

"Why would I make it up? Play that thought out for me."

The knowledge engineer thinks he has a bite, gives him slack. Dred decided, just slap at the bait, give him a tug. "On the face of it the guy seems pretty ethical to me. What makes him unethical?"

"I could never get into specifics."

"But you think he's involved in the virus?"

"I couldn't say for sure. He absolutely has the know-how."

"So do you."

"Ray's had problems with the company. He was almost laid off last year. Harvey will tell you that if you ask him."

"And you have no problems with the company?"

"I love it here. I could never do anything else."

And now simultaneously a call came in from Harvey Monahan in Westville, and one of the white-shirted knowledge engineers from the group out at the big table entered without knocking, both with the same news, that together, linked up, always in communication via landlines and satellites and microwave and everything else, including the infrared connection to HRA, they'd found virtual proof that yes, the program had been residing in ADC computers since Sunday afternoon, that its clock delayed its performance till late Monday morning, spitting out the letters in FUCK YOU to every terminal in ADC's AI division. The virus now seemed to have taken its leave, but it had revealed enough of itself to have become much better known.

Doug Kiskel appeared pleased but not surprised. He handed the phone over to Dred.

"Harvey wants a word," said Kiskel.

"Harvey. Nice work." Kiskel was rising, leaving.

"Yeah, no thanks to me. Matter of time, that's all." The great bear voice sounding tired and indifferent. "You're with Kiskel now?"

"Just left." And, in case he was still within earshot: "He's been really helpful."

"Good. I'm calling because we gotta meet, four-thirty. Somerset Club. You know it?"

Three blocks from home, the Somerset Club was the standard against which all other stuffy men's clubs in Boston and hence North America were measured, and not the sort of place he imagined Harvey Monahan having much truck with.

"Yes, I've been there. Why the Somerset?"

"That's where Mr. Cooper wants to meet. It's his meeting, it's his club."

"Burt Cooper."

"Right, you, me, and the CEO, this is one for your scrapbook. See you at four-thirty, sharp."

Dred left the office and found Kiskel back at the big table with the guys in white shirts, and they were slumped over from exhaustion, very much relieved. Kiskel rose and came to him, could not let him depart without an attempt at conciliation, which took shape as an inept apology for not wanting to say too many negative things about Ray Niles. Kiskel said that now that the virus had expended itself he would go home and catch up on his sleep.

Reporters in the lobby were crowding with excitement around

Betty Ohlmeyer, getting the word that the bug had been squashed. Or so it appeared, she added.

Outside, Channel 5 had their van and what's-his-name, the short guy with the Grecian Formula sandy-colored hair, was doing a standup in front of the building, probably unaware that for now there was no longer a problem with the virus. Dred found himself walking in view of the camera and crossing only a few feet behind what's-his-name because that's the way the sidewalk was built and the grass was roped off. Sorry, fellas. They asked, "Another take?" and the short guy said, no, what the hell.

5

It was almost eleven-thirty when Dred stepped around the Channel 5 news crew to the side parking lot and found Kevin in his old Audi.

"First thing is the dumpster girl," he said, as Dred got in next to him and closed the door. "Eighteen stab wounds."

"No ID on her?"

Kevin shook his head. "Precinct captain says she was black. He thinks it's drug-related. Eighteen stab wounds, I don't know. Sounds like an old boyfriend to me. Now. I also got CNA and more on Carmody."

CNA is Customer's Name and Address. For Kevin Ryan or Frank Cirione, getting a CNA was one of the easier investigative tasks, presuming the source at the phone company was still doing his job. With CNA from the phone company source, you could then go to the Registry of Motor Vehicles and get Social Security numbers, which would lead you to credit information and nearly anything else you needed. Dred found Harvey Monahan's business card in his pocket, wrote "Carmody" on the back.

"Great."

"It's 26 MacElroy Street in Brighton, near Brookline, he's behind in his rent but he pays his phone bills, he's got no priors, no

MV violations, he's twenty-seven and, get this, he works for the Mass Pike as a toll collector. That's the day job."

Dred jotted the address, then, "toll collector."

"So I did a little more digging, I got his schedule, he should be on the four-to-eight shift, the Allston-Brighton tolls, today."

"Great. Thanks a lot." The four-thirty meeting at the Somerset Club would make it tough to see much of Carmody ahead of time. "Anything on Holland or Proctor?"

"Yeah, this narrows the field. Holland's in New York. Proctor's in California. They were roommates until January, the band croaked, they broke their lease and left town. Gone."

"Okay."

"You might want to know, when I did Carmody's CNA? Your pal Stevie shared the same phone number. Unpublished, but listed."

This was very big news indeed. "Shared?"

"As in they lived there together."

"When did the sharing stop?"

"Late January. She had her name dropped, with no forwarding number. So maybe Carmody knows."

"This is great, Kev. Thanks."

"Yeah, I guess. Well, I gotta have lunch in Charlestown, better move." This was said with some anxious chagrin. At last Kevin confirmed what Dred was about to guess. "Yeah, Sheila."

"Careful, old boy."

"Couldn't believe it, she loosened my sap last night."

"She doesn't work?"

"She's looking."

"I'll say she's looking."

"Well, we were pretty tight back then."

"I'll let you go." Dred started to open the door, got halfway out.

"Dred. Her husband, Billy Lagan, I've met the guy, I know who he *is*. He's not a good choice. Aw, hell, I'll tell you later."

" 'Bye. Take it easy."

"Yeah."

When the Audi disappeared from view, Dred stepped into a pay phone to call Carmody again, hung up when the message machine came on. Then he called his own office machine, punching double zero to get his messages.

Hearing again his long-winded, no longer amusing message about voltage surges and his TX-20, he decided it would soon have to be replaced. The only message was from Erica. "Dred, it's almost lunchtime, can we eat? Are you around? Kurt and Tony are leaving by themselves this afternoon, and I'd like to see you."

He picked her up on the street in front of Harbor Towers. She had on her old Nike hooded sweatshirt and navy sweatpants and running shoes, with her long, wheat-colored hair tied back. Except that her eyes were red and her throat a little blotchy she looked fine, had a big smile for him. She had wanted, after this latest fight with Kurt, to go running and take her anger out on her legs. But at the last minute she'd changed her mind, preferring instead to get drunk with her brother-in-law. Who she thought looked very tired and underfed and maybe not in the mood to drink in the middle of the day.

"Let's not worry about me, but let's get *you* drunk," he suggested, as he took the Subaru down the ramp onto the Expressway and then onto the Mass Pike headed west. Erica agreed, and she said going west is fine, she had a friend out there with a house on the Concord River and they could just go for a walk.

He noticed that it was becoming in fact a very beautiful day, with the sky softening into a warm milky blue, that warm wind from yesterday freshening again. T-shirt weather.

Tony, she said, was ripshit, storming at them: how could you guys have a fight just before the plane leaves? This is not a one-hour fight, this is a ten-day fight because I'm going to be stuck with just one of you, that's how you'll do it. One of you will stay home. The kid sure knew his parents. Privately, Erica told Kurt, as he was turning his back for the last time, see ya, buddy, this is it.

"What did you fight about?"

"Nothing. We just fought."

"I'd like to see my nephew. When he gets back, I guess. I miss him."

She had her hand on his forearm, squeezed it. "Dred. Kurt almost hit me."

"Not Kurt."

"Almost. We've come that far."

Far enough, Dred thought, stunned by the image. True, Kurt had been merciless with him as a kid, but Dred couldn't remember when he'd ever raised either his voice or his hand in real anger against him. Whatever the anger that was in him now, Kurt was a master of self-control. If he could be abusive, it was in quieter ways that you hardly noticed.

The vision of his brother striking Erica sickened him. She was too smart for that, too fine a person to be hurt.

For just a second he thought of Stevie and saw the attack again. It flashed in his mind, he quickly blotted it out.

"That's what I've decided," she said. "Tony knows it. Before the plane, I told him, you have to get ready for a change. Secretly you've been preparing yourself, which is good, because soon it's going to happen."

Outbound on the Pike they reached the Allston-Brighton tolls. There were at least twelve booths here, maybe the broadest expanse of toll-collecting on the Pike, from Boston to the New York State border. If he was ever going to get to Tom Carmody, it would have to be right here, today between four and eight.

"Kurt and I, we joke about abuse," Erica said. "I burn dinner it's food abuse. I shift the gears wrong in the car, it's car abuse. Then Kurt makes a fist in front of my face. The word *abuse* didn't come to mind. Just divorce."

"Let's get you a drink. In Concord."

At about the time that Kurt and Tony were probably in Fort Lauderdale changing planes to fly to Marsh Harbour in the Abacos, Dred and Erica moseyed into the lounge of the North Bridge Inn for a late lunch and drink. Most people had finished and were leaving.

Erica wanted a Lillet, very cold. He had a dark beer, which wasn't cold enough. Second time around, he had a very cold Lillet with her, enjoyed its sweetness. And some cheese and crackers and clam chowder and rolls and a salad on the side. He was starving and ate hungrily and quickly ordered another bowl of chowder. Just what he'd tried to eat last Thursday with Stevie when everything had gotten in the way of his appetite.

Erica felt fine, her skin deblotched, just a healthy pink flush of spring air and Lillet. He talked to her about Florida and the Bahamas, his old stomping grounds, how much he liked the Abacos. She talked to him about him, that he was just a real pal who was important to her. Finishing her Lillet, in a moment of silence she leaned forward and touched his hair, tweaked it where it grew long behind the ears. Getting just a little gray, she said. There was more Dutch in Kurt perhaps, with his brown hair starting to recede; more Spanish in Dred, out of the one one-hundred-twenty-eighth available to him, with his thick, very dark hair.

These things, she teased him, mean women problems.

"I've fantasized about you," she said. "But I know it could never be more than that."

"I think that's right."

"It's a nice fantasy," she said.

He smiled.

"Kurt and I. It's been months. He has such awful hours anyway. Not since my birthday. I'm thirty-nine, and not once has it happened to me as a thirty-nine-year-old."

"Erica, I'm sorry about all this." He would love to change that for her, and knew he couldn't.

"Dred, someone must have told you about your eyes. I haven't but someone else must have."

"I'm not sure," he said, lying. Someone else had, several others had, that he had nice eyes.

Erica snickered disbelief. "You'd remember. You have the nicest, gentlest eyes, even now when you look all beat to hell."

"Thanks, I think."

"Do you want to go somewhere and make love?"

"Yes, but no."

"You sure? I do."

"I'm sure. If you'd never met Kurt it would be different."

"Of course. Boy, your eyes are so nice."

"You're feeling good, aren't you," he said. "That's why we came."

"We could go to the Old North Bridge and get lost in the woods. Belated Happy Birthday from Dred."

"Erica. I've thought, wouldn't it be great, with you. And I've thought that frequently. And I know we couldn't ever do that."

"We could if you'd let it. If we could induce amnesia for you. Have you ever thought, okay, I'll forget who I am, I'll be someone else today?"

"I'm sorry, pal," he said.

"Okay," she said. "We'll just have a little walk or something." She ordered another Lillet, her third, and her eyes started to well up. She left the table and came back a few minutes later with her eyes red from crying and wondered if they could leave.

Now driving toward the Old North Bridge, along the Concord River, they found her friend's house, someone named Monica who'd just gotten divorced and who owned this huge place with acres of meadows rolling down to the river. Monica was somewhere in the tropics, the place was deserted. The ground was spongy underfoot, it was almost mudtime out here, almost too wet to walk in her running shoes, his sneakers, but they tried it anyway and got down to the river. Monica, she said, was ready for a roommate if it came to that, the house was huge and Erica could have her own wing with a kitchenette. You'd get off on Monica, she's wildly beautiful. Lovely old colonial farmhouse, added on to, with barn and studio. The Harbor Towers condo, she and Kurt had agreed, would be sold. Kurt would love to move back to Beacon Hill. Tony would go back to prep school in California and everything would be divvied up very nicely, there was plenty of money to go around, plenty of love for Tony, it wouldn't be so bad, really, to end the marriage and start over again. Enormous fat willow tree up ahead with a rough circular bench built around the trunk. Dred and Erica sat facing the sun, their legs touching. Erica rolled back her shirtsleeves, dangled her hands between her legs, talked about life alone and how good it could be. Closed her eyes, lifted her chin to the sun, became silent as Dred's thoughts turned to Stevie and Tom Carmody and the band

and Doug Kiskel with his blue parka, and Ray Niles and now the meeting coming up with Cooper. The river was shimmering with feathers of this southerly wind skittering across its surface. Erica leaned against him. She was big-boned, wide-shouldered. Skin on her forearm smooth, lightly freckled, hairless, and he'd noticed before this thick vein that wrapped from the smooth creamy underside of her arm around the top and down to her wrist, funny how some people, both men and women, were veiny and some weren't, perhaps it had to do with thickness of the skin. This full vein invited his forefinger to touch it at the wrist and trace it curling up her arm and around underneath to the crook of her elbow, and like a curious child he did. Erica's hand was between her legs.

"Hug me?"

He wrapped his left arm around her wide strong shoulders, under her arms and his hand on her breast as her body started to move in easy rhythms against the force of her right hand between her legs. His face close to her ear, he kissed her ear gently, then her jawbone with her head thrown back. She moved slowly, all these muscles tightening in exertion against the temptation to burst into higher gear, he could feel her body fighting that urge. He retreated from his own urge to continue kissing her, simply held her, his hand immobile on her full breast. This was, he imagined, a slow dance of very carefully perceived pleasures into which he had few insights. Perhaps she had thoughts of him, or perhaps just of warm sunlight and soft spring air and the river shining, and her own strong body. He felt fine being only this close. It fascinated and pleased him that she was so unembarrassed with this most private of indulgences, that to do this she had to keep him in a fine balance of intimacy and distance. Now she moved her other hand inside and uttered a moan of deep pleasure, her right arm swinging around him, pulling his face back into hers. No kiss, just cheeks pressing. This was all hers, she said, nobody else's, and it felt just wonderful. But no more talk now. Long seconds of pure silence with the warm breeze in their hair and her labored breathing, with her body beginning, he thought, to jerk toward orgasm. Her hand digging into his ribs.

"Oh, I wish you could do this. We."

This great spreading willow budding lime green overhead, so beautiful, and lowering his gaze to her upturned face and long white throat, her face flushing with blood, and she said it was happening now, in long waves, her fingers clawing his skin at the ribs and his face pressing her cheek, this orgasm was long and convulsive with her legs jerking out but her voice never rising above a constricted cry. When it ended she was limp against the tree, her face pale and skin translucent, a ghost, as she might appear in death, an empty vessel. Head falling gently on his shoulder and nestling there.

"Thank you."

"I love you, Erica."

"I love you, Dred. If only I weren't married to your fucking brother."

On the way back into town on Route 2 she slept. Traffic was building from the east; he was driving against it, the sun behind him, now planning to arrive at the Allston-Brighton tolls on the Mass Pike just at four o'clock. There he'd try to make introductions with Tom Carmody before the meeting at the Somerset Club on Beacon Street thirty minutes later with Burt Cooper and Harvey Monahan. Timing would be tight.

Now, going south on Route 128, there was trouble ahead. Brake lights lit up everywhere. An accident, a mile ahead, just before the exit onto the Pike.

It was serious: an overturned car in the median strip with ambulances just leaving, State Police cruisers all over the place. It was about five minutes past four with traffic still bunched up at the Pike exit, and another ten-minute ride from there to the toll plaza.

Maybe he should just pass on Carmody for today and meet with Harvey and Burt Cooper. Carmody would still be taking tolls after the meeting, and tomorrow, and the next day. Fine. Except that Carmody seemed infinitely more important right now than Burt Cooper.

Erica was curled onto her side with her knees pulled up to her chest, dead to the world. She had cried some more, and kissed him, and wished for another drink and then just fallen asleep.

His hand was on her leg. "Erica, gotta wake up." He had to jostle her, which he didn't like to do. "Erica."

"Dreddy."

"Gotta wake up. Time to rally."

"Uh uh."

The breakdown lane was filling with cheaters, zipping by his right side. In a minute it would be clogged, no better than the other four lanes. His hand on her very fine firm ass, he gave her a solid squeeze.

"I need you. Your pretty blue eyes."

"Why?"

" 'Cause we're going to do some creative driving."

Erica jerked her body bolt upright, swept the hair from her eyes. "What? Oh, please."

"Check the right, okay? We gotta move."

She seemed alert enough to help, found a gap for him, and he swerved sharply into the breakdown lane in front of an enormous semi that leaned on its huge instant-headache horn.

"Jesus, Erica. You didn't see him?"

"I thought he'd slow down. I'm still asleep. Why are we doing this?"

"Gotta see this guy who knows Stevie. He works at a booth." Ahead it was another two hundred yards to the ramp onto the Mass Pike, with the breakdown lane flooding solid red ahead with a swarm of brake lights. Under the circumstances pavement was a mere nicety, not essential to forward movement. The apron of grass on the side was just wide enough, but unsettlingly steep.

"I take it time is a factor here," she said.

"Can you get in the back seat right behind me?"

Without asking why, she lowered her seat and scrambled into the back and to the left, the uphill side. "You think it really makes a difference?"

"Less chance of you getting hurt. If it gets too steep and we roll."

"Thanks a lot."

Now at a dead stop behind another tractor trailer rig. "Here goes, hang on."

Off onto the grass beside the truck, just inches from his huge tires and leaning hard to the right, having their combined weight on the left side felt better as he pushed the Subaru up to thirty miles an hour heading for the ramp.

"They're looking at us like we're crazy," she said.

Ahead he would have to go around to the right of a speed limit sign and an exit sign and then some kind of a drop from the apron over a curb onto the ramp itself, where traffic was normal.

"Shit," he said, crabbing around both signs. Front-wheel drive helped.

"What, shit."

"Might lose my oil pan on this one. Damn. Will they let me back in?"

"They look angry. I don't think so."

"We're going to bump, hang on." An eight-, maybe ten-inch drop from the grass over the granite curb onto the ramp—Dred gunned it, and the Subaru leaped across the curb, a loud crunch from somewhere underneath.

"Any loose metal on the road behind us?"

Erica was looking back. "You're okay."

At the first toll there was a long line at the one manned booth. The Exact Change lanes were open and the wooden gates, as was often the case, were missing. He found what loose change he had in his breast pocket and tossed the coins in a blur toward the bin without losing speed, not caring that he missed, the alarm signaling that he was once again in some small debt to the Commonwealth of Massachusetts and its limitless array of fee-collection agencies. Erica was pulling herself back into the front seat as the Subaru was shuddering up to eighty miles an hour in the far left lane, engine whining its little lungs out at the top end of fourth gear. An extra gear right now would have been appreciated.

Over the noise he told her about Carmody and his four-thirty Somerset meeting with ADC's Burt Cooper—which right now was in some jeopardy.

"It's like an audience with the Pope," she suggested. "It's not nice to be late."

"I guess I'm crazy," he said. "I gotta get to Carmody first."

Traffic thickened ahead and he started to slalom through it, cutting sharply from lane to lane. It was an axiom of driving in Massachusetts that anarchy was the only productive strategy. Here on the Pike the high-speed left lane was jammed up behind someone doing forty-five. As often as not, cars moved faster in the middle lane, fastest in the far right.

The toll plaza loomed ahead, one half mile.

"Which one is he in?"

"Beats me. Look for a guy in his twenties, fair-haired, preppy, wire-rimmed glasses. Very unlikely type for a toll collector."

"Inbound or outbound?"

"No idea. We'll find him."

"Dred, you could pull over and just walk up to him, don't they have a place for you to park there, on the side?"

Over a rise and down in front of them the plaza spread out.

"Apparently not." The only option was simply to go through the tolls. Three manned booths on the right side, three Exact Change booths in the middle, two more manned booths on the left and these orange cones set up to give outbound traffic more booths. He chose the right side, the middle booth, a black woman. Guy on the right was old. Guy on the left was Oriental. Gave the woman a dollar.

Asked her: "Tom Carmody working this shift somewhere?"

"Yeah, just saw him," she said. "Over there somewhere, outbound side." Big smile, she waved generally toward the other booths on the far side. Gave him his change.

"Now what?" Erica asked.

"U-turn."

She shielded her face as he turned on his flashers and leaned on his horn, then cut hard left across the full gaping maws of the other toll booths as cars started to spring out of them, like racehorses from their gates, only to find this battered old yellow Subaru wagon, a venerable Boston *death-car*, the kind you *don't challenge* because one more collision won't hurt it, *broadside* to them creeping toward the far outbound lanes. This, the busiest toll plaza in the state with the most traffic at the peak of rush hour, with hundreds of commuters in their usual ugly combative moods. And, boy, did they show it.

Erica hiding behind her hand. "I don't know you."

"You just said you loved me."

"I do but I don't know you."

Ahead was the lineup of orange cones and beyond, many hundreds of cars spreading from three lanes into twelve or more at the outbound toll booths, stacked ten deep at each booth. Finally the Subaru was there, straddling the line defined by the orange cones, maneuvering to head west again, the opposite direction. The first two westbound booths were manned, but neither one was Tom. Then another four lanes of Exact Change. Tom had to be on the extreme far side.

"Erica, this is the worst possible news. Tom is way the fuck over there. Has to be."

"Please, God, no."

"I've come this far." Again there was no place just to dump the car for a minute or two to walk across all these spaces. Right in this lane a limousine was jockeying, the driver ignoring him but perfectly aware that this rusty little yellow tin box from Japan posed an immediate and dire threat. Dred darted ahead in a space in front of the limo, the limo surged forward, hit its brakes, the driver went nuts, a uniformed chauffeur, rolled down the dark-tinted window. Erica ducked down to hide or protect herself. The cars hadn't hit but it could not have been much closer. An inch or two.

"I can explain, pal," he was saying to himself. "There's this girl, see."

Safely ensconced in front of the limo he waited his turn to pay the toll collector, a very Irish-looking guy in his fifties with a collar that was too tight.

"How ya doin'?" Dred greeted him, handing him his last dollar.

"Pal, you're a real creative driver, I saw the whole thing. Be careful, I can call the cops from here. Lucky I'm in a good mood."

"Yeah, I'm lost. Keep the change."

"You may need that," Erica said. "I'm broke. No pockets."

"Relax, I've still got twenty cents, we're rich."

Through the booth, and then another, "Hang on, Erica, here we

go," and slashing hard right with horn blaring right across traffic
again, broadside toward the far end of the tolls on the wrong side,
the outbound side and somewhere over here was Carmody, he had
to be, these other cars couldn't *believe* what was happening in front
of them, even in Boston, and now on the far side Erica was alert and
looking.

"Preppy guy, wire-rimmed glasses," she said.

"Which one?"

"Last booth, just leaned out."

"Okay. You're gonna have to get to a phone." So many cars
honking at him he could hardly hear himself speak.

"Where?"

"Pay phone, right over there." Screaming at her over the honking. Phone booth right at the curb just past Carmody's booth. "Call
the Somerset Club and tell them I'm running late."

Erica was hiding behind her hands. "I'm going to have a nervous
breakdown *right here*."

"No, not now. Here we go." At the last booth a BMW leaped
out and just missed him as he started to *back in*, which was the only
possible way to get face to face with this guy. Boy, this was history,
backing into a toll booth clogged with traffic, and with no money
left! The guy behind in his Audi was incredulous, but conceded to
the crazy man and backed up, forcing others to retreat behind him.
All these people were letting him back into the booth figuring he
must be morally obsessed with paying his toll, wherever he'd come
from.

He dug into his pocket to retrieve two nickels. "For the phone,"
he said, sticking them in her hand.

"Somerset Club," she repeated.

"Right. And remember all this so you can tell your grandchildren."

"I have too much to tell them already."

Now she was out of the car, pulled her Nike sweatshirt hood up
over her face and went for the phone booth. She looked back at him
as if to ask: Do I really know you?

Here was Tom in his official Mass Pike starchy green uniform.

Peering down through his granny glasses at a Boston driver crazed by disorientation.

"You backed in. That's amazing."

"You're Tom Carmody."

Squinting at him. "Right."

"I need to talk about Stevie Bear."

If the request unsettled him he would not show it. "Mister, all I can give you are directions, the time, and the weather."

"What if I don't move till you give me something else."

Tom didn't like hearing this. He leaned out the booth and gestured ahead as if giving directions, never looking at him. "So you're the guy who called my machine, right? Same voice."

"Right. I'm a private investigator."

"I see. Okay."

During this the guy in the Audi had had enough, leaned hard on his horn, and was yelling out his window. Tom yelled back, get lost, try another lane. The Audi and the cars behind him gave up on this booth, canting left to sluice into the next lane.

"Tom. I think this young woman may be in some danger. I want to help her."

"I could just shut down the lane," Tom said. "Then my supervisor inside sees the red light on the board, he comes out and all hell breaks loose. I tell him I'm being hassled."

"Please don't do that, Tom. I damn near killed myself getting here, okay? This is important. I've got to find Stevie."

"Why?"

"I want to help her. She's mixed up in something."

"You're telling me," he said. "I don't know where she is. She moved out a couple months ago."

"Where's she live?"

Tom rolled his eyes. "Look. Pull the car over there, to that space."

Dred lurched forward and pulled the Subaru out of the traffic to a parking area right next to the phone booth. Erica had just finished her call and came over to him.

"I told them your car died, right at the tolls. A Mr. Monahan is sending a cab right over. He says Cooper is anxious to see you."

"Terrific. Stick around, I'm almost finished."

"Okay."

He followed Tom back to his booth.

"Can't come in here," Tom said.

Dred was talking through a crack in the door. "Where is she, you know where she lives, tell me."

"I wish I did but I don't." Tom simply wouldn't turn to look at him. Making change again, here you go, thank you, have a nice day.

"You're not helping, Tom."

"You haven't talked to Jerry, have you?"

He didn't know the name. "Maybe, maybe not."

"Aw, fuck it all anyway. Yes, sorry, thank you, have a nice day."

"Tom, I want to sit down and talk to you, okay? We can have a beer."

"I've stopped drinking. Yes, ma'am, I'm talking to someone else, here you go, have a nice day."

"Stevie Bear. What's her real name, I'll find her."

"Man, that *is* her real name, from the time she was six."

"There's a lot you're not telling me, Tom."

"You got *that* right. I'm busy now."

"Okay, okay, me too. You're off at eight, let's meet at eight-thirty."

"Shit," said Tom.

"Eight-thirty, your place. Be there."

Back to the Subaru, Erica was waiting, she'd been dealing with some asshole Pike civil servant who wondered what they were *doing* here bothering a toll collector, she was trying to be charming but he was having none of it. She abandoned him, hopped into the car, and Dred was ready to hit the road again, pull another seriously traffic-obstructing U-turn. Let's get out of here, she thought, this place is *very strange*, awful people, congenitally unhappy and disapproving, so what if it's March in Boston, it's bizarre that these people are so deeply unfriendly. And it was now twenty minutes of five, she said. In her jogging clothes she had no money, he had no money, he pulled back out into traffic and wormed far across to the first eastbound booth on the other side of the orange cones, rolled down the window to speak to this large, strongly built, registered-nurse-type woman, taking off his sunglasses so she could see that his eyes were kind and he was not a bad person. "I've done this a lot today," he said, "and I'm all out of money so I'll just have to keep going if you don't mind."

She didn't understand any of it but it didn't matter because he was rapidly accelerating through the booth away from the toll plaza, the last such checkpoint on the Pike, it was free from here on to the east, into downtown Boston, the highway wide and white and largely free of traffic right now, inbound.

Erica said the cab Harvey was going to send here probably wouldn't come. He had to agree: cabs in Boston typically don't show up when they're supposed to.

He squeezed her leg, cheer up, no more toll booths. She wanted to know more about Stevie, this girl, what it was that this was now becoming, what Tom had said. He could respond truthfully with a variation on an old theme, something his father was fond of saying later in life.

"I'm learning more and knowing less."

On Beacon Street across from the Somerset Club they stopped and switched places. She would take the car to its Willow Street parking space, leave the keys under the seat, and then take a cab back home and pay at the other end. They would talk tonight by phone. Before eight or after eleven, he said. She took him by the shoulders and he pulled her close and kissed her softly on her mouth, on her closed eyes. And thanks, he said, for being my partner and saving my ass.

Thanks for today, she said. The river. The sunshine.

It was almost five when he stepped inside the long front hallway of the club. The coat check man, brittle-boned and slow-witted and foul-tempered as Dred prayed he wouldn't become in old age and assumed he would, took forever to find the drawer that held the emergency Somerset Club clip-on necktie, didn't bother to ask if he was a member or even a guest. Suddenly around the corner here was Harvey Monahan, in a suit, taking him by the elbow.

"Jesus Christ, you know the last time anyone kept Burt Cooper waiting? What's the story?"

"Cab didn't come. I fixed the car."

"Let's get going, Burt's getting very impatient. He's got a meeting at six with the Governor. Which he shouldn't miss."

Dred was unimpressed. More precisely, he was unimpressed with the special needs and obligations of celebrity status. There was room, and reason, for admiration of those who had become Big Names through their own brains and hard work, but the heart didn't flutter and the knees didn't knock.

"I'll be wanting a drink, Harvey."

"You look like hell. Where have you been? Just be aware, ADC stock lost three and a half points today."

"C'mon. Not really."

"Really. Christ, I hope I don't have to fire you."

They stopped in the bar and Dred ordered a dry martini with a black olive as Harvey moved off into the next room, the dining room, to let Cooper know their wayward operative had arrived. The Somerset Club was everything he remembered from his last visit with one of Elaine's pals, everything anyone would expect of such a place. So very fine and very old, with enormous chandeliers dangling from twenty-foot ceilings and monstrous blackening portraits of famous dead Brahmins here in the land of the bean and the cod where the Cabots talk only to God, and the place smells of last night's cigars and today's Welsh rarebit, soft food for the tired gums and irritated bowels of Boston's best and brightest.

Dred recognized Cooper instantly—the man had become a familiar face around Boston, a recognizable rich and famous person. He was an unlikely Somersettian, a new arrival far outside the tight inner circle of *Mayflower* descendants. Fifty years old, but built like an ex–Olympian wrestler, cinder-block body, square-jawed with closely cropped iron-gray hair. A quick, very strong handshake and cursory commiseration about his broken car and not a hint of a smile or the least bit of visible pleasure in meeting him. But Cooper was placated by a distant bond of blood, or so he thought:

"My mother's great-grandfather was named Salazar. His family was from San Sebastián. And there were cousins named Balcazar."

"Yes, sir. Quite possible. Just might be."

They'd been drinking coffee. The martini was woefully incorrect right now.

"As long as you're having, I'll have," said Cooper. "Harvey?"

"No, thank you, sir."

The waiter seemed to know that Cooper was Cooper and never took his eyes off the three of them. Cooper's rum and water, a double, arrived with laudable alacrity.

"In your absence Harvey and I have had a chance to catch up. I was out of town when all this started to happen. And unfortunately I'll be leaving almost immediately for a meeting with the Governor."

"Yes, sir."

"This is fundamentally not a technology problem. It's a business problem. ADC is many millions of dollars less valuable today than it was yesterday."

"So Harvey just informed me."

"I understand you just got on the case. How long before you think you can catch this person? If that's in fact what you do?"

"No, sir, I simply try to gather evidence. I'm a private investigator. I can't catch him, as such."

Of all the luminaries in high tech, Cooper had given the impression of being one of the most gregarious, rarely missing an opportunity to be photographed or interviewed and forever evangelizing the ADC gospel of hanging out on the ragged edge of futuristic research and development in computers, making them do things they could never do before. In this milieu he consistently wore the wide smile of success. But not here at this table, not tonight. He seemed very sad.

"Too bad. No doubt you've learned a few things," Cooper said, polishing off his drink and rattling his ice.

"Yes, sir, a few things."

"You and I can talk about that," said Harvey. Cooper glanced at his watch, grimaced, rose from the table and laid his hand on Dred's shoulder to keep him seated.

"Don't get up. If the Governor could wait, I'd make him."

"I'm sorry about my car trouble."

"So am I. Let me just say a couple of things that need to be said."

It was a physically uncomfortable situation. Cooper was right behind him, standing. Dred had to crane his neck to get even a peripheral glimpse of the man's bulk.

"Harvey and I have spent quite a bit of time reviewing what he knows and what he thinks we might do. I will tell you, Mr. Balcazar, that one of those options, seriously discussed, was the notion of identifying this sick man and having him utterly disabled as a threat to my company. Had you been here on time you would have been a party to that conversation. For some reason I now feel a little less desperate. But I have something to tell you. If you're successful in securing sufficient evidence against this unhappy soul, I will guarantee you a position at ADC, on your own terms, as a security consultant, with the kind of salary that will make your life very comfortable indeed."

So it was just a pep talk. A waste of time. "Yes, sir."

His hand on his shoulder again, the avuncular touch of a man who had just hinted at contemplating murder. Under no circumstances would he ever work for this man, or his company, full-time. Or for any other computer company. Or for any company at all.

"It has become manifest in this industry that surefire technological security is fundamentally impossible. Security has to be in our hearts and minds."

"I understand. There's no mechanical way to protect a machine."

"Humans will always be smarter. When we know how to protect humans from other humans, only then will we know how to protect machines from humans. So long. I hope we'll meet again."

Even with his increasing exhaustion, Dred could not help hearing the alarm bells going off in Cooper's final sentiments.

Harvey had risen for Cooper's departure and was now reseating himself. "He seems to like you, which is a good thing under the circumstances. And which is remarkable, considering your five o'clock shadow *and* arrival."

"Extenuating circumstances." Dubious flattery, to be liked by a man so anxious to protect machines from humans.

"Obviously he wants a speedy resolution to this problem."

"Can't blame him."

"Okay, good. Based on my own research, I've got pretty strong suspicions already."

"So do I." Polishing off his martini. "You first."

Harvey drew a deep breath. "Incredibly enough, Doug Kiskel."

Yes, very possible. "Tell me why."

"You look at the guy's credentials, he's one of the few people smart enough to pull this off. He came out of Cal Tech and then the AI group at Stanford, SRI, and arrived at ADC at the age of twenty-five and now ten years later he's the guru of the whole AI research effort. This bug has acted very differently from your typical hacker-style virus. Only a very smart person could've created it."

"So what's his motive?"

"I don't know. No idea. Isn't it possible there isn't one?"

"No, not really."

"Dred, I see this as the era of the senseless crime. Serial killers. People who act out of blind rage."

"Kiskel doesn't strike me as one given to rages, blind or other-wise."

"So he hits us quietly, noiselessly, with a virus."

"What about politics?" Dred asked. "A lot of this AI stuff is related to defense, right? Star Wars?"

"From our end, only very generally. We're not making software that's directly commissioned by the DoD. Our technology, yes, but not our programming. Anyway, I've known Doug Kiskel ever since I came over to AI three years ago, and I don't have a sense that he's a political animal. He doesn't give a shit about that stuff."

"So what does he give a shit about? He's single, right?"

"Yes."

"Girlfriends? Social life?"

"Not much that I'm aware of. I don't see how that—"

"Does he hate the company? Is this possibly some sort of ven-detta against ADC or one of the higher-ups?"

Harvey didn't think so. "The man gets paid a lot of money to do almost anything he wants. He said, I want to work on a higher-level language, we said sure, no problem, so he spends most of his time on Miriam and its extensions. If he said, hey, I want to sit here all day and jack off, we'd say, fine, Doug, whatever makes you happy. Once you're hired as an individual contributor, what we call an 'IC,' you're your own boss." Harvey paused for a second. "You really think the man needs a motive?"

"Yes. Even if it's just to prove a point. Or to make jacking off more fun."

"Doug has proven himself time and time again. He doesn't need to show us anything."

"What about grabbing some headlines? Not his name, just his artwork? Some people will do that."

"I keep thinking, Dred, this guy's too smart for that. He's too grown up, he doesn't have those kinds of hangups. I don't know what his motive is. All I know is I can't think of anyone else who's got the brains to pull it off."

"Okay. That's worth hearing."

"And right now the virus is dormant. But I bet it's coming back, it has that look of coitus interruptus. Just one thing, though, about Kiskel. Work is everything to him. And there's some question that he's really under pressure to get ready for the AI conference in Washington. It's incredible, with this virus slowing everything down, that he's so calm."

Harvey was getting itchy to leave. He lived in Westville, not far from AI-3 and his teenaged son was in a basketball tournament that he absolutely was not allowed to miss, they'd been having a rough time of it lately, father and son. Tomorrow he wanted to meet with Dred again. They left the Somerset Club together, neither one a member, neither knowing how to pay for or sign for the drinks, hoping the club maître d' would figure it out, assuming somehow he would.

Back home he resisted the urge to have another martini, put on the Doctor Glassheart demo cassette again, very low, and went to his desk, fishing out the yellow legal pad sandwiched in the pile of

AI reprints and magazines that Elaine had given him. He wrote the name Ray Niles had given him: Sandy Murchison, Arlington. The suburban phone directory gave him the only Murchison in the town, Viola. Sandy's mother. He dialed.

On their tape there was Mozart in the background, clashing with Glassheart, and then a gravelly voice heavy with boredom: "You've reached the Murchisons. Neither of us is available now, so leave a message either for Viola or for Sandra."

He told this dark and gloomy voice that a friend had mentioned Sandy Murchison as someone who might help him with some research, that he'd be willing to pay. He left his name and office number.

Staring at the pad, he wrote "Jerry?," the name Tom had blurted out from his toll booth. Then the phrase "SB left in Jan." He wrote "26 MacElroy—Carmody," found the street on his city map and circled it with his pen. He wrote on the pad, "Thank Erica." Then a stream of things that needed bringing together: ID audio cable? Bears in Ohio. Man 5'10" to 6'2"? Strong. SB comes home Wed. Lab analysis of green thread. *Backoff* text file vanishes from comp.

From his top drawer he removed the tiny poly Ziploc bag with the springy coil of plastic green thread inside, took it out, and once again eyed it closely under his loupe. Very bright Kelly green—this had to be from the guy's jacket.

He wrote: green poly, Thurs. Heavy black leather, Sat. Same gloves both nights?

The phone interrupted his effort to stitch any of these together. It was a distantly familiar voice that lacked a name, the kind of guy who assumes you know who he is. "Yeah, Dred, you shoulda seen yourself on the tube. That was so fucking dumb, walking right by the camera, if you're trying to do this undercover."

Chummy abrasive familiarity insulting.

"Todd? That you?"

"Yeah, for Christ's sake, get with it, it's only been since Friday. Boy, if you're trying to keep a low profile you're blowing it. Stayed late at work tonight, we were in the lounge for the news, myself and a bunch of the other guys, and here on Channel 5 is the virus story, and Dred Balcazar coming out of ADC."

"It's not undercover. It's straight stuff, no secrets."

"You probably didn't know we got messed up by the same thing."

This was strange news. "How?"

"Well, we're on the Internet with ADC and a lot of other people, too, we're always using their stuff, and—" A disturbance in his house, he was muffling the mouthpiece but the anger and profanity came through anyway. Yelling at either his kid or his wife, Alexis, dinner can wait. He was back. "Yeah, anyway, the guy, whoever he is, stuck this bug into the network, it came right into my office today. Didn't wreck anything, it just slowed us down."

From Cambridge to Westville and to the world, including Bedford and Todd Shaler's office and his work in space research, whatever it was.

"Todd. The Internet. That's military?"

"Some of it. It's either military, commercial, educational, or government, depending on where you want to go. I do a lot of military stuff, but it's not as sexy as it sounds, don't get carried away. But this virus definitely got onto the Net and it makes everyone nervous. Didn't get into the Milnet, but shit, some of the stuff we're doing is pretty high level."

"Yeah." As long as he was here, he might be helpful. "Todd, real quick, I just heard the term 'downloading' today. In conjunction with the word 'immortality.' Any thoughts on that?"

A little whistle through his teeth. "Downloading as such isn't any big deal, it's just a term, but downloading like with a capital D, that's what you're talking about, when they mention immortality. That's all fantasyland stuff. That's sort of the final step in AI, it's electrodes on the brain and the whole nine yards."

"What do you mean, electrodes?"

"Meaning, Downloading with a capital D is converting the brain into software, that's it in a nutshell. The Downloaders think that might happen in the next fifty years or so. Not my lifetime or yours, probably, but maybe our kids'. The supernerds get together and talk Downloading, and who knows, maybe it can happen. I don't want to be around for it."

"It's a real issue then."

"Yeah, it's an issue, but it's only theory. Don't sweat it, it's science fiction, it's stuff to dream about. Nightmares, more like it."

"Thanks. That helps."

"Okay. Hey look, Balcazar, if you ever try to call me, do it at work, okay?"

It was hard to imagine calling Shaler for any reason at all.

"Why's that?"

"I'm moving out, I don't know where. Alexis and I have talked, everyone's in agreement." Now a shift in tone. "Danny, you go in with Mom in the kitchen while I talk, all right? Attaboy. So Balcazar, that's the story. I'm looking for a place."

"Sorry to hear it," he said absently.

"Alexis, she's got this new group of women, flapping their gums, they meet twice a week and it's all about our bodies our minds and how to talk to men and all that bullshit. Gimme a break."

Dred grunted. It was hard to imagine how Alexis could be any worse off.

"So I'm going to try to make a go of it with Honey."

"Honey?"

"Yeah, my friend I was telling you about. Seeing her tonight. She says she could see it, going straight, being with me."

"That's nice."

"Yeah, well, it's not ideal, believe me. She kids herself, she says she has the cunt that's lunched on a thousand pricks and she's right, I wonder who's been in her and who's done what to her, but what the hell I really do like her, and she says she really likes me, she treats me well and she's pretty damned smart and for Christ's sake she's *sane*, unlike my ridiculous wife who is so crazy now she's scaring the children."

"Todd, maybe Alexis should get some help." And then you.

"No, I don't mean crazy that way. Just weird. But what the fuck, you don't know women, why'm I wasting my time?"

"Yeah."

"Gotta go. Good to see you on the tube. I said, hey, *I* know that guy, that's Dred Balcazar, he's a detective! Even with the sunglasses I could see it was you."

"Yeah, well, good luck with Honey."

"It's not luck, it's love. She loves me, I can tell. But I'd never move in with her, not where she lives. I have to get reestablished first, then invite her to move in." Yelling again, okay I'm coming, hold your water. What a sweet man. "Okay, gotta go. 'Bye."

" 'Bye."

He hung up, went to the kitchen to fire up the coffee maker, and trotted downstairs to the bathroom to have his second shower of the day—to get rid of the city dirt and confusion, and to shave for the first time since Monday morning. There had been some notion after his first shower that skipping his usual shave would be in some indefinable way to his benefit. Metabolically, perhaps. Slow down the clock, like a long relaxing Sunday without shaving, mildly hung over, staying mellow. It hadn't worked that way today, he'd been jumpy right from the start, from Elaine's blitzkrieg right through all the craziness on the Mass Pike to Burt Cooper's stentorian plea that we protect machines from people.

They were right, all of them, he did look like hell. Tuckered out. Crow's-feet and the beginnings of lines under the eyes, his stubbly beard flecked with white. His father at fifty had developed great bassett hound bags that made him look *so tired*, even if the ladies loved him for his wise sadness and weariness looking like that, it was the sort of hereditary collapsing of flesh Dred could easily do without.

Ray Niles has no ethical center. Uttered to him as he stood next to that book about Downloading: Centering the Ethics of Immortality. If Kiskel had been ad-libbing, toying with him, why?

He heard on the stereo upstairs the wash of noise from "The Love I Dread." The lyrics were incoherent, so much blathering.

Shaving with those twin blades that are twice as likely to draw blood, he nicked off another two or three millimeters of his sideburns, which normally, mostly out of general neglect, still retained much of their mid-seventies length, almost down to the earlobe where the hair became bristly and more speckled with white. A minimal effort at water conservation was to shave with the sink full and the taps off, and only because the water was off could he hear the phone upstairs. A quick wipe of his face, towel around his neck, two stairs at a time and he was at his desk just as the tape kicked in on the fourth ring.

"T. D. Balcazar?"

A heartbeat of recognition. "Frankie! Shit, man." Frank Cirione, live and back home.

"So I play hard to get. So what. I'd rather be in the tropics."

"You were in England."

"Yeah, well, I lied about being in the tropics. England. All I got was a sunburn at the end of my nose."

"Welcome back, good to hear your voice."

"Yeah, I touched down an hour ago and already I'm at the office and criminy, here's Kevin hard at work after hours and I can't believe it, my genius buddy Balcazar's got another case! The ADC boys came through for you."

"You work too hard, Frank."

"Yeah, do I care? So ADC is this computer company that called like three weeks back, and Kevin fills me in about this girl and a rock and roll band and somebody tried to cool her right in your kitchen, and how not much else makes sense. So I'm off my case and I'm working on yours, I need the variety. And Kevin tells me he got a hot tip and pulled a fast CNA on, which one is it? Yeah, the *paisan*."

"Who?"

"Kevin's yapping at me. Okay, he's gotta wait his turn. But this girl, named Bear? Nothing. You tried the Registry of Motor Vehicles? Your voting lists? Phone company is not the be-all for every living soul in Boston, so—" Kevin was trying to break in again, harassing Frank. "Just a minute, I ain't talked to him in months." Frank came back to him. "Now Kevin tells me he thinks you can do all that tomorrow, do the Registry. And he tells me he thinks you might have a bug in there, in your phone line or maybe even in your computer. I mean, either one of us can get into it, if we know what to look for. You think your computer's bugged?"

This hadn't been a serious consideration. "I don't know, Frank. This whole thing's pretty strange—"

"Yeah, well, so am I and so are you and so's the fuckface who tried to kill the girl, so let's not take any chances, we can check it out for you. Kevin can do his tone sweep, too, 'cause maybe the sonofabitch just wanted to get in to tap your line, instead of the burglary, you follow?"

If that was really the case, a lot of things would make more sense. "Yeah. Frank, you mentioned *paisan*."

"Kev wants to tell you that. So maybe we can do the sweep tonight? Kevin says yes. The sooner you wrap this case the better for everyone. I could use you on the Strohecker thing, I gotta tell you about this when I get the chance. I go away for a few days, I get unindated with messages. It's still Tuesday and it feels like it's been Tuesday for three days. Problem is, the neighbor just made my client. Which is a bad break because I'm convinced he didn't do it, it was the boyfriend."

"I should hear about this sometime," Dred told him.

"Kevin should've filled you in. Ann Strohecker. Westchester County, went to bed two weeks ago and woke up dead. DA thinks her husband did it. That's David Strohecker, my client, the one the neighbor made as the guy who walked out the front door at two in the morning. Indictment right around the corner. Thing is, she had a boyfriend and the boyfriend fits the crime, not my client. Boyfriend's in England, that's why I was there. Thing is, she also had a skull fracture which the ME initially thought was the cause of death but I snuck in and saw the full autopsy and we've got fractured cricoid cartilage *and* fractured hyoid, but I just don't buy it because my client's got wicked tennis elbow, he can't lift a can of beer let alone do that kind of damage to somebody's neck."

None of this made much sense right now, this New York State society crime. "Frank. I hope you don't need me right away."

"Couple of weeks, maybe. See, I need someone who can hobnob undercover with the hoi polloi, with a big vocabulary. In exchange, I can help you out on your thing. Jesus, Kevin's pissing in his pants he wants to talk to you so much. Okay, so we'll talk later tonight, okay? Maybe come over, do a sweep, grab a couple of shooters, okay?"

"Okay. Welcome back."

"Dred." Kevin was slightly out of breath.

"What's this *paisan* business?"

"Okay, remember my source at Jamais Vu last night?"

Sheila, of course. "Yes."

"She said the guy at the mixer, the sound board last night, was this guy Jerry DiGiacomo. He does a lot of engineering for local bands when they make tapes. He worked with Doctor Glassheart."

Jerry. The guy Carmody mentioned. Dred was trying to remember what picture he had of the sound man, sitting in the back of the room not far from their table. Unclear.

"So I know this about him," Kevin continued. "He has an apartment, in the North End, lives with his younger brother. No priors. Lot of parking tickets. Otherwise, I got a long list of callbacks I'm waiting for to fill in the blanks. And he works some nights at Jamais Vu, some at the Nameless Lounge, but now my source at the Registry gets me to my credit check source, just before she leaves for the day, and *she* gives me the guy's work address, which turns out to be some high-tech place over in Tech Square, right where I saw you this morning." A pause for Kevin to catch his breath. "You with me?"

"Weird, Kevin."

"Tell me. So I called the number, the place is named something I didn't write down 'cause I can't pronounce, and then Research Associates."

"Heuristics. HRA. They're a division of ADC."

"Those are the magic words. Bingo. Rock and roll meets computer virus."

"So it seems. What's he do there?"

"Not a whole lot. Security guard, five bucks an hour. He does Sundays and Mondays noon to eight, and a couple of graveyard shifts. Like Wednesday morning, midnight to eight."

Dred was writing all this down.

"You there?"

"Yeah. Kev, what's the guy look like? I never got a good look at him."

"Hell, I *talked* to him last night, remember? We're old pals by now. Just before we left, I said, you know a singer named Stevie Bear? He kind of shrugged it off, but I thought, yeah, sure he knows her, he probably mixed their tape. So, description: he looks sort of Italian. Little bigger than you, not as big as me. Big enough to trash your apartment. Big enough to kill the girl."

6

Number 26 was the second-to-last house on MacElroy, a one-way street of cheap asphalt-shingled duplexes that seemed hardly able to sustain their own weight. The porch light was on and the front door ajar. An old rust bucket Toyota with Massachusetts plates sat out front, its passenger door swung open, spouting rock music. The hatchback lid was raised, revealing stacks of boxes and loose clothing. Affixed to the unsoiled rear license plate was a fresh January registration sticker. Just above it, a car dealer's nameplate: "West Side Toyota, Toledo."

From the street Dred could see through half-closed venetian blinds subtle shifts in patterns of light and dark as Tom Carmody moved about from room to room, staying away from the front door. Dred poked into the back of the Toyota, rummaged quickly through boxes of books, magazines, records, and old undelivered mail. Bundled with a rubber band, the mail was variously for S. Bear, Mr. Steven Bear, Ms. Stevie Bear from music companies, a Montana livestock supply store, a seed catalog, A-1 Temporaries in Boston (a window envelope with her name typed in carbon: a W-2 form perhaps), and an abundance of junk mail from Toledo. Thumbing deeper into the box, he found three old November issues of *Time* magazine addressed to J. DiGiacomo, 26 MacElroy.

Except that DiGiacomo lived in the North End with his younger brother, not here.

"You never told me your name." Carmody had come out on the porch, in sawed-off dungaree shorts and sneakers without socks and a ratty gray T-shirt that proclaimed in faded churchy typeface that Jesus Did It His Way—an evocative sentiment, but ridiculous apparel for a night this cold.

Dred pronounced his name three times before Carmody could either believe it or remember it.

"You don't have to snoop in my car. I told you I'd help."

"Yes, thanks," Dred conceded, turning to face him. "Your lease expire tonight? Looks like you're taking a long trip."

"I'm a tenant-at-will. And if you want me to help you, we gotta hurry it up, okay, because I am taking a long trip and I'm doing it tonight."

The emotional crack in his voice betrayed him: he wasn't just going away, he was going away *mad*. Beneath the overhead light in the hall his skin was blotchy and his eyes were red behind his moon-shaped lenses, and in this condition he looked very young, and not quite big or strong enough to make a fit with the guy from Saturday night.

"You can sit down if you want," Tom said with a flick of his hand, but here in the living room the couch was littered with record albums and sheet music and the only chair had a dish of cat food on it, cat food with milk that had gone sour and curdled. "You can move that dish. Katie left Saturday, I don't know where she went. She runs off for a few days, then comes back. Sorry the place is such a mess." He perched on the arm of the couch, squeezing his bony white knees together.

Against the long wall was a low bookcase without books in it, just junk and papers and dust. And in the middle of the room was a brass-hinged trunk half-filled with laundry.

"This shouldn't take long—I'll stand."

"Okay."

On an end table was today's paper, partially tucked under a hi-fi catalog but definitely folded open to the story of the virus at ADC. "Two things. First, all about Stevie, where she lives—"

"Maybe I need to know who you're working for first. Or what the deal is. She might be in some danger, is what you said. How do I know that the danger isn't from you, that you're a cop or something?"

"I'm a private investigator—" Dred began.

"You said the word *danger* out there on the Pike, the damn word's been ringing in my ears ever since. You gotta understand that. For everything that made us friends, that's one thing that always scared me about her, how she let everything just fall right into her life and . . . shit, I'm all bent outa shape." Now Tom got up and headed for the kitchen. "Gotta get a beer, 'scuse me."

He'd said at the toll booth he'd stopped drinking. "I thought you quit," Dred called after him, but now he was coming back with the bottle of beer, twisting its cap off. He drank with his head thrown back, guzzling, and his Adam's apple bobbing.

"No, man," he said, wiping his mouth clean, "I just took a break from it. Damn that's good. I've been so obstinate for so long."

Obstinate. For Frank Cirione to use the word "unindated," or toss out a term like "hoi polloi" and mean the opposite was not surprising, considering not much formal education and his enthusiasm for creative use of the language. But in missing the word "abstinent" Tom now fit in a little better as someone who *could* be a uniformed civil servant at a toll booth, in spite of his diffident, schoolish kind of looks. He was a pleasant-faced boy—he really was a boy, a very young twenty-seven who was utterly lost trying to be an adult.

"You mentioned Jerry back at the toll booth. Jerry DiGiacomo."

The knees squeezing together. "Right."

"I mentioned Stevie and you immediately mentioned Jerry. Why?"

"I didn't connect them, not immediately. It was only after I saw your ADC badge clipped to your belt. I'm not a total idiot, okay? People drive through the toll plaza, I like to look inside their cars,

see what's going on. Just a game. So I saw your badge, and Jerry
had the same kind of badge when he worked there."

"Worked? He's still there, Tom. At HRA, he's a security guard."

"No shit. But before, he was at ADC in Framingham, and he had
a red badge like you. When he was a big-time software engineer. I
figured you already knew that. This *is* about the virus, right?" Suddenly he leaked a smile of some minor self-satisfaction. "Maybe I
should just stop."

Yes. There are times when the best forward speed is full stop.

"I'm thinking, Mr. Balcazar. ADC must be paying you a lot for
this virus thing. You can imagine what I make as a toll collector and
a drummer who doesn't have a band."

Full stop: DiGiacomo used to be a software engineer. Carmody
was leaving town. Carmody had lived with Stevie until January;
from his brokenhearted rhapsodizing, they probably were more than
just roommates. And now Carmody wanted money.

Dred moved past him toward the far end of the living room and
the door to the kitchen and the hall leading to two bedrooms and a
bathroom. From the hall he turned and glowered. "Tom, I'm not
going to pay you a fucking dime."

Carmody sniffed back at him, "Then you'll get what you pay for."

"I've told you she's in danger. I'm in a position to help her."

"Two hundred bucks, Mr. Balcazar. I'll tell you everything I
know."

"You bastard."

Again, full stop. Dred was profoundly tempted to test every ounce
of skill he had at intimidation, perceiving this kid's bravado to be
whisker thin. In the deep right pocket of his leather jacket his hand
closed around the coiled-up piece of audio cable he'd grabbed at the
last minute when leaving the apartment. Later, he intended to check
it against cable at Jamais Vu, get some expert opinion on exactly
what it was, where it might have come from. Right now he was
sorely tempted to dramatize for Tom, in some fashion, what had
happened to his ex-roommate. But he held off. Tom's jaw had
dropped, his eyes widening, seeing that his guest was having some
trouble controlling himself.

"You couldn't have liked her very much," Dred muttered finally.

Tom's chest was heaving, prologue to another emotional eruption.

"She's in danger, and you can help me help her, but you won't, because you're looking for some kind of revenge. What happened? She leave you for DiGiacomo?"

Tom closed his eyes, shook his head. Lips quivering. "I'm sorry," he whimpered.

Those three issues of *Time*. "Either Jerry lived here for a while, or he wanted to. Am I right?"

Again Tom shook his head, swallowed repeatedly to clear the phlegm, took a huge breath. "He was going to move in. Stevie told him no."

Confident enough about a move to send *Time* a change of address.

"That's when he had his breakdown," Tom added. "I'm not saying any more. It just isn't fair."

Dred moved back into the middle of the room. "Okay, Tom, let me tell you a little about myself. As detectives go, I have a few things to learn. But one thing I do know is that I'm an arrogant sonofabitch and just on principle I don't like to negotiate fees with witnesses. Either you want to help me or you don't. At the same time, friends of mine have told me that I'm pretty generous, I'm always picking up the tab, I'm not totally hung up about money. You with me?"

Tom nodded, his wet eyes blinking, yes.

"So possibly I send you a check of some sort. But it's my decision, not yours. I'll decide 'if,' and I'll decide the amount. Being shaken down by witnesses—that's never happened before. And it isn't going to start here."

Tom nodded.

"Okay. So let's continue. Jerry had his breakdown. After Stevie told him no, don't move in."

He nodded. "And now I'm not saying any more."

"Fine, don't. I'll ask, you nod or shake your head, I'll look around a little, you don't have to compromise yourself at all, okay?"

"Maybe," he said.

"So let me flesh it out: he stays in his North End apartment with

his baby brother, he keeps his high-stress job at ADC in Framingham, and then—he snaps.''

Tom nodded again. So far so good.

"Maybe he gets hospitalized. Maybe his work suffers so much
ADC wants to lay him off. Somehow he drops thirty rungs on the
ladder of success to security guard—hell, he gets a uniform, he keeps
his medical coverage, he works odd hours so he can do his music,
nice deal.''

No response from Tom. Dred stepped away to the back hall and
turned the lights on in the big bedroom. Single bed, made up but
messy, more boxes on the floor, drums and cymbals stacked in the
corner. One of the boxes was full of Doctor Glassheart stuff—
posters and fliers like the one he'd liberated from Jamais Vu, demo
cassettes, a master reel of tape in a pizza-sized box. Candid five-by-
seven black-and-white photos of some kind of a recording session,
with Bill and Tom and Hank, and then another guy who had to be
DiGiacomo draped all over Stevie in the control room part of the
studio, both of them mugging goofily for the camera. Several shots
of these two. This man was about her age, built like a fullback, with
thick, wavy black hair and surprisingly friendly eyes, a nice face.
Audio cable dangled like black spaghetti from a board behind them.

Also in this box was a folder stuffed with business papers: a lease
agreement for a room as rehearsal space, form letters from record
companies saying thanks but no thanks, a bill from Jerry DiGiacomo
for his mixing services, eight hours for three songs, N/C. No charge
for the band with the lead singer he loved. Dated October.

And in a shoebox was mail for Tom Carmody, some of it with
computerized forwarding labels from Columbus, Ohio. Columbus.
A very long haul from Toledo.

"I'm being helpful just by letting you do this," Tom said, making his presence known in the doorway.

"Yes, you are, Tom. I'm indebted."

"If you do decide to send me a check, what kind of range are you
thinking?"

Dred held up one of the five-by-sevens to show him. "Seems like a nice guy. Back then. Guy has a psychic break, though . . . I don't know."

"Are you thinking like a hundred bucks? In that area?"

"But he's probably smoothed out on Lithium or Elavil or something, or some antipsychotic." Which would make a sustained outburst of pure rage unlikely.

"Maybe, maybe not," said Tom.

"I can find out by myself, thanks." Dred rose, pushed him aside with his body as he stepped into the hall, then through into the other bedroom, which must have been Stevie's, turned on the overhead light.

Completely empty.

"She left nothing," Tom said.

Just pinholes in the white plaster walls where she'd hung her pictures and posters. "For the money you want you're not giving me dick," he said, opening the closet door. Even in here there was nothing. "Who did your cleaning?"

"She did."

"Where'd she go?" Still in the closet, he found only a piece of matchbook cover from the upper shelf, which he pocketed. Behind him Tom persisted in saying nothing. Back at the toll booth Dred had almost liked him, but now he felt the anger building up in him, his heart pounding.

"Where did she move to?" he asked again with such pained, measured restraint that no one could mistake his state of mind.

Carmody, though obviously scared, would not back down. "I'm leaving for my brother's place in Harrisburg in a few minutes. I have to finish my packing. You need to go."

"You alarm me, Tom, how big an asshole you are. Incredible that she had anything to do with you."

"Not very much, actually."

Dred stepped past him, hurried into the kitchen, rummaged through drawers until he found the right weapon—a heavy-bladed carving knife. Tom was right behind him but suddenly spun away with a weak cry, backing into the living room.

"It's not for you," Dred sneered at him. "It's for your car."

And he was out the door, across the porch to the steps, down to the street. He slid on his back under the rear bumper of the Toyota, the tip of the blade ready to jam up through the thin steel skin of the gas tank.

"No, please! I'll show you her place. She asked me not to tell anyone, that's why—"

"But for the right price you would." Dred jabbed the knife against the tank. Not hard enough to pierce it.

"Please don't!"

Dred hit the tank again. "I've just figured you out. This is how you get back at her. You know she's in danger, you figure, okay, she owes me." Again, the knife, but this time clanging it against the filler pipe, of much heavier gauge steel, just to scare him. "Damn, this is going to take a while."

"I *told* you, I'll take you there."

"Hate to do this, Tom. Pisses me off. Also pisses me off that she had to sell you her car. Right? Car's worth eight hundred, maybe a thousand. What you get it for?" Clang, into the filler pipe. "Progress, nice little dent."

"She needed the money. She didn't have a regular job. Look, I can show you her place."

Clang. "How much, asshole?"

"Two hundred. That's all I had."

Clang. "Almost there. That's a helluva deal."

"How'd you know it was hers?"

Tired of lying on his back, Dred wormed out from under the car, stood up, held the knife forward at groin level, Tom with his back against the car. "Good guess. Dealer plate says Toledo, where she used to live. You got a brand-new January registration, just when life started to go sour for Stevie, when she moved out, when she needed cash. So here's the balance sheet: you owe me at least six hundred dollars in quality information."

Tom's body went limp, as if finally unburdened. "I've been so lonely since she left," he said at last. "It is so *lonely*, not seeing her."

———

A few minutes later Tom had thrown on a sweatshirt and gotten into the Subaru to guide him to this place, her crash pad.

"Go out, take a left. It's real close, right next to the Pike. I don't even know the street name, it's just a huge old warehouse and there's a room on the second floor and she looks out over the Pike, right near the tolls where I work. It's not an apartment, understand? It's a fucking storage room. And the place stinks, it smells like a *school*. 'Cause it's a warehouse for printers' supplies and school stuff and there's huge boxes of ink and mimeograph ink and chemicals. It's always dark up there, the main door's locked, she's never there. She might've moved out. She's *never there*. I called her at work a couple of times."

"Where. Where's that."

"She's a temp. A Kelly Girl type. To talk to her I have to find out where she's working and call her there and when I get her she won't talk to me. Now take a right."

"A-1 Temporaries," Dred thought aloud, remembering the window envelope that looked like a W-2 form.

"Yeah, that's the place. So you already know some things."

"Some."

"Stevie, gotta understand, she's hard to know. Can't blame her, she's been so fucked up. Her father, he left when she was about six."

"Her father left."

"Yeah, right, because her mother was really weird. So what I heard was, when she was six her father left and, okay, take a right at the lights. So her father in Montana, I forget the town, was a cop and I guess got in all kinds of trouble, Stevie didn't talk about him much, she never sees him, but after he left, her mother really lost it. She came down one morning, Stevie did, and her mother is making breakfast and says, 'Oh, by the way, I don't like the name Polly, I'm changing your name to Stevie. I hope you don't mind.' Can you believe that? She says, 'Tommy, the crazy lady changed my name!' So can you believe it? Age six and you have a new name? She used to be Polly, she had to get used to a whole new identity. Here it is, turn right." A street with the sign torn off the post, paralleling the Mass Pike, riddled with potholes. Warehouses and vacant lots.

Down here a white brick two-story building, a football field long with the entire second story huge multipaned windows, many painted black, some broken.

"Polly. But now her real complete formal name is Stevie, all legal and proper. Not Stephanie or anything, just Stevie. This is in Montana after her sister's already left."

Dred slowed the Subaru to a crawl.

"She's not there," Tom said. "Again."

Stopping by the far corner of the building, Dred stepped out and went to the door, satisfied himself that it was securely locked.

"You know who owns this building?" he asked when he got back into the car.

"No."

"What about another man? Not you, not Jerry, but someone else?"

"No idea. With Stevie, you'd never know."

"When's the last time you saw her here?"

"I'm telling you, it was January. Two months at least. I mean, we came to this city together as pals, from Ohio last spring, and we moved into the apartment and I thought all along everything was fine and it wasn't. Right after Christmas she decided to move out. Shit. She had no money, I said, where you going to move? And she said like a friend of a friend got her this room for like a hundred a month. Can you believe someone like her living in this hovel, I mean *choosing* to live here?"

Frank Cirione was infused with a constant supply of energy, from his first cup of coffee to his final nightcap; it flirted with, but never quite became outright distress. Even in the worst situations his excitability really was a kind of *convulsive enthusiasm*, not loss of control. Not ever, not now, as he waited on the steps of 118-C, his enormous white Lincoln town car beached halfway on the sidewalk, the car he called "Moby."

It had been a few months since they'd seen each other, but Frank didn't much care, it was late and he wanted to get right to work. He had in his hand a black cordless handset, evidently linked to his cellular car phone. "Yeah, so here's the thing, I got Kevin out of bed, he's pulling OT at the office, he's got the Sweeper thing, and we have to choreograph this ahead of time because once we're inside we can't talk like this, just in case, we'll have to write notes and do charades."

Dred was just about to unlock the door. "Frank, if he bugged me, I'm already so compromised I haven't got a chance. The horse has been out of the barn for five days."

"Yeah, well, just what did the horse say?"

"Forget it, he knows my whole life. Even more if it's the kind that picks up room conversations."

"Yeah, more often as not it usually is. So let's go find the bug but let's not let him know we're finding it, all right? So what if you got loose lips? That's good, that shows you're a normal guy. But from now on it's not normal, it's search and destroy. We'll talk damage assessment later. First thing is, let's disconnect your answering machines."

Inside the front hallway Frank apparently changed his mind and, for anyone who might be listening, noisily established himself a long-lost friend just arriving from out of state who desperately would appreciate a shooter or two and maybe some music to unwind. Say, is this my bedroom? No, Dred replied, going to the bedside phone and turning the answering machine off, it's mine, yours is upstairs in the living room on the couch, you're lucky to have a roof over your head, a deadbeat like you. Sure, sure, you miss me so much you're at a loss for words, humor is always the hiding place for heartfelt emotion. Let's get a shooter.

Frank now had his bourbon in a little juice glass and Dred was turning off the office answering machine upstairs, then putting on a cassette of the Crusaders with Joe Cocker. Frank was touring, poking around. The computer in the office, the phone and machine, the kitchen cordless phone and its wall cradle. Hitting the upright piano with the four note theme of Beethoven's Fifth, quickly scanning the TV and VCR and stereo in the bookcase around the fireplace.

Now downstairs to the bathroom with the door closed where with the water running in the tub there was no chance of being heard. Bathrooms, he had learned from Frank, are the least likely places for bugs. On his cordless patched through to his car phone on the street Frank dialed up Kevin at the office on the private unlisted line and said they were ready, do the residential number first, which rang on the bedroom phone and the cordless in the kitchen.

In a few seconds the bedroom phone started to ring.

"Clever, ain't it," Frank said, turning off the water and stepping out of the bathroom, giving him the cordless to listen to The Sweeper accelerating from 300 to 2000 cycles, like something out of *Star Trek* when the engines are overheating and Scotty's telling them they're about to blow. The phone kept ringing in the bedroom and upstairs in the kitchen, fifteen, twenty times until the sweep climaxed and ended: no tone-activated transmitter on that line.

More relaxed in the kitchen, Frank finally got Kevin back on the phone. Christ, man, don't go away, now do the office number. Frank poured himself a refill, strolled into the office as the phone began ringing. On the desk he found the Doctor Glassheart flier, studied it, pointed to the picture of Stevie and did a thumbs-up, wordless approval, then a quick aside. "Ten years ago this coulda been Ann Strohecker. Real pretty."

The office line kept ringing. It seemed to take longer and ring louder than the house phone.

Joe Cocker started singing "I'm So Glad I'm Standing Here Today."

Dred asked, "She really looks like Ann Strohecker?"

Frank wandered back into the living room and sat down in the swivel chair at the piano. "Same damned innocent face. Real cutie."

The ringing stopped.

"Was that two thousand?" Frank asked Kevin in a whisper.

Again Kevin seemed to have wandered from the phone.

"Stop scratching your balls and talk to me. Did it go to two thousand?"

Frank's sigh of relief was obvious when Kevin returned. "Okay, good. Don't go home yet, we got more to do, I'll call you back." He turned the cordless off, spun around in the chair and downed the rest of his drink. "All clear. Damn, I drink too much."

"Yes, you do, Frank, and so did I."

"You'll get over it. So lemme work it out: Thursday night this asshole busted in to steal your computer. Saturday he busts in to kill the girl. Monday he returns the computer to your front door, and it's got some threat written into it. Which has now disappeared. So he's been here enough times so he owes you rent, and we still don't know him from shit. So let's say part of the reason he came here was to bug you. In which case, if he knows his stuff he'd probably use a phone bug, not a room bug. But maybe he *doesn't* know his stuff, so he's tacked up a little itty-bitty transmitter somewhere. So tomorrow I come back with a Sniffer. Same idea as The Sweeper but they call it The Sniffer, it detects transmitters. But somehow I think he wouldn't do that, the phone bugs are much, much better, you get *everything*, he should know that. So what about the computer? See, I think a transmitter in a computer is a bad match, a lot of interference for one or the other, and I wouldn't be talking like this if I thought he'd done that. But just to ice the cake I'll come back with The Sniffer tomorrow, okay? Tell me about this girl, what's her story? Boy, she's pretty."

Frank had another shooter and Dred, cradling a glass of ice water and a twist of lime, explained most of what he knew about Stevie Bear, leaving out that he was extremely attracted to her, and tried to get Frank up to speed on the names—Tom Carmody and Jerry Di-Giacomo and Ray Niles and Doug Kiskel.

"Okay, but this kid, this pretty girl, there's some trouble here. Where is she now? Is she okay?"

"Tell me, Frank. What's on your mind?"

Holding up the flier, studying her. This kid has the face. Ann Strohecker had the face. Many other women had the face, too. Frank had theories about whiskey and wine and pasta and Confirmation and Cadillacs and the Irish and women, and this theory was, a woman like this, like Stevie, with a face like this is asking for trouble and she don't know it. A woman with a face like this. That's the theory.

Frank was up again, prowling back into the other room toward the piano. "Hey, listen to me, Dred. I'm saying, look, you and I we come from good New York stock but we're different. I'm totally Italian and a street kid and you're some kinda high-class mutt, I don't know, and you didn't come home every night like me wondering if your old man would still be alive. So now I'm a Boston detective, I have to trust my instincts, and there's something intuitive you get, you know, you have a sense, you say about this girl Stevie, hey, there's trouble here. She's got the vibes."

"Frank, I really like this girl."

Dah dah dah duuhh, Beethoven's Fifth on the piano. "Boy, you're acting like the drunk, not me. How can you really like her? You seen her once? Twice? What, you gonna be infatuated? Sure, why not. My wife. I love my wife, I really do. Am I in love, infatuated? Hell, don't pressure me on that, I'd have to be less than honest. Now Ann Strohecker, there's a woman I'm in love with, you wanna know the truth. Except I didn't meet her till she was dead. Seen her pictures all over the house, love letters to her boyfriend, photo album, and her autopsy, and you don't think but for a few twists of fate she could be *my* wife, I coulda been in love with her? So I'm saying, big deal, Dred, maybe you're in love with this girl you just hardly met and she's still alive, right? We haven't got any evidence that she ain't. And I'm in love with this woman whose life I know very well and she's dead. You lead, one to nothing."

Midnight: it was now Wednesday. Tuesday had started with wanting to throw a beer bottle at Bunny McMahon's head, just now ended with Frank Cirione's insistence that he was in love with a murder victim. Damn good thing to have it over. Thursday, tomorrow, Frank reminded him, was the first day of spring, the equinox, thank God, because winter drags on forever in Boston. Frank wanted to move to someplace warmer. Like Baltimore. Start over. But in the meantime there was the Strohecker case, and this weird piece of work from ADC.

Frank left at one, having exhausted his fantasies of living in Baltimore with a different woman who looked exactly like Ann

Strohecker, after he had called his best midnight locksmith, Old Reliable Barry Brown, to meet with Dred at one-thirty for a quick and dirty low-risk B&E at a residence in a warehouse on Howard Avenue—what Dred's city map told him this nameless street next to the Pike was named. Arriving there on time, Dred parked the Subaru around the corner out of sight, and waited five minutes listening to the whoosh of traffic on the Mass Pike until he saw lights approaching, a red Datsun pickup, which then moved past him on the street. He flicked the Subaru's lights just once, got out of the car to be seen by the pickup as it did a U-turn and stopped, and Barry Brown got out, a compactly built black man, younger, dressed completely in black and toting a heavy tool kit. This was a freebie, he said, he owed Frank, something that had to do with his getting into law school, and now at the big black steel door he said, no problem, it's a simple lock, and went to work with a thin wire probe and a tiny penlight. Dred moved to the edge of Howard Avenue to watch for any traffic, keeping Barry in peripheral view, the firefly dance of his penlight. In a few seconds Barry straightened up, packed his tool box, and came out to him.

"All set."

"Thanks a lot. That was fast work."

"Yeah, no problem. Quite the shitty neighborhood. You say this is a residence?"

"Guess so. Soon find out."

"Need me ever again, call anytime." Barry took out his wallet, gave Dred his card. "After hours it's time and a half. This offer good only till I pass the bar." He was serious, didn't smile.

"I understand. Thanks."

Barry had left the door slightly ajar. Dred took the flashlight from his glove compartment and moved inside, immediately finding stairs through a door up to the second floor. It was one huge storage room, mostly empty except for pallets at the far end, and yes, Tom was right, the place did smell of school, of mimeograph fluid. There was enough light from the streetlamps on the Pike to navigate here without the flashlight, toward the far end of the building and a wall with two doors. The left door opened to a bathroom, its porcelain sink mottled with ink stains and handprints, a wastebasket overflowing with those brown paper hand towels that absorb like wax paper. A fragment of inky soap. Everything was bone dry, no other signs of use, just a toilet with rusty water and this tiny sink. The other door was to the room where Tom said she had been living.

Only a thick double-bed-sized mattress askew on the floor and a single rust-stained pillow. No pillowcase or sheets or blankets. A faint odor was layered on top of the ink smell, mildly familiar and human. Maybe it was old perfume. With the flashlight he explored all corners of this small room, found nothing, not a scrap of paper, a receipt, nothing. There was one electrical outlet, no phone plugs.

Dred lay down on the mattress, hands behind his head, staring at the ceiling and the two windows facing the Mass Pike, the prismatic sweep of car lights overhead. Shifting his body to get comfortable, discovering there was the slightest depression here, just a sense of where her body had possibly been on this mattress, information that, because it was just as easily imagined as perceived, wasn't really information at all. Only a sense that she had been here and slept in the middle of the mattress, which would suggest that she had slept alone.

He wondered about a thermometer of such magical precision that it could measure in tolerances of billionths of a degree, could determine the temperature of this mattress or this pillow in a perfectly stable environment, would indicate that, yes, a human being had last been in contact with this material a month ago February nineteenth, the ambient temperature is a stable perfect 43 degrees and this pillow comes in at 43.0001 degrees, human contact never is traceless, never really disappears, it decreases asymptotically always approaching the condition before the contact but never quite getting there, never 43 degrees again. So also the effect of a handshake, a kiss, a bead of perspiration caught by the tip of his tongue. Forty or fifty years later it is still there, a full-time preoccupation for a dozen or so brain cells still firing off a synapse or two even as we're dying and we think we've completely forgotten.

Casual cursory human contact, the heating effect of a human hand on a cold doorknob, does approach over time the infinitesimal, but

Dred now felt with Stevie it was going quite the other way, the opposite mathematics of expansion and increase. Brief contact had spawned full-time preoccupation for his full consciousness. Stevie was becoming more a composite of other people's responses to her, less who she was when he'd been with her at the Athenaeum, the Oyster House, in his apartment when, as Lauren Michaelec, she could hardly be certain herself who she was.

Like the depression left by her in this mattress: it could never really be known, corrupted by his own weight upon it. Things are as they are seen, are made when they are touched, are nourished by the mind, cease when forgotten.

This would be explored more by a computer someday. An artificially intelligent computer that is programmed to wonder.

When he awoke, it was still dark. He left the storage room, made a mental note that the company here, noted on the boxes of mimeograph ink, was ITL School Supplies, Inc., found his way downstairs, and pulled the big metal door closed so that it locked behind him. He got in the Subaru and headed for Tech Square in Cambridge. It was almost four o'clock in the morning.

At Heuristics Research Associates and at American Data Corporation's AI-5 building across the block the lights still burned, a twenty-four-hour quest for ever more obscure knowledge. And inside the lobby of HRA it should be Jerry DiGiacomo on the midnight-to-eight shift.

Dred sat in the Subaru sucking deep breaths, passingly curious that the only other car on the street, three spaces ahead of him, was a classic VW bug, repainted robin's-egg blue and with a permanent list to port as if its left-side springs had snapped. Bumper sticker: God is coming and is she ever pissed.

At last he was ready. He left the Subaru and ambled toward the front door.

Inside, the name tag confirmed that this was indeed Jerry DiGiacomo, but he clearly was not the same man in the photographs cheerfully flirting with Stevie. The face was thinner, the cheekbones pulling at the corners of his eyes, eyes that had no life in them. The Mediterranean gloss to his skin had dulled to flat manila. Physically, he was easily a match for the Saturday intruder, the arms and shoulders and hands large and strong enough to have done that kind of damage. But was there any will left in this man? Any capacity left for hatred, for sabotage, for murder?

Looking at Dred, examining the name on his badge, watching him sign in under "Irregular Hours for Employees," DiGiacomo should have leaked the smallest hint of recognition that the man before him was both his prey and his pursuer. But he didn't.

"Okay, you're all set," DiGiacomo said, giving him back his card.

"Yeah, well, here we go, I hope I can get some work done without the Internet fucking up again. Holy shit! I hope everything's up again. What are they saying, are we okay tonight?"

"I don't know, they didn't tell me."

"*Man*, that virus is a showstopper! Look at me, do I look like someone who enjoys redoing the same goddamn programming every night? Do I? Huh? I've had it, man! In heuristics, continuity is everything. Understand? Continuity! And I haven't had any continuity all week!"

This was the principle of the *provocative anomaly*: Say something at least imprecise, at most irrational, and get the other guy into it. Even if the guy seemed a million miles away.

DiGiacomo would not get into it. Dred moved over to the glassed-in bulletin board, something familiar catching his eye: the Doctor Glassheart flier for the January gig at Jamais Vu. DiGiacomo must have been the one to post it. Why had he not, in recent weeks, removed it, just to obscure the link between ADC and Stevie Bear? Why the ever-thickening trail of bread crumbs?

"Mr. DiGiacomo," he said in a tone more grave, "what do you know of heuristics?"

"Much more than I need to," said DiGiacomo.

Dred spun on his heels. "Really?"

"Yes. I used to do a lot of programming that involved heuristics." The voice was flat and bored.

"Heuristics, of course," Dred ventured, "is a brand of common sense. A rule of thumb, as it were. If you were a computer, or even a person in this band here. Rule of thumb for a successful band: advertise."

"Yes," said DiGiacomo. "Correct. If it's an axiom that works, then it's heuristic. I take it you're new at this."

Dred could feel himself winding up. "*Very* new—I have a lot to learn. Axiom: women always fuck things up. True? Women are like viruses, they just infect everything. My own girlfriend is like that." He was surprised to be saying this, but figured improvisation is like that, it just *comes out*.

"I suppose," DiGiacomo said emptily. Now something caught Dred's eye as he looked past the security desk to the corridor with elevators on the left and on the right an alcove for hanging coats. A water fountain beyond it, and rest rooms. In the alcove hung a bright green jacket.

"Excuse me," he said, stepping around the desk and into the corridor. The jacket was new, Kelly green with white trim, part of a white shamrock showing, a familiar stock item at any downtown tourist shop—a Celtics warm-up jacket.

With one hand on the faucet to mask any noise he might make, Dred fingered the right sleeve of the jacket, inside the cuff, snaring a loose thread and jerking it free. He leaned over for a sip of water, smacked his lips, found a toothpick in his shirt pocket and wound the thread tightly around it. He returned to the lobby.

"Jerry." Very softly now. "Didn't you do some work with that band?" He turned toward the bulletin board. "Doctor Glassheart?"

A flicker of interest in the eyes. "I've worked with a lot of bands, yeah. I still do."

"Did you work Saturday night?"

Now twisting anxiously in the swivel chair, DiGiacomo craned his neck to try to read the last entry on the sign-in sheet.

"Balcazar," Dred told him.

"Balcazar. Why you asking me these questions?"

The bread crumbs were thinning out; Dred chose to be straight with him. "I'm an investigator. I've been hired to work on this virus thing."

"Oh, man." DiGiacomo swept his hand through his hair. "Not me—why'd they send you to *me*?"

"They didn't, it was my own idea. I need to know—were you here Saturday night, or with a band?" Or prowling around Beacon Hill.

"I don't like being grilled like this," he said, his voice quaking.

Much softer, Dred leaned in. "Jerry, it would help me to know. I'm just following some leads, that's all."

"Yeah, okay. Saturday night I was home. With my brother."

He might as well have said he was alone at the movies. Just to finish the thought: "So who was here, on duty?"

His hands trembling, more frightened than he should have been, DiGiacomo fished around for the schedule, told him the guard Saturday night was Jacqueline Kazmeier, and yes, he agreed to keep this conversation in confidence. That was it, that was enough, Dred believed he had everything he needed for the time being. Now he moved to the elevator, stepped in, and went up to the seventh floor.

The corridors were lit overhead, but there was no sign of life. In the corner facing ADC's AI-5 building an empty conference room beckoned, its door open, and at the window a cameralike object on a tripod faced out through an untinted rectangle of glass. This was the HRA infrared transceiver that communicated line of sight with its partner across the street at ADC. Except that outside a large dark mass dangled a few feet away, obstructing the line of sight. Four heavy ropes, and a window-washing scaffolding with buckets, was suspended from some unseen cornice over this window.

He sat down at the head of the clean white formica oval table, rested his head on his hands to think, viewed the eight or nine empty chairs around the table and imagined them filling up with Niles and Kiskel and also DiGiacomo and Carmody, and Stevie. And Elaine and Erica. And everyone would be talking at once. "Please, one at a time," he muttered as his eyes closed and he drifted off to sleep.

When he awoke a half hour later he discovered another after-hours visitor to the seventh floor. She must have weighed three hundred pounds, the lower half of her bulk poured into enormous blue jeans, the upper half swaying inside a heather-colored UMass sweat-shirt as she lifted first one tree-trunk-sized leg, then the other, in a painfully slow attempt to traverse the length of the central corridor to reach the elevators. Coke-bottle glasses, mouse-colored unkempt hair, in one hand a filterless cigarette, in the other a kind of cassette tape, smaller than a VHS video. She would complete six or eight steps before pausing to catch her breath and, simultaneously, para-doxically, draw deeply on her cigarette.

If she had any response to his being here with her, approaching from the other direction, she didn't reveal it. He, however, was so-bered by the presence of a woman who, although not much older than he, was obviously beginning to die. Hitting the elevator call button, he faced her, smiled, offered a quick hello; she ignored him as she hesitated again to smoke and catch her breath, still only half-way to her goal, breasts as big as birthday cakes, bouncing.

Now she seemed to cast a glance at his ID card, clipped to his belt. Hers was missing, unless it was somehow secreted under a drooping fold of flesh. Gagging on her final inhale, she crushed the cigarette out on the carpet, took four more steps toward him as the elevator signaled its arrival. She spoke, at last. "Big deal, no ID. You gonna throw me in jail?" A squeaky, sandpapery voice, rough with antagonism. And very bored. The voice on the answering ma-chine he'd called yesterday.

So this was Sandy Murchison.

The elevator doors slid apart and stayed open. "I don't know what you mean," he said.

"You're management. I don't give a shit, but you'd better."

The doors squeezed shut. Dred hit the call button again.

"You go," she said. "I'll take the next trip."

"I'm not management. I'm free-lance."

"With a B-1? Not bad. 'Bye." The doors were open for him, he smiled again at her and stepped in. Hearing her thud ever closer, in spite of her unfriendliness and her good-bye, he held the Door Open button and waited until she came into view, now clutching the cassette thing to her stomach and breathing very hard.

"Thanks," she said, still scowling.

"Are you okay?"

"You don't wanna know. I'll make it home, then we'll see." She moved into the elevator with him, her whole body heaving to take in air, hard to imagine the exertion of muscle required to move all the flab out of the way so her lungs could work. Pudgy hand clutching the cassette—a Walkman-sized clear plastic box with a finger-thickness of tape inside, fully rewound. There was an ADC label on it, obscured by her hand.

As the doors closed and they started down, she noticed him staring. "Do you care? Gonna call security? Don't bother, 'cause I'm pals with that guy down there, he'll just slap my wrist, send me home, and I'll be thinking, fuck you. Fuck you"—she squinted through her glasses to read his name on his ID card—"Mister who-ever, boy, that's a name to crash a program."

"Let me test myself for a second," he said. "You've been laid off. But you're back here moonlighting." Why not finagle a few extra days of your pet project with a sympathetic security guard down in the lobby?

"Brilliant. Wanna know the truth, they screwed me. You're free-lance, you don't care. But that's what they did. Who wants Kate Smith to be their best brain in complexity theory? Thursday, my last day here, I'da done anything to get my job back. Now I don't give two shits. But damned"—and here she gave an acknowledging jiggle to the cassette—"if one sonofabitch in particular is gonna get away with it. You wouldn't know. You don't know this business."

The elevator slowed, their weight increasing (she just felt the G-force of an added fifty pounds), then it stopped and the doors separated.

"I'm learning. Every business seems to have the one sonofa-bitch."

His lead didn't draw out the name. "Fuckin' tell me about it," she said, and, as he'd wished, she now held the cassette in her chubby right hand dangling off the fat of her side, and as she moved to step off the elevator so did he, bringing his knee sharply up into the plastic case and dislodging it, sending it clattering onto the marble floor of the corridor.

"Shit," she said. "They break."

"Sorry," he said, bending down. The ADC label was hand-marked in black felt pen: 3EXT.MRM. He stood up and cheerfully returned the cassette to her, making sure that, in the lobby, Jerry DiGiacomo hadn't noticed, and actually was surprised when two people who had no business being together in fact, at this ridiculous hour, were getting off the elevator.

"Here's my buddy," she said with a nod to Jerry, "risking his new job so that justice may prevail!" She waddled slowly up to him. "My last night here, pal. Gimme an interoffice mailer, will ya?"

"You've finished?" Jerry asked her with evident interest, as though they really were friends. Dred stayed back a few steps to watch as DiGiacomo produced a mailer for her.

"All done. Four hours is plenty, I'm sick of this place."

Four hours: so she'd arrived just after Jerry had started his shift. Dred moved one step closer. She was writing weakly, daintily, on the mailer, "B. Ohlmeyer," the research vice president who'd acted as press spokesperson yesterday morning. The next line was hard to hear because her voice, as if mimicking her handwriting, sank to a near whisper. "It just isn't tractable, just like I thought," is what he thought she said.

DiGiacomo looked past her to Dred. "You're a friend of Mr. Balcazar here?"

She turned back, eyed him with some doubt. "I don't know. Seems harmless enough. Are you, Mr. Balcazar, a trusted site?"

"He was quite confrontational with *me*," DiGiacomo told her.

"Really? You've been bullying my buddy Jerry? Shame on you! His brain is not healthy, you know."

"I needed to ask some questions," Dred replied.

She turned back to Jerry, leaned across the desk to tousle his hair. "It's not his mind I care about anyway," she said. "It's his hardware."

Her lecherous quip went over Jerry's head. "Sandy, this man told me he's investigating the virus."

"Oh, dear," she said. "Maybe I've been too helpful." Now she sealed up the mailer and handed it to DiGiacomo. "She better get this. Soon." Then she leaned forward and planted a huge wet kiss on the top of DiGiacomo's head.

She turned to start for the revolving door, Dred moving a few steps ahead of her. Jerry said, " 'Bye, Sandy. You can come back anytime I'm here."

"Can't do," she said without turning around, heaving one huge leg in front of the other. "All done." Then, to Dred: "You gonna help me across the street? I don't need it."

"No. But I'm very interested in what you're sending to Betty."

"I'll bet you are. You the one who called my machine and didn't leave a name?"

"Yesterday evening," he said.

She struggled through the revolving door after him and was completely winded by the effort. "Harvey Monahan's called several times." Sucking air. "I'm sure you both have me all but convicted."

"Incorrect. Someone else gave me your name, as a resource. A lead. That's why I called."

"And followed me here."

Dred shook his head. "I came here for other reasons."

"So maybe you think it's Jerry. Which would be equally wrong."

"Why?"

"Instinct," she said with a knowing smile. "I can tell. He's a very sweet boy. A little overworked, some personal problems, and suddenly his brain turned to crawl space. Sure, he could write a virus, he could write a virus like Shakespeare writes plays. But set it loose? Nah. All the hostility got burned out of him."

"Personal problems. Like a girlfriend?"

"Fuck this. Why'm I talking to *you*?"

"Sandy, I know about them. But they broke up last fall, right? And they haven't seen each other since November. Am I right?"

She wouldn't answer, but the question clearly troubled her, as if she knew a great deal more of Jerry and his old girlfriend than she would admit to. "Jerry's not your man."

Very possible. "Sandy, we need to talk some more."

"I'll call you. You left your number."

She did not take his outstretched hand. He crossed the street by himself, noted again the old Volkswagen bug, started up the Subaru to head home, giving her a final wave as she stood monumentally still in front of the main door to HRA. At a few minutes before five starlight over Tech Square was yielding to the first light of dawn, day and night in Boston now virtually equal in length on the eve of the equinox. The wind had shifted northerly out of a cloudless sky, a gentle morning wind but with a wintry bite to it, it was still technically winter, just one more day.

7

At eight-thirty Wednesday morning, the day Stevie said she would be back from Ohio, he shook himself awake after three hours of wretched sleep that came over him in waves of little nightmares. Again, dreams of black wire—snaking into her bed and coiling loosely about her before constricting murderously. Dreams of her legs sticking out of a dumpster. Three hours of virtually useless sleep, panicked that he was running out of time. A-1 Temporaries loomed as an important source: only they would know when she'd last been in touch. Only they would know where she now lived.

Beaucoup coffee just to *begin* pretending it had been a normal night. Scooping out lots and lots of Folger's into the little white baskety filter thing for eight cups, which everyone knows is more like five or six cups, a normal supply for a busy day.

Groggily he groped about in the office closet where he kept his squash and tennis rackets and vacuum cleaner, sailbag stuffed with nylon line and brass fittings and weather-stained charts from Florida, tackle box and unused fly rod, cardboard box that probably (uselessly) contained the Subaru's original (now nonfunctioning) alternator, until at last he found, in the farthest dark corner under boxes of books and under his battered old Olivetti, the mahogany box that contained his modest but adequate microscope. He set it up on the desk, bending the lamp down and close in, rotated the lens turret to 300X, its most powerful magnification. First, in its little Ziploc bag, the thread from the break-in. Now, uncoiling the second sample from the toothpick, laying it next to the first.

Similar green translucent plastic hoses. Very similar diameter, color, edge definition. Identical.

But to be sure they'd have to go to one of Frank's labs.

In the kitchen the coffee was burping and belching its final drips, a full black cylinder in the pot. He procured his first mugful even as the basket was still emptying itself, its dregs drooling and spitting onto the hotplate. Then back into the office to his phone.

"A-1, how can we help you?" A guy, unctuous and singsongy.

"Hi, yeah, need to find Stevie Bear, she worked for me a while back and I have this *ring* of hers, she left it behind."

"Hold on, please." On hold. Still on hold. Why did he say *ring*? Still on hold.

Now a woman's voice: "Who are you holding for, please?"

Oh, shit, one of these. "Some guy who's pathologically cheerful."

"Hold, please." We are not amused.

Quite possibly they would have work for her today. Certainly they'd have her current address.

"Yes, hello. You say *who* left a ring?" The singsongy guy again.

"Stevie Bear. She's one of your temps." Please help.

"Bring the ring in and we'll make sure she gets it."

"Oh, no. Not *this* ring, man. I don't think she'd want that."

"We'll be happy to send it to her." Happy happy, how can we happily help you?

"Look. Can you just give me her number and I'll save you the trouble?"

The guy went away, leaving him on hold to finish his coffee until he returned once again, bearing ugly news. "We can't give out home numbers and we've had no contact with Ms. Bear this week, I don't know why. But bring us the ring and we'll make sure she gets it."

"Thanks."

Two more mugs of coffee, a fast shower and shave, and he was out of the house, tweed jacket and tie and charcoal gray Brooks Brothers wool overcoat, shoes shined, the Doctor Glassheart cassette and promotional flier in his pocket along with notepad and pen. The first stop was ITL School Supplies, occupying the second floor of one of Boston's few remaining downtown *fin de siècle* brownstone office buildings, the place crowded with rolltop desks and boxes of unknown inventory, not a soul in the place under fifty. Instantly it smelled like the warehouse—the mustiness of ink and anomie, rusty plumbing, clock-watching.

He explained to the president's secretary who he was and that, in his considered professional opinion, the young woman who had recently been using their warehouse as a crash pad, known as Stevie Bear, was, currently, a missing person. Myrtle, the secretary, didn't know about Ms. Bear or anyone recently living at their warehouse. The president, Harold Harbison, pince-nez and bow tie, was tied up on the phone in his glassed-in office with his accountant—an uninterruptable call. Tax time, you know. Dred described Stevie to Myrtle, apologized for the cliché: pretty, blond, late twenties. She was instantly intrigued: yes, this young lady had come through an agency and it would be the treasurer, Dave Twomey, if anyone, who would know about the warehouse business, but Mr. Twomey was out getting Danish. She wondered what kind of trouble the girl might be in, wasn't it possible people had just lost track of her? On her first day, a week before Christmas when A-1 had sent her over, Myrtle had shown her the ropes about bookkeeping, the word processor, the checkbook, and there was the very clear idea that this girl was *so sad*. Just about to burst into tears all the time. Must be the same girl, she thought.

She led him around a corner to Twomey's open office door, suggesting he leave a note. The office was classic old Boston small business, too many cardboard boxes and loose papers, stacks of things everywhere, old oak desk against the wall, an ancient leather swivel chair with a seam just beginning to leak cream-colored wool stuffing. Very formal family photo of Dave and wife, pretty people in their early thirties, and two little girls and a sheepdog. A photo of a beachscape. And another photo of his wife in boots and jodhpurs next to a very fine-looking horse. Expensive lifestyle for a guy who sells mimeograph ink.

"It occurs to me," she said, "that Mr. Harbison probably doesn't know of this situation."

"Really?"

"Well, Mr. Twomey did this once before." She looked past him as the front door opened and Dave Twomey arrived carrying boxes of Danish. The interview was over.

"I think South Street Stationers can probably help you," she declared as Twomey sidled past them. Dred grabbed an envelope off a desk and quickly scribbled down his office number, handed it to her.

"Call me?"

"I'll try," she said. Then, louder: "Three blocks that way, take a left, can't miss 'em."

Of course Herb Fielding remembered Dred's Monday visit to Vidco and the article he was doing on artificial intelligence, but he was reeling from a creative clash with his young spiked-haired associate, Sam, and didn't think he could spend much time *or* energy helping him out this morning on such short notice, what with this big slide show they were doing. Dred told him he simply wanted to view the program one more time, if he might.

"Well, fine, let's get you set up," Herb said, leading him down the hall to an editing room. "*Shame* ADC is having so much trouble—surely you know about their virus problem."

"Read something about it, yeah. Tough luck."

The editing room was also a tape library, floor-to-ceiling shelves packed with black cassette cases, each sporting the Vidco label and title of the project or client, arranged chronologically. Herb settled him at the control panel.

"ADC. Last summer, here it is."

"Herb. Out of curiosity, any idea what ever happened to that woman? Lauren what's-her-name, who worked on this?"

"The Wicked Witch? I *do* believe she's on the Coast, which I know will disappoint her."

"Any idea when she left?"

"Here, let me just stick this in." He leaned over him, grazing his shoulder as he inserted the cassette into its player. It was not a nice feeling. "Must have been last summer. Yes, I'm quite certain. You know, someone else was asking the same identical questions just a few weeks ago, I didn't know she had such a following. She's such an extraordinary *bitch*."

"Someone else."

"Hm. Now, everything's turned on. You push play to play it— do you have a VCR at home?"

"Yes, it looks similar."

"Essentially the same. If you have any questions, just call Moira out front. Dial zero." Two cassette players, two monitors, telephone, big audio board with a zillion knobs and meters just like the one back at Jamais Vu. In touch with the world, right here in this tiny dark room in Charlestown.

"Thanks. You mentioned 'someone else.' "

"Hm, I don't really recall. Anyway, we must have lunch, I'm sure we'll have things to talk about."

After he left, Dred started the tape to see if by any remote chance there was anything in the program that could help him now: a brief appearance by Kiskel or Niles he might have missed the first time. With the fast-forward button he sped through the opening titles and an introductory informal chat by the program host. At the same time, he dialed Moira and asked how to call out. Nine, she said, no problem. Dred called his office machine, it rang three times and was answered by Frank Cirione.

"Mr. Balcazar's line."

"Shit, Frank, you get up early." It was nine-thirty.

"Leave me alone, I got home at one, went to sleep and woke up at two and I been up ever since. I been worried about the both of you, you and the girl. Look, Kevin and I are here, he's doing the Sniffer all over your place downstairs, we haven't got anything yet. We're just about to start the upstairs. I gotta get to Westchester this afternoon, they just arrested my client last night, they're arraigning him today, I *know* he didn't do it, and all the time most of what I'm thinking about isn't him or Ann Strohecker but instead you and this girl and what the fuck is going on. Okay, Kevin says you're clear on your stairwell, he's poking it up into the cornishes, he gets nothing. So what is it? Why am I not thinking about my own case, my client and the woman I love?"

Cornishes. In time, Frank could have his own dictionary. "I don't know, Frank." Fast forward to one of the knowledge engineers speaking in his office, "scoping the task domain." That meant, he was saying, figuring out just how much the software should *know*.

"Look, we been here all of fifteen minutes and you got some calls here. You want to hear them? Here's the first," he said without waiting for a response. Moving the handset close to the answering machine speaker. Alexis Shaler, introducing herself as the wife of his friend Todd. In Bedford. Extremely distraught. Can you please call?

He jotted down her name and number next to Sandy Murchison's on the torn-off scrap of the Boston *Globe*. The knowledge engineer's face was frozen on the monitor, his mouth caught sneering, his lips stuck between awkward syllables.

"She's a peach, huh?" said Frank. "Kevin's in the kitchen, so far you're fine. Okay, so the next one I heard while I was here, you had your volume up—Dred, you got *problems* with basic security here, know what I mean? If there's a room bug in here somewhere it just might be picking up your goddamn phone tape as your calls come in, see? Okay, so here's the next one."

Harvey Monahan from ADC at nine-fifteen, please call him right away at AI-5 in Cambridge, and the number.

"That your client?"

"That's him. Better go, Frank. Got a lot to report."

"There's one more here."

"I'll call you back, don't go away." Dred hung up.

Fast-forwarding through this guy to a scene where they're all gathered in a conference room, the camera moving around from man to man, and at the same time he was dialing the main number at AI-5 and asking the operator to page Harvey Monahan.

Sweeping around the room, the camera blurred past Doug Kiskel, same beige ratty sweater, with his hands to his face tugging at his cheeks from exhaustion, boredom, the microphone just barely picking up something he was saying into his palms, even so this guy dominated the room.

"Harvey Monahan." The familiar big bear voice.

"Harvey, it's Dred."

"Eat shit," he said. "That's what it's telling me right now, Dred. It's telling me to eat shit in huge capital letters." Dred was rewinding to the beginning of that shot, playing it back again in slow motion as Harvey was ranting, something about *Charlotte's Web* and the pig and the messages in the web that he'd just finished reading to his youngest kid.

"I remember it, I don't remember the words in the web," Dred told him, studying Kiskel looking exhausted and annoyed with his fingers rubbing deep into his eyes pulling at his lower lids.

"Some Pig. Terrific. What I wouldn't give for something friendly for a change. Instead we get Fuck You and Eat Shit, I might as well be in the men's room at North Station. No damage though, it's just another interrupt. Ray's at work on it here at AI-5. We don't think it got out very far on the Internet."

"Where's Kiskel?" He was here on the screen in front of him, just fed up with the meeting, a regular guy.

"He's back in Westville, AI-3. On the phone with Ray, coupla other guys."

Kiskel's voice on the videotape started with something like *We made it we can*—and then the camera swept by him to someone else who started talking over him, who was saying, *it's got to be tractable*.

"What's he think?" Dred asked. "Or what do you think?"

"I just don't know anymore. He's working *so hard* to fix it."

"Harvey, hold on a second, I'm watching something, I gotta pay attention. Don't go away."

Back rewinding to the start of the shot, with the volume up and playing at normal speed. *We made it, we can unmake it.* Then the next guy, *it's got to be tractable*. The same word Sandy had used.

"Where are you?" Harvey asked. "What're you doing? I might need your help."

"I'm watching an ADC training tape. Niles and Kiskel are in it,

Kiskel is in a meeting looking bored and they're talking about undoing what they've been doing."

"Look, can you come over this morning? The far-off chance we can meet and make some intelligent deductions?"

"Right." Once more, still oblivious to the camera, Doug Kiskel mumbled into his hands, "We made it, we can unmake it," a pronouncement of pure defeat, weary with cynicism. "Harvey, these guys are in a meeting, this is from last summer, and it's going badly and they have to *undo* a lot of work."

"So? Look, can you get down here?"

"Sure. But tell me quick: what's 'tractable'? What's it mean?"

"Christ, Dred, that's something from complexity theory. What's that got to do with this fucking virus?"

"Something, I'm not sure yet. Look, gimme fifteen, twenty minutes."

Dred hung up and watched the rest of the meeting scene, remembering it now from Monday as the place in the program where the featured knowledge engineers are introduced, Kiskel and Niles not among them. The narrator confirms that this weekly project review meeting is not going well, a lot of the work they've done already will have to be scrapped. Learning to fail is an important part of creating successful artificial intelligence. Learning to make it, and then to give it up.

He let the program continue while he redialed his office number. Frank and Kevin were continuing their Sniffing.

"All clear so far, kitchen and living room," said Frank. "Moving into the office, he's working the moldings and cornishes and the tops of the curtains. Very basic Buck Rogers stuff, this is just a tin shoebox with an antenna sticking out of it, a meter, a calibrater. We're talking very fifties. So tell me why it's two bills. It's two bills 'cause private detectives are *rich*, right, Kev?"

"Frank, there was a third call."

"Right, but it's just a hang-up."

"Can I hear it? Maybe there's something there."

"Right-o. Lemme find it. You as tired as I am? I'm getting the twitchy lid. Doctor said it might be caffeine poisoning but I think it's just no sleep. Eyelid twitch."

Dred knew about his own twitch, the uncontrollable fluttering of lower eyelid skin flap, the one Nature made to be most visible and embarrassing. Back to the monitor, they were showing the outside of the AI-5 building in Tech Square and going inside to another brainstorming session, Kiskel not there. But Sandy Murchison was, briefly but unmistakably taking up the space of two men for a quick cameo. God, she was even bigger then!

"Okay, here it is," said Frank. He played the tail end of Harvey's call, a few seconds of dead air, dial tone, and a beep again.

There were two quick tones following the beep.

"That's it," said Frank.

Dred hit the operator button on the phone twice. It was the same tone.

"You do that?" Frank asked.

"Yeah. Frank, someone's been listening in on my messages."

From behind him, he hadn't heard the door open. Here was Herb. "As a matter of fact, my friend, I'm free for lunch today, if you are."

"Excuse me, Herb, I'm on the phone, won't be long." Then to Frank: "I got problems."

"So sorry," said Herb.

Dred turned in the chair to face him. "I can't have lunch today, maybe next week."

"Okay, saaarreeee." And he left with his chin thrust forward.

"So they got your code?" Frank asked.

"Dumb. Really dumb. The code is double zero, the factory setting. Jesus, it's so *dumb*." Sure, it was easy: in his outgoing message he told them what model machine he had. Any idiot could discover the factory setting for the remote code and give it a shot. Kevin had warned him—change the remote code. Dumb.

Dred raced through the rest of the video program, found a quick walk-on by Ray Niles near the end, no further appearances by Kiskel or Sandy, and now to the credits with the name *Lauren Michalec* on the screen. He froze it, studied it.

Frank was giggling. "Kevin's trying to goose me with the fucking antenna! Now I remember why I hired him."

Kevin's voice, leaning into the phone. "To satisfy his profound homosexual cravings."

"I've seen bigger dicks on cockroaches," said Frank. "Hey! Stop that!"

Dred hit rewind, turned the monitor off and waited for Frank and Kevin to calm down. "I'm leaving for ADC in just a second. We gotta talk, Frank."

"By the way, through all that, there's no bug in your computer, just like I thought."

"No transmitter."

"Right," said Frank. "No transmitter. Too much interference with all those electronics in there. My guess."

"Where is he now?"

"Wiggling his buns over by the north windows, over your curtains. We've got nothing, not a damn thing. This is a very sensitive machine."

"Why would he bug me when he can simply play back all my messages?"

"Dred, boy. Messages only give you one half a conversation."

"If you're smart enough, that's all you need. I really screwed up. Damn!"

"Dred. Be like me. When it gets tricky like this, take a coupla hours off, think it through. Ease the strain on the brain."

"I wish I had that kind of time, Frank. I don't."

"Well, me too. I'm catching the eleven o'clock to LaGuardia. Might be back tomorrow but Friday's more like it. Kevin? Yeah, he's got it, nice work."

"Got it? How so?"

"He's done. Place is as pure as a baby's bottom. Bugless. No *Playboys*, no scumbags, you're looking pretty pure yourself, we've seen every inch of your apartment. Whoops, Kevin says you got ants in your kitchen, you're a lousy housekeeper. 'Course he's got a pony tail and an earring so he's really *into* stuff like that."

"Frank, I think I'm going to need his help, can you put him on?"

"Hey, love slave! Boss wants to talk to you!"

Dred reviewed for him the business with the double-zero caller.

"Shit, man!" said Kevin. "Want me to change it? I'm right here, standing over the damn thing."

"No. Let's leave it; otherwise he calls again, gets no response from the machine, we've shown our hand."

"Right, good point. How 'bout just turning it off?"

"Kev, *any* change and we've shown our hand. And if she calls and there's no answer, I'm sunk. She's the central thing here, not the virus, am I right? Death threat beats vandalism any day, right? Stone breaks scissors?"

"So it stays at double zero. Too bad."

"Kev, listen. Carmody doesn't know where she lives. Hunch tells me DiGiacomo doesn't either. The outfit that owns this warehouse where she lived doesn't know dick. There's only one place that would have to know at least her phone number."

When Dred described his call to A-1 Temporaries earlier that morning, Kevin instantly perceived he'd been too polite. Better to go there in person, he said, flash some ID, look very much the part of an ex-bouncer from a South Boston Irish pub, and not leave until he had hard information.

And another thing: in his top desk drawer were two samples of green polyester thread that needed tests, to see if they came off the same garment. Kevin found the samples right away. Later he wanted to talk about "his source at Jamais Vu." Meaning his ex-girlfriend Sheila Corrigan and the long lunch he'd had.

They called this The Playpen, a common work space with half a dozen ADC terminals and lots of counter space for engineers visiting from other buildings, for demonstrations, or just for a change of scene, playtime, here on the eighth floor of AI-5 in Cambridge. At the keyboard was Ray Niles, behind him were Harvey Monahan and Betty Ohlmeyer, and all three of them deep into what the screen in front of them was saying.

"Still waiting for the last letter," Ray said, today sporting a Patriots sweatshirt. Harvey was slipping: no tie today, his white shirt-tails already pulling out.

"Today we're keeping this to ourselves," Betty said. "That's straight from the top." Nattily attired in suit and snug-collared blouse with red bow.

"Meaning Cooper," Harvey told him.

Betty straightened up. "I got about a hundred people waiting for me down in the cafeteria. You gentlemen are welcome, if you'd like to witness a desperate attempt to calm everybody down. Harvey?"

"In a while. I need to talk to Dred first."

"Okay, but they really do need to hear from you. And, Ray, when you have the fingerprint, will you have me paged right away?"

Not looking up from the screen, he nodded with a hint of impatience that she was distracting him. "You'll be the first to know, Betty."

She grabbed her valise and started for the door, catching a quick look at Dred, who was urgently signaling her to step out of earshot to talk. With some reluctance, she followed him out.

"Okay, what is it? By rights Harvey should be here."

"If I can't break some rules, I won't do you any good."

She grimaced. "We're working on this problem almost 'round the clock, and I'll confess, relatively speaking, I haven't seen very much of you."

He had to shake this one off. "Betty, I need to ask you if you've gotten your mail yet this morning."

"Mail? My office is out in Westville, I don't get mail here. Why?"

Why couldn't ADC live in one town like a normal company? He persisted: "Quite by accident yesterday I made the acquaintance of a woman who used to work here." *Yesterday* carefully chosen; it was impossible to know if more specific information might open a can of worms.

"Come with me, I've got to get to this meeting." They turned the corner and headed for the elevators.

"I believe this is important. I learned that yesterday she sent you one of these cassette things, whatever they're called." Boxing its dimensions with his hands.

"You're describing a twenty-megabyte cartridge. Why?"

"This woman wants you to see it because, as I heard her say, it's—the word is—*intractable*."

The abrupt use of the word itself gave her pause, even if, as Harvey had implied, she didn't know her bits from her bytes. Clearly she did.

"She specifically used the term *intractable?*"

"Yes."

"This would be, no doubt, Sandy Murchison."

Dred saw no reason to deny the fact. "Yes. It would."

At the elevators she hesitated before pressing the call button. "Sandy was one of our top people in complexity theory, and an excellent compiler writer. If she's analyzed something as intractable, it probably is." Offered in a mild whine of irritation—that Sandy was too often correct and this could be a problem.

"Meaning?"

"Intractable means, in complexity theory, that it's too complicated to do its job. It can do very simple things, but that's it. And it cannot be compiled. Do you have any idea what's on that cartridge? If she sent it just yesterday, I doubt I'd have it this morning. Boston to Westville, overnight." Of course, Betty assumed an external mailing from the outside world, where Sandy now lived, not interoffice from HRA.

"Betty, may I ask, was your relationship one where she felt certain of your trust, your support?"

"Yes, I think even during the exit interview she felt positive toward me. Men in general, I might say, were a problem for her."

Conceivable. God is coming and is she ever pissed.

At last Betty pressed the call button. "Well. I'll just have to wait to see what it is. It could be an old project she wanted to wind up. Still, it bothers me. If she was working on tractability analysis yesterday, she had to be on the network, and she's been laid off for almost a week. That's the part I don't like."

"Why was she let go?" he asked.

"That has to be confidential, I'm sorry."

He followed her into the elevator, going down to the third floor.

"Not just because she's an enormously unpleasant person?"

Poker face. "Lots of people were laid off, for a variety of reasons. But it really does bother me—once she's gone, she shouldn't have access to the network. Where did you meet her?"

The elevator door opened and she stepped off.

"We didn't meet. We bumped into each other."

Betty was instantly annoyed with him. "*Where*. Inside ADC?"

"Not far from here. Betty, I have an obligation to her," he lied. "And I don't consider her a suspect."

Above her collar her neck started to crimson. "Consider this, my friend: your principal obligation is to me, to Harvey, and to ADC."

"I'm sorry. I wish I could do better right now."

"She couldn't have been within our buildings. It's just not possible." Dumbfounded, angry with him, biting her lip as the doors closed between them.

Going up. Twenty-megabyte cartridge, able to hold lots and lots of programming, acres of it, packed into a box that could fit in your vest pocket. 3EXT.MRM. Harvey had used the term *extensions* when talking about Miriam, extensions as little piggyback programs to make the main program work better. Sandy said she'd been working on the thing for all of four hours. Midnight, the starting time of DiGiacomo's shift: she'd befriended him, this was her first chance to get in the building that day.

It made some sense: the virus hit the news Tuesday. Sandy went to work right away, the wee hours of Wednesday.

Upstairs in the Playpen, Ray and Harvey were leaning in to the terminal screen. A staticky voice said something about a new directory; Dred realized it was Kiskel, on a speakerphone next to the computer terminal where Ray sat. Kiskel was in Westville at AI-3, twenty-five, thirty miles away.

The terminal appeared to be behaving itself. "You said there's one letter to go. Still waiting for it?"

Ray grimaced at him wearily. "Yeah, it's playing hide-and-seek. Soon as I have a buffer full of commands it'll jump me." He continued entering those commands, doing things Dred knew he'd never in his lifetime have the energy or time, let alone aptitude, to comprehend. Away from the speakerphone, Ray said to him, "Amazing parallels here, I'm still waiting for the second T. Fuck you. Eat shit. They're both seven letters. In each case it's the seventh letter that repeats, so for both there are just six different letters. The *U* and the *T* repeat—maybe this means *nothing*. We think it's the same identical program except it's got a faster clock on it, this has all happened in like an hour or so. Hold on, I gotta go to work here, and anyway I've forgotten how to talk. Harvey, help the man out?" And with that irrational high-pitched laugh Ray went back to work with Doug Kiskel on the speakerphone in Westville, continuing their incomprehensible technical dialogue punctuated by Ray's astonished protests ("Why do you want to do *that*?!") and subsequent bursts of nervous laughter, "Oh, of course, *now* I see."

Harvey escorted Dred to the far corner of the room. Leaning forward, Harvey spoke in a deep, sonorous whisper, a little too close to his face. The virus kicked in around nine o'clock, spitting out its anagrammatic message on monitors throughout ADC in Cambridge, Westville, and Framingham—only these three AI buildings and nowhere else. With the very first interrupt they were ready, and they'd finally chosen to go off-line, cutting contact with Internet and all other outside data communications networks, hoping that their prompt action had stifled the virus's spread. Unlike Fuck You, which had leaked out of ADC and now, they knew, had temporarily contaminated chunks of the Internet at a number of sites outside the company.

Betty had mentioned *fingerprints*. Yes, Harvey said, they were actually seeking the virus program itself, which apparently was ferried in electronically on a packet and now resided somewhere in the mainframe memory banks. Once it was found, they would disassemble it and see whose fingerprints were on it—there are ways of finding out when and where it was made and where it came from—if you can find the program itself. A packet, Harvey was saying, is a bit of a file, like a page from a book, that travels from one computer terminal to another, and viruses can be made to cling to them, to get a free ride. A remora on a shark, that kind of thing, a parasite.

The simpler Harvey tried to make all this for him the less Dred tried to understand it. Diluted for the layman, it had limited value anyway; fully expounded, one expert talking to another, it yielded only certain fragments that aroused his curiosity and then dead-ended at a wall of jargon. The main problem right now wasn't so much the riddle of the virus as it was the invasive proximity of Harvey's face—just too close with the lights too bright overhead, the man's exhausted eyes roadmapped and thyroidally buggy and his lulling baritone too breathy against the backdrop of Ray Niles's increasingly excited voice bending over the speakerphone.

Excitement that suddenly caught Harvey's attention. "Progress?" "Think so," Ray said, his fingers pecking frantically at the keyboard, hesitating, and then, "Huzzah, Dougie, huzzah!" Dred mouthed these words, wondered at Ray's volatile affections, his hostility toward Kiskel, the suspicion and jealousy—that Doug Kiskel was a superior mind to his in all aspects of artificial intelligence and that in spite of anything else he was worthy of hearty congratulations for helping walk Ray through all this mess, by *phone*.

"Think I've got the hook," Ray said, now spinning in his chair. "Can you guys excuse me for a minute? I'm going to need complete quiet. If I screw up I'm *finished*!" Harvey got up, Dred followed him out into the corridor down toward the kitchen until they were out of earshot, and Harvey stopped, slumping against the wall.

"Dred. Let me find a way to convey to you my state of mind."

"I think I can guess."

"Look. I'm really a technoweenie, a grownup version of Ray Niles, I'm a math person who somehow got kicked into management. You're the philosophy guy, right? So tell me: why should I trust anybody?"

"Maybe you shouldn't."

"Not only Kiskel, but Niles as well. You. Betty. That's where my mind is today. Okay, let me see if I can pour coffee and talk at the same time." In the little kitchen he succeeded in filling two mugs in spite of a telltale tremor in his hand. "When ADC got its AI division going way back when, it of course had to adopt the IC staffing structure. The Individual Contributor, guys who go off and do their own thing that's just part of one big project. So in AI we have maybe eighty, ninety knowledge engineers who are all ICs with a very liberal schedule of deliverables. There are meetings, of course, these guys do get together to swap ideas or get feedback, but essentially they're all one-man shows. Like Ray Niles overseeing vision work for robotics. And Doug creating extensions to his natural language."

"Miriam."

"Yeah, Miriam. Cheers, I hope I don't leap out of my skin, this is my seventh or eighth, I forget."

The coffee was heavy and oily from the bottom of the pot, pure poison. Harvey cringed as he drank, led him out into the hall to the big conference table where two days ago a dozen or so knowledge engineers had successfully disassembled Fuck You.

"No one's really seen Miriam, right?" Dred needed to be sure. "No one's seen it work?"

"Just some very basic things—nothing impressive. She gets the big unveiling in Washington, at the conference next month. I'm not worried about that. I'm worried about trying to understand who knows what. The thing is, I don't *know* how much Ray knows about, say, robotic vision. Only Ray knows, only Ray can begin to describe what he knows. I don't *know* how much Kiskel knows about natural language. Only Kiskel knows or can try to tell me. Even Betty doesn't really know what they're doing, and she's their boss, for Christ's sake."

"So only the knowledge engineers know what they know."

"Yeah, and you get into the high-level guys like Kiskel and Niles, it gets pretty rarefied."

"You say Kiskel's been working hard on this virus all morning."

"Yeah, it *seems* that he and Ray are doing it together by phone, but you hang around there long enough, you get the idea: Kiskel's really in charge, they're looking at the same stuff on their terminals and Kiskel's doing most of the brainwork. Why? Not because Ray isn't pretty smart himself, it's just that Kiskel is a whole shitload smarter. Easily smart enough to create a virus and then appear to try to disarm it."

"Harvey." Now Dred caught himself, on the brink of invoking the name of Jerry DiGiacomo—someone Harvey should know. But immediately he thought better of it, that it was too early.

Harvey needed to complete his own train of thought. "Dred, listen to me: when Kiskel says something is *so*, there's no one there to say it isn't. So we have to go with it because ninety-nine percent of the time he's right, it's confirmed later. You can see what I'm up against."

Now Ray Niles came out into the hallway and urgently waved at them. "Can you come see this?" For the first time since Dred had met him, the man was smiling in a way that suggested he was *not* about to cut loose with his hysterical whinny.

The last *T*, Niles claimed, had come and gone without destroying any memory, and here frozen on the monitor, he explained, were the lines of programming code behind the words *Eat Shit*. For the first time the bones and arteries of the virus were unwrapped, submissive and unprotected, from its skin. Thanks very much to Doug Kiskel. The code meant nothing to Dred, but Harvey smiled approvingly and said, "Looks like you got it."

"Don't go away, back in ten minutes," Ray said to Kiskel on the speakerphone, then hung up. Leaning in to squint at the screen, Harvey confessed that this was very sophisticated code. Impressed by what he saw, Ray was delighting in pointing out obscure intersections of logic and math that made the architecture of this virus so elusive and so potentially dangerous. And here, he said, is a major fingerprint, *routing information* that linked it unequivocally to an HRA computer across the block.

"Guy tried to hide it, but he just couldn't."

"Have to take your word for it, Ray," Harvey said.

"Please do. It's HRA all right."

"You sure?" Harvey asked.

"Positive."

"How did it get here?" Dred asked.

"On the IR transceiver. It's the only way, there just ain't no alternate route."

Harvey edged closer to the screen. "Any idea when it was written or when it was transmitted?"

Ray was shaking his head. "Not yet. I might be able to figure it out if you give me an hour or so. With a little help from Westville." Meaning Kiskel.

The Playpen phone rang, Betty Ohlmeyer for Harvey. The meeting was about to start, could he come down to the cafeteria and lend a hand? Two minutes, he told her, they'd just broken through on this thing, they had the fingerprint they were looking for. Dred could hear her squeal of excitement over the phone. Ray could hear it too, remarked that this was Betty's "best shriek," reserved for special successes.

Harvey wanted to get moving. "Can you save all this stuff?" he asked Ray.

"As we speak," he said, banging at keys. "This sucker is *ours*."

"Will you tell Kiskel?"

"I'll call him right now. Dougie and I have *lots* to talk about, I'm not going to crack all this code on my own. But, *boy*, this feels good." And he laughed.

Heading for the elevators, Harvey was attempting to straighten his shirt, jam the shirttail back into his pants with trembling, frantic hands. "So you see what we've got now, Dred? A bug that started at HRA."

"Ostensibly," he said.

"Of course it started at HRA. Kiskel and Niles agree, that's what the fingerprint says. So it must be as it seems to be. Right?"

"If they say so."

"Then you see what we're up against. Christ Almighty."

There, through the window, he could make out a slice of the HRA building where Dred had been just six hours earlier with Jerry DiGiacomo and Sandy Murchison. And right here, mounted on the wall, was the AI-5 infrared transceiver pointed at HRA.

"Right," Harvey confirmed for him. "That's how the two buildings talk to each other."

Dred's attention was drawn outside toward distant objects: there was something about this transceiver's view of HRA and the building's rectangular dark bulk. Something that was different. Something missing or something extra.

"Harvey, how about an independent computer genius, from another firm?" They got to the elevator, punched down to the third floor and the cafeteria.

"Lord deliver me, it's hard to imagine anyone second-guessing Ray Niles. Impossible to beat Doug Kiskel. These guys wrote the book."

"How about Miriam? How long's he been working on that?"

"Intensively, since last fall."

"And these extensions?"

"Yeah, that's the new work he's doing just to make it better, faster."

"And you haven't seen any of this? Ray hasn't seen it?"

"Not till it's done. That happens next month, in Washington. Dred, you're not supposed to worry about that kind of thing."

"Harvey, I have to. Believe me."

In the cafeteria the kitchen staff had been excused and it was standing room only for Betty Ohlmeyer, apparently just now getting past her opening remarks. The rogue program, as she called it, had done no permanent damage either here at ADC or out on the Internet, as far as they knew. Still, it had disrupted critical work in AI. Its message was offensive and ugly. Worst of all, it had spawned a plague of disinformation, rumor, and innuendo. More than likely, she said, it was the creation of someone within the "general ADC family," in which case they were dealing with a vicious and destructive personality.

In this final phrase Dred imagined the target of Betty's suspicion, heard the heavy thudding of Sandy Murchison's feet in the pristine corridors of ADC.

For the short term, she said, everyone's primary responsibility was to continue work as if nothing had happened and to keep today's recurrence of the virus a secret.

She turned and introduced Harvey Monahan, VP of Security for the AI division, visiting today from AI-3. Harvey could give more details about the virus itself.

Harvey began to speak cagily about what they did and didn't know, that *probably* but not certainly the program was authored by a person in the ADC family. The best news was that a "group of our best knowledge engineers" had captured the program, disassembled it, and were now inspecting its code, looking for clues.

Soon the speech dissolved into questions and answers, increasingly technical and incomprehensible. Dred understood none of it. Even Harvey's voice was losing its coherence, becoming so much environmental noise, like a continuous rumble of distant thunder. Things were falling out of place; faces around the room were starting to quiver in a bizarre sort of herky-jerky slow motion, forcing him to lean back against the wall by the cashier's station, to try to shake the feeling loose. Poison in the bottom of the coffeepot? Then Harvey would be affected, too, would have to start feeling the same way. But Harvey looked perfectly healthy. The wall was eerily abuzz with the resonance of his voice.

A terrifying thought rushed through him and tingled in his extremities: since his arrival here moments earlier he was not aware that anyone in the room had so much as looked at him. His eyes had wandered to all corners, had picked out and explored a dozen faces, Harvey's included. But no reciprocation. They didn't see him.

By tensing his muscles and breathing deeply, he calmed down a bit, felt sane enough to know it was time to get out. Still unnoticed by Harvey and everyone else, he turned and walked out of the cafeteria, to the elevators, down to the first-floor lobby and outside onto the street. A cold wind was blustering in from the north. Deep, slow breaths all the way to the parking lot and his car.

He got in the car, closed the door, and leaned the seat back a couple of notches, lowering the visor to block the sun rising high over Heuristics Research Associates. Where, right now, the window-washing scaffolding was suspended along the adjoining wall of the building. Two blue-uniformed guys were working with buckets and squeegees, seven stories up, no longer blocking the infrared transceiver.

That's what was different about HRA.

Perceiving and processing this extremely simple piece of information relieved some of the pressure in his chest, distracted him momentarily from any serious questioning of what was and wasn't real.

"Hey." It was Harvey, tapping on his window. Dred rolled it down. "You all right?"

"Sorry, I felt really queasy, I had to leave."

"Too bad, seems to be going around. My kids just got over it. Anyway, you didn't miss a whole lot, just a lot of gnashing of teeth. But Ray just came down and said he and Doug just cracked the internal clock on the thing. You should know—they say it was transmitted at four this morning, with a time delay on it."

"They sure?" This was not possible.

"As sure as they can be."

Dred glanced up again at the window washers seven stories up. "Harvey, I don't believe this. They're taking us for a ride and we don't even know it."

"Excuse me?"

"You've been suspicious of Kiskel all along, and *now* you believe him?"

"Dred, Ray and Doug *together* found the clock. I have to trust *something* of what they say."

"Okay." To keep things simple, concede for the moment.

"Soon as you get a chance, I'd like you to check it out at HRA. Anyone who was in the building at four in the morning. Okay?"

"Right."

"That's just the *Eat Shit* virus. Now they're hunting for the clock on the *Fuck You*."

Dred wearily went through the mechanics of starting up the car. "Harvey. Do me a favor and just stick around AI-5 today, okay? Leave the gumshoe work to me, don't talk to anybody, don't move." It was time to drive to Westville. "Everything just got very complicated."

Harvey paused before acceding. "All right. But you should check out HRA and the sign-in sheet."

At last Dred could smile. "Harvey, he's playing you like a Stradivarius. I gotta go."

Harvey mouthed, "Who?" but Dred gunned the car sharply toward the entranceway and the street.

First, to Massachusetts Avenue and Harvard Square, then continuing toward Arlington Center, where, at quarter after eleven, he stopped to call his office machine. He punched double zero after his ineptly composed outgoing message and got a fresh chorus of messages. First, a quick update from Kevin.

"Heading over to A-1 Agency, I'll get the address for you, stay tuned. Hey, maybe she's back and wants your body, who knows?"

And a second message.

"Mr. Balcazar, this is Alexis Shaler again. I hate to disturb you, but please do call me, I need to talk to you about my husband, it's very, very important."

And a third.

"Mr. Balcazar, I *hope* this is the right number. Anyway, this is Myrtle D'Angelis at ITL School Supplies? I have to talk quietly because Mr. Twomey's not far away and he's on the other line so I have to make it quick. So, anyway, about that pretty girl you were asking about? From the agency? Naturally, I hope she's okay. I thought even that first day he had kind of a crush on her, he's really quite a rascal. But I wanted to tell you—"

Silence for a second.

"Sorry, he just got off the phone, I'll have to call back later. Don't call here please."

Triple beeps indicating end of messages, without an audible double zero. For the time being, the messages were secure.

In the glass of the booth color had come back to his face. He took several deep breaths, tightened his fists and relaxed them, felt his muscles toughening, relaxing, and again, and again. Freed from the abnormality of too much intelligence concentrated in one place at AI-5, he felt renewed and solid, connected again to the earth and feeling fine.

He got back in the Subaru and continued west.

8

Dred pulled the Subaru very carefully into the driveway behind the big old Chevy station wagon where Alexis Shaler was sitting behind the wheel, inhaling hard on a cigarette and filling the car with her smoke. Except for one furtive glance in the mirror when their eyes momentarily met, she ignored him. Finally, when he stepped out of the car she got out too, cigarette in one hand and an enormous beer stein in the other. It was a struggle for her, she was drunk and had to prop herself up with one hand on the car. Her dark hair was tangled and matted, and she wore that same shiny green overcoat from last Friday when she'd been standing in front of her car scolding it like an obstreperous child.

"Mrs. Shaler. I'm Dred Balcazar."

She smiled at him, crooked teeth but friendly. "I know. I seen your Yale picture in the yearbook. You don't look so different." After she drank from the stein, her lips were smeared with red juice. "You want a Bloody Mary? I make 'em big and strong." Despite her condition he couldn't help liking her, her openness and her broad Midwestern accent.

"Can't," he said. "I've got a long day ahead."

"Well, you come into the house anyway. You can start the meter anytime, you just been hired."

"I didn't come here to get work. Thanks anyway, but I'm too

busy." He followed her into the open garage to the back door.

"I got the money," she said, going into the hall and the kitchen. "Even though it don't look like it. And it don't."

"No thanks, really. I don't want you to hire me."

She spun around and moved a step closer to him. "Well, you're a good-looking guy, all right. A little craggy maybe but you'll age well, I bet. How in the Lord's name you end up being friends with a pig like my husband?"

Friends. Todd was stretching it. "Well, we were in some of the same classes. Todd's an interesting guy," he said, fudging.

"He's not gonna see the sun rise tomorrow, that's for sure. That's why I want to hire you so you can tell me the truth about what a sack of shit he really is." Immediately he felt compromised, that she'd made public a threat against his life. She dumped four or five ounces of vodka into her stein, following with straight tomato juice and a quarter lemon, unsqueezed. No ice.

"I think we need to talk about this. In such a way where I'm not learning about any crime you may be contemplating."

She drank hugely, then dabbed at her lips with a soggy wad of paper towel, seemed not to hear his warning. "Don't sit down over there," she said, indicating the breakfast nook by the bay window, still cluttered with the detritus of at least two previous meals and smelling of sour milk. "The kids can't keep the food off their seats, I swear they'd rather sit on their food than eat it." Now with a wicked grin she took his right hand, his fingers, in hers. "I'm not making a pass, just relax." She pulled his hand to her side coat pocket, patted his palm against some small hard lump inside it. "Feel that? It's something *baaad*."

"Smaller than a grenade," he said, immediately wondering why, for she burst out laughing and leaned on him, throwing an arm around his neck and leaning on him.

"Oh, Mr. Balcazar, you are a *scream*." And disengaging, she stepped back but kept her eyes on his face. "A grenade, wouldn't *that* be a sight! No, put your hand right in there." She was guiding his hand down into her raincoat pocket, but he quickly pulled it free, grabbed her so suddenly by the crisp green plastic of her shoul-

ders that it startled her, spun her around and steered her toward the
hall leading out of the kitchen.

"Alexis, figure it out, you've got to learn the rules. You don't
call a detective with desperation in your voice and then do what
you're doing. You don't make threats, and you don't reveal any
weapons you might have on your person." She was muttering incoherent protests as he pushed her into the den, toward the Barca-
lounger. "Now maybe you've got a little gun in there, and maybe
you don't, but as soon as you show it to me I'm bound by law to
remember it when you get hauled into court on a weapons charge or
assault or murder or whatever you might be fantasizing."

She landed awkwardly, with one leg sprawled over the arm of the
chair. "I need my drink to help me with my fantasy," she said,
struggling to get up. "He's not at work, that virus thing closed it
down, and he's over with that whore he's got, and simple enough
I'm gonna kill him. I got it all planned so when the kids get home
from school the neighbor will be here to take care of them while I'm
at the police station. I don't care if I go to jail—" She lurched over
the arm of the chair and onto the floor in a heap. "He's *not* gonna
get it that easy, the miserable fucker!" She was up, stumbling into
the kitchen. "I don't care if I go to jail. I don't care if you're a
witness."

On a footstool by the little fireplace was the familiar volume, the
Yale yearbook opened to the class pictures, the B's, he was the first
of the B's, and there was a pink dribble of spilled Bloody Mary on
the page facing this all-but-forgotten photo, with his much shorter
hair and already, at age twenty-two, his face sporting a carefully
cultivated look of sublime indifference.

She caught his eye from the kitchen, standing by the sink. "You
look nice in there. You're cute. You're the only one Todd ever mentioned. You're the only one I seen from the book, and I'll tell you
you're a whole lot cuter now."

She was leaning into the sink splashing cold water on her face,
running her fingers through her hair, a sweep of her glossy green
arm knocking half a dozen dirty glasses off the counter clattering
onto the floor. He came in, stooped down, and started picking up

the glasses. Slugging down the Bloody Mary, she burbled at him, "Don't do that. It don't matter."

"Let's get it together, okay?" he found himself saying, feeling increasingly useless with her, wondering why he was on his hands and knees gathering up dirty glasses knocked to the floor by a woman he'd just met. She needed a vacation in a bad way, from the sour-milk stink of the house, her nagging kids, and ridiculous husband.

"Please don't do that," she said again.

"Alexis. Aside from telling me all this, what do you need from me?"

She started to whine. "I *told* you. Tell me he's the shithead I've always known. There's nothing else to surprise me."

When he said nothing she started to become angry.

"Here's the gun I'm gonna use." Resting in the palm of her hand was a tiny derringer, as he'd suspected, scarcely more than a toy but still a sufficient close-range weapon. He stood up and brought the last two glasses to the sink, very natural action, as she stepped aside, but still close enough so he could quickly seize it from her. "It's loaded. It's his. He plays with it. And he says you couldn't hit a nigger at noon from five feet. Imagine living with him for fifteen years and he starts talking like that. Couldn't hit a nigger at noon from five feet. Never talked like that before. I hate that kind of talk."

"I'm sorry, Alexis. I'm sorry your husband is the way he is."

He did not make a move to grab the gun, and he did not know why. From what he could see he was confident the hammer was on safety, but the way she held it he couldn't be absolutely certain. Now she stepped farther back, just to find clear counter space on which to support herself.

"If I stuck it right into his tit, could it kill him? It's got a hollow point in it, but it's real short."

He nodded, yes, of course, at close range the derringer could kill him, hollow point or not, the gun was made for point-blank shooting, not for target practice. The barrel was not much longer than his little toe.

"Damn, I gotta be drunk enough to shoot him and sober enough not to miss. I gotta be right up against him, this thing jammed into his fat *tit*."

"That's right. Otherwise you'll miss. Can I make a drink for myself?" He reached for the vodka bottle, rinsed out one of the dirty juice glasses.

"Dad told me I should go ahead and do it," she said, and drained the last of her drink, Bloody Mary juice trickling down her chin.

"People are entitled to their opinions. But now that makes two people who'll go to jail."

She laughed. "Mr. Balcazar, my daddy's dead. Can't go to jail if you're dead, right?"

He was not totally disinclined to believe that she might have recent communication with her dead father, especially with a little help from the bottle. "Do you speak to him often?"

"In the car. That's where he died, three years ago right in the front seat. We were driving, just the two of us, he had a nap and he never woke up when we got back into the driveway. I've heard his voice in that car. I hear him talk to me. He says Todd is no good. He's always said Todd is no good. Now Todd says, your father's right, I am no good, that's why I'm leaving you. Well, Mr. Balcazar, Todd may be no good, but he's the only damn husband I got and he's not going to get off that easy. I'm going to his whore's house, I know where she lives, and his car will be there and I'll go inside." She pulled the hammer back on the derringer, releasing the safety, and took a step toward him. "I'll have the gun just like this, and come right up to him and stick it right into his fat squishy tit."

Even dulled by booze her body seemed to stiffen with the excitement of the violence she contemplated, the milk-white skin of her throat blotching red and the heartbeat there, tapping from within, visibly quickening. Another step toward him, and when the little barrel of the derringer grazed his shirt between his jacket lapels Dred slowly lifted his left hand in an arc, in one sweep deflecting the gun and holding her wrist away from him. She did not contest him. "I wasn't going to hurt you," she said.

"You're damn right."

"You're a very nice man, a fine man. I was just *showing* how I would do it." She seemed about to cry.

"I want you to let go of the gun now."

But now, surprisingly, her grip tightened on it, she choked back the feeling that was about to make her cry and started babbling. "If only I'd married someone like you, someone who's not all fat and smelly like Todd."

"Just let go of the gun."

She was wildly strong hanging on, but instantly released the derringer when he locked his grip on her wrist with somewhat more force than was really needed. The gun dropped into the sink, splashed into a mixing bowl filled with batter-colored glop.

"Shit, thanks a lot, Tarzan. You men. You always, in the pinch, it's always us against you."

"I didn't come here to fight you, Alexis."

"Yeah, so. That's what it comes down to."

"With Todd, maybe, not me."

"You didn't know about Todd, that he's been holding out on me, the fuckhead. He's been playing the market, did he tell you that?"

"No. I hardly know him."

"That's not what *he* says, he says you're old friends. Didn't he tell you? The fuckhead takes half his pay and buys stock, and Monday he starts selling it off so he can go to Tahiti with his whore. Listen to me, Monday they shut the place down at work, 'cause the computers got all messed up, and the asshole left work and spent the afternoon with the whore and they made a deal, I'm sure that's what they did, because his broker called here late in the day asking for him, and told me the whole thing, he wanted to verify all these sell orders. I played innocent and heard it all. The fuckhead's got almost a hundred thousand in stock and he never told me."

She had moved over to the breakfast table and sat in one of the cereal-and-milk-encrusted chairs. Dred fished the derringer out of the pancake batter glop in the bowl and started to wipe it clean with a paper towel.

"Alexis. You don't have to kill someone to end a relationship."

"C'mon, don't make me laugh."

He wrapped the derringer in a little sandwich bag, stuck it in his pocket. "I know a good divorce lawyer who'll get some of that money back for you, keep you out of jail. Call me when you've thought it over. In the meantime, I'm going to take this with me, if you don't mind. You stick it in someone's chest, the way you did with me, no matter how drunk you are, it's assault with a deadly weapon. Take it easy, I gotta go."

"Maybe I got another. What if I told you there's *five* more where that came from?"

He walked out, leaving behind her unanswerable question and the little juice glass of straight vodka he had poured for himself, planning to toss it in her face if she'd gotten too cute with the derringer. Now, driving away, he wished he'd had at least one good healthy swig, to phase out crazy Alexis and her haunted Chevy wagon, to bolster himself for another bout with the virus at ADC.

North from Bedford to Westville two towns away he found himself on a road clogged with lunchtime traffic and ineptly synchronized signals at a huge suburban mall he'd never heard of. There was no industry out here that wasn't high tech or related to high tech. Even DeMarco's Mobil Station, classic 1930s stucco architecture, sported a very new sign of Saab and BMW logos and proclaiming, for the freshly affluent, *Foreign Car Repairs A Specialty*. DeMarco's offered the only outdoor phone booth on the strip. It was twelve-thirty. Punching double zero, he listened through the three messages from Kevin, Alexis, and Myrtle, heard his own remote call with code, and still nothing else. Still secure. But no word from Kevin on getting Stevie's address from A-1 Temporaries.

Back in the car, headed north. In time the strip petered out into used-furniture stores and mattress outlets, took a few wide turns and became country again with open farmland and woods. Recalling what had just happened with Alexis Shaler, he wondered if with a clear head and enough sleep he might have acted differently and been a better counselor. He imagined that every day, conceivably, a million couples on earth break up, all but a handful without violence. Erica moves out to a riverside farmhouse in Concord. Elaine resumes her splendid North Shore isolation, comforted by family and gin. But Alexis sticks a derringer into Todd's fat tit and blows a hole in his heart, which vents like a whoopee cushion.

Glassheart. Who named the band? Who foresaw hearts breaking like crystal, splintering into slivers of tears? What was Stevie Bear's heartbreak? Leaving Montana at sixteen to wend east, to love and lose who knows how many men? Including a one-nighter with a glossy-haired mimeograph-ink salesman, a quickie payback for the free crash pad in the warehouse that smelled like school? Stevie was Dave Twomey's kind of gal, that's what Myrtle would be wanting to tell him. That's the kind of trouble Stevie allowed to fall, unfiltered, into her life.

What was obviously Sandy Murchison's blocky interoffice envelope lay buried under magazines and other mail on one of three vacant chairs meant for visitors to Betty Ohlmeyer's spacious and handsomely decorated outer office, the prized top-floor corner location at Westville's AI-3, currently command-posted by a sweet, button-nosed redhead named Ginger, or so her nameplate declared.

From his vantage point in an adjoining cubicle, Dred could see that liberating the envelope from this area would be tricky. It would commit him to the hazards of a new strategy that, once seen from the outside, would make him look at least dishonest if not foolish: that he believed the cartridge contained a tractability analysis that might be central to the case—an analysis undertaken by a just-fired, foul-tempered circus fat lady of spurious reputation. And that it would be far better to keep the evidence out of the hands of his client, Betty Ohlmeyer.

Who was already losing faith in him anyway.

ADC had limited his range by charging him with the passive tasks of snooping and advising. To accept what he already knew, they would need hard math to convince them, an ineluctable fence of binary certainty to trap them with their own doubts and force them to confront the embarrassing truth that one of their own, one of their best, was very likely the one who was so cleverly screwing them.

Guarding Betty's closed office door, Ginger was building a small tower of pink slips, on one of those message skewers, while her boss was off somewhere with Burt Cooper, unable to appreciate just how popular a woman she was today, with her entire department (sprawling beneath her in Westville and afar in Cambridge and Framingham) vulnerable to sabotage. Tethered to her duty, Ginger was not likely to wander off and leave Betty's chairful of mail unwatched.

So. On more than one occasion as head bartender at the Port o' Call in Lauderdale-by-the-Sea, because the owner was a stickler for the fine points of the law, Dred had been forced to use novel methods to clear the lounge at its required 2 A.M. closing time. Most effective was the old standby of life-threatening terror, billowing smoke from a normally harmless men's room wastebasket fire made convincing with the addition of grain alcohol and lots of Styrofoam and plastic, followed by the requisite cry of "Fire!" A wastebasket fire as a diversion was stupidly simple, but here in the ultraclean, fastidious environment of a big computer company it would do the trick very nicely, here in this uninhabited cubicle with its computer terminal freshly removed, the desk still home to things the previous owner hadn't bothered to claim. Lots of paper and a handful of virginal floppy disks. A sturdy metal wastebasket.

Matches had to be rescued from a desktop far across the room, one of the last smokers at American Data Corp.

There was just enough distance, and partition insulation, to crumple and arrange the fuel without being heard. But to make certain, he peered around the corner at Ginger on the phone. Sitting in the chair next to the heap of mail was Doug Kiskel. He'd slithered in noiselessly, was scratching out a long note to Betty. With whom, he was explaining to Ginger, he had planned to meet at this time.

The fire would have to wait. Kiskel stood, the top of his head just visible over the wall. He left the note with Ginger and turned to go, his footsteps padding by on the the other side of the partition. Now Dred eyed the target for his match, a loosely rolled column of onion-skin stationery carefully exposed at the bottom of this heap of paper and crumpled floppy disks. He lit the match, found the curl of onion-skin, saw the flame grab it and flare up the column of the roll. Leaving quickly, ducking around the far side of the cubicle, he came swiftly into Ginger's view, wrapped himself in a wide and genuinely happy smile.

"Hi," he said to her. She was just getting off the phone.

"Hello. Sorry, Mrs. Ohlmeyer's not here right now."

"Oh, I thought she was expecting me."

She was poking into the office appointment book. "Your name?"

He could not hear it, see it, smell it. He slurred the name "Gavorkin," and added, "We confirmed yesterday."

"Ga-what?" Ginger asked, her freckly hand reaching behind her ear into her hair and scratching. Dred started sniffing the air.

"Do you smell something?" he asked, not smelling anything.

Ginger sniffed. "No. Like what?"

"Smoke," he said, still not smelling it.

Ginger sniffed, her nostrils twitching rabbitlike, a redheaded bunny face. "Yeah. Something's burning."

Dred still didn't smell it. But, turning around, he saw the first thin haze of evidence lifting over the partition of the cubicle, proof that, indeed, ADC was on fire. Now he smelled it. Boy, she had a good nose.

"Lady, I think we've got a fire here." Come on, damn it, burn, cut loose.

"It's in the cubicle," Ginger said, utterly serene, as if there were no fire at all. Who are these people? Who trains them in common sense? "Let me call security."

"Don't you have an alarm?" he asked. "Security's down on the first floor, it'll take too long."

"Oh, yeah, maybe we should." Now the smoke was thickening, veined with black from the floppy disks, didn't everyone see it? "Where is it?" She was standing up, looking around. "One of those break-the-glass things. That's what we need."

"Ginger," he said, beginning to feign real panic. "This is an emergency. Your company is on fire."

"Yeah, it's getting really thick. I wish I knew what to do."

At last someone else smelled it, saw it, screamed, "Fire!," again and again, and the entire floor began to respond in widening waves of concern, consternation, and finally fear, with the smoke billowing out over half the ceiling and the ADC lemmings spilling out into the corridors. Dred said, "C'mon!" to Ginger and led her to the site of the fire, where some men had gathered and were trying to smother the blaze. Then he quickly doubled back, alone, to the outer office, the chair stacked with mail where he grabbed the bulky interoffice envelope, tucked it into his briefcase, and headed for the elevators.

"Doug. Can I have a word?"

Dred had forgotten that Doug Kiskel was, objectively, a handsome man who would be quite appealing to women, in an unthinking, visceral kind of way. Elaine, for one, would be predictably intrigued. Now there's an interesting-looking man, she'd say, I wonder what his secret is? Light skin, pale hair, and startlingly bright, almost electric blue eyes. A large, powerful man who today was rested, clean-shaven, dressed in jeans and open-necked yellow shirt, with a necktie rolled up in his shirt pocket. The fire and a halfhearted evacuation had come and gone, the virus problem once again was the main topic of chatter in the corridors, and here in a little windowless room on the fourth floor that was his Westville pied-à-terre Doug Kiskel was hardly able to collect enough interest to turn around and look at him.

"Give me a minute," he said, pecking at the keyboard. "I'm a little strung out by all this, between the false alarm and the virus."

"It wasn't a false alarm. There was a real fire." Dred set his briefcase down.

"Really? I wouldn't know. Ray and I, we've made real progress. Sit back, relax, and watch this." With a few flicks on the keyboard his printer whined into action, spitting out two lists of names. "We've found the time and place of the second virus. Heuristic Research Associates—"

"I know, at four this morning," Dred finished for him. "Harvey told me."

"Yes, good. Now a late-breaking addendum is that we've just done the same for the first virus. Same place, HRA, this past Sunday evening at six. What I'm printing out is a list of those people who were signed into HRA at those two times. Look at the names. You should see one that's familiar."

Under the heading *Wednesday 4 A.M.* his own name topped a short alphabetized list.

"The first virus, 'Fuck You,' was sent Sunday at six P.M. The second virus, 'Eat Shit,' was sent Wednesday at four A.M. Both had clever time delays. Now look at the names and see who was there both times."

With a flourish he tore off the printout and handed it to Dred. There were six or seven names on each list. But no repeats.

"Right," said Kiskel, his face now beaming with contempt. "Nobody."

"Unless the person you want didn't sign in."

"Lovely thinking. The *only* person not required to sign in after hours is who? The security guard himself. A security guard who, as luck would have it, worked both shifts on Sunday and Wednesday."

"Interesting."

"I've got to tell you, Balcazar, I've spent a lot of time the last few days trying to get into the guts of the virus and take it apart and figure out how to stop it before it wrecks a lot of important work, including my own. And I've been doing a lot of stupid little things just to keep all hell from breaking loose. But *this* bullshit"—he slapped at the sheet of names in Dred's hand—"this is kindergarten stuff *you* should be doing, not me."

Dred summoned an ounce of fawning sincerity. "Thanks for your help, Doug. This is all very recent news, the HRA connection—you can understand I haven't really had a chance to digest it."

"I've *assumed* that because you were there at that time this morning, you were closing in on this guy. You say that's not the case?"

"Not really, no."

"Well, then, there's no time to waste." All by itself the printer cranked up again, spit out a line or two of text over which Kiskel leaned, blocking it from view. "And Harvey Monahan sends his deepest thanks."

"Harvey?"

"I just sent him this stuff by modem. And he just wrote back."

And now a feeble protest, calculated to sweeten Kiskel's ire. "Doug, I only wish you'd come to me first. Harvey should hear this from me—"

Kiskel cut him off with a derisive snort. "From what *I* hear you've spent the last three days with your jaw down at your knees oohing and aahing over a technology you've been futilely trying to understand, that you will never understand, that we didn't hire you to understand. And all the nontechnical obvious *surface* things that will tell us who this shithead is, all those typical things any gumshoe should know—*we've* been doing that work for you. You're not doing your job. And as a result we're not doing ours."

Kiskel did have a point. He was also extending an invitation for more groveling.

"I'll try to do the best I can. But I'll need as much help as you can give me, especially—"

"With or without my help, maybe you can't do your job, not really, without actually being one of us. I imagine you're looking for someone with motive. That's what Harvey might be expecting from you. Perhaps this security guard has a motive. But perhaps not. If I were in your shoes, I wouldn't be sweating motive."

"Tell me why not."

"Because of what I know that you don't. Listen for a second: in the extensions I'm doing on Miriam, my natural language project, I've incorporated many principles of the mathematics of chaos, which you may have heard about, because that's how natural language *is*, that's how we communicate and act with each other. We communicate in rhythms that suggest repetition, but in fact they're aperiodic—always unique. Forces that unpredictably push and pull, that are themselves driven and restrained. The result is turbulence. I suspect this crime is the work of such a mind. Turbulent in its logic, turbulent in its emotion."

"I have to deal with fundamentals, Doug. And one of them is motive."

"You don't listen, do you? Start thinking that motive is malleable, shaped by convenience. Think of the exhilaration of destruction. Think of getting your name in the paper. Happens all the time, doesn't it? Isn't that motive enough? Just before you walked in I heard a news bulletin on the radio of a murder, right out here in the 'burbs, and the way it was described I suspected there was no real motive there. Nothing that made sense. How different is that kind of senseless crime from, in this case, injecting a virus whose principal command is 'copy me, again and again,' until nothing else is left but *it*, by the millions?"

Kiskel turned his computer off, silver flashing to a point of light, then black. "The exhilaration of destruction fits with the suspect. There's some question about his mental stability."

"This security guard. Do you have his name?"

"Too late, Balcazar. Harvey's on the brink of going to the Attorney General to get a warrant. It'll be front-page news and you'll still be grappling with the obvious."

Dred composed his most convincing scowl. "I saw this guy just eight, ten hours ago." A quick glimpse of the list of names again confirmed that Sandy Murchison was not one of them. Fortunately, she'd slipped in and out of HRA this morning, with Jerry's help, unannounced.

"I suggest you call Harvey," Kiskel was saying, packing papers into his briefcase, preparing to leave. "He may want you to do a background check on this fellow. We already know he came over from another division of ADC, that he was formerly a software engineer of some skill."

"Meaning," Dred continued for him, "he's easily capable of writing a virus program."

"If that isn't the eureka of the day, nothing is. In the meantime this security guard has an eight-to-midnight shift tonight, and I for one don't think he's quite through with us."

Dred cleared his throat and did his best to appear mildly discomfited. "I'm going back to Cambridge," he muttered.

"You first," Kiskel replied, the disquietingly familiar hand on his back, steering him out of the room.

Dred believed that Doug Kiskel would be one elevator trip behind him, sufficient distance not to suffer the company of this slow-witted detective but close enough to watch his movements as he left the building to go to his car. Briefly chatting with the security guard before leaving, Dred confirmed his suspicion, peripherally spotting Kiskel emerging from the elevator and taking a seat by a table with a telephone and a clear view of the parking lot.

Outside, these huge lobby windows were tinted a deep indigo, reflecting forest and fields and the great dairy farm beyond, effectively a one-way mirror for anyone inside. Two dozen steps from the front door was the Subaru. And now, next to it, the robin's-egg blue Volkswagen beetle with Sandy Murchison heaving her enormous attention-getting self out of it.

"Mr. Balcazar." She lit up a cigarette. In her hand was an ADC interoffice envelope identical to the one he now had in his briefcase. "We gotta talk." The smoke mixing with the steam of her breath.

His plan to get to a pay phone temporarily thwarted, Dred moved toward her, making sure he was directly in Kiskel's line of sight, blocking as much of her as possible. But without question Kiskel was watching. "Sandy, someone inside is not happy to see you here—and don't look over my shoulder." She'd just started to.

"Sorry," she said with uncharacteristic civility.

"Is that in fact a tractability analysis?"

"Yes."

"Of Miriam?"

"Yes. Its extensions."

"Showing that it doesn't work?"

"It doesn't compile. Right. I never sent it to Betty. I couldn't."

He did not bother sharing with her his mortification that he'd almost burned the building down to steal the wrong envelope. Observed, they had no choice but to perform for their audience.

She was getting ahead of him. "I changed my mind last night.

Betty Ohlmeyer's not the right person to see this, she wouldn't understand it. But you might."

"Sandy, we're onstage. Can you act?"

"*What?*"

"You've got to pretend you're meeting me for the first time. Shake my hand, look worried."

He extended his hand. At last she took it.

"Hello, shithead," she said.

"Good start, you're very suspicious of me."

"Stevie Bear, Miss Honey Pot, she's mixed up in this, isn't she?"

Dred nodded, said between clenched teeth, "Now show me this envelope, wave it around, gradually start to get mad."

"Jerry thinks she's in trouble. He's right, isn't he?" Good job showing off the envelope, looking angrier.

"I can't say. Now take out the cartridge, tell me how important it is, it's gonna cost me money to see it."

"Mr. Balcazar," she said in a full stage voice, taking out the cartridge clearly marked 3EXT.MRM. "This is really important and it's gonna fucking cost you a million dollars."

"Do not look toward the building. Just at me. Now I'm going to reach for it, and you're going to pull it back." He did, and she withdrew it, holding it to her breast.

"A million bucks!" she said. "Who cares if the girl's in trouble?"

"Hide the thing behind your back, wag your finger at me, give me a hell of a lecture about anything you want, and listen carefully to what I have to say." She shielded the cartridge from him, backed away closer to her car door, wagged her finger at him, repeatedly mouthed, "Fuck you."

"Sandy." He stepped toward her threateningly. "In an hour or so, call my office phone, leave this message on my tape: You've thought it over, you changed your mind, the money I offered is okay, and, yes, you will come to meet me at the Athenaeum tonight at nine. Say it: the Athenaeum tonight at nine."

"The Athenaeum tonight at nine. That's that library on Beacon Hill."

"Right. Nine o'clock, Athenaeum. In reality, you won't come. Important not to come, okay? Also important that you stay away from your house for the rest of the day, just to be sure, okay? Okay. Now you can lecture me. Give me what for."

"It's Doug Kiskel who's watching?" she asked.

He nodded. "No more questions, lecture me."

"You sonofabitch working for these imperialist capitalist fart-breath greedmongers, you can't come up with a shitty million bucks to get proof that one of your own people is wrecking your software? Jesus Christ, Balcazar, you're a cheap bastard and you know what?"

"Good—keep it up," he said.

"Imperialist fascists . . . " She squinted past him, toward the building, shook her head. "Damn, we gotta talk—"

"No, keep the pressure on—"

"Look, Jerry had it figured out. That prick in there, he must be the one that hit on Stevie. Jerry said Stevie met some other guy at ADC. Who came to see the band. Jerry said he'd seen him some-where before, he was an ADC guy. *Him*. Jesus! So it's the same old—the same century-old shit, it's a woman." Her words hung in the cold wind. "That's what it comes down to: another woman drives another man nuts." The vapor from her breath dissipated as she started to turn away, jamming the cartridge back into its envelope.

"Sandy. Wait." She turned back. Her eyes had welled up, about to cry. "Please, hold up the envelope one more time, and make like a phone call, with your thumb and little finger to your face, like you're going to call me."

Slowly, resolutely she did as he asked, mimed making a phone call, receiver to her cheek.

"Is that it?" she whispered.

"That's it. Stay away from home. Thank you."

"So tell me sometime what this bullshit's all about." She turned and struggled into the car, which groaned with the impact of her heft. Dred waited for her to leave, threw up his hands in mock de-spair, chanced a glimpse back at the inky glass of the lobby win-dows and was quite certain he perceived Kiskel looking at him and now turning away.

Forty minutes later Dred dashed through the outer lobby of ADC in Cambridge, card-keyed himself through the glass doors, and almost collided with Harvey Monahan on his way out.

"Harvey!"

Harvey was equally harassed, frantic, in no mood for trifles.

"Dred, we're way ahead of you. Not that it's your fault—"

"I need ten minutes of your time, that's all."

"No go. I've got a three o'clock meeting at the Attorney General's office and I'm already late."

"Five minutes."

Harvey didn't want to bargain. Dred was on his tail coming back into the lobby. "Ray, Doug, and I—we found what we need. Guy I'm meeting is John Medeiros, he's the assistant A.G., and he says he can get a warrant right away. I can't be late." John Medeiros was a familiar name, a friend of Frank Cirione, old war-horses from somewhere back in time.

"Two minutes. Please."

He stopped before reaching the main entrance, must have seen the urgency in his face. "Jesus. What the hell. Let's go back inside. Two minutes is all I've got."

Past the elevators they found an alcove which was home to a large display, apparently describing what artificial intelligence was and how it worked at ADC. Dred had not seen this before.

"So am I after the wrong guy?"

"Harvey, there are too many inconsistencies. Kiskel sent you names of people who were inside HRA at four this morning."

"Right. That's why—"

"And I'm at the top of the list."

"Yeah, I noticed. I thought, what the *hell* is Dred Balcazar—"

"Harvey, I was on the seventh floor in *that* corner"—he spun and pointed through the window at the building across the street—"and at four in the morning the IR transceiver was totally blocked by window-washing equipment. *All night long* it was blocked. There were no transmissions between the two buildings at all, all night long. I saw it, and we can check with maintenance to back me up."

"Hold on. It could've been sent by phone, very easily."

"Talk to Ray about that. Doug and Ray got routing information on the virus, and they both insist it was via infrared, on the network. They're *certain*."

Harvey was processing this information. It made him unhappy.

"You're sure about the window-washing stuff?"

"Totally, completely, absolutely."

"Damn. Suddenly I don't get it."

"Part Two," Dred continued, "because I'm short of time. Tonight I'm acquiring total absolute proof that Miriam doesn't work. That it's intractable."

Harvey squinted at him quizzically.

"Mathematical, *binary* proof. Miriam cannot be compiled."

Harvey lowered his face into his hands and rubbed his eyes. "You've learned the lingo, haven't you."

"Enough. I had to."

"This is from Sandy Murchison?"

"Maybe."

"All right, details later. And you think Kiskel's part of this?"

"Possibly, yes."

"And I don't have enough on this Jerry DiGiacomo for a warrant?"

Down the corridor through the glass doors in the lobby someone seemed to be waving at him. "My two minutes are up, Harvey. And I think I see my partner." Baggy overalls, motorcycle jacket, ponytail and earrings and all, Kevin Ryan was grinning ear to ear with each hand raised high and holding something small, clear plastic. Ziploc bags.

Dred mimed picking lint off his jacket—the thread samples? Yes, Kevin nodded, then wiggled them like little fish, spread them apart and with a firm shake of his head indicated *no*. Not the same. They're different.

"Dred, I'm asking you: I go to John Medeiros, suddenly I don't have enough for a warrant?"

"You've got enough for a warrant, but it won't hold up."

"That's a 'no,' I take it."

Kevin was pacing; beyond him was Moby, hugely conspicuous by the front door, illegally parked. "I'm telling you, the evidence is still coming in."

"Okay, I'll call and cancel," Harvey said with weary resignation. "Jesus, I was driving in the last nail."

"If you can be free at eight o'clock tonight, it would be a big help."

"Eight o'clock tonight. Where?"

"Boston Athenaeum, on Beacon Street. I'll call you with the details, as soon as I figure out what they are. Medeiros should be there too."

He finally pushed out the magic word: "Okay."

"Great. I'll call you."

Dred cut past him, burst out into the lobby to greet Kevin.

"I had to track you down. Sure as hell I'm not going to talk to your tape. Can we go outside, have some privacy?"

In a moment Dred was settled in Moby's front seat. Kevin had the engine running and the heater on. He passed over the two thread samples in their bags, which he'd marked in red pen *A* and *B*.

"To the eye they're the same, but the spectrographic thing says they're not. And this ain't the police lab, this is from the fabulous Dr. Hofstedder and his high-tech basement."

"I don't know him, Kev."

"In time, my son, in time. Anything to do with fabric, he's very very good, and if you're in the crunch he'll blow off everything else to do your job. Which is what happened. I said, this has got to be quick. He said fine. He says they're the same rayon-polyester blend, but the colors are different. Just a *hair*. They're both Kelly green but one's a little more Kelly green than the other. *A* is the one you already had in a bag. *B*'s the one you had wrapped around the toothpick."

"*B* is off a Celtics jacket," Dred told him.

"Well, maybe *A* is, too. A different jacket, a different manufacturer, hell, maybe just a different dye lot. *Definitely* a different jacket. You have any idea how many Celtics warm-up jackets there are in this town?"

"Don't want to think. If they're different, that's all I need."

"Yeah, fine. Unless this guy has a whole closet full of them."

"Kev, I need to assume he doesn't. Somewhere I've got to make some assumptions. I don't see DiGiacomo as a collector of Celtics jackets."

"Yeah, well, *assume* makes an ass out of you and me, right? The main thing you want to know is, sample *A* is from the jacket that broke into your apartment Thursday night. Sample *B* isn't."

"Right."

"Okay, now you wanna go over some other things? You look beat."

"I'm nuts," Dred agreed.

Kevin slipped him a folded piece of paper: A-1 Temporaries letterhead. "You can thank Sheila for this," Kevin was saying. Handwritten on it was the phone number, and the address: 15 Horton St., Somerville, Apt. #1. "She strolled right in with some cockamamy story—"

The elation he felt was both thrilling and numbing. This was the best piece of news in a week.

"—so right after my trip to Hofstedder's lab I cruised right over, scoped it out, it's a first-floor apartment and it's got the name Bernstein on the door, but inside in the living room I saw a guitar case and an amplifier. So I did a CNA on the number and it's Rachel Bernstein, no listing for Stevie Bear. I figure Bernstein's the roommate. Then, on a wild hunch that Stevie found this place through a friend at work, I called A-1 back again, and sure enough they employ a Rachel Bernstein, and she's on vacation this week down in the Caribbean."

"Great work, Kev. Unbelievable."

"Yeah, here's the best part. While I'm on the phone with A-1, down the street walks someone wearing a scarf I *know* I've seen before, I didn't get a look at her face, but I know that scarf and I thought, shit, she's back. Carrying groceries. Blue-and-white scarf."

9

He was prepared to explain every last detail of the tortuous path he'd followed to find her here, how it all started six days earlier when he noticed calluses on the fingertips of her very lovely left hand—the index finger of which she now held to her lips: shh, don't talk, don't explain. The paragraph he'd prepared would for the time remain his secret.

She was just a little surprised to see him. Surprise became her—as did his blue-and-white scarf, tucked under her lovely blond hair. Removing the scarf from her neck and placing it around his own, he inspected the faint purple line that, with raised chin, she allowed him to see.

The radiators were banging and hissing, but the house was very cold. In the front hall she pulled him close enough to hear her feeblest whisper, "No talk. I think it's bugged," and he almost kissed her but refrained as she turned away into the living room, going to the stereo, fishing through a stack of cassette tapes. On a small table in the front hall were her wallet, airline ticket carbons, two keys on a chain, chewing gum, a travel-worn pack of cigarettes. The tickets were round trip, Boston-Pittsburgh-Toledo, leaving early Sunday morning and returning at 1 P.M. today. She was watching him, signaling yes, it was okay to look at these things, a shrug of her shoulders as if he could not be blamed for needing proof that, for once, was unequivocal. The airfare was very cheap, clearly some sort of Supersaver ticket bought well in advance.

Derek and the Dominoes' "Layla" erupted on the stereo.

Also, an in-flight magazine, and under it a self-mailing parking ticket. Tuesday 10 A.M. in Toledo, Ohio, registered car, the violation coded as blocking a fire hydrant, $25. "Laylah."

She came over to him, flashed her middle finger at the parking ticket, then grabbed him by the scarf and pulled him down the length of the hall into the bathroom, closing the door behind them and leaning into the shower to turn on the faucets. She peeled off her navy blue sweatshirt. Under it she wore a candy-stripe snug-fitting cotton shirt that flattered her breasts. She kicked off her running shoes, threw one arm around his neck, and pulled his ear to her mouth.

"I'm filthy from the trip. Gotta have a shower. Need a shower?"

He shook his head. The tips of her breasts under this soft cotton grazed him, now pressing into the rough, stiff tweed of his jacket. "That's twice that you've run off on me."

"You didn't call the police?"

He shook his head again.

"I love you, T. D. I really missed you. And I'm sorry you don't trust me." She began working at the buckle of her belt, but he took her hand and held it, their fingers intertwining between them.

"Why do you think you're bugged?"

"My phone sounds funny. I'm tired of being careless."

The shower steamed with too much hot water, fogging the air; droplets beaded in her hair, her eyebrows, a drop condensed on the bridge of her nose and trickled onto her cheek, a vagrant tear coming to rest in the fine, thin fuzz above her lip. He kissed her there, then slowly released his fingers from her hand and stepped aside, inviting from her a look of amazement—he would let this moment get away?

He tapped his wrist: it's getting late. He pulled back the shower curtain and turned the water off.

They drove in the Subaru toward Beacon Hill. She had readily accepted his belief that she would be safer elsewhere, but once they'd driven out of the neighborhood she'd become increasingly wary of his questions. He fell silent, permitting her all the time she wanted to speak. At last she did, of Tom, and Toledo, and coming to Boston last spring.

"I imagined myself being kidnapped," she said. "This nice sweet boy whisking me away, against my will. Change my name, erase the memory tape, undress my ego. That's the fantasy I had, that's what Tom could do for me. But he was too childish and sweet, and then I had Jerry come along to kidnap me from Tom."

She herself looked childish and sweet, with rose-tinted sunglasses and a suede jacket he hadn't seen before, smoke-colored and with its collar up, and around her head a colorfully striped taffeta scarf.

"And who did you ask to kidnap you from Jerry?"

She was quiet. "You know as much as you need to."

"Somebody hurt you, damn it."

"It's over, it doesn't matter."

"Tell me sometime about this thing you have with the police." Her dad the cop, leaving when she was six.

"Maybe. Sometime," she said.

"You can't tell me who he is?"

"As long as I'm not sure about everything, I made a promise."

"Damn! Stevie, you gave him *everything*."

"A little help, that's all."

"Right—to distract me, get me out of my apartment."

"T. D., I was told you'd made videotapes that had something to do with spying, industrial espionage. I believed it. That's why I did what I did. I was a little gullible, but it didn't matter because it was the last favor I was ever going to do."

"For him. You can say it."

"Okay. *For him*. I blew it."

Over the bridge by the Museum of Science traffic was thickening going into the city. Stop-and-go, and it wasn't yet four o'clock. Stevie was biting her lip, already weary of the interrogation. The guy almost kills her and she can't say his name, says it doesn't matter, consigns it all to the accumulating garbage of past mistakes. She confesses her fantasy of kidnap, which seems more a harsh word for rescue, fails to anticipate how rough, with a guy like Doug Kiskel, rescue can be.

"I made a mistake. You don't have to ask me any more questions."

"All right," he said softly. "For now."

He remembered now her keen interest, Thursday at dinner, in whether he'd ever used a video camera. He'd said no, absolutely not. It was the last fragment of conversation before Elaine's phone call, when, as Lauren Michaelec, she had so abruptly walked out. True, she was right, for the time being he didn't have to ask more questions. Elaine's call hadn't scared her away; it was the sudden knowledge that Kiskel had lied to her. Knowledge that scared her right out of the Oyster House.

No more questions. Except, what was it that drew her to Kiskel in the first place? That he was another in a parade of men who told her how wonderful she was? Who was fascinated by her? Whose affection might become obsessive, attraction at its most dangerous—and, conceivably for her, its most beguiling?

"You are different, T. D. From other men."

"I hope so," he said immediately, picturing the other men she had known, and immediately regretting the arrogance implicit in his reply.

"I've been very careless."

"Stevie, don't apologize, not to me." He was thinking now of Kevin's warning: assume makes an ass of you and me, it was very possible Jerry DiGiacomo could own more than one Celtics warm-up jacket from different manufacturers or with different dye lots.

From that moment in the parking lot when Harvey Monahan had declared that Kiskel and Niles had fixed the origin of the virus at HRA at four in the morning, Jerry DiGiacomo and his alibi for Saturday night had become a non-issue. Niles had *insisted* that the infrared transceivers were the only way to communicate between HRA and AI-5, the only way computers could send their little packets back and forth over the network. But those times when Kiskel had manipulated him, Niles had been wrong; could he also be wrong about the infrared business? One of ADC's top knowledge engineers, *wrong* about something so basic and mechanically straightforward?

Nothing was ever absolutely certain in the computer business. They'd said it several times—one approaches perfection but never can be known to achieve it. If Niles was wrong about the infrared, Kiskel could actually be innocent. His odious performance right after the wastebasket fire, his furtive window-seat view of the parking lot charade with Sandy Murchison—neither had any solid evidentiary use. Kiskel had, in fact, initially waved a finger of suspicion at Niles himself.

Certain of nothing, Dred negotiated the back streets of Beacon Hill.

"It's pretty up here," Stevie said, her cheek against the glass.

"Yes."

"I'd like to live here someday."

He turned onto Willow Street and into his parking place.

"Or maybe in the country—"

"Please stop." He killed the engine, turned to her. "Stevie. Don't fuck around. You've got no idea how I've been trying to help you."

She stared straight ahead through the window.

"The guy who broke in Thursday night stole my computer. He returned it Monday night with a death threat. Against you. He said if I didn't back off the ADC case he wouldn't mess up the way he did Saturday night."

The smallest tic at the corner of her mouth. "Guess I'm not surprised."

"Saturday night or not, I'd still take this very seriously. I've busted my balls for you, I've played beat the clock for the last three days trying to find out who you are and what the hell's going on before you got back, and as you can see I just barely made it. And nobody knows about you, not the police, not my client, not my ex-girlfriend—"

"Just you."

"Just me. And my two partners."

She frowned.

"They're with me on this. They have short memories."

She turned to him. "I'm sorry."

"Let's go inside. I've got a lot of work to do." He grabbed his briefcase from the backseat, they got out of the car and turned the corner up Willow toward Acorn Lane. She surprised him by tucking her hand under his arm.

"I can explain some of this, okay? My sister in Toledo. This is her third marriage. She's lived in about a dozen states. She marries men who like to move around. I told her, and we talked about it a lot, I want to get out of Boston. I told her, it's too much and I can't deal with it. And I told her about you. That you'd saved my life, but more important that you were a good guy. Just a good guy."

"Thanks." A trace of acid in his voice.

"My plan was to come back, get my shit and leave, go back to Toledo, then take it from there. Sis said, Stevie, you were sixteen and you left Montana. You went to Kentucky, then California, then Texas, then Ohio, then Boston, and if you can't hack it in Boston you can't hack it at all. Here's my crazy gypsy sister who's got no moss growing on her, I'll tell you, she sells houses like a realtor, and she says stick it out, stay put. Coming into Logan, I looked down on Beacon Hill with all that red brick and I thought maybe I saw your house. Right here."

On the front steps, he opened the door and ushered her in.

"And I had this picture of you way down below in this house, and I knew you'd be waiting at the other end. I mean, I really do like you."

"Fine, I appreciate it. Except that you've been no help at all." He dumped the briefcase on the Parsons bench, draped his overcoat over the back, and started upstairs. She followed.

"T. D., believe me, it wasn't till we landed that I knew the right thing to do was to call you. Sorry, I could've called from Ohio, but I was gonna blow the whole thing off and leave town. I just changed my mind like an hour or two ago, in the landing pattern."

At the top of the stairs he turned, saw her plaintively looking up at him from two steps below. "You *called* me?"

"Yeah, from the airport. You didn't get the message?"

"No."

"How'd you ever in a blue moon find my house? *Damn*."

He tossed his tweed jacket on the living room couch and was instantly in the office fast forwarding over the old messages from Kevin, Alexis, and Myrtle, until he found Stevie's voice: "Hi, it's me. You probably want your scarf back, right? Okay. So I'm not really Lauren, but I'll explain when I see you. I just got in, I'm at Logan, it's about one o'clock and I'm getting a cab home right now. I want to see you, okay? And I promise I won't run out on you this time. So come on by to 15 Horton Street in Somerville, on the first floor. I can give you directions if you call." And the phone number that A-1 Temporaries had so assiduously guarded.

"Christ," he said. "How simple it can be."

She'd come in behind him. "How'd you ever find me? I don't exist in this town."

"Later." There was another message following, from Sandy Murchison.

"Hello, Mr. Balcazar. This is Sandy." As he might have expected, in her most lugubrious voice. "It's about two o'clock Wednesday. I've thought it over and I've decided to accept your terms. As you suggested, I'll meet you tonight at the Athenaeum at nine o'clock. And I'll have the tractability analysis with me. Thank you. I will see you then." Very fine job. Dred sincerely hoped, as they'd planned, that she didn't mean what she'd said.

"Sandy. I met a Sandy who sounds just like that, like she's always going to a funeral."

"Stevie, wait."

Following her hang-up, the few seconds of dead air and a dial tone, another call came in.

Two beeps: double zero.

Whoever he was, he'd finally done his duty and called to take messages. He knew she was back, he knew where she lived, he knew she was still in touch with Dred Balcazar.

"What's the analysis thing she said? Is that computers?"

"Take a load off, Stevie. Tour the house, read a book, make a drink, put your feet up, and if someone's at the door let me answer it. I've got some work to do before we go to the library."

Better if he hadn't extended such a broadly worded invitation to make herself at home. While he telephoned Kevin and Harvey Monahan and then John Medeiros at the Criminal Bureau of the Attorney General's Office, Stevie raided the bar, toasted him with vodka on ice for his sleuthing skills, downed it quickly and made another, became ever more the mischievous child. He could hear her prowling all over the house, from upstairs in the living room, downstairs to his bedroom and the guest room crammed with Elaine's junk, as she poked through all his things and at one point presented herself in his office sporting his old black Stetson hat, which looked very good on her considering it must have been two sizes too large, drawstring snug under her chin. She strutted off and plinked something out on the piano, took out his guitar and tuned it for him, brought him a freshly poured beer which he had to decline under the circumstances, explored his books and his record collection, came back and kissed him on the top of his head as he finished his final phone call.

"I feel wonderful being here."

"It's library hour," he said, picking up his briefcase. "Let's go."

With the black Stetson, sunglasses, and taffeta scarf bunched around her neck she was not recognizable to the guard as last week's Lauren Michaelec. Dred cheerfully signed her in as his cousin Eliza Balcazar from Houston, taking a tour of the nation's most redoubtable private library. It was five-thirty, a half hour before its usual closing, but tonight, with the Walt Whitman lecture at eight o'clock, the front doors would remain open throughout the evening.

In the grand lobby he glanced upward to the balcony and the row of office doors separated by bookshelves, these elements approximately configured as he recalled them. The plan would work only if he could obtain the use of two adjoining offices on the mezzanine level, overlooking the grand lobby floor. From about eight till nine. With just a little arm-twisting, John should help clear the way.

"John Brewster?" said a sharp-nosed young woman at the circulation desk whom Stevie was watching with curiosity. "He's hosting the Whitman lecture, I believe. He shouldn't be here till seven-thirty or so, I don't imagine."

Brewster. A last name was finally delivered to him.

"Anything I can help you with?"

He remembered that in the corner at the end of the row of offices was the Children's Reading Room. "I need to speak with that attractive young black woman who reads the children's books."

Stevie had her fingers around his arm, squeezing into the bicep at the word "attractive."

"Yes," said the sharp-nosed woman with a hint of disapproval, "that would be Kari Collins. They should just be finishing up by now."

"Thanks."

"I'm lost," said Stevie when they had stepped away toward the staircase under the balcony. "And I'm not in the mood for Dick and Jane."

He drew her out of sight into the stacks. "I've got to make a few arrangements. It would be better if I did this alone, okay?"

"All right."

"I'll meet you in a few minutes. Fifth floor?"

"Same place?"

"Same place."

She nodded, smiled. "I'll save you a seat. I'll save you the whole floor."

She took the elevator, and he took the stairs to the balcony, walked its full length to the Children's Room; there were just three little kids, kindergarten age, he guessed, listening with rapt attention to a story from this very thin young black woman, hair in cornrows, lacy ivory-colored blouse. Next to the Children's Room was an office, its door ajar. This was hers, he thought, with the Alvin Ailey poster on the wall. He set his briefcase down and leaned into the

Children's Room to catch her eye. When she looked up he pointed to her office, signaled that he wanted to talk, but no hurry. Although they'd never really met, she smiled and mouthed an "okay," then continued her story, about Jody discovering she was lost and alone, starting to cry.

Jody, it happened, was a kitten and her mother eventually came back and found her and all ended well, but the story had dragged on in long, painfully slow syllables with Kari supplying sound effects of wind and finger motions of rain. Three mothers had gathered in the grand lobby below, checking their watches impatiently. At last Jody was safe, the storm was over, and the three toddlers tumbled out of the room and dashed along the balcony toward the stairs.

Dred introduced himself to Kari, who took his hand and apologized for running late.

"Do I have your child?" she asked, escorting him into her office.

"No, it's something else. I'm a reader here and I need a special favor. John Brewster suggested I talk to you." Posters of dragons and princesses, dinosaurs and Muppets. "I need to conduct a confidential interview tonight, and the room I'd reserved just fell through. My hope was to use a room just like this, close to the lobby, and I was wondering if it might be free. Just for an hour or so, from eight to nine."

Kari examined his face with a stern intensity that alarmed him. She must have seen that he was exhausted, the circles under his eyes, the odor of a long day of unrelieved tension. She must have been thinking: "Who is this guy and what does he really want?"

At last she consented with a smile. "Fine. It's a little messy . . ."

"It's perfect," he said.

"Okay. The key will be here on the desk, and the door open. Just leave the key at the circulation desk when you're done."

The office looked to be of fairly recent drywall construction.

"Thanks a lot."

She straightened some papers, cleared an area around the telephone. "If you need to make local calls, this is a direct line. Help yourself."

"Thank you, Kari, this is a big help." Occasionally it happens this way, he thought. A complete stranger trusts another complete stranger. Now for the hard part: "The next room over. Any chance that's available, too?"

Puzzled, she arched her eyebrows.

"See, I may have more than one person coming, and I'm thinking about a place for him to wait."

She laughed gustily as she reached for her coat hanging on the back of the door. "Well, if he doesn't mind waiting in the bathroom—it's always unlocked."

As soon as she said good-bye he ducked into the bathroom, a tidy lavatory with toilet and sink and mirrored medicine cabinet recessed into the wall between studs, its back panel presumably snug against the inner wall of Kari's office. He would need to test the acoustics, but with its door opened the medicine cabinet should act something like a crude loudspeaker for conversations in the adjacent office.

He retrieved his briefcase from the entrance to the Children's Room and took the elevator to the fifth floor, walked across the dimly lit main reading room, completely abandoned, to the narrow staircase leading up into the stacks to the balcony alcove where Stevie should have been, and wasn't. From his perch on the table, George Bernard Shaw surveyed the scene in splendid isolation.

The enormous Goethe anthology, incredibly, was still splayed out on the floor by the chair where she had dumped it that Monday afternoon. The three issues of *American Science* remained neatly stacked on the table. No one had been here in ten days.

The thick green leather of "his" chair, where he had first seen her, was cool to the touch, unvisited.

She had entered the elevator from the grand lobby, that was for sure. But in the twenty minutes or so since then she could have taken herself just about anywhere. Was she exploring another floor of the library, just to kill time? Was she looking for him? Or had she changed her mind, *again*, and just disappeared?

Dred vowed that, when all this was over, he would treat himself to a full week of not worrying about what some woman might or might not be thinking.

He decided on a cursory tour of all five floors of the Athenaeum.

If she was even remotely interested in meeting up with him, she'd want to be in plain sight somewhere.

He turned away from the alcove to head back into the stacks. Just before the first row of shelves was a dark corner of space he'd never noticed before, a heavy oak door slightly ajar. A thin ribbon of weak light coming through from a faraway source. An attic, or storage room of some kind.

Setting down his briefcase in the hall, he stepped toward the door and called her name in a whisper. No response. He eased the door wider, reached around the corner for a wall switch, found none, and now pushed the door all the way open and moved into the room.

He thought he heard movement nearby, was about to call out her name when something jabbed him in the small of his back.

"If you value your kidneys, don't move." Stevie. "Hands out in front, like a sleepwalker. Two steps forward."

She jabbed him again and steered him out into a long hallway toward a distant ceiling light. Shelves on either side piled with boxes, books and magazines, busts and vases.

"You're a clever guy, T. D., but you leave your stuff just lying around. I got this out of your briefcase downstairs on your bench."

The derringer, from Alexis Shaler.

"This is very unlike you, Stevie."

"Fat lot *you* know," she said. Also unlike her was this lapse into a broader, twangier Western accent.

"There's only one round in that gun, and it probably wouldn't kill me."

"Hurt a lot, wouldn't it?"

"That it would."

"Keep walking."

He did. He also, as a test, slowly lowered his arms.

"Keep 'em up!"

"Stevie, you know I'm not armed."

"Yeah, but you're sneaky quick. Stick 'em up!"

He did. Of all the configurations of guilt he'd imagined, none had involved her—beyond her unwitting complicity the previous week. He still wasn't convinced.

"I thought I had it sorted out."

"Yeah, well, think again, smart boy." And then she giggled. "Golly, this is the tiniest damn gun."

"It's a riot, isn't it?"

She recovered quickly and snarled at him: "Over here. Be quick about it." Cutting through the shelves, they came to a clear space on the floor, fenced in with stacked boxes, a huge slab of thick orange-colored foam rubber in the middle.

"You probably think you know this library, don't you? Come here every week, you *should*." Another hard jab with the barrel of the derringer. "Well, I'm an outlaw, and I'm naturally inquisitive, and when I was in my other character last week I tailed that faggy guy at the desk when he took a break, and I followed him right up here, and darned if that beak-nosed girl who's down at the desk right now wasn't up here waiting for him, just ripping her clothes off. I sneaked in to verify my suspicion and they never saw me. So this is it. This is the official Athenaeum copulatorium."

"And?" he asked, slowly turning around, lowering his hands.

"There've been too goddamn many interruptions. Sometimes it takes a little cold steel to make a point." The derringer was on safety, chamber empty, she tossed it into a box of old magazines and threw a headlock on him. Empowered by sheer determination, she successfully wrestled him to the floor.

She'd also filched his vintage World War I leather-sheathed hip flask from the kitchen, topped it off with vodka, and pretty much emptied it by the time they left the Athenaeum to return, arms around waists, to Acorn Lane. He had one small swig himself, to toast the pure raw nerve of her performance. He felt wildly unabashedly happy with her, relaxed and peaceful. She was crazy, but he loved it. She rested her head against his shoulder as they walked, the black Stetson hanging behind her neck.

"I had you dead to rights, T. D. No *way* you were gonna walk past that door—either you were coming in or I was gonna ambush you. You were gone so *long*, I thought, oops, there's a problem.

The more time I had, the more I could rehearse. I also knew, Jesus, as soon as I stick this thing in his back, he's gonna whale me with an elbow and knock my front teeth out, so I had every muscle tensed to jump back about six feet if you turned on me. But somehow I figured you wouldn't."

"I think I was too scared to try anything."

"Shit, you were not," she said. "You were cool as a cuke. Or maybe in shock."

"In shock."

"I don't think I had you completely fooled, though."

"Close enough, kiddo. Pretty good acting job. Once again."

"Sure. When I lived in California I took classes."

The only drag on his mood was the briefcase, light in his hand but otherwise a deadweight against his euphoria. Sliding around inside it was the interoffice envelope, as yet unclasped, containing the twenty-megabyte cartridge from Betty Ohlmeyer's office—the cartridge that was not Sandy's tractability analysis. Clunking around with it was the derringer minus its single hollow point round. He thought carefully of these things, began to anticipate different ways the evening could turn out. Clinging to him, Stevie was cheerfully engaging in a one-woman debate on the role of alcohol in her behavior, concluding that, without it, she might not have had the gumption to use the gun to subdue him. Sober, she most likely would have jumped him and tried to overpower him, using what she conceded was her God-given "considerable physical strength."

The remark brought him out of his thoughts and he happily pulled her very close. They turned onto Walnut Street, zigzagging into the neighborhood. Lamplight washed over her, darkening and brightening as they moved along, the light playing tricks of color in her hair and on her skin. In a pool of light they stopped, and she grinned at him wickedly.

"You thinking the same thing?"

Her skin was still flushed from their attic encounter, the most wonderful experience with a woman ever in his life. To think the same thing, and do it again: they had curled completely into each other, her mouth all over his neck, collarbones, and chest, her pleasure revealed in squeaks and whimpers. His mouth played with her hair and her ear, the golden fuzz at her temple and the hard line of her jaw, his tongue wanted to lick the down from her cheek and the color from her left eye, see through its smokiness, its vitreous mask. She was so strong! And so clever, like a dancer, with the rhythms of her muscles urging him to dance the same dance. It was easy to be perfect with her, effortless to love her.

"You are, aren't you?"

"Yes."

"But you're on the rebound, don't forget."

"Hell, no," he said, "it's been a very long time."

"I need to be careful with you."

Careful! She'd wanted to pull it all out of him in a rush of triumph, as if she believed he'd stored his whole life for this moment, her fingers kneading the backs of his thighs to draw him more closely in. But he'd thought *bluefish*, and fooled her, wanting to love her in his own time, whispering in her ear *easy*, feeling the little nod of her head, her body slowing.

"Stevie." He watched her lower her eyes. "Don't make me nuts, not tonight."

"And the same to you," she said with a weak smile. "Maybe better that we don't."

His eyes probed the subtle curl of her mouth, her hair, her throat, and he suddenly reacted to the smallest twinge of concern for her, a galvanic charge racing to his fingers.

"Hey," he said.

"What?"

There was nothing wrong here, not really, but she was wearing his Stetson off her head and the drawstring looked not entirely comfortable around the base of her neck, an ounce or two too tight, creasing and reddening the skin. Higher on her neck, under her jaw, she still bore the evidence of Saturday night's attack. His heart quickened; illogically but decisively he took the hat and lifted the drawstring over her head.

"Hey, that's mine for the night," she protested.

"People don't wear cowboy hats on Beacon Hill."

"I'm a guest."

"A dangerous guest at that."

"Hey, c'mon! You're the guy who keeps guns lying around."

"You're the one who used it."

"Little dinky thing with no bullet in it."

"What'd you do with the bullet?"

"Chucked it off into your neighbor's bushes. Hope you didn't need it."

"If I ever do, I'm changing jobs."

"Then why do you have it?"

"It's not mine. It's registered to somebody else."

"Oh," she said. He took her arm and urged her more quickly to his house. He decided then and there that if there was to be any future for them at all, he would have to explain what he fervently hoped was about to transpire tonight at the Athenaeum.

Using the last of his wood stored in the pantry, he built a large fire, which now flared and crackled in front of her while she rocked lazily in his Hitchcock rocker and sipped a mug of strong tea. He'd started out gently, with a very general description of his investigation into the virus attacks at ADC, but soon he was using names—Harvey Monahan, Ray Niles, Betty Ohlmeyer, Doug Kiskel, Sandy Murchison—with no telltale signs that she recognized any of them, except Sandy, whom she'd met somewhere before but couldn't remember where.

He expounded on artificial intelligence, liberally tossing around the jargon with no attempt to explain it. When he mentioned knowledge engineers she wanted him to stop.

"Do we have an understanding?" she asked. "I thought we did."

"Well, I think we do, if it's this: you have a pact with this guy and you feel you can't get out of it. Even though he seems to want you dead."

"The understanding is, I'm just not *sure*. Damn, I wish I was."

"Stevie, I've thought it out, and you *have* to know: he was wrestling with you, he was all over you, you could *feel* him, you could smell him."

She shook her head, denial that was too adamant. "If I knew for *sure*, believe me, I'd be the first one to—" She cut herself off, drank her tea. She just didn't like talking about it.

"Okay, this is my first big case, we won't talk about him, we'll talk about Joe." He pulled the fire bench over and sat facing her, thought carefully how to reveal just the right amount of information. "Joe is very smart. He's a software guy. He's created this enormously complex artificial intelligence software that some of his colleagues believe just doesn't work. Joe needs to present it all at this huge convention in Washington in April. If it doesn't work, he looks like an asshole. Joe creates a virus. He makes the virus do square dances around all his company's software for three days, just to show off. But Joe really has it programmed so it'll actually trash his own work." Programmed also, he now imagined, to instruct the main computer not to make backups of his daily work on it, for several days in a row.

Very softly she said, "Joe's pretty strange."

"Yes, but his plan makes a certain amount of sense, if you can imagine it's like a form of suicide." He let the word hang in the air before continuing. "Now. One of his colleagues puts together a computer analysis of his software, proving in cold mathematical terms that Joe's work is a flop." He considered showing her the ADC interoffice envelope with the wrong cartridge in it. But it was in his briefcase, downstairs on the Parsons bench. Unlatched. "Another thing: Joe also figures out how to intercept my phone messages. He hears a message from this colleague saying she'll meet me at the Athenaeum to give me this evidence, tonight at nine. And he also hears *your* message, when you called me from the airport."

At last she made eye contact with him.

"Stevie. If Joe's the guy you've become entangled with, he knows you're back in town, and now he knows your current address. If he didn't know before." Which he probably did.

"This isn't fair," she said, her face scrunching a little.

"Look, kiddo, I think maybe Joe will pop into the Athenaeum tonight. To try to mess things up— as innocently as he can. He's very shrewd that way. He *has* to be innocent, because he's been dropping a lot of evidence to frame somebody else. Thursday night. Thursday night he left traces of fabric in the kitchen. Green polyester. Kelly green. *Celtics* green—a virtual perfect match to a Celtics jacket. You may know someone who likes to wear Celtics jackets."

Of course she did. But he hated pulling this kind of rank on her, hinting that he knew more about her than he'd said.

"Stay with me. Saturday night, while I was trying to bust through the wall, you were in a wrestling match with this guy who could've dispensed with you a lot faster than he did. He had a chance to use one of my own kitchen knives, but he didn't, and he could've killed you with his hands, but he didn't. He imported his own weapon—not rope or a necktie or anything so pedestrian as that, but electrical cable, the kind you'd find in a recording studio or a rock and roll place. There's more. This guy also arranged for the virus programs to *appear* to have been sent from an ADC building at times when a certain security guard—let's call him Jerry Di-Giacomo—when Jerry DiGiacomo was on duty. There. Now you begin to know what I know."

She shut her eyes against what she was hearing, threw her head back. "Oh, God."

"Stevie, I've been working my butt off all day to keep Jerry out of handcuffs. Maybe he's crazy, but he's not *that* kind of crazy. I don't think he'd go after the company, and I sure as hell don't think he'd go after you."

"If you know all this, why do you need me?" She rose from the rocker and started to move toward the hallway.

He stood still, lowered his voice. "Because I don't know it. I just think I do."

"You just have to do the best you can, T. D."

"It's my first big case and I need your help."

"I can't give it to you."

He suspected why, but needed to pretend otherwise. "Stevie. Tell me Doug Kiskel became your friend, kidnapped you from Jerry, got an alias for you and lured you into a conspiracy to burglarize this place. Then you learned he'd lied to you, you challenged him, he intercepted my phone messages and discovered you were coming here Saturday night and mostly to protect himself but also out of insane jealousy he tried to kill you. Tell me you didn't know he was obsessed with you."

Her hands went to her face.

"Tell me you harbor the slightest doubt that it wasn't Doug Kiskel, that you still admire him for his mind and his affection for you even if his motives are twisted—even if he's trying to frame your old boyfriend. You have to think I'm just a little bit wrong, don't you, to keep protecting him?"

At least she was listening and feeling what he was saying, that his last lingering doubts about his deductions were just part of it.

"I'm going to have to go," she said, taking a deep breath.

"Again?"

"I wish I could tell you more."

"Me too."

"Can I get a cab?"

He drew a breath. "Out on Beacon Street, two blocks. They go by all the time."

Now she stopped, turned. "This fellow, Joe. When he comes to the library tonight. Do you arrest him?"

"No. Maybe we get additional evidence against him. Then we get a warrant, we arrest him tomorrow."

"So. He's a free man tonight."

He nodded. "Stevie, use your head, don't go home, go to a friend's house—"

"I have a new home that only a few people know about, and it's my *home*, and I'm not going to be scared out of it." She clenched her jaw, punched the air with her finger. "I fought that sonofabitch, I fought him with everything I had, even when I thought, 'Hey, there's no way out of this one, you've had it.' I didn't give up."

He saw it in her eyes and understood that her love, her fears, her kindness, and her rage were all tangled together. He could also see that she was thinking very hard.

"I really do love you, Stevie," he said.

She blinked a few times, bit her lip.

"Will you call me? Please?" he asked.

She nodded, turned, and eased slowly downstairs, out of his sight as he remained motionless in the middle of the room. She took her time, rustling about in the front hall, getting her coat and scarf and perhaps his Stetson and other things. After a couple of minutes she opened the door and was gone.

"Let me get this straight," Harvey Monahan intoned in his most resonant radio voice. "John Medeiros and I are going to stand in this tiny bathroom with our ears to this medicine cabinet to try to overhear a fired ADC employee, of doubtful credibility, speaking to you in confidence about some doubtful programming analysis she's done on Doug Kiskel's software?"

"Almost. With the cabinet door open, both of you should hear pretty clearly without straining, and, as you can see, there is a seat in here."

Harvey smiled knowingly at John Medeiros, who looked very tired, having come straight from work. "We can take turns."

"Charming," said Medeiros, a short, stocky man whose Portuguese ancestry was evident in his burnt-umber skin and thick black hair.

"Gentlemen, we're doing this because very few people understand complexity theory and we don't have time to decode all this to get a warrant." Once again Dred waved the bogus twenty-megabyte cartridge before them, fingers concealing the label, abstrusely marked INF.ENG. "We need Sandy Murchison to talk to me in utter confidence, to tell us what's on it. She trusts no one at the company. She barely trusts me."

"It's something, Dred. But not much." Harvey was still trying to appease Medeiros, who was very unhappy to be here, even if he was just one block away from his office on Ashburton Place.

"Officially, I'm not here, okay?" Medeiros reminded him.

"Yes, sir, I know. I think we should take our places, it's getting late." It was almost eight-thirty. "One last thing: please don't come out unless I give you the word."

"Okay, Dred," Harvey acknowledged with a wry grin, closing himself and the assistant Attorney General into the bathroom and locking the door.

Dred stepped around the corner into Kari Collins's office, stuffed INF.ENG back into the ADC interoffice envelope and set it very carefully on her cluttered desk next to the telephone. Over the envelope he placed a sheet of Athenaeum stationery, slightly askew so that the envelope was still identifiable beneath it.

He sat down in the desk chair. With the office door wide open, he had a clear view of anyone coming into the grand lobby below. Anyone coming in would also have a clear look at him, seated in the only office with its door open and lights on. It could be a short or a long wait. A few minutes after nine, he'd think about calling it a day.

At the far end of the grand lobby the lecture hall's doors were swung apart, revealing the last few rows of a fair-sized crowd still attuned to the speaker's discourse on Walt Whitman. Up here on the mezzanine level his words were a dull and restful drone, but occasionally the hall vented bursts of laughter or buzzings of exclamation. From time to time John Brewster would appear in the doorway checking for latecomers, but the lecture, scheduled to end at nine, was already half over.

"Quick sound tests, one more time," Dred spoke at a normal level.

"Hear you fine," came back Harvey's muffled voice through the wall.

At that moment he heard the Athenaeum's huge front doors open, footsteps in the outer lobby, too rapid and agile to be Sandy's.

It was a short wait. "I think we have a guest," he said.

As soon as he'd gotten his bearings in the grand lobby and seen that a lecture was in progress in the adjoining room, Doug Kiskel turned in his direction and spotted him. Dred stood up, pretending not to see, lifted his briefcase onto the desk as if packing to leave. When Kiskel's feet clacked across the floor, Dred poked his head out the door to show sufficient surprise, then retreated as Kiskel bound up the stairs to the balcony.

"I'm kind of amazed to see you here, Doug." Dred had no choice but to step aside as Kiskel pushed into the room.

"We have some things to discuss." His eyes darted about the room, flashed at him with an antagonism Dred had not seen before.

Dred set his open briefcase on the floor. "I was just packing up to leave. I've just finished a meeting—"

"I know about your meeting. It's happening at nine. Twenty minutes from now." Soon he would have to notice the bulky ADC envelope under the library stationery, inches from his hand leaning on the desk. "That's why I'm here."

"It was scheduled for nine, yes. But there was a conflict, and we moved it up an hour. I've had my meeting. The person has come and gone."

Perhaps. "We'll see." He was absorbing every detail he could in this office. Looking for a tape recorder, a microphone?

"I'll have to admit, Doug, I'm impressed you know so much about my schedule. I imagined my meeting would be confidential."

"Balcazar, your very participation in this investigation is affecting the conduct of the crime. I've had to work very hard to know who you're talking to, and when, and where. It's after eight o'clock Wednesday, Jerry DiGiacomo is sitting innocently at the front desk in HRA waiting for a chance to slip into one of the offices to do his thing again. And for *you* to choose this hour to be five miles away, to meet with a social dysfunctionary like Sandy Murchison—it staggers me."

"Doug, if you're so convinced HRA is the source, why not just disconnect the infrared transceiver?"

The question, so obvious, momentarily rattled him. "Too many people rely on open communication with HRA, all day long."

Finally his eyes flicked downward at the desk, then recovered. He'd seen the envelope and he started to pace.

"So. She's come and gone. I'll accept that. Too bad—I happen to know she's become very friendly with DiGiacomo. I think she knows a great deal about all this. I think it would be very helpful to me if I talked to her myself."

"Possible. But I really have to get going." Dred started to rise.

"Balcazar, wait. If Sandy gave you anything useful, I'll need to know about it. I've got a lot at stake here."

"She was only minimally helpful."

Doug was increasingly jittery, pacing. "After your meeting, where did she go?"

"She said home."

"She left how long ago?"

Dred quickly calculated it was worth the risk to let Kiskel believe Sandy was now home, ready to be called. "Fifteen minutes, maybe. She'd be home now. Just."

"Gotta talk to her. You have her number?"

"Not handy," Dred answered. Harvey must have found it modestly entertaining so far, but there was a long way to go. "I really have to get back—"

"Balcazar, please wait. I think you'll find this instructive." He took Kari's phone in his hands, punched a number. "This guy should be arrested by now, I don't know what's held it up. You're such a good detective, you should've discovered a link between DiGiacomo and that woman you had dinner with, the night DiGiacomo broke into your apartment?"

Dred couldn't believe Kiskel would be this daring.

"It never occurred to me last week's burglary has anything to do with this. I certainly haven't tied it to DiGiacomo. And the woman I had dinner with is simply a friend who has no ties to this case at all. And for you to have this kind of information raises serious questions—"

Stiff with arrogance, Kiskel waved him silent. "Ray, it's me . . . Don't ask. Quick favor: can you dig up Sandy Murchison's home telephone number out of the old book?. . . Okay. Then give me a call back. Keep ringing, I may be some distance away." Doug told Ray the number of Kari's phone and hung up.

With expert nonchalance, Kiskel placed the telephone squarely atop the ADC envelope.

Dred had to construct something of Kiskel's reasoning for this move. The telephone wobbled awkwardly for a second or two; its positioning was calculated. Niles would be calling back very shortly.

Brilliant.

A ringing phone requires a weak current. Which would create a magnetic field.

Why steal the cartridge, as Dred had assumed he would, when it can be so readily and "accidentally" erased by the electromagnetism leaking from a ringing telephone?

"To finish," Kiskel continued, "I have a source who's been keeping an eye on you. DiGiacomo and your woman companion that night were once close friends, both in the local music scene. DiGiacomo, as you know, was once a top programmer and compiler writer in another division of ADC. Before his breakdown. Very capable of writing a virus program."

"Doug. I think you should know. Sandy Murchison delivered to me tonight a twenty-megabyte cartridge that contains a tractability analysis of Miriam. It proves that Miriam is a dud."

The phone rang.

"Oh?"

Two rings. "You've gone to a lot of trouble to implicate an innocent man."

"You don't suspect DiGiacomo?"

Three rings.

"No. I suspect you."

"So what? That evidence will soon be complete garbage."

Four.

"You better get the phone."

"Why should I, when Ray Niles, for once, is doing just the right thing? Let's just let it ring, okay?" Five rings, then six. "It takes a while."

While the phone continued to ring, Dred assumed the air of a man who knows when he's been beaten, mumbled wearily, "So. You win."

"You should know, Balcazar, it might take fifteen rings to finish it off."

"Even with the phone directly on top of it?"

"It's a weak magnetic field."

Dred didn't move. And for the first time Kiskel appeared to sense that something was out of place. On the twelfth or fourteenth or fifteenth ring, he angrily picked up the receiver.

"Yes. . . . No, forget the number, I don't need it. . . . What?" As he listened to Ray he grabbed the ADC envelope and started to rip it open. "I don't know, Ray. I just don't know. Hold on." He turned to Dred. "Right on schedule, the virus is back. And it's eating everything in sight—including my work on Miriam." He pulled out the cartridge, saw the label, INF.ENG. "What is this shit? This is Ray's work on his inference engine."

Even while Kiskel had been on the phone Dred had heard the commotion below, someone barging into the grand lobby, arguing with John, a heavy, gruff female voice.

"You *prick*." Glaring up at them, Sandy Murchison lumbered as fast as she could toward the stairs. In her hand, very obviously, was the best of her life's work stored on tape.

Kiskel was still dealing with Ray Niles. "Ray, all hell's breaking loose here. Talk to Balcazar."

Ray in mid-sentence: "—I've got Miriam up but it's like she's rotting, the whole thing is collapsing—*damn*, this thing is *strong*—"

Dred dropped the receiver on the desk and was out of the office, shoving past Kiskel to meet Sandy on the balcony.

"Bad move, Sandy. Jesus Christ—"

"Where is the fucker?"

He was out of the office onto the balcony, going for the cartridge in her hand, grabbing her and wrestling with her, slamming her against the bathroom door. Dred had one arm hooked through Kiskel's elbow to try to wrench him loose, but the three of them had twisted around against the railing, just as Sandy jerked eighty pounds of right leg, leading with her knee, into Kiskel's crotch. Kiskel howled in pain. The bathroom door flung open, Harvey and Medeiros lunging at them, but it was too late. The railing was no match for Sandy's bulk, it groaned and cracked and Dred felt her fat arm around his neck as all support gave way, and, for only as long as it takes to understand and appreciate the euphoria of being purely weightless, he was.

The last second of his consciousness blurred senselessly with the moment of his awakening. Crashing glass and splintering wood, a great weight on his chest. Harvey's weasely face bent over him. A cop kneeling by him, the badge glinting from an overhead light. A deep cry of surprise from Sandy Murchison. Many, many people all around him. Sirens.

Now a guy with a tiny flashlight, an EMT, beamed it in his eyes and asked him to look one way and then the other. Someone wanted him to wiggle toes and fingers. Raise his arm, bend his knees to bring his legs up. At the same time he was aware of other, more feverish activity not far away.

"Harvey."

"I'm here. How ya feeling?"

"Shitty. Where's Kiskel?"

"We don't know. He got out of here pretty quick. But he's our boy, all right."

Dred smiled, feeling a tingle of relief and gratitude.

"That was a helluva show you guys put on. Medeiros couldn't believe it. He went back to his office to do the paperwork."

"Arrest."

"You bet."

One of the EMTs moved his face in. "Mr. Balcazar. You seem to be okay—no visible signs of fracture, no concussion. But we'd advise a trip to the emergency room, just to be safe."

Dred carefully raised his head to look around. The other, more active group, was moving out the front door with Sandy Murchison's body on a stretcher.

"Will she be all right?" he asked the EMT.

Harvey moved in. "She died."

"C'mon." The balcony was ten, maybe twelve feet up.

Harvey avoided his eyes. "Sorry. She broke her neck, it was instantaneous. And she also took a big chunk of glass through her femoral artery."

"Mr. Balcazar, we have another ambulance waiting," said the EMT. "We can put you on a stretcher now."

"No."

"Sir? You were out about ten minutes."

"Yeah, and the last time I went to an emergency room I had a cut on my arm that needed a dozen stitches and I waited for an hour and a half. Thanks but no thanks."

Harvey smiled at the EMT. "He sounds okay to me."

With help he straightened up to a sitting position. His head swam. Out on the street, a siren screamed. When his vision was clear he saw wood and glass all around him.

"What's all this?"

"This *was* our display case of pre–Revolutionary War ledgers and diaries," said John Brewster, leaning in. "Which I'm sure was demolished for a very worthy cause."

"The woman died, asshole," said Harvey. "You can rebuild your precious case."

Now the patent leather shoes and light gray wool overcoat, bending down to him. "Balcazar, right?"

"Right."

A kind-faced man about his own age. "Work with Frank Cirione?"

"Yep."

"I'm Lieutenant Mullen, homicide. Roy Mullen. We'll need a statement from you, if you feel up to it."

"Tomorrow, if that's all right."

Mullen had taken his notebook out and now slipped it back in his pocket. "Fine. Just to confirm: this guy's name is Douglas Kiskel?"

"Yes."

Mullen turned to Harvey. "This has to do with that computer virus I've been reading about?"

"Lieutenant, can we do this tomorrow, when we're all thinking straight?"

"Sure. But we have an apparent homicide, and I may not want to wait for a warrant from the A.G.'s office, understand? I can pick this guy up tonight. Let me get some of the vitals, okay?" Harvey conceded and stepped aside with him.

"Easy does it," said a cop, taking Dred's hand to help him to his feet. He winced as pain shot into him just above the hip on his right side. Near his feet was Sandy's cartridge, its case cracked and soaked with blood.

"Harvey."

Harvey turned away from Mullen, saw the remains of the evidence, but shook his head. "We don't need it, Dred. Miriam's not an issue anymore."

Outside, Sandy's Volkswagen bug sat on the sidewalk, its engine idling. The police were wondering what to do with it, but Mullen was yelling, "It's the victim's car, don't touch it."

It was starting to snow, tiny sleety flakes that would become thicker and heavier through the night, a real nor'easter. The weather was no discouragement to the crowd that had gathered, their faces flickering blue from the dozens of police lights, wondering what sort of nastiness had sullied one of the city's most respected and proper institutions. Something more dire, perhaps, than a long overdue book.

The pain was still sharp in his right side, where he must have hit something when he fell, and he needed Harvey for support. He patted his jacket pocket, felt the jangly lump of his key chain. His briefcase was back inside, still on the floor of Kari's office, completely empty and not very important right now.

"I could take you to the emergency room myself, if you'd like," Harvey said.

"Appreciate the offer, but no thanks. I gotta know what happened. Kiskel took off?"

"Yeah, who knows where. Not home, I imagine."

"And the virus got to Miriam, and anybody else?"

"Too early—we don't know yet. After we get you home I'll call Ray—"

Dred stopped in his tracks. "Do that now, okay? I can get home myself, but maybe you've still got problems at work."

"You sure?" Harvey seemed relieved by the suggestion.

"Jesus, Harvey. Let's not all of us go crazy."

He laid his hand on Dred's shoulder. "I'll call you. Thanks for everything." Harvey spun around and raced back up Beacon Street toward the crowd and the blue lights.

Once inside the front hall he knew he didn't have the energy to make it up the stairs. In his bedroom he grabbed his phone, found Stevie's number folded up in his pocket on the A-1 Temporaries notepaper, and called.

He hung up after ten rings.

He struggled into the bathroom to take three extra-strength aspirin for a headache that was starting to feel unlike any other he'd known: a chisel exploring the entire inner surface of his skull. He lay back on the bed, focused all his concentration on being perfectly certain of three things: first, that when leaving the Athenaeum earlier with Stevie she handed Shaler's derringer back to him and he placed it again inside his briefcase. Second, that upon their return to his apartment he had deposited the briefcase unlatched on the Parsons bench. And third, that upon opening his briefcase inside Kari's office, preparing for Kiskel's arrival, the derringer was noticeably absent.

She had tossed the single bullet, a short hollow point, into the neighbor's bushes. Or so she had said.

He felt confident about these things, but he also believed that his mind might not be working entirely correctly. He rolled over, eased himself off the bed, and tried his best to stand up straight without collapsing from the pain in his side. He succeeded, but only because the headache was far worse.

Outside, the snow was thickening, making walking very difficult. Driving, even with front-wheel drive, would be equally interesting.

Whatever his injury was, it made it almost impossible for him to use his right arm to shift gears; he steered feebly with the fingers of his right hand, used his left to get into second gear and stay there.

Thankfully, traffic was very light and no self-respecting city cop was out in this kind of weather to bear witness to his spectacular contempt for traffic signals between Beacon Hill and Horton Street in Somerville.

She died, Harvey said. A suitably compact declaration of Sandy Murchison's finest single performance, after so many years of being complicated and unfathomable and unpleasant. Her last conscious wish was to live, her final reflex to grab him around the neck and, in falling, embrace him. He could have died, too. Sandy could have awakened with Harvey leaning over her, saying to her, "Dred? He died."

She died. Tomorrow Lieutenant Mullen would have his chance to report the news, finding Stevie's body in a dumpster somewhere with her legs poking out. Kiskel wrapped a cable around her neck and pulled with all his might until, after several long minutes, she died. She was very smart, this woman, but Kiskel was smarter. His will to destroy her was stronger than her will to survive.

Almost ten o'clock. Horton Street was a blur of snow swirling in yellow cones of soft streetlight. Number 15, Stevie's house, upstairs and downstairs, was darkened.

He parked in front, eased himself out of the car, into the snow, and onto the shelter of her front porch, her home, where she had every intention of living for a few months or a year or more, in peace. Her door was locked, and no one came when he rang the bell.

He turned the Subaru around and eased his way back home. Suddenly he was aware that some of the pain in his lower side was not from a bruised kidney or cracked rib or torn muscle, but from hunger. He had no appetite at all, but he was famished, having eaten nothing all day long.

Erica came over immediately, ferrying food up the stairs into the kitchen from the taxicab down on Acorn Lane, installments of a gourmet Italian dinner she'd picked up at Galucci's, having called ahead moments after he'd telephoned her. Veal Marsala and veggies and salad and a strange ravioli appetizer and antipasto, plus a nice-looking Chianti Classico to follow the martinis he was mixing. All the hot food into the oven in their cozy cardboard boxes. He sipped his martini cautiously, still unable to muster an appetite. He stirred the coals in the fire, turned the Hitchcock rocker and the wing chair around to face the warmth, put on some Ravel very low, *Daphnis et Chloé*. Erica came out with the antipasto on a platter, and they sat and drank another round and ignored the food.

He admitted to himself that he could not readily get through this evening alone. The pain in his side had eased to a dull ache, his headache was subsiding, and his deepest longing now was for company. He knew he could never be too far from friends, could never be the solitary adventurer, the solo mountain climber or reclusive poet.

Her calmness comforted him. She wanted to know everything that had happened, but also wanted to wait until he felt he could talk about it. Tomorrow, perhaps. One of the people in the case had died in a fall. He had been shaken up. His friend Stevie was not at home and he was worried. At some time Erica asked him, "Is it possible she's not in any danger?"

He said, "It's possible I'm wrong about all of it. That they're both up to their eyeballs in some monster conspiracy and know exactly what they're doing. And they're having a helluva laugh."

It must have been around eleven that he was on the couch and Erica had come over to stroke his neck and his back, very gently. He was aware of the late news on TV, very low, Erica prone on the rug watching, as he faded in and out of consciousness and believed they were talking about a million dollars' worth of damage at American Data Corporation in their artificial intelligence division. Erica was rolling over, calling to him, and he opened his eyes long enough to realize it was true, here was Betty Ohlmeyer droopy-eyed on camera making a general statement about sabotage, Burt Cooper not being available for comment. One particular AI project, the "Cadillac" of their current research efforts, had all but been asphyxiated by an extremely powerful virus program quite different from the two others that sneaked into the network earlier. A lot of work forever lost. Betty used the word asphyxiated.

Tom and Sally were the co-anchors who might have been married, he couldn't remember, and they tried to cover for the lack of detail in this story, there just wasn't enough information right now, ADC was still estimating the loss. More on the morning report at seven.

Nothing yet about blood and broken glass at the Athenaeum.

Erica was shaking the sleep from her head as Tom and Sally talked about this fast-moving snowstorm, four to eight inches but high winds and lots of skidding, it could be a tough commute in the morning. And now the story of a handgun killing, and pictures of the Minuteman statue, Capt. John Parker and his musket, cutting to police and EMTs carting someone in a body bag out of a house. Lexington, that afternoon. Suspect identified as thirty-one-year-old Honey Blaine, who turned herself in to police after allegedly shooting and killing thirty-eight-year-old Todd Shaler of Bedford. Police say the suspect is known locally as a prostitute, and it is believed the victim, husband and father of three, was one of her customers. He was shot once in the face with a nine-millimeter semi-automatic. Naked and dead at the scene, the suspect's home.

Sobbing, hiding her face, Honey Blaine was being led away from the cameras and helped into a police cruiser. Wide-shouldered, dark-haired woman with blood still on her own face and neck but clean powder-blue dress. Camera in this room looking at rumpled bedclothes bloodstained and now up at the ceiling where there's a hole in the plaster made by the bullet after exiting the victim's head. Ironic, Sally, that Shaler was a computer software engineer working in artificial intelligence for the government.

"What's going on?" Erica asked him. "You know this guy?"

He was up and in the kitchen splashing water on his face.

"I wish I felt well enough to be really drunk tonight."

Erica turned the television off. "You *knew* him?"

"Not very well."

10

Kevin Ryan had warned him ahead of time this would be a classic South Boston Irish pub, and he was right, especially on the Friday night before St. Patrick's Day. The place radiated a weird mix of Irish angst and a raucous joy that was both baseless and transitory. Few Irish in Boston were at peace with themselves in a bar. And if so, it wasn't for very long.

Kevin was an exception. He'd been knocked around as a kid, spent a year or two at a Department of Youth Services detention center, had his share of battles with the law, but from the time Frank had taken him under his wing he'd become ever more the wise young man, ever more tranquil in his bearing. It was actually beginning to work for him, but life was not yet perfect.

"Thing about Sheila," he was saying over his beer. "She married Billy Lagan because she didn't think she was pretty. She grew up thinking she wasn't pretty, and Billy told her she was and he'd buy her things. Which, being a developer, wasn't hard for him. What I always wanted to tell Sheila, and never did, was she was beautiful. You think? You saw her over there at Jamais Vu. Am I right?"

She was very attractive. "You're right."

"Which gets me to her and me. She says Billy's shooting blanks. She wants a big Irish family. We have lunch. We go back to her house and one thing leads to another. I use her bathroom and in the medicine chest—I mean, who doesn't poke into somebody else's medicine chest? In the medicine chest I find a thing of foam. That did it, right there."

"Kevin, that doesn't mean a thing. It could've been old—"

"Don't kid me. Look, to be honest, I was flattered. I really was. But that's not what I was in the mood to *give*. I wanted to help her, I didn't just want to screw her."

"Yeah."

"Sheila and I were very, very close and I never told her I thought she was beautiful."

"She's beautiful, all right," Dred told him, meaning it because at Jamais Vu he really did think she was.

Kevin was facing the door of the pub, flashed a wave.

"Here's Frank. He's got a big envelope. And he looks pissed."

"Frank often looks pissed, but you never know if he really is."

"Hey, Frank," said Kevin. Frank slid into the seat next to Kevin, slapped the envelope on the table.

"Do I look happy? No. Why not? Because an hour ago my client changed his story. *After* I flew to Westchester and held his hand and told him, 'Don't worry.' Tendonitis, right? That's tennis elbow, in the parlance of your hoi polloi, right, Dred? Tendonitis or no tendonitis, the power of hate gave him the strength to do it, it was him all along. What an asshole. And I loved you, Ann Strohecker. In another life, in another city, with me from a different foreign country, maybe we could've made it. And Christ, the boyfriend's still in England and he's laughing at me. Yeah, whatever they're having," he said to the chunky woman who came to get his order. "Any old beer." Back to Dred. "So, my friend, I lose, I win, I lose, and on and on it goes, *ad infinauseam*, we just end up in a tie."

"Don't expect to finish first, Frank," said Kevin.

"Maybe I do, Kev, maybe I really do. So you, my friend," he said, looking at Dred. "We just got a minute or two before Mullen comes over."

"Mullen's coming here? This is social, I don't want to do business with Mullen. I did that yesterday."

"Yeah, well, he's got more stuff, he's getting into this. Sorry, I had to bargain with him to get an early draft of the autopsy. I swapped the best info I could get from the ME for a meeting between you and Mullen. You're sharp, you can handle this."

Thirty-six hours ago he could hardly tie his shoes. Now he had to be smart for this wily lieutenant from homicide. *He's got more stuff.*

Frank took a stapled form out of the envelope and handed it to Dred. "It's not all filled in. But you get the idea."

Preliminary finding was suicide. Doug Kiskel had held the gun to his right temple and fired. Spatter of gunpowder burns all over the right side of the face and press contact wound indicated point-blank range. Bullet lodged in the middle of the cerebrum. Gun held in the right hand, muscular contraction at moment of death locked fingers tightly around it. Death occurred between midnight and one o'clock Thursday morning, in the back seat of the car owned by the deceased.

"Think the girl knows anything about this?" Frank asked.

"Girl doesn't exist, Frank," Kevin insisted quietly.

"I know, I know. I wish I knew the fuck *why*."

"Because," Dred was saying, "she was used."

"Hey, I forgot her name already. So how 'bout you? You can walk okay now? You gonna be a hundred percent so you'll be back in the loop?"

"After the weekend," Dred replied. The doctor this morning had confirmed that at the worst he'd bruised a rib and torn a muscle. He was very, very lucky indeed. But he was also very tired and not inclined to take on more work for a few days.

"Finished with the client, right?" Frank asked him.

Dred nodded. "This morning."

"He's a happy boy? Considering?" Meaning happy with the agency.

"Happy enough. But the virus fooled everybody, including me."

Frank and Kevin exchanged looks: Dred was supposed to be the resident genius with his staff.

"They're still doing the postmortem over there. But what Kiskel did was stick his main program, what they call the 'Mother virus,' right inside Miriam. That's why it was so hard to find. The mother released its baby viruses on Monday, Tuesday, and Wednesday. The last one was the killer, the one that destroyed everything. They figure about a million bucks, all together."

"But what about the backup business?" Kevin asked. "If the company backs up its software—"

"Miriam didn't get backed up. Mother instructed the main computers not to back it up. For several weeks it told the main computers, 'Turn the Miriam backup bits to OFF.' Nobody saw that. Not the techies, not Harvey, certainly not me."

"I'm lost," Frank admitted.

"The only thing Mother couldn't destroy was, guess what?"

"Itself," Kevin said.

"You got it. That's how they found it." Dred turned to Frank. Imagine a dragon trying to eat itself. Somewhere it has to stop, right?"

Frank didn't care for the image, returning to his favorite subject. "Women," Frank was lamenting, "what do they want?"

The chunky waitress set his beer down and answered him. "A smile and twenty percent."

"Thanks, sweetie. I'm talking in general."

"I don't know, Frank," said Kevin.

"Neither do I," said Dred.

"I'll tell you what they want. They want commitment."

"Some do, sure," said Kevin, "and some don't. Here comes Mullen, party's over."

Before any of them could react, Lieutenant Mullen was headed toward them in his gray overcoat, young face, hollow brown eyes, the earliest stages of a double chin jiggling as he walked.

"Hello, Frank."

"Roy. You've met these two."

"Gentlemen," he said, sitting on the bench next to Dred. They nodded, grumbled a greeting. Mullen fingered the autopsy report on the table.

"This isn't final, you all should know."

"It's proof that he's dead, though," Kevin said, a little too darkly, Dred thought.

Mullen turned to Dred. "Again, thanks for coming down to the station yesterday. I know you still have some pain."

"No problem, it's better."

Mullen reached into his pocket, drew out a clear plastic exhibit bag and placed it neatly in the center of the table. "There's the weapon." Mullen watched him carefully.

Shaler's derringer.

Kevin laughed. "It's a frigging *toy*." Kevin and Frank knew nothing of this weapon, of Todd or Alexis Shaler or the tortuous path of circumstances that had brought the gun from Alexis's kitchen all the way here to South Boston.

"Frigging *deadly* toy," Mullen corrected him. "The round was a hollow point."

Frank chortled. "You could off yourself with eight aspirin. Same chance."

"It killed him, Frank," Mullen said somberly. "But the thing is, it wasn't his gun. That's why I'm here."

At that moment Dred knew the next move was his. The gun had almost certainly been traced by now, the trail of evidence was too dense.

"I know this gun," Dred told him, trying to think fast.

"Really?" said Mullen, wide-eyed. "I had no idea. Tell me."

Really? said his partners' faces.

Confident he wasn't thinking too fast, he said, "It belonged to Todd Shaler, in Bedford."

"Right so far—that's just what the FRB told me. I'm impressed."

As a matter of procedure they *would* trace the weapon through the state's Firearms Record Bureau, discovering to their dismay it belonged to a man just killed. "Shaler was a contact for me, in the virus thing, a technical expert. I met with him, I met his wife, I discovered they were having a very difficult time personally and I feared his wife was violent enough so she might use this gun against him. I confiscated it from her Wednesday morning."

Both Kevin and Frank were listening very intently.

"You realize that your friend Shaler was the guy who got shot and killed by the whore? In Lexington?"

"Yes, Roy, I do."

"You can see why I'm intrigued. A computer genius commits suicide with a weapon owned by another computer genius, who's a murder victim twelve hours earlier."

"I can see. And I can tell you how Kiskel got the gun."

"Do."

"Wednesday night at the Athenaeum, when Kiskel was in the office with me, I had my briefcase with me. It was open. This little derringer was in a sandwich bag, in the briefcase, tucked into one of the pockets, where it had been since I'd left Shaler's house. When Sandy Murchison arrived, I came out of the office for a moment to see what was going on. After that, everything's a blur, because that's when Kiskel became violent and we were pushed off the balcony. But certainly he had time to notice the contents of my briefcase, and take the gun." Dred drank his beer deeply, finishing it off.

"The gun was visible in your briefcase?"

"Must've been. Roy, trust me, the last thing on my mind there at the Athenaeum was this dinky derringer that may or may not have been a functioning weapon. It was simply something I did not want Alexis Shaler to have in her possession. I'd been carting it around all day."

"And you? You have a pistol permit?"

Frank was incensed. "Cool it, Roy. This guy just cracked a mother of an industrial sabotage case, and he kept a crazy woman from shooting her husband. Whaddya want, anyway?"

"Frank. Excuse the chauvinism, but a gun like this, women use. I tried to picture a big healthy guy like Kiskel sticking this thing against his skull, and it looked goofy to me. You follow?"

If anyone followed, no one said anything.

"Ask yourself why, when all hell was breaking loose in the Athenaeum place, he went for the weapon. Overwhelming impulse to kill himself? I mean, there's just a coupla things that bug me. Kiskel's car was parked down in an industrial area, Howard Avenue in Brighton, okay? Fine. His body in the back seat of his Mercedes. Also in the back seat is a grocery sack. In the sack is the guy's jacket, and a piece of electrical cable of some kind."

"First I heard of this," said Kevin.

"Me too," said Dred.

"Souvenir Celtics jacket. And the kicker is, some female head hairs, blond, not his, on the seat. I don't know how fresh. But I have to wonder, was he out on a date? Did he get stood up? Did he put the moves on, get rejected, then get instantly very depressed, so he shot himself? That's what I was thinking. *Now* I'm thinking, after what Dred says, that he grabbed the gun from the briefcase just outa desperation. No plan—he was just frantic to defend himself."

"Roy, what if he's such a world-record jerk that it doesn't matter?" Kevin challenged.

"It matters. And I thought one or two of you might know something I don't. Before I consider we recommend an inquest."

"Not me," said Kevin.

"Not me," said Frank.

"It all suggests suicide," Mullen went on. "Press contact wound, powder burns, all that shit. Then we trace the gun to this Shaler guy. Then we think about the blond hairs. We get confused—we think, just maybe, there's a woman in here somewhere."

"Kiskel staked his whole career, his life, on his work," Dred began. "Everything revolved around this program he was writing, Miriam."

"Who the hell is Miriam?" Mullen asked.

He could feel his anger building, did his best to contain it. "Listen to me: Miriam's the name of his program. He created this very fancy program, and when it was too late he learned that it didn't work. Months, years even, on something that doesn't work. He was due to unveil the thing at a huge convention in Washington next month. Fat chance. When he knew it didn't work, the only way out was to destroy it. With a virus, making it look like the work of some nut. Wednesday night it all comes crashing down: even as the virus is destroying his work, he unwittingly unmasks himself to both a company executive *and* an assistant Attorney General. Seconds later, he assaults a former colleague who falls to her death. So now he faces manslaughter. His work is destroyed, his job is lost, he's suddenly a felon—Kiskel's an unstable guy to begin with, Roy. What the hell would *you* do after all those things happen at once? Go out on a fucking *date*?"

Kevin sneaked him a thin smile, an arched eyebrow. Mullen slowly nodded, reached for the evidence bag, and jammed it back in his pocket.

But Frank was still curious. "How 'bout prints, Roy? Anybody's prints on there but his?"

"Nope, just his," he sighed. "The hell with it. You're right, Kevin. The guy was an asshole."

He got up.

"So long, Roy," said Frank.

" 'Bye, Frank. Gentlemen." He started out, hesitated for a second, then changed his mind and kept going.

Kevin eyed Dred, whistled through his teeth. "Championship."

Stevie had said so convincingly that she had tossed the hollow-point bullet into the neighbor's bushes. The sentence had rolled right off her tongue.

"You should know about this girl," Stevie Bear's roommate Rachel Bernstein was telling him over cups of chowder at the Hampshire House that same night. She sipped her wine gingerly, as if the rim of her glass were infected with germs, then dabbed her lips with a napkin. Of course: Creamy New England–style clam chowder leaves that awful telltale smear on glassware, and Rachel knew it. She had strong, nicely geometric features, her skin pleasingly glossy from a freshly acquired Caribbean tan. Her eyes were deep and intelligent, her words educated. Her manner was humorless and severe, a teacher anticipating a rude remark from a pupil. "Stevie lies."

"She lies?" Was that possible? That a woman so beset by the consequences of her indiscretions should ever resort to untruths just to keep her ass out of a sling? Of course she lies.

Rachel nodded somberly. "Nothing . . . serious. Remember, I knew her only a few weeks as a roommate. I knew her *vaguely* prior to that, through the temporary agency. But she would trip over her own falsehoods. And I'd catch her at it. And she'd be embarrassed."

"Did she speak to you honestly about her life?"

"Sometimes. But of course the great lie was Thursday, when I got back a day early and found her still in bed at two in the afternoon, and she looked so banged up. The greatest lie was 'It's over with him.' I've seen it before, some women never know how to end it, and Stevie's one of those."

"How was she banged up?" he wanted to know.

"Scratches on her face. Bruises on her neck—she said forget it, it's over. But I say it isn't. It doesn't matter that she hopped a bus for Ohio that night, that she wrote me a fat check for rent and utilities, that she *physically* took herself out of Boston, out of this situation. For someone like Stevie, it's never 'over with him,' because there are hims just like him everywhere, and she'll find them. That's the greatest lie. It's not over with him, because he'll be waiting for her in Toledo."

"This guy she was seeing—"

"I told you on the phone yesterday I never laid eyes on him. Never knew his name beyond Doug. Just Doug. He never came in the house. He'd pull up outside and they'd go off." She squinted at him as if she'd just met him and was studying his face. "You're more than just an old friend, aren't you?"

"Yes," he admitted.

She allowed herself a self-congratulatory snicker. "So you both lie."

"I guess."

"Well. I'll miss her. She was a load of laughs. As long as she wasn't all hung up on some *man*. No offense, but men can be so awful. They were awful to her. I'm glad she's gone, so I don't have to watch it anymore."

Saturday afternoon Elaine called him from Bermuda, her last day, after a round of golf with Tally's brother Gordie, who had come down from Boston completely on a *whim*. They'd had gobs of fun.

Dred barely remembered the name Tally and didn't care about the brother Gordie. Elaine's voice was sunny and enthusiastic, declaring Gordie to be very nice, divorced last year, no kids, seemed to laugh at the same jokes, and such a wonderful teacher of golf when you don't know the first thing about it. She hated the prospect of coming back, especially with all the weird weather they were having in Boston, and was it absolutely beyond the realm to consider actually living down here? Still, she said, she hoped when she got back she could see him. Okay?

Sometime, he told her.

After hanging up, he felt in terrible need of fresh air, threw on his leather jacket and headed out for a walk on the Common. The snow Wednesday night had changed to rain, freezing Thursday and Friday, thawing again today, another blast of teasing warmth from the southwest. It was remarkable that on the Common the end of winter was the ugliest of all seasons, the cycles of snowmelt spawning old litter and cigarette butts and hundreds of these little piles of brick-red dogshit in neat coils. The pigeons and panhandlers were out in force, but it was good to see that there were also happy families from out of town and college kids with Frisbees and the occasional proper Bostonian matron with her multipurpose Bonwit's bag. And on a bench far away, a wheat-haired, leather-clad young woman was idly strumming a guitar, enticing a passerby or two to linger long enough to drop change into the top hat at her feet.

He moved close enough to know that she was not Stevie, but she was pretty nonetheless and the music she played was lovely. For the moment the music was all he could be certain of, music that was clear and sweet and crafted with real skill. Everything else was becoming a great gray fog, an expanding enormity of what he didn't know.

Her song ended, the passersby passed on, and a man who was obviously her boyfriend lifted the hat on the bench next to her, sat on her other side, and put his arm around her shoulders. They sat this way for a long quiet time, as still as sculpture, while he imagined himself to be the man and the woman to be Stevie, an old trusted friend whom he loved and with whom he could sit this way for long moments and say nothing.

It would be wonderful, but it would be a fantasy with a woman who never sat still long enough to be understood and, therefore, to be fully trusted. She ought to feel safe enough now to level with him and accept what he knew of her—that she was sneaky smart. Smart enough to have figured out that he'd become her accessory, helping to arrange some of the pieces for her: his "carelessness" in leaving the weapon on the Parsons bench yet a second time; the little gun, which he'd told her belonged to somebody else, all but placed in her hand; his suggestion that Kiskel might be thought of as suicidal. It would be wonderful to have her appreciate these things and call him up to talk about them in complete honesty.

Dred turned away and headed back toward home. He needed to rest up for tomorrow morning, to have the energy to deal with Erica and her decision to move out of Harbor Towers to the farmhouse in Concord. She wanted to wait for Kurt and Tony's return from the Bahamas, to get them settled before telling them what she was forced to do. Kurt would not make it easy for her; Tony would be utterly crushed. There was no way around it—Sunday was going to be a miserable day.

Crossing Beacon into the brick and cobblestone enclaves of Beacon Hill, he spied a familiar figure ahead of him.

"Willie!" he called out.

Wilhemina Cuthbertson turned with a puzzled grin. "Dred Balcazar. Out for a walk, just as I'd hoped."

"Excuse me?"

"*Well.* You certainly weren't at home, so I imagined you'd be taking the airs of this wonderful afternoon."

He caught up with her and soon saw that something was troubling her.

"You wanted to see me?"

"Of course! You must have seen the photo of the man in this morning's *Herald.*"

He did not regularly see the *Herald.* The *Globe* had covered the story with no pictures. "Afraid not. Which man is that?"

"The one who shot himself in the head! Didn't you hear about that?"

"Oh yes, now I remember. From that computer company. The virus business."

"Dred, I just *know* it's the same man, from last Saturday night. The one who was prowling all around."

"That's very strange," he said, showing just a trace of interest. "You said you saw him only from behind. That you never saw his face."

"Ah ha! But I did catch a glimpse of his *reflection* in your downstairs window glass. It *must* be the same man. So what in Heaven's name was he doing here? I wanted to inquire of you, before calling the police. That Lieutenant Mullen they interviewed."

"Willie." He hooked his arm within hers, gently eased her forward along the sidewalk. "I'll just bet you and I together can come up with a theory."

"Oh, marvelous!"

It shouldn't be too hard to come up with something that would keep her from making the call. "Tea? I've got some Earl Grey."

"Perfect for an afternoon like this, yes."

Something like: getting her to describe the photo in the paper, then to step in and contradict it, confessing for the first time that he'd seen the man himself that Saturday night, close up, sometime after the hydrant incident. Like: the man had a heavy handlebar mustache, absolutely for certain. Something.

He'd lied to Willie before and won. She'd asked him: why do you drive a Japanese car when it's so important to support American car manufacturers? It was a gift from his mother, he could hardly turn it down. Oh. And why is that lovely Elaine Prescott not working with you anymore? She still is, but we communicate now by computer and telephone. Oh, how *advanced*. And: you're an intelligent, well-bred, and attractive young man, why don't you date more young women from the Hill, like Natalie Fennelman or Cynthia Fiske? The woman I'm dating is from Florida, and she's on a long cruise and I need to wait until she comes back. *Oh*, how romantic.

At his door she was bothered by a speck of dust in her eye, removed her glasses to rub it away.

"There," she said. "Tea and mystery await us!"

She definitely hadn't worn glasses the Saturday night of the hydrant. Completely relieved, he ushered her inside.

"I forget—you usually wear glasses," he said.

"Generally. Sometimes I'm a bit lazy about them," she explained.

For the moment he smiled, cheerfully took her coat, and closed the door behind them.